Grand Central

GRAND CENTRAL
TERMINAL

Grand Central

ORIGINAL STORIES OF POSTWAR
LOVE AND REUNION

Melanie Benjamin · Jenna Blum · Amanda Hodgkinson
Pam Jenoff · Sarah Jio · Sarah McCoy · Kristina McMorris
Alyson Richman · Erika Robuck · Karen White

With an Introduction by Kristin Hannah

BERKLEY BOOKS, NEW YORK

THE BERKLEY PUBLISHING GROUP
Published by the Penguin Group
Penguin Group (USA) LLC
375 Hudson Street, New York, New York 10014

USA • Canada • UK • Ireland • Australia • New Zealand • India • South Africa • China

penguin.com

A Penguin Random House Company

This book is an original publication of The Berkley Publishing Group.

GRAND CENTRAL

Berkley trade paperback ISBN: 978-0-425-27202-2

An application to register this book for cataloging has been submitted to the Library of Congress.

PUBLISHING HISTORY
Berkley trade paperback edition / July 2014

PRINTED IN THE UNITED STATES OF AMERICA

10 9 8 7 6 5 4 3 2 1

Cover photographs: couple © Alfred Eisenstaedt/Getty Images; Grand Central © Michael Poehlman/
Getty Images; crowd © iStock/Thinkstock; texture © iStock/Thinkstock; clock © iStock/Thinkstock.
Cover design by Sarah Oberrender.
Frontispiece art © iStockphoto.
Interior text design by Tiffany Estreicher.

CONTENTS

Introduction by Kristin Hannah   vii

Going Home   1
     by Alyson Richman

The Lucky One   39
     by Jenna Blum

The Branch of Hazel   77
     by Sarah McCoy

The Kissing Room   113
     by Melanie Benjamin

I'll Be Seeing You   147
     by Sarah Jio

I'll Walk Alone   181
     by Erika Robuck

The Reunion   217
     by Kristina McMorris

CONTENTS

Tin Town   255
    by Amanda Hodgkinson

Strand of Pearls   289
    by Pam Jenoff

The Harvest Season   321
    by Karen White

INTRODUCTION

I was born in sunny Southern California, in a time when the world was a simpler, quieter place. I rode my bicycle to the store and bought bottles of soda and Pop Rocks. My friends and I built forts in our manicured backyards and spent Sundays at the beach with our moms, wading in the water, splashing each other. The sun was always shining in my little corner of the world. Dads worked during the day and were rarely seen; moms couldn't be ditched no matter how hard you tried. When the sun set, we all raced home on our bikes and gathered around a dinner table where there was almost always a hot casserole waiting.

I was a preteen when the Vietnam War changed the landscape around me. Suddenly there were protests and sit-ins and marches on the weekends; the police wore riot gear against college students. The nightly news was about body counts and bombs falling in faraway places. Then came Watergate. Nothing seemed safe or certain anymore.

I came of age reading about distant planets and unknown worlds. On my nightstand were novels by Tolkien and Heinlein and Bradbury and Herbert. I was a voracious reader, with my nose always buried in a book. I was constantly being admonished to quit reading and look up around me—especially on family vacations. In my high school years, it was Stephen King who held me in the palm of his hand and whispered to me that evil existed, but that it could be battled and beaten . . . if only one was strong enough, if only one truly believed. And I believed.

It wasn't until later, when I grew up and got married and had a child of my own, that I began to see my life in context, to see how different the sixties and seventies and eighties were from the years that came before. I think that's when I fell in love with World War II fiction.

World War II. Today, that's all it takes for me. Tell me it's a novel set during the war and you have a better than even chance of snagging my attention. Add that it's epic or a love story and you have me ordering the book in advance.

There's something inherently special about that war, at least as it is seen by the modern reader, which is to say, in retrospect. World War II was the last great war for Americans, the last time that good was good and evil was evil and there was no way to mistake the two. It was a time of national sacrifice and common goals. A time when we all agreed on what was important and what was worth fighting and dying for. Women wore white gloves and men wore hats. Through the prism of today's contentious times, it seems almost impossibly romantic and polite. In our modern, divided and conflicted world, many of us long to glimpse a forgotten time, where the right path seemed easier to identify and follow. The "Greatest Generation." That's what we see when we look back now. It's no wonder that stories about the men and women who lived and loved during that era seize our imagination and hold it so firmly.

World War II, like most wars, has been primarily defined by men. We learn in school about the battles and the skirmishes, about the bombs and the missions. We see the photographs of men marching on beaches and advancing up hillsides. We study the atrocities that were committed and remember the lives—indeed the generation—that was lost. But only recently have we begun to pay attention to the women.

In the World War II novel that I am currently writing, a female character says to her son, "We women were in the shadows of the war. There were no parades for us and few medals," and I think that's really true. In too much of our war fiction, women are forgotten, and yet the truth of their participation is fascinating and compelling and deserves to be at the forefront of the discussion about the aftermath of the war. Women were spies and pilots and code breakers. And of equal importance was their place on the home front. While the world was at war and the men were gone, it was the women who held life together, who gave the soldiers a safe place to return to. Many of the stories herein are focused on women and their lives on a single day in 1945, when the war was over but far from forgotten. Everyone had to readjust their lives after World War II—the men coming home, the women trying to return to a life that had been changed beyond recognition, the children who remembered nothing of peacetime. These are the themes and issues that continue to resonate with readers today.

I was enthralled by the short stories in this collection. This talented group of authors has taken an intriguing premise and coaxed from it a seamlessly integrated group of stories. In it, a single day in Grand Central Terminal—entrance to the melting pot of America— becomes the springboard for ten very different stories, which, when read together, weave a beautiful tapestry about men and women and their war years. In some, the characters are finding new lives after devastating losses; in others, the characters are battling the terrible effects of the war and trying to believe in a better future. In all of them, we see the changes wrought by World War II and the battles that often needed to be fought at home simply to survive and begin anew. And through all the stories is the melody of loss and renewal, the idea that something as simple as a song played on a violin in a train station can remind one of everything that was lost . . . and everything one hopes to regain.

Kristin Hannah
New York Times bestselling author of
Home Front and *Winter Garden*

Grand Central

SEPTEMBER 1945

Going Home

ALYSON RICHMAN

For Stephen, my violinist.
With special thanks to Joane Rogers.

He wasn't sure whether it was the vaulted ceilings or the marble floors that created the building's special acoustics. But on certain afternoons, when the pedestrian traffic was not too heavy, Gregori Yanovsky could close his eyes, place his chin on his violin, and convince himself that Grand Central Terminal was his very own Carnegie Hall.

Months before, he had discovered his perfect little corner of the terminal—the one just before the entrance to the subway, on the way to the Lexington Avenue exit. It was far enough from the thunder of the train tracks, yet still busy enough for foot traffic to yield him a few spare coins every couple of minutes.

He'd arrive early each morning from his apartment on Delancey Street and ascend the stairs of the subway with his shoulders back and his head held high. Something about carrying a violin case made him feel special amongst the throng of commuters. For concealed within his velvet-lined case was the possibility of magic, of music, of art, which no mere briefcase in the world could ever contain.

And although his suit jacket, with its thin grey flannel, was a far cry from the more stylish ones from Paul Stuart or Brooks Brothers worn by the men who arrived daily on trains from Larchmont or Greenwich, Gregori felt he transcended the shabbiness of his shirtsleeves. His elegance came instead from the simplicity and precision of his movements. The way he positioned his instrument against his collarbone. The graceful manner in which he lifted his bow. These were not flourishes that were taught in a finishing school or at suburban family meals.

He and his instrument needed each other, like partners in a waltz. Without the other, there could be no music.

As a child in Poland, Gregori had watched his father, Josek, soak his hands in milk every night to soften his calluses after a day of splitting wood. Josek had learned the craft of barrel making from his own father but secretly had always dreamed of making musical instruments instead. The barrels made him money and so kept food on the table and a roof over his family's head, but music fed his soul.

On Friday nights, Josek invited anyone with an instrument into their home to fill it with music for his wife and child. Gregori still remembered his father twirling him around the room, as a neighbor played the balalaika. Years later, he would recall his father's laughter. He could have tuned his violin on the sound of it. It was a perfect A.

During cart rides to the city of Krakow, with his father's barrels loaded in the back and young Gregori sitting in the front, father and son would hum melodies together. Sometimes Josek would pull the cart over outside of a church, just to let his son listen to the organ music being played. Gregori seemed to come alive every time his father exposed him to melodies of any kind, whether it was the folk music of the village or the Mozart wafting out from one of the music schools in the city. Even more extraordinary was the boy's remarkable ability to hum back any melody he heard, without missing a single note.

One night, when the rain was coming down so hard it sounded to Gregori as though the roof might collapse, there was a knock at the family's door. When his mother opened the door, she found Josek's friend Lev standing there under the doorway, with a man she did not recognize.

"We've been caught in the storm," Lev said. "The wheel on my cart came off."

He motioned to the man standing next to him, a hat pulled over his eyes. "I was trying to get my wife's brother, Zelik, back to his home."

Zelik raised one hand in greeting as he shuddered in the rain. In the other hand, Gregori's father noticed a small dark case, shaped like a silhouette. Instinctively, he knew there had to be a violin inside.

"Come in before you ruin your instrument," Josek said, waving the two men inside. His wife took their wet coats and hung them by the fire, while Josek and Gregori watched as Zelik placed his violin case on the table and unlatched it. Everyone gasped when they saw the glimmering instrument, which thankfully had not been damaged by the rain.

Gregori would never forget the sight of Zelik taking his violin out from his case, withdrawing the instrument as though he were a sorcerer. He still remembered that impending sense of magic as Zelik placed his chin on the edge, lifted his bow, and began to play. Zelik captivated everyone with the music that soon came forth in swirls and arabesques; the notes filled the room and thundered over the storm outside.

Zelik tapped his foot on the floor and bobbed his head from side to side. If joy had a sound, Gregori heard it that night from Zelik's bow gliding over the strings. When the young man eventually put the instrument into Gregori's hands, instructing him how to grasp the bow, all he could think about was learning to play it himself. The instrument had the capacity both to speak sorrow and to sing joy, all without a single word.

The next morning, after the sun reemerged and the wet timber and muddy roads began to dry, Zelik gave Gregori one last lesson. Gregori cradled the instrument in cupped hands. He slid his palm across the violin's long, slim neck and fingered the tuning knobs. He felt as though he was touching beauty for the first time.

Zelik could see immediately how the boy's hand naturally gripped the bow and could hear how he had a natural ear for melody. Zelik also sensed that, behind his closed eyes, Gregori didn't just feel the music; instead it came forth from him as though he were breathing each note. As he grasped Josek's hands, thanking him for giving him and Lev shelter that night, Zelik whispered into the man's ear, "Your son has a gift. Sell what you must, but get him a violin and find a way to get him lessons. And do it as quickly as you can."

Josek was able to get his son a violin in exchange for twelve pickle barrels made from his very best timber. After he saved enough money to feed his family, Josek used whatever funds remained to have a music teacher from a nearby village come to give Gregori lessons. The boy learned quickly how to play his scales, and then went on to more complicated études and sonatas that normally took other children far longer to master. Every so often, Josek would also take him into Krakow for a lesson and the opportunity to play with a piano accompanist. By the time he was ten, he could play all of the Mozart concertos. And when he was fifteen, he took his first stabs at the Mendelssohn.

But as much as he loved the music of the classical composers, after the weekly Shabbat dinners, Gregori always played the music of his shtetl. His fiddle work made his mother smile and his father pour the neighbors another glass of wine.

As he became older and his skills advanced, he started to dream of one day playing in Krakow's prestigious Academy of Music and in candlelit recitals throughout Europe. But these dreams ended one night with the sound of breaking glass and his mother's screams.

Before, the essence of his youth was a bowl of soup, a slice of bread, and his parents smiling to the sound of his violin. But that night, it was the sounds of terror and hate. Even fifteen years later, as he played in the safety and grandeur of Grand Central Terminal, the dark memories of his final days in his village often returned to him. The sight of his father being pulled from the house by an angry mob. The smell of burning barrels. The cries of his mother in the dark as the villagers torched their house, as his father lay bleeding and motionless on the ground. The word "Jew" slicing through the air like a scythe, uttered like a curse.

Gregori stood there watching, a voyeur to his own family's destruction. All he wanted to do was rush over and kneel by his father, and remove the splinters of glass from his head, which looked like a broken gourd. He yearned to cradle his father in his arms and bring back the warmth that was flowing out of him, causing him to turn blue before Gregori's eyes. But the boy's limbs would simply not move. It was only when the family's house was set ablaze that he felt his legs moving beneath him. They moved not by reason, but by instinct, his body lurching into the fire to save his violin.

———

Less than a year afterward, seventeen-year-old Gregori walked through Ellis Island. He had been sponsored by an older uncle whom his mother had not seen in years. In one hand, he carried a small leather suitcase, and in the other, he carried his violin. And beneath the material of his trousers were angry red patches of burn marks that wrapped around one leg. The scar looked like fire itself, a permanent red torch set in high relief against his skin. An eternal reminder of that horrible night.

His uncle had sponsored Gregori not purely out of compassion but also because he believed the boy's music might draw customers to his restaurant on the Lower East Side. The first night, Gregori pulled out his violin in that crowded apartment on Delancey Street and serenaded his new family. The women let the dishes pile in the sink unwashed, their bodies instead anchored to their chairs as he played. As Gregori's uncle scanned the room and saw the women transfixed, he was confident he'd have every table at his restaurant full by week's end.

———

Nearly every night for three years, Gregori played countless mazurkas and tarantellas to diners enjoying their bowls of borscht and plates of stuffed cabbage. In some way, he enjoyed the warmth of the restaurant. The customers and their families reminded him of his Shabbat performances back in the shtetl. But it was hardly the type of playing Gregori had dreamed of when he was younger. As a new immigrant to a country that seemed so wealthy and full of prospects compared to Europe, Gregori wanted to find a way to harvest every opportunity. He didn't just want to serenade men and women over his uncle's pierogies and cabbage his entire life. He still carried the dream of playing on a stage alongside an orchestra, something that he had not yet had the chance to do.

So when he noticed an advertisement in one of the trade papers that a customer had left behind one night, indicating that the New Amsterdam Theater was holding auditions for musicians interested in their pit orchestra, Gregori took it as a sign. An opportunity waiting to be seized. He mustered up enough courage to go to the theater. There weren't as many men there as he had expected, as such a great number of them were off serving in the war, a fate he had escaped because of the severe scarring on his legs. Still, there were so many talented musicians who came out to audition that when Gregori was offered a place as one of the second violins, it felt like a dream come true.

Even with his new job, Gregori still had his mornings and most early afternoons free. He chose to rehearse in the one place in New York he discovered he loved the most. Right in front of the entrance to Vanderbilt Hall, across from Murray's pastry cart and Jack's shoeshine booth. Grand Central Terminal, his own favorite stage.

The extra money he received from busking was nice, of course. Some days it barely covered the cost of his subway fare and lunch, but Gregori loved playing in Grand Central for many more reasons than the few dollars it added to his daily income: the acoustics, the vaulted ceiling with its turquoise plaster and gilded constellations, and the kinetic energy of the commuters. He found it thrilling that he was surrounded by so much motion, that he was in the epicenter of a thousand merging worlds. He could sense the rumble of the subway beneath his feet, and the wind from the train tunnels that blew in and out from the brass doors. Here, waitresses mingled with soldiers returning from the war, and bankers in chalk-striped suits sprinted next to the men who worked the elevators in their skyscraper offices lining Fifth Avenue.

There were also those few minutes each morning, when he leaned down to sprinkle the first few coins into the velvet of his case to encourage others to do the same, that he could hear the pattern of the foot traffic. It was a symphony to his ears. He could hear the gallop of a child's patent leather shoes against the marble, the soft shuffle of a banker's oxfords, or the drag of a wounded soldier's crutch as it thumped against the floor. But one day he heard a patter of footsteps so unlike all the others he had heard over the years pounding against the marble that he felt a small twinge in his heart. The steps were light, almost airy, as if the heel of the shoe were barely touching the ground. Without even looking up, he could hear the spry, leaping sounds of a dancer.

He lifted his gaze and noticed a beautiful woman walking in his direction. She had just come up from the subway, her green silk dress fluttering like the ruffled edge of tulip leaves. Her face appeared to him in a flash: the pale skin, the dark hair, and foxlike eyes that looked almost like they belonged to another place. Not a typical American, in the way he thought of Americans, though he knew every person here could claim ancestry from abroad. But in Gregori's mind, the American face belonged to those of English or Irish descent, with their small-carved features and peaches-and-cream skin. This girl instead had the high cheekbones and coloring that reminded him of the girls back in his village. But really she could have been from any country in Central or Eastern Europe, he thought. Hungarian or Lithuanian. Polish or Russian, maybe. Or even Czech.

Her footsteps had slowed, and now she stood only a few feet from him. She had stopped in front of the pastry cart that sold glazed doughnuts for a nickel and apple strudel for a dime. Around her pooled a dozen other commuters eager for something sweet before their morning's work consumed them.

Her long legs and shapely back were evident through the silk of her dress. She wore her black hair in soft curls around her face, just like the starlets in the movies. But her movements were somehow old-fashioned and slightly tentative, the way a person who wasn't born in America might search for the right coins in her purse, or how someone new to Manhattan might pull slightly away when someone's sleeve brushed against their own. He noticed a difference in the way she moved when there was no one around, compared to the way she moved when she was thrust into a group. The ease was replaced with caution. As if beneath the carefree veneer there was something more complex, something she kept hidden behind a radiant facade. This did not deter Gregori. On the contrary, it increased his fascination. The contrast was like music itself. On the surface, an untrained ear would hear only beauty when he played something like Albinoni's Adagio in G Minor. Only a few would also hear the sadness that floated from the strings. Two contradictory emotions, braided like rope, the true essence of a human soul.

————

Gregori quickly pondered the best way to gain her attention. He had yet to begin his playing that morning, and as he stood holding his violin in his hands, his mind now raced as to what music to select. He desperately wanted to find a way to reach her, to make her stop—if only for a moment—and take notice of the music intended just for her.

It quickly occurred to him that if he could find something that reminded her of her homeland, it might be enough to make her pause and linger just a bit.

But time was ticking away as he watched her pay for what looked like a small piece of strudel now safely tucked inside a wax paper bag.

His heart was racing. He knew that Mozart had never failed him with the crowds, so he began playing *Eine kleine Nachtmusik*. It was popular enough that even if she weren't from Austria, she still might recognize the melody and walk over to him. Then, once he had finished, he could ask her where she was from and their conversation would come naturally, just like a dance.

He played with half-closed eyelids, not wanting to remove his gaze from her for even a moment. As his bow moved across the strings, his body bouncing to the music, he saw her dip her fingers into the wax paper bag and pull out her pastry. But even though the melody got livelier, she barely seemed to take notice of him.

Gregori watched, crestfallen, as she headed toward the Lexington Avenue exit, her hips moving beneath her dress as she pushed through the heavy, brass-edged doors.

As Liesel crossed over Lexington, past the Bowery Savings Bank branch and the newspaper stand, she kept her stride brisk and glided by any older pedestrians who would have slowed her down. One thing she prided herself on was her punctuality. She didn't like to keep Mr. Stein waiting. If he requested she arrive by one thirty P.M., she'd be at his building a few minutes before. Just enough time to fluff out her hair and smooth down her dress.

Nor did she want to arrive at his office with bits of apple strudel on her lips. So she quickly finished her pastry and, on the corner of

46th Street and Lexington Avenue, took out a napkin and blotted her lips to make sure there were no crumbs. She took a compact out of her purse and swept a dusting of powder over her face. Then, as she had watched the other dancers do a thousand times, she reapplied her lipstick before taking one final look in the compact mirror and snapping it shut.

Liesel was happy that Leo Stein's office was on Lexington Avenue, not on Broadway like most of the other theatrical agents. This meant that she had to take the 42nd Street shuttle from her sewing job near the theater district to get to him. But it was a route she loved because it enabled her to pass the only pastry kiosk in all of New York that had apple strudel exactly like her mother used to make. If she had an extra few minutes, she'd walk toward the central concourse and enjoy the pastry under the gilded images of the zodiac, those finely painted constellations resplendent in a sea of blue.

Liesel loved the very vastness of the rotunda, with its cathedral-like opulence, and the way the light streamed through the east entrance's arched windows and illuminated the commuters in a sepia-soft glow. It was a place where she could feel both alone and safe amongst the crowd. And even more poignantly, it was where she could imagine a chance meeting or a potential reunion with the family she still refused to accept as lost.

———

It was hard to believe it had been over five years since she had seen her family and that there had been no contact with them since the last letter arrived.

"The time will go quickly," her mother had promised her as she packed for America.

What her mother had told her was true. Time had gone by

quicker than she'd imagined, but it wasn't without a lot of work on her part. Liesel had done everything she could to keep herself as busy as possible. She didn't want to have time to think, because during those pauses, it was hard not to imagine what terror had befallen her family.

What she also loved about Grand Central Terminal was that everyone there was off to another place and they all had a sense of urgency to their journey. This was compounded by the fact that there were clocks everywhere: brass-rimmed clocks fastened onto the marble walls, the famed one in the center of the concourse, and downstairs by the tracks, there were clocks suspended from the ceiling. Some had art nouveau embellishments, and others looked like larger versions of watch faces. But no matter the style, the clocks all gave a sense that one had to keep moving, and Liesel liked this. It enabled her to focus on her responsibilities. When she wasn't dancing, she was sewing. And when she wasn't sewing, she was dancing, either at her ballet studies or performing at the supper clubs that helped pay her bills.

She had never imagined that she'd be able to make enough money dancing to support herself, but Leo Stein had changed all that for her. She would always be grateful he had taken her on as one of his girls. His agency was on the third floor of a slim grey brownstone that had been converted into small offices. Upon arriving, she buzzed the doorbell and climbed up the narrow stairs. She could smell his cigar smoke from the first landing.

Leo Stein, Talent Agent was carved on the dark wooden door. She entered without knocking.

"Hello, my *sheyna meydel*," he called out to her. "What a sight for sore eyes."

She sat down across from his desk, folding her hands in the

green silk folds of the dress that she had made herself the week before.

"So, today through Friday afternoon it's rehearsal on this side of town, at Rosenthal's studio. Not over on Broadway for a change . . ."

She nodded. She appreciated how he treated her with kindness, never overtaxed her, but would instead take her other obligations into account when assigning her work. So he arranged for her to work in the supper clubs on Friday through Sunday, meaning that aside from the rehearsals to learn that weekend's choreography, she was still free to do everything else: the sewing for her boss, Gerta, and the ballet training she refused to give up, even though it provided her with no income yet. It just meant she was busy all the time, which was exactly what Liesel wanted.

Leo handed her a rehearsal schedule. "Check back with me later this week on your way to Rosenthal's. I think I might have something at the Crown Club for next week, but it's not confirmed yet."

She smiled. "Well, you know I'll be ready when you need me, Mr. Stein."

Leo reached into the desk drawer. "You never stop, do you? One of the hardest-working girls I know. To think, if you wanted to do this full-time, how much of a commission I could make off of you!"

"I don't want to break my promise to Gerta." She smiled and fluttered her eyelids, not to be coy, but because she enjoyed being especially sweet to him. "And I can't disappoint my teacher, Psota, either."

Leo nodded. He knew very well that her teacher, Ivan Psota, was the one who had gotten her out of Czechoslovakia in time.

"Yes, yes. I know how much you owe him. That's why I don't push you like I do the other girls."

"I'm very grateful, Mr. Stein."

"Just be thankful that you look like my daughter." He shook his head, placed his cigar on the ashtray, and reached for his desk drawer.

"I've taken out my commission, but the rest is for you, sweetheart."

She glanced quickly at the hand-drawn numbers and Leo's rolling signature on the bottom. Twenty-five dollars. Enough to pay her room and board, as well as some to put away in case the Red Cross was ever able to locate her family and she could bring them over.

Leo glanced at his watch. "So, Rosenthal's studio. It's on 38th and Lex. Better get going. You need to be there by two."

Liesel had twenty minutes.

"Thank you, Mr. Stein." She said the words carefully and respectfully, ensuring, once again, that he could hear the gratitude in her voice.

———

Liesel knew she had many things in her life to be grateful for. And one of the main ones was her dance teacher, Ivan Psota.

When she started grade school, her mother's clients began commenting with increasing frequency that Liesel was born with the physique of a dancer. It wasn't just that she was slim, for that was the case for most young girls her age. It was the length and proportion of her limbs that gave her a natural gracefulness that set her apart from her peers.

Her mother had sewn costumes for the prestigious dance academy in the city for over a decade, and Liesel had spent most of her childhood seeing her fit the girls for their corsets and tutus. Her mother used a special closet in the back of the apartment to store her baskets of beads and yards of tulle. And although Liesel's mother began to teach her to sew from the time she could hold a needle and thread, she imagined her daughter receiving the applause, perhaps even traveling with the troupe, rather than behind the scenes making the costumes for the stage.

Her mother brought her in to audition for the conservatory the minute she was old enough to try out. The sight of the school's famous ballet master, Ivan Psota, was hard to forget. He had the dark hair and broad smile that befitted Hollywood. And his well-tailored suits were anchored by two perfectly arched feet, which were encased in black slippers and moved with great elegance across the wooden floor.

The other girls, who were a few years older than Liesel, all flushed in his company. They knew that this man was already regarded as one of the best dancers in their country, and had also recently begun to hone his skills as a choreographer. Yet he saw something unique in young Liesel, thus ensuring she was accepted to the dance conservatory for the following year.

Liesel's mother, concerned that the rigorous program at the dance school would deplete her daughter's energy, always made sure she had a kitchen full of Liesel's favorite food. Each day, before she left for the conservatory, Liesel would find a freshly baked apple strudel and a glass of milk waiting on the table for her.

"Make sure you eat before you dance," her mother would remind her.

But Liesel never needed reminding. From the moment she saw her mother's baking, she found herself sitting down with napkin in hand.

For the next five years, Liesel would study dance under Master Psota. He had brought an element of glamour and prestige to the

conservatory when he began there ten years earlier, at the age of
twenty. Liesel was indebted to him not only because he trained her
as a dancer, but for something far more important, and for which
she knew she could never repay him.

Psota had helped save her.

———

From the very beginning of her training, Psota had taken a special
interest in Liesel. He noticed her perfectly arched feet, the natural
lightness to her step, and, even more unusual for her young age,
her sharp mind, which remembered his choreography. He believed
that if she continued to work hard, someday she might make it to
the ballet corps.

But in the spring of 1939, when Liesel was seventeen years old
and at the height of her training, Hitler marched into Czechoslovakia.

"I can no longer keep you at the conservatory," Psota told Liesel
after calling her into his office. "You know I'd do anything to keep
you here . . ." He stumbled to catch his breath, and his normally
bright and lively eyes looked as grey and lifeless as plaster. "But it's
the law now." He fingered a memo on his desk. "I've been ordered
to dismiss all my Jewish students."

Liesel sat in Psota's office, a photograph of him surrounded by
one of his dancing troupes resting on his desk. The girls were in
black leotards, their bodies strong, athletic, invincible. She dug a
nail into her palm, thinking the jab of pain would prevent her from
crying in front of him.

"Liesel, I wish I had the power to change this . . . but I don't."

"I know, Master Psota . . ." she could barely whisper.

"But I'm not going to let Hitler win. You're still going to dance,

Liesel. I mean that." He straightened in his chair. "I've asked someone I met in Monte Carlo last summer to help you, a man with a lot
of wealth and power. He has many contacts in the United States
government, and I've written to him to see about getting you a visa."

"I don't understand. Why would he help me or my family?"

"His name is Carl Laemmle, and he's a German-born Jew . . .
He founded a film company called Universal Pictures, in California."

The names didn't mean anything to Liesel, but from the sound
of Psota's voice, she knew it was something impressive.

"He's already helped a lot of Jewish families in his hometown
in Germany and other places in Europe. Many of them are on their
way to America as we speak. I've written him personally to ask
him to also sponsor you. I've told him not only that you dance, but
that you're also a great seamstress and learned how to make costumes from your talented mother. He has many contacts in California and New York, so there will be work for you when you
arrive."

Liesel felt a lump in her throat. She couldn't believe that her
teacher would go to such lengths to get her out of a country that
now so clearly no longer wanted her or her family.

So many of their neighbors had stopped talking with them.
Once her father's shop was shuttered closed by the new anti-Jewish
laws, most people shunned them.

But a sudden fear gripped her, as Psota had only mentioned
there being work for her in America. "And my parents?" she ques-
tioned, her voice barely above a whisper. "Will he sponsor them as
well?"

He turned his gaze away from her, looking past the long French
doors of his office. On Psota's desk she noticed another photo-

graph, this one of him as a boy with his parents, when he was close to the same age as she was now.

"No," he said softly. "He can only sponsor you . . . I'm very sorry."

Before she could get the words that were forming on her lips, he anticipated what she was going to say.

"Liesel, I've already spoken to your parents. I actually discussed it with them before I even wrote to Mr. Laemmle." He stopped speaking for a moment, and his eyes once again left her and settled on the ground. "They realize what's going on here. They want you to take this opportunity. They want you to go. To America."

———————

By June, Liesel had her affidavit and visa. As per Mr. Laemmle's instructions, she would leave for Antwerp, and from there she would take a boat to New York. That afternoon, as she said good-bye to her parents at the train station in Brno, her mother reached into the basket she was carrying and pulled out a package.

"What is it?" Liesel asked, her voice struggling to keep back her tears. For the first time in her life, Liesel's feet felt heavy, as if someone had poured cement into her soles. She wanted to anchor herself to the street and tell her parents it was impossible for her to leave them.

"I made your favorite," her mother said, tears forming in her eyes. "Apple strudel . . ."

Liesel took the package, and in her hands she could feel a little bit of the warm fruit seeping through the cloth.

"Now I can pretend that you're just going off somewhere to dance," her mother said, forcing a smile.

Liesel sensed how fragile the long loaf of strudel felt in her hands.

"I'm afraid it might break before I eat it."

"It doesn't matter if it splits apart, my darling. Even if it separates into crumbs, all the ingredients are still there."

Her mother's hands reached over and clasped Liesel's.

"It's just like Papa's and my love for you."

———

Liesel arrived in New York not knowing a single word of English. She did know some German, though, which would serve her well, as Mr. Laemmle had arranged a sewing job for her with a German Jew who owned a costume atelier in the theater district. As for her ballet classes, Psota made sure she could study in the evenings with a former Kirov dancer, a Madame Polyakov, on the Upper West Side. But each night, no matter how tired Liesel was from her sewing work or her ballet, she lay awake worrying about her family back in Czechoslovakia.

She had written countless, increasingly desperate letters to her parents back in Brno but had only received one back since her arrival in New York. That letter, sacred to her now, she kept folded carefully in a small box in her dresser drawer.

Our dearest Liesel,

As I write this to you, I imagine you with your bright eyes, your joyful smile, and your leotard and dance shoes close by. This is what a mother does to warm her heart. We have seen Master Psota, and he tells us that Mr. Laemmle has made good on his

promises to you. That you are working and still studying your
ballet. Papa and I can't tell you how happy it makes us to know
that your life in America is moving forward.

We have received your first letter and do not want you to
worry so much about us. Psota has made sure I stay busy sewing.
He has the dancers visit me before curfew, and only one or two of
them come each week so as not to raise suspicions that he is
helping supplement our income. Franny and Tomas Kohn have
chosen to go to a place outside Prague called Terezín. They say if
we go there, it will be safer than staying in the city. Papa hasn't
yet decided if we will go, too. How much longer we have to choose
before they choose for us, I do not know. But please do not worry
about us, miláčku. *Knowing that you are smiling across the*
ocean gives us sustenance. I pray we will see you soon.

All our love,
Mama and Papa

She had read the letter so many times that the paper was now
in danger of tearing at the folds. Because she had only been able to
bring a small suitcase with her, Liesel now had so few tangible
things that connected her with her family life back in Brno. She
had two dresses that her mother had sewn for her, a small leather
photograph album that captured scattered memories of their family vacations in the Moravian countryside, and a recording that
Psota had brought to her the night before she left, which she had
carefully wrapped within the layers of clothing in her suitcase.

That last night, when her mother had tried her best to make
something from what little they had left in rations, Psota came to
their apartment to say good-bye.

When Liesel opened the door, he was standing there in his elegant suit. In one hand he held a bunch of flowers for her mother, and in the other, a record that he gave to her.

"It's a going-away gift," he told her. "Dvořák's *New World Symphony*."

She knew it well. It was a favorite of the music students at the conservatory who shared part of the building with the dancers, and Liesel had heard it several times floating through the walls of the practice halls. The composer was a Czech who had written it while living in New York and conducting the Philharmonic. The symphony was filled with melodies that were inspired by Native American music and by African American spirituals that Dvořák had heard in America. The second movement was especially beautiful; one of the boys at the conservatory tried to impress her after rehearsal one day by telling her that it had inspired another American composer to create a song called "Going Home."

"An appropriate gift," she said, smiling and kissing him on the cheek. "Thank you so much. I'll treasure it."

That night, after they ate the simple potato dumplings that her mother had prepared, her father took the record Psota had given Liesel and put it on the Victrola.

The music had a layering to it that befitted the evening. In it she heard the longing for one's homeland, infused with a ray of hope.

"Dvořák wrote it when he was in America, Liesel."

"I know," she said quietly.

"I've thought about choreographing a ballet to it . . ." His voice drifted. She saw him close his eyes, as if imagining the choreography. All of them later hummed along with the theme from the second movement.

That night everyone seemed to welcome the comfort the music

offered. It filled the space where words failed them. And later in New York when Liesel could not find the peace to sleep when haunted by fears of what had befallen her family, she would think of the beautiful strings and the English horn in the second movement and consider it an invisible thread that connected her heart to her family back home.

Liesel shared her small apartment with another girl whom Mr. Laemmle had also helped bring over from Europe. It was sparsely furnished, with just two beds and a kitchen table and chairs. But after a year of working for Gerta Kleinfeld's costume atelier, Liesel had enough money to buy a secondhand Victrola from a consignment shop, without feeling guilty that it would draw too much from the money she was saving to one day bring her family to America.

On the nights the pain of being separated from her family was unshakable, she would put on the Dvořák recording from her teacher back home and imagine all of them in the living room again, her parents' soft hands within reach.

Once the day began, though, she was too busy to allow herself to feel melancholy. She spent hours stitching hems, taking in bustiers, and adding embellishments to the costumes of women who performed at supper clubs. This was the bread and butter of Gerta's business. And after she finished at Gerta's around one P.M. each day, she would try to take an afternoon class at Madame Polyakov's dance studio to practice her ballet, using a portion of her wages to pay for her lessons.

Liesel was grateful she had learned a skill from her mother that could pay the bills. Within Gerta's sewing studio, chorus girls, with their elaborate hair and makeup, white smiles, and perfect curls, stood in front of the mirror as Liesel pinned their fittings so their costumes enhanced their figures. At the conservatory back home, she had danced in nothing more than a leotard and tights, with her hair swept back into a bun.

But in the crowded and noisy confines of the sewing room, Liesel learned the art of transformation. Her mother had taught her about ballet corsetry and whaleboning, but here in New York she learned about waist nippers and other items that could transform even the slightest girl into a goddess.

Over the next several months, she began to develop a close relationship with the dancers who were sent over to Gerta's for fittings. The girls liked Liesel's light touch with her needle and thread, and the way she understood, from her own years of training as a classical dancer, how their bodies moved while they performed. She knew how important it was that their costumes not only flattered their bodies but also held up while they danced.

"Raise your arms up," she would say to them in her broken English. "Arch your back . . ." She gave them cues to enable her to alter the costume so it would not shift or gap while they stretched their bodies and moved across the stage. She understood that nothing was more distracting for a dancer than to feel that her costume might come undone.

About a year after she arrived, one of the girls, who was named Victoria, struck up a conversation with her.

"You always move so elegantly," she told Liesel. "You move just like a dancer . . ."

Liesel smiled. "I do dance. But only ballet." She took a pin from her cushion and slipped it into the hem of Victoria's skirt.

"I knew it!" Victoria laughed. "I could see it, just how you moved across the room. Shoulders back, neck long . . ."

Liesel laughed.

"Plus you have great legs." Her eyes ran over Liesel from top to bottom. "Why, heck, you should be dancing with us, not holed up in here!"

Liesel bent over to find some more fitting pins and to take in Victoria's costume. She was standing near the full-length mirror and was trying to adjust the corsetry to fit Victoria's tiny rib cage.

"I have no stage background," Liesel said. "Just my time at my school back in Europe and the classes I take here after work. I'm lucky to have this work sewing . . ."

"Don't be silly," Victoria answered. "I can see with a little makeup and some work, you'd be fantastic on the stage. Your posture is perfect, and the dances are really easy. We're just background beauty for whoever is singing that night. It's not hard at all, especially compared to ballet . . ."

"But my English . . ."

"You don't even need to talk! Just to understand the directions . . ." Victoria was beginning to move her arms about.

"Careful," Liesel said, slightly amused by the suggestion she could be a dancer in New York City. "I don't want you to scratch up your arms with all these pins."

———

That afternoon, after Liesel had made sure her costume looked like a second skin, Victoria handed her Leo Stein's business card. "Give him a visit," she insisted. "You're as much of a dancer as I was when I got started.

"Shouldn't lock a body like that up in a sewing studio all day. Tell him Victoria Creegan sent you. It's only three blocks from here. Go pay him a visit during your lunch break."

———————

It was now nearly three years since she had begun dancing at the supper clubs. The money she had saved from her paycheck and from her sewing, which she hoped to use one day to bring her parents over, remained untouched. But terrible reports were now coming out of Europe. Rumors of concentration camps and of Jewish families being rounded up and sent to places in Poland.

She spent so much of her day with a silk-screened smile imprinted on her face and her body propelling itself to embrace the laughter and music around her. But when the makeup was wiped off and her sequined dance costume put away, the black-and-white photographs in the newspapers were a haunting she couldn't shake.

In those moments when she was alone, her body propped up in bed and a borrowed book she was using to study English on her lap, she saw her mother saying good-bye for the last time through a forced smile, and her father still holding on to her bag for a few more moments. She didn't want to look at those horrible photos in the paper and believe her parents could be amongst the piles of bodies or reduced to dark ash. She wanted instead to look at the family photograph that sat on her nightstand and believe that they were still just as she had left them. Father in his dark brown overcoat and stylish fedora, and Mother always with something warm and sweet in her hands.

———————

For two days, Gregori searched the crowds for the girl in the tulip green dress. He scanned the parade of dark suits and white shirts, and the women in their autumn costumes of felt hats and kidskin gloves. He listened to every footstep and took breaks between his playing in order to study the faces that stood in line for Murray's pastries.

In the course of a day, Gregori saw several hundred commuters walk past him and his violin. Some stopped briefly to listen to him play, and a number of them dropped some change into his velvet-lined case as a token of their appreciation. But he still couldn't shake the image of the girl with the light, dancerlike footsteps and the face of an old-world beauty.

Then, that following Tuesday afternoon, a little after one P.M., he saw her again. It was definitely her. Her unmistakable face. Her legs. That smile. The footsteps light as air.

This time, he knew he had to be quicker with his bow and start playing immediately. She had not responded to Mozart, so Austria was quickly erased from his mental list of possibilities for her homeland. Germany was the next obvious choice. It gave Gregori the option of one of the three "Bs": Bach, Brahms, or Beethoven. Both Brahms's and Beethoven's violin concertos would allow him to impress the girl with his talent, but he could also play the "Ode to Joy" theme from Beethoven's Ninth Symphony and ignite the crowd. Perhaps the attention around him would be a way to draw her near?

He saw a slight twirl as he began to play. Her heel had pivoted gracefully as she turned from Murray's with her wax paper bag in her hand, like the miniature ballerina in a music box he once saw in an antiques store near his apartment. A twirling girl made of porcelain no bigger than his thumb with a postage stamp–sized skirt made of tulle.

He saw she had looked in his direction, but she did not stop as he hoped she would. He was sure that she had reacted to something in his playing, though. He had seen her twirl, a movement of pleasure and a visceral response to the music that had come from his bow. It was an improvement from the last time, he told himself, trying not to be deterred. This time, as she walked toward the door, she turned her head and gazed back at him briefly. Her smile pierced his heart, a bounty more rewarding than all of the coins in the world.

As Liesel headed toward Mr. Stein's office, she felt a buoyancy in her step that had nothing to do with the sunshine hitting her face or the fact that she knew she'd soon be getting her next paycheck. Something in the music she had just heard coming from the violinist in Grand Central had made her feel happy and alive.

She hadn't heard the "Ode to Joy" in ages, and its inspiring melody lifted her. What had he played the last time? she now wondered. Was it *Eine kleine Nachtmusik*? She remembered hearing that music countless times wafting from the cafés late at night in Brno. This violinist's playing was enchanting. She'd heard lots of the buskers in the subway stations since she arrived in New York, but most of them chose works by contemporary composers such as Gershwin or Duke Ellington, probably because they thought those were the pieces that would inspire people to reach into their pockets. But this man seemed to prefer the music that reminded her of Europe.

As she walked, Beethoven's notes lingered in her mind. She thought of her former life back in Brno, and those days at the dance conservatory where the music students often tried to gain the attention of the most beautiful dancers by playing their instruments with as much passion as possible.

———

Those years were the sweetest in Liesel's memory. A time when she not only began cultivating her love of dance and music, but also when she thought it would all go on like that forever. A life of culture and art, and of friends and family.

During her last year with Master Psota, she witnessed him at the height of his creativity as he choreographed Dvořák's *Slavonic Dances*. He spent hours with her and five other girls from his master class calling out the intricate footwork. But even with the door to his studio closed, the beautiful music played by the chamber orchestra filled the entire school.

———

She was surprised at how much she was now looking forward to the rehearsals at Rosenthal's dance studio. They provided a few consecutive days where she could grab one of Murray's pastries and again be serenaded by the handsome violinist who seemed to be playing just for her.

On Thursday afternoon, after a morning of sewing at Gerta's, she walked up the stairs from the subway to the Lexington Avenue exit side of Grand Central, and she could already hear him playing around the corner. She thought he was playing a violin concerto, maybe by Mendelssohn, but she couldn't be sure. But one thing was certain: as soon as she heard the music, she could feel her body start responding to it. The notes were like little pulleys within her. She could feel her limbs wanting to stretch, and her feet wanting to point and flex. In her mind, she could imagine herself dancing as if she were on her own private stage and this man she didn't know was her accompanist.

The line for Murray's cart was not as long as it usually was, and as she walked past this nameless musician, she turned her head and smiled at him. She saw his eyes look up from his instrument, his own lips curling into a smile to match her own.

"Next!" Murray's sharp voice called out from behind the counter of his cart.

"What do you want, doll? An apple strudel like always?"

"Yes," she said, blushing. "But one of these days I'll have to try your doughnuts."

"You look more like a strudel girl," he said, smiling, and handed her the wax paper bag. Already he was on to the next customer, and she turned to look at the wall clock just above the entrance that led down to Vanderbilt Hall.

She had less time than she thought. She now had only ten minutes to get to rehearsal at Rosenthal's on time.

As she quickened her step to exit the terminal, she could hear the violinist begin to play a piece by the Polish-born composer Chopin. It struck her as an odd choice, as even she knew the piece sounded far better on a piano than on a violin.

It didn't occur to her that he was playing it just to see if she might respond. To see if she was from Poland, like he was. That he was searching to find something that would remind her of her home, wherever that may be.

———

That afternoon, Liesel continued to think of the violinist who always seemed to play in the same part of the terminal, and whose musical selections began to bemuse her. She had not yet been able to see his face in its entirety, for his instrument had obstructed a clear view of his features. But Liesel had definitely seen his eyes.

They had fastened onto her like a magnet. Even now, she could remember the weight of his gaze.

Rosenthal was barking orders at the girls to remember their steps.

"You're going to descend the stairs, with your arms laced through your partners' . . ." he commanded. "Remember to smile. Remember you need to keep your legs in sync with the others . . . I want everything seamless . . . Girls!" He raised his voice and glared at one of the girls who was chatting with another dancer. "Three days until this has to be perfect. So let's concentrate and get going!"

Liesel kept quiet and made a mental note of the choreography. It was simplistic to her, nothing compared to the intricate work that Master Psota had created.

She looked up at the clock and saw it was almost four P.M. Before she headed to the Upper West Side to Madame Polyakov's, she could dip into Grand Central and see if the violinist was still playing.

————————

By three thirty, Gregori had already packed up and left to get to his night job at the theater's orchestra pit. As he pushed through the doors to Lexington Avenue, he couldn't stop thinking about the music he chose to play for the girl that day.

Although she hadn't yet come over to him, at least today she had looked in his direction and smiled. This, he had to tell himself, was a good sign.

He knew selecting one of the *Polonaises* was a poor choice for him to play. It sounded terrible on the violin, given that Chopin wrote it (and virtually everything else he had composed) for the piano. But he thought that if she were Polish, she would have appreciated his feeble attempts to play something from her home-land. He racked his brain to think of what else he could play the next time he saw her.

He still had a few pieces left in his repertoire to evoke the different countries she might have come from. Anything to get her to stop for a few minutes.

He imagined that if he could do this, he would play the piece until the end, as if he were serenading her. And when he finally rested his bow, he could actually speak with her. Perhaps maybe even ask her to lunch at the Automat nearby.

He pictured a map of Europe in his head and thought about where to try next for her potential homeland. Russia was easy. Tchaikovsky. Gregori loved showing off his skills with the violin concerto, but the love theme from *Romeo and Juliet* would awaken the warm feelings of any girl, particularly a Russian far from home. If she were from a place like Bulgaria or Romania, then he was in trouble, though. No great composers from either of those countries. Maybe he could ask one of his uncle's diners for a suggestion for a folk song from there. And Hungary, like Poland, would also prove difficult. There was Liszt, of course. But he was another pianist, whose best works didn't translate well to violin. But if he tried that route again, after the Chopin debacle, wouldn't she now see that he wasn't playing for the money, but, instead, just trying to send a message that was only for her?

He hoped he'd see her again tomorrow and get another chance. He had already noticed her respond with her feet once to his music, and the last time he was sure he had gotten a smile. He also wondered where she might be rushing off to every afternoon. His mind created several scenarios, but none where she was locked away in an office with nothing but a typewriter and a phone.

———

As Gregori headed home to change his clothes for his orchestra job that evening, Liesel decided to dip one more time into the terminal and see if she might catch another performance by the violinist. But when she walked through the doors of the Lexington Avenue entrance, she didn't see him. Across from Murray's pastry cart, there was an empty spot, like a vacant stage that now was only squares of gleaming, pale marble. Liesel was surprised at her own sense of disappointment in not seeing him there.

She saw the shoeshine man busy with a customer, his back hunched over and a rag brushing off what looked like a middle-aged banker's now sparkling wingtips.

A woman was tugging her two children in the direction of the tracks, her son with his cap crumpled in his hand.

She looked at the empty space and her mind began to wander. There was the sewing at Gerta's that needed to be done, the performance on Friday night, and the final rehearsal for that tomorrow afternoon at two. Liesel saw Murray look up from his pastry cart. The trays were nearly empty.

"No more strudel," he said with a smile. "But I have a few more doughnuts."

She was hungry and knew it would be better if she had a sandwich or something healthier. But she had yet to try one of his doughnuts.

"Two sweets in one day?" She laughed and walked closer to the counter. "My waistline might not be able to take it."

"You must be joking," he said as he reached to take one and put it in the paper bag. Liesel removed a dime from her coin purse.

"It's on me, honey . . . A little taste of America to sweeten your day."

———

The following afternoon, she left Gerta's at lunchtime and went to Times Square to catch the shuttle for Grand Central. Mr. Stein had another check for her, and then she would go on to Rosenthal's for the last rehearsal.

In her hand was the contract for that evening.

Dates of performance: September 21–24, 1945
Start time: Be at theater no later than 5 P.M.
Performance at 7 P.M.
Payment: $10 for each performance

She folded the paper and slipped it into her purse. In her bag, she had packed her black ankle strap shoes, a waist nipper, and two pairs of hosiery, just in case one got a tear.

"Off dancing again?" Gerta had asked her as she got ready to leave.

"Yes. I've left all the costumes on the racks with the names of the girls attached. Everything's up to date."

"It always is with you, *meine liebe*," she said in German, "my dear."

"See you Monday," Liesel said as she opened the door to leave.

"Unless I get around to seeing you perform." Gerta smiled and lifted her head from her sewing table. "One of these days, I will!"

Outside, the taxis were honking their horns and a couple on the sidewalk was locked in an embrace. As Liesel walked toward the subway station to catch the shuttle to Grand Central, she felt her hours at Gerta's falling away from her. Her neck lengthened, her spine straightened, and her feet sprang to life: it was as if the seamstress had instantaneously transformed into the dancer.

———————

Gregori had been tired from last night's theater performance. But after a strong cup of coffee and a hard roll from the deli beneath his apartment, he had gotten to Grand Central and began to tune his violin.

The day was hot and overcast. He was too warm to wear his suit jacket, so he folded it carefully and placed it against the wall behind him.

By eleven A.M., Gregori had begun with Vivaldi's Concerto in D Major. Though originally intended for the lute, it had been transposed for the violin. Everyone loved the romantic largo. It stirred something within them and the tips were generous. Gregori wondered if that might have been a better piece with which to have serenaded the girl in the tulip green dress, though he doubted that she was Italian.

At noon, after a small lunch break, just as he was trying to think of what to play next, he saw her come up from the stairs, just out of the corner of his eye. There was hardly a soul around her, so he could focus on her completely. In her silver grey dress, she looked like a fluttering dove, one who had long limbs rather than wings. He was sure she paused for a moment to look at him.

As he gazed at her, she looked as though she was suddenly standing at the threshold of two worlds. He took his violin and placed it under his chin, his eyes stealing one more glance at the beautiful girl in the soft-colored dress.

It was then that the perfect music came immediately to him. The melody that seemed to befit her fully: the second movement of the Dvořák *New World Symphony*.

His eyes shut and he lifted his bow. He would play the piece as though it had been created out of his own longing and the deepest recesses of his heart.

The music swelled within his violin like a starburst of emotion. His body swayed, and his head moved from side to side. The music was pouring from every aspect of his soul. He realized he was playing it both for himself and for the girl, two strangers in New York who were neither Americans nor completely refugees. But a pair of souls finding themselves caught between each of those two worlds.

Liesel's feet had momentarily locked underneath her as soon as he started playing Dvořák's haunting melody. Her mind rushed with memories of that same piece being played back in Brno.

It was as if this nameless violinist had peered into her soul and found the one piece of music that encapsulated her journey to America. He played with such depth that one didn't even miss the sounds of the English horn from Dvořák's original score. His playing brought her back to her parents and her teacher, and to the warmth of the living room she had left so many years before. She felt not just nostalgia and longing, but now a sense of possibility as well. Something in his playing made Liesel believe he had chosen this piece just to reach her.

For years she had studied how to interpret music so her limbs could move in synchronicity with the score. Now Liesel felt herself being pulled in his direction, a choreography that was between them alone. "How did you know?" she whispered, as her eyes locked onto his. In his gaze, she saw not only warmth, but also the recognition that this music had special meaning for him, too.

As Liesel moved closer, he set down his bow and smiled as if the stars from the Great Hall had suddenly aligned. With tears in her eyes, Liesel took her last steps toward Gregori, her feet fixed at the edge of his private stage. And when she finally stood right there in front of him, she knew she would never leave.

The Lucky One

JENNA BLUM

For my dad

I.

GRAND CENTRAL TERMINAL, NEW YORK
Thursday, September 20, 1945

~ 1 ~

It was late September when Peter saw the woman who looked just like his mother, sitting in the Oyster Bar near one of the grand architectural columns that reminded him of the Hotel Adlon in Berlin. She was eating something Peter's mother would never have put in her mouth because it was *treyf*—a shrimp salad. Peter quite liked it, as he liked most things forbidden by his mother's childhood teachings. He cleared the woman's dining companion's soup bowl—the remains of the restaurant's nominal dish, oyster stew, pooling tepidly in the bottom—then stopped, the bus tub held at his waist level, and just stared. Despite her consumption of shellfish, this woman had to be Jewish. She was, to use the English idiom for it, a dead ringer for Peter's mother. Salt-and-pepper hair braided around her head. A rose-colored dress. Pearls. A fur stole, although the day outside was quite warm and the air in the Oyster Bar soupy. The woman's nose was the delicate blade of a fish-boning knife, her exquisitely ruched skin the texture of a peach the day before the fruit rots and its mortal sheath slides off. The term in German was *Doppelgänger*; it meant "double goer," one's exact counterpart, and in literature, Peter remembered from his university days, a confrontation with one's *Doppelgänger* signified imminent death. But what did this mean, spying not his own ghost but his mother's?

The woman, sensing Peter's stare or his lingering presence next to the table, looked up and over, and Peter saw with deepening shock and fear that the woman even had his mother's eyes, his own eyes, deep set and blue green. Peter fully expected her to say, *"Ach, Petel, your beautiful hair! It's far too long,"* and then to reach over, brush the locks off his forehead, and say to her friend, a corpulent man with black-rimmed glasses, "Did you ever see such golden curls on a boy? A gift from my mother, so wasted on him. Isn't he the lucky one," and then she would sigh dramatically and smile at Peter with the greatest tenderness. This *Doppelgänger*, however, did nothing of the kind. Her face, at first inquiring, tightened into an irritated expression. She looked him up and down and seemed on the verge of saying something sharp when her traveling gaze fixed on Peter's left forearm. Peter himself glanced down, although of course he knew what was there. The bus tub had pushed up the sleeve of his white shirt, unbuttoned in the heat of the kitchen, to expose the small, crooked greenish line of death camp numbers.

The woman looked quickly away from the tattoo, then back, then at Peter's face. She forced a smile that sat ill on her features and angled forward to say something to her dining companion, the dead fox face of her fur stole dangling perilously close to a little silver tureen of Thousand Island dressing. Peter sneaked his hand onto the table to retrieve this just in time and shifted the bus tub to better conceal his number. The woman and her dining companion were both examining him now, trying to look as if they weren't looking while their glances ticked from Peter's arm to torso to face to legs, checking for visible infirmities from the camp: missing teeth, perhaps, or broken, ill-set bones; a lopped-off ear; the blue nails and protruding ribs of malnutrition.

Peter rehearsed in his mind what he would say next so it would emerge in perfect English, with only the slightest taint of German—*You mean to tell me this kid's a Jew who talks like a Kraut?* one of Cousin Sol's friends had said recently at the country club. *Now that just beats all!*

Peter reached for the woman's bread plate, smattered with crumbs and butter.

"May I clear this for you, madam?" he asked.

II.
LARCHMONT, NEW YORK
Thursday, September 20, 1945

 2

After his shift was over, Peter took the New Haven line back to Larchmont, to the house in which he was living now—Cousin Sol's. Sol's Tudor mansion in Westchester was similar enough to Peter's childhood home in the affluent Charlottenburg suburb of Berlin to make Peter feel as though he were in a dream in which everything was familiar, yet deeply, deeply wrong. Both houses were large and half-timbered, with stone foundations. Both were surrounded by extensive, well-manicured grounds. But there the likenesses stopped. The view here was not the River Spree and the Schloβ Charlottenburg but the Long Island Sound. The very rock upon which Sol's house sat was different, huge boulders flecked with sparkling stuff, which Sol's gardener had told Peter was called mica. The plantings were exotic imports, bonsai and Japanese maple trees, tropical bushes with lush pink blooms, not the groomed topiary and raked gravel paths of Peter's youth. There was even a man-made waterfall chattering artfully down a dark, mossy rock channel to splash, finally, into a kidney-shaped swimming pool, painted aquamarine at the bottom, whereas the showpiece of Peter's parents' grounds had been a tennis court. Peter's wife, Masha, would have much preferred this pool, Peter thought, with its Hollywood intimations; she would have sunned herself alongside it in her polka-dotted suit and cat's-eye sunglasses, while the girls . . . He wiped his forehead on his sleeve as he mounted the stone steps to the terrace, the day humid and sultry with whirring insects, and used the key Sol's wife, Esther, had given him to let himself into the Larchmont house kitchen.

Inside, the house should have been cool, its temperature lowered by the rumbling window boxes Peter had been told were called air conditioners, but when he stepped into the kitchen he found it steamy with the bland smell of boiling vegetables. The maid, Ines, stood at the sink struggling to debone a large bluefish Cousin Sol had caught the past weekend in Long Island Sound, while Esther shucked ears of corn into a waste bin she had set in the center of the floor, on the Spanish tiles. More bounty from Esther's garden was piled on the counter, awaiting its turn to be cleaned and stripped: cucumbers, eggplants, and zucchini the size and circumference of Peter's arms. Peter had never seen such huge vegetables before coming to America and found them somewhat alarming. Didn't their size detract from their flavor? he had asked Esther when he first encountered her coming up the garden path in her straw sun hat, with a basket of tomatoes the size of infants' heads. Esther had laughed, showing her lovely, healthy white teeth. *Not at all*, she had said. *That's how we like it in this country—the bigger the better in America.*

She had allowed Peter to help the gardener lug more bushels of giant squash up to the house but had been mortified by Peter's suggestion that, since he was a trained cook, after all, he help assemble the produce into tasty dishes. If Esther was not much like Peter's mother, Riva, in stature and demeanor, she was similar in two other ways: she was a gentlewoman married to a man much louder than she, and she would not countenance any man working in her kitchen. Peter was not especially surprised to find this sentiment about his lowly profession had followed him across the ocean; Peter's father, Avram, had been the same way. It had been Avram's greatest personal disappointment that his son had not followed him into the practice of law, although before the Nazis had kicked Peter and every other Jew out of university in 1939, that was precisely what Peter had been studying. Peter had been so grateful to his oppressors for disrupting his education, so energized by his unexpected liberation, that he had for once not waited for Avram to arrange for him another position; instead, Peter had taken a Gentile friend's offer to work at the Hotel Adlon as a prep chef. By then, everyone agreed, it was lucky Peter had secured employment at all, though it was a pity that the only son of one of Berlin's most prominent families had been reduced to a kitchen boy. Even Avram had to accept it, and it was at the Adlon that Peter had discovered his surprising love and aptitude for cooking. He was careful to present a long face at home, but internally he rejoiced; until later in the war, he had secretly, stupidly thought the Nazis coming to power was the best thing that could have happened to him.

Now Peter turned away from the sight of Ines butchering the bluefish, though his hands itched to wrest it from her; he had learned early in his stay here, during a luncheon in the glass-walled room Cousin Sol and Esther called the solarium, not to offer culinary suggestions. No sooner had Peter tentatively mentioned that he could show the maid a way to clean the fish so scales would not end up in the bread, the cranberry mold, and the milk than Cousin Sol had smashed his highball tumbler on the glass-topped table and roared, *GodDAMNit! I will not stand for any relative of mine doing neb-bish work under my roof!* So Peter smiled now at Esther and said, in careful English, "Good afternoon, ladies. I see we are at work on the evening menu. What do we make?"

"What are we making," Esther corrected him. She was a tiny woman with short hair curled and teased to stand up as though she had recently suffered a fright; she wore a flowered caftan, several lengths of polished stone beads, and bright red lipstick, a waxy imprint of which she left on Peter's cheek when she craned up to kiss him hello. Peter reminded himself to wipe it off later, when he was out of her sight. "I am making rat-a-tou-ille," Esther said, pronouncing it carefully, "a vegetable stew—have you heard of it?—although it's for tomorrow, not tonight. The flavors blend together better if you make it a day in advance. Tonight we have the club, remember?"

Peter thought, then nodded. At least twice a week they dined at Cousin Sol's country club, and equally often they attended a fundraiser for Cousin Sol's excellent causes; tonight the two would be combined.

"Very good," said Esther. She took a long drag of a cigarette smoldering in a jade turtle-shaped ashtray amid the zucchini. The kitchen manager at the Adlon, Peter thought, would have threatened to break one of Esther's fingers off had he seen her smoking near the food.

"Your new tuxedo is in your room," Esther said, smiling at Peter; she had the lipstick on one of her front teeth, a red smear, but it was a radiant smile nonetheless. "Ines picked it up from Sol's tailor earlier, didn't you, Ines?"

"Yes, madam," Ines said, not glancing up from the fish. Ines never looked directly at Peter, nor spoke to him; her English was even more limited than his, Peter had observed, confined mostly to answering her employers in the affirmative or the negative. But sometimes when Cousin Sol and Esther were both out, Peter had overheard Ines discussing him on the telephone or with the gardener—sucking in her cheeks and slapping her ribs to pantomime a skeleton, starvation; clicking her tongue, issuing liquidly rapid pronouncements punctuated by much head shaking and sighs of *Ai! Ai!*

"Mr. Peter's suit is on his door," Ines said now, and Peter thought briefly of the humiliation of visiting Cousin Sol's tailor, trying on one of Sol's tuxedos, and having the tailor, a little man with a big mustache, tell Esther, *There's no way we can take this much in. Sol's got at least ninety pounds on this guy. We'll have to make him a new one—* then glancing up from Peter's feet with eyes aswim with sympathy.

"Did you eat?" Esther asked Peter now, and Peter said yes, thank you, he'd had lunch at the Oyster Bar. Esther shook her head and snuffed her cigarette. "That's not enough," she said, flinging open the refrigerator. "Here, here's some nice whitefish dip, and I think I've got some crackers—oh, would you like a peach? Last of the year—or some cookies?"

Peter smiled but again said no, thank you. When he had first arrived in this country, he'd been astounded by all the food—the abundance of it, the dizzying rainbow array, the fact that you could eat whatever you wanted whenever you wanted—and he had been ravenous all the time. Now, most days, his stomach felt like a shriveled walnut.

"At least some ruggelah," insisted Esther, pressing on him a plate of the small pastries, containing a prune spread and peppered with chopped nuts, that Peter had never seen before coming to America. *He doesn't know ruggelah?* Esther had said to Cousin Sol, astonished, and Sol had shrugged and said, *How many times do I have to tell you Avi and his family didn't observe.*

Peter took the ruggelah and a glass of milk to be polite. Esther patted his cheek, then pinched it, although Peter, at twenty-six, had not allowed his own mother to do this for at least fifteen years. "So handsome," Esther said, her eyes filling with tears, *"mien scheena Jung!* What those *goyim* monsters did to you," and she ripped off a sheet of what Peter had learned was called paper towel and blew her nose. "Go, go," she said, waving him away with this makeshift handkerchief, "go for a swim, lie down, rest. We've got a big evening ahead."

~ 3 ~

In the shadowy foyer beyond the kitchen, Peter stood with the plate of little mouse-shaped pastries in his hand, indecisive. Behind him, a grandfather clock identical to the one Peter had grown up

with bonged the quarter hour. He estimated he had forty-five minutes before Sol arrived home, flush with Crown Royal whiskey and
either triumph for having walloped his fellow commuters in the
club car at bridge or rage because they'd emptied his pockets.
Either way, Peter didn't particularly want to be in Sol's path. He
considered the pool; there was indeed time for a swim, and for a
moment Peter envisioned changing in the pool house with its
striped towels and pleasant smell of chlorine; floating on his back
in the man-made turquoise lagoon, listening to the waterfall, and
gazing up into the canopy of the huge oak that spread its branches
over the pool. Although the last time Peter had done this, he had
heard rustling in the wild reeds that divided Sol's property from
his neighbor's; turning his head from where he lay on the inflatable
raft and shielding his eyes, Peter had spied the two little girls who
lived next door, peering at him and whispering. When they realized they'd been found out, they fled, fleet and shy as deer, but not
before Peter had seen they were almost exactly the same age as
Vivi and Ginger, his twins . . .

He decided against the pool and began walking through the
house. The rooms were hushed and crammed with treasure from
Cousin Sol and Esther's numerous prewar trips abroad: Japanese
scrolls and golden Buddha statues; Russian dolls and Persian rugs;
Esther's Venetian glass collection. There was a lit display case containing what Esther had explained to Peter, her penciled eyebrows
again rising in dismay and pity at his ignorance, were Jewish arti-
facts: antique *dreydls* and menorahs belonging to Sol's grandfather;
a *tallit* once owned by a famous rabbi. There was a harp in the
living room and, in a specially designed nook, a Steinway grand
piano that, to the best of Peter's knowledge, nobody played.

He wandered, trailing his fingers over glossy surfaces and coming up dustless, his feet gliding soundlessly over the Oriental carpets like a ghost's. At some point, he must have put down the pastries, but he couldn't remember where. These memory lapses still plagued him, although they were growing less frequent; shock, Sol's physician had said, when Peter had first arrived in New York: the aftereffects of starvation and all Peter had been through. With rest and good nutrition, they would diminish over time. They seemed to be doing so, Peter thought; he had little trouble retaining orders at work, for instance, although every so often he still got on the wrong train or left a book in Esther's refrigerator, and once, most frighteningly, he had woken in the middle of the night and for several panicked moments had not been able to remember his own name.

At the end of a long hallway, next to Ines's quarters, was the room Esther had assigned to Peter: the Loom Room, or so Peter had nicknamed it because his cot shared the small toile-papered space with Esther's giant loom, on which she spun yards and yards of mohair. Peter went into this room and shut the door behind him, and there, on a hook, as Esther had promised, was Peter's new tuxedo. Slowly, Peter stripped to his underwear and took down the suit, but instead of putting it on, he draped it over the loom and stood looking at himself in the full-length mirror on the back of the door. His body glimmered mostly white in the light refracting off the Long Island Sound, winking blue beyond the window—the Loom Room being one of the few in the house that received direct sun. Like his memory, Peter's physique was not quite back to its prewar shape—or, to be more accurate, the body he'd had before Terezín and Auschwitz. Prior to deportation, even during rationing, Peter had actually been quite strong, a by-product of working on the kitchen line at the Hotel Adlon, a job that had required stamina, strength, and nimbleness. How Masha had loved to tease him about this, running her hands silkily over Peter's back and shoulders and biceps, remarking on his resemblance to the American actor Buster Crabbe. *My husband, Flash Gordon,* she said, kissing his neck, *my own personal Tarzan!* Peter had groaned and rolled his eyes, although he secretly preferred the comparison with the jungle hero to the awful two weeks Masha had decided he looked more like Errol Flynn and made him grow a pencil-line mustache. *You just want to see me in a leopard loincloth,* he teased her, and on their honeymoon he had been astonished when Masha produced just that, a ridiculous spotted length of fabric she had sewn herself and that Peter had wrapped around his head instead of his groin, like a turban. *Come to me,* he had said in his best Sheik of Araby accent. *You are my slave. I paid ten thousand camels for you!* and he had chased Masha shrieking around the luxurious hotel room, both of them scrambling on and over the bed like children, knocking over lamps and chairs. How they had laughed and laughed . . .

Peter stripped off his underwear as well, flicking contemptuously at his penis. Useless appendage, all the more so because it still worked, awakening him in the mornings and sometimes at night with its tumescence, throbbing—to what purpose? *You're young,* Sol's physician said. *There's little permanent damage; you'll bounce back quickly. You're one of the lucky ones.* Peter pulled on fresh briefs and the crisp new shirt, covering the purple scars on his rib cage and back, souvenirs from an SS officer dissatisfied with how quickly Peter had been laying gravestones from the nearby Jewish cemetery to pave a new road at Terezín. *Watch out,* Peter remembered the man saying as he beat Peter with his truncheon. *Move faster, faster! Or I'll kick you in the ass.* Peter had had the benefit of understanding the man, who spoke Peter's native tongue, unlike the prisoner next to Peter who, not comprehending, continued to move too slowly to suit the officer, who then unleashed his dogs. Even here, in the Loom Room, Peter sometimes woke abruptly from a dream of having to step over and over the ropes of intestines steaming and steaming on the gravestones.

The house vibrated as the garage door rumbled up in its tracks, a novelty Peter had yet to adjust to, and a minute later Peter heard Cousin Sol bellow, "Esther, I'm home." There was Esther's higher staccato voice, then the crack of ice cubes being freed from their tin tray and the clink of them hitting a glass. Sol demanded, "Where's my tux? Did you get it back from the cleaners?" More Esther, her words indecipherable but her voice drawing closer now; she was probably trotting to keep up with Sol, slightly behind him as he thundered along the hallway. "What?" Sol said. "The whitefish. Bring me some of that. I'm starved." The Russian dolls-within-dolls clattered on the table next to Peter's cot as Sol's heavy footsteps thudded closer. Sol could have been Peter's father's twin, separated at birth and spirited to America: short, stocky, powerfully built men you could hear coming from a hundred meters away, their mouths plugged with excellent cigars that they removed only to issue forth smoke and opinions. Self-made men, each with his own law firm; men of influence, self-described. At least, Avram, Peter's father, had been until the Nazis dismantled his business; even then, Avram had continued to funnel money and influence into organizations that carried Jewish friends off to distant countries. Later, after the Nazis took Avram away during the Night of

Broken Glass and put him in Buchenwald, Avram still proved stubbornly unsinkable; he returned—unlike so many others—and kept up his illegal activities, this time channeling Cousin Sol's funds into resistance networks in the newly established ghettos of Poland. *We will NOT leave,* Avram bellowed, whenever Peter's mother, Riva, brought up the subject. *You want me to bow to those thugs? Our family was practicing law in Berlin when their peasant grandparents were wiping shit out of their asses with their hands. Our family does NOT run.* It wasn't until the Nazis removed Avram for the second time, to Buchenwald again, Peter later discovered, and then to Lodz and finally to Birkenau, that Avram was finally quiet, leaving only Sol to carry on his good work.

"Where's the *nebbish*?" Sol was saying now, almost directly outside the door to the Loom Room; he would be standing, Peter deduced, near the entrance to Sol and Esther's master bedroom suite. "Is he home from the city?" and Esther said something affirmative in her anxious tones, and Sol said, "Does he have his suit at least?" and Esther assured him yes, and Sol said, "*Schlemiel* the busboy. After all I've done for him. My cousin Avi would be turning in his grave—if those Nazi bastards had left him one," and Esther said something like, *Shush, he'll hear you!* and ice cubes clinked and rattled as Sol handed her his glass. "Get me another one of these, would you?" he said. "Go get ready. We leave in half an hour." A door slammed. The floor creaked as Esther trotted quickly off down the hall. Peter looped his tie around the collar of his tuxedo shirt and went to his cot. He turned his head to the toile-papered wall; the slanted eye of a red deer, pursued by lords and maidens on a hunt, stared at Peter, sinister with inscrutable meaning. Peter lay back and shut his eyes against the evening sun.

~ *4* ~

By the time they arrived at the golf club—not the White Stag, which looked very much to Peter like the Schloβ Charlottenburg, but the Briar Rose, which allowed Jews—Cousin Sol was well *in the bag*, as Americans would say. Peter had picked up many such phrases for inebriation from the Oyster Bar kitchen staff: *soused*, *oiled*, *sloshed*, *three sheets to the wind*, and the most imagistic, *pie-eyed*. Sol was all of the above. He stashed bottles of Crown Royal in convenient locations throughout the Larchmont house; Peter had come across the navy blue velvet bags with their gold script and piping in Sol's phonograph cabinet, the breakfast nook, the pool house, and the powder room off the foyer—in this instance beneath the skirt of the knitted lady who was meant to conceal toilet paper. Sol also apparently kept a bottle in the glove box of the Volvo he drove, for handy tippling while traveling. The roads in Larchmont were serpentine, wending among huge rock outcroppings and alongside the shoreline of the Sound, and they were made all the more curvaceous by Sol's creative driving. At one point, Sol had not only crossed the yellow center line, a fairly frequent occurrence, but scraped the Volvo up against one of the boulders, making a squealing sound and causing Esther to grab Sol's arm and scream, *Solomon, you'll kill us!* and Sol to shake her off, roaring, *GodDAMNit, Esther, leave me alone! I know what I'm doing.* The resulting gash along the side of the car was deep enough to earn a startled look from the Negro valet at the club's front door, before the large bill Sol slipped him recalled him to his senses. Peter was not so fast to recover; he had not been frightened at the prospect of a crash, but he was nauseous, and the club's lobby seemed to tip and tilt before his eyes until he got control of his gorge.

They were all streaming toward the dining room, Sol's friends and colleagues—the *machers*, Peter had heard them called, the movers and shakers, doctors and lawyers and business owners who founded schools and gave to charities. They stopped to clap Sol on the back, to kiss Esther on the cheek and smile at Peter as they made their way toward dinner. The hallway was lined with flower arrangements in recessed alcoves and hung with portraits of the club's presidents, Sol prominent among them; the carpet was lush and gold patterned and the wallpaper gaily striped mint and flamingo pink; the chandelier tinkled overhead. The artificially cooled air was redolent of liquor and a hundred ladies' perfumes. Peter followed Esther to their table in the dining room overlooking the golf course and suddenly found standing before him a dark-haired woman his age, wearing pearls and a bright yellow frock. "Peter," Esther said, "this is Miss Rachel Nussbaum. Rachel, this is our cousin Peter I told your mother about, from *Europe*," and Esther pinched Peter's arm through his tuxedo jacket.

"How do you do," Peter said and bowed slightly from the waist, and Miss Rachel Nussbaum's cheeks instantly stained the color of raspberries. She smiled at Peter when he pulled out her chair for her; she was shy, it appeared, and graceful as she folded her full skirt beneath her, and utterly lovely—as unlike Masha as she could be. Masha, who had not been lovely, who in fact had been plain, long faced like a foal, but who had been so full of life she practically crackled with it, throwing off sparks. Masha with her flashing eyes and teeth, the first things Peter had noticed about her in the kitchen at the Hotel Adlon, and her surprisingly robust laugh and her one vanity: her beautiful, beautiful Veronica Lake hair . . . Peter smiled at Miss Rachel Nussbaum as his tablemates settled themselves into padded chairs; he feigned interest when she spoke, asking, How did Peter like America? What did he think of this Indian summer? but in answer Peter said, *"Bitte?"* and *"Entschuldigung Sie?"*—*Pardon me?* leaning forward and cupping his ear as if he were hard of hearing, and soon, as he had intended her to do, Miss Rachel Nussbaum lapsed into bewildered silence. Esther, who of course knew Peter's English was fairly good despite his truncated time at university, witnessed this charade from a seat away and shook her head; she murmured, "You have to live again, *bubbeleh.*" But she reached over and patted Peter's hand.

The first course was presented by Negro waiters in white gloves: a rather wilted Waldorf salad. Peter was not fond of apples amid his greens nor the aberration called American mayonnaise, which Peter knew came from plastic tubs instead of being freshly made, so he stirred the concoction with his fork as conversation swirled about his head. The usual topics, golf scores and politics, disobedient servants and clothes. Peter knew most of his fellow diners at this large table: the elder Nussbaums and Webers, the Steins and Rosenbergs. But there were a few he had not been introduced to, who cast puzzled glances at him until it was whispered to them who he was. Then their faces changed, assuming either expressions of magnified pity or the same oblique, crawling curiosity Peter's mother's *Doppelgänger* had displayed this morning in the Oyster Bar. Peter kept forking through his lettuce. He was used to these looks and had been ever since May, when the first *Life* magazine with the Margaret Bourke-White photos had appeared on the newsstands, the headlines proclaiming NAZI ATROCITIES and AT THE GATES OF HELL! above black-and-white images of skeletal prisoners and entangled corpses. Poor Esther had been unhinged for days, following Peter through the corridors of the Larchmont house, shaking pages at him and demanding, *Is this what it was really like in there, Peter? Did you see this? How about this? Or,* Gottenyu, *this?* Peter had excused himself and gone to the Loom Room, pleading exhaustion. He had not so much as glanced at the images. He didn't need to. He had seen the corpses in color.

Peter's right-hand seatmate, Dan Rosenberg, elbowed Peter in the ribs. "So how do you like it," he boomed, "working for the *alte kakker?*"

Peter tried to translate this as Dan waited, exhaling whiskey and impatience. Dan was Sol's age, the age Peter's father, Avram, would have been: in his midfifties, with a bald, spotted head and amazing purple lips like two cuts of liver. Dan lifted his highball glass toward Sol, seated across the round table. "WORKING FOR SOLOMON," he enunciated, as if Peter were slow-witted, "IN HIS LAW OFFICE."

"Ah," Peter said. "I do not work with Sol. I work in a restaurant."

"BUT I WAS TOLD YOU WERE A LAW STUDENT," Dan said.

"Long ago," Peter said. "I work now in the Oyster Bar in Grand Central Terminal. You must visit. We serve excellent Oysters Rockefeller."

Dan appeared to find it suspicious, Peter's backward slide from legal scholar to kitchen servant. He shot a look at his wife, Belva, and tapped his temple.

"ANYHOW," he said, "SOLLY'S A MENSCH. YOU'RE LUCKY HE SPONSORED YOU, WITH SO MANY OTHERS STILL IN THE CAMPS."

"Dan!" Belva Rosenberg gasped.

"I meant the DP camps, not the other ones," Dan muttered, and subsided into his drink.

Conversation resumed. Swans glided past the floor-to-ceiling windows, on the golf course's artificial lake. The Negro waiter replaced Peter's salad with a pallid salmon plank reposing among flower-cut radishes. Peter toyed with the fish, wishing very much he were back in the kitchen with the staff rather than in this upholstered seat. He would show them how to properly treat this fish, baking it in parchment paper, and then when they took their break he would join them as they smoked behind the rhododendron bushes near the loading dock, as he had seen them doing. He would have enjoyed working at this club, so convenient to the Larchmont house, but of course Sol would not hear of it. Peter wondered daily what had become of his friends in the kitchen at the Adlon: he had not had a chance to say good-bye to them; he had been at work one day and deported the next. Perhaps they were all still there, and maybe the Adlon was now the way it had been, the grandest restaurant in the best hotel in all of Berlin. Peter knew it was unlikely—he had heard the Adlon had been bombed—but he still held it in his mind like a photo, its marble columns and mirrored walls, the movie star patrons who sent Masha into a frenzy. Peter had once spotted Henry Ford, and a white-haired gentleman he was sure was Albert Einstein smoking in the lounge, but Masha had been more impressed by Clark Gable and Frau Marlene Dietrich, the Negress singer Josephine Baker and the actress Louise Brooks . . .

The salmon plates were whisked away and crumbs swept from the table by the white-gloved waiters. Then silverware chimed against glasses as Sol ascended to the podium at the front of the room, carrying his Scotch. There was applause. Sol dipped his head. "Thank you," he said. The lights dimmed.

"Many of you here know me," Sol began, and somebody yelled, "We sure do, Solly!" prompting laughter and a scolding susurrus of *shushing.* Sol waited tolerantly. In the spotlight, his complexion was so ruddy from golf and fishing he could have been mistaken for one of the Negros serving dinner. Peter had recently overheard Esther confide laughingly into the telephone, *Solomon has such a tan I woke up last night and screamed; I thought there was a* schvartze *in my bed!*

"We gather here tonight after the High Holidays not just to enjoy each other's company but to find yet another way in which to make amends, to give," Sol told the now-quiet room. "And the need for giving, especially now, is boundless. You all know I am a very dedicated man. I've been on the board of the Jewish Distribution Committee for thirty years. Saly Meyer and I, we saw the writing on the wall for European Jews before anyone here ever even heard the word *Nazi.* We funded the emigration of Jews to Canada, to the Americas and Palestine. We raised money for Jewish schools, hospitals, and orphanages. Because we knew what would happen to our people." He paused to sip his Scotch.

"In 1944, I was appointed by President Roosevelt himself to the War Refugee Board," he went on, in the same rolling tones Peter had heard him once use, at a smaller dinner party, to announce, *I was instrumental in bringing Polish ham to this country!* leading Peter to wonder whether Sol equated the saving of European Jewry with the importation of luncheon meat. "It is my job to ensure safe passage for Jews devastated by the war to this country and to help them set up new lives," Sol said. "Here tonight we have just such a young man, who has lost everything," and Sol gestured in Peter's general direction with his Scotch tumbler. "This young man is my family," Sol said. "His father, Avram, was my beloved cousin. We played together as boys when our families summered in the Alps, and as adults, when the Nazis started pushing our people into ghettos, Avi and I . . . Avi . . ."

Here Sol set down his drink. He removed his glasses and took out his handkerchief. This happened every time; the tears were genuine, Peter knew, which made them all the more terrible. All over the darkened room people wept in sympathy. Noses were sniffled, then honked. Peter could feel Miss Rachel Nussbaum gazing at the side of his face, her eyes a liquid glimmer. Peter knew what would happen next: Sol would tell the story of his own lost family, Peter's parents. A screen would roll down behind Sol and slides would be projected onto it, clicking one after another: of the ghettos and camps, then of the raw Displaced Persons settlements, Jewish sickrooms and community centers, Jewish children emaciated and lost. There would be cries of sorrow and outrage. Sol would emphasize that the good work, far from being over, was just beginning. Checkbooks would be removed from inner pockets and opened, supplementing the already high price of dinner. And as the pièce de résistance, the proof, Peter would be summoned to stand with Sol in the spotlight; he would be asked to remove his cuff link and roll up his sleeve to expose the tattoo. Now, Peter slipped off his tuxedo jacket in preparation. He sat back in the dark and awaited his cue.

5

Peter made his escape as soon as he decently could after the show, when he thought he would not be missed: while dessert, scoops of vanilla ice cream melting in silver cups, was being served and what Sol called *schmoozing* was going on. Although Peter slid along the circumference of the room, a tearful lady waylaid him and told him that her whole family, her aunts and uncles and all their offspring, had all perished in those awful camps—all, all!—and she had cried on Peter's starched shirt a little, and then he was free. He slipped into the hallway and walked quickly with his head down toward the closest set of double doors leading out onto the putting greens. But then, "Hello," said the quiet voice of Miss Rachel Nussbaum; she was standing by the exit in her yellow dress, gazing out at the misty night. "Would you care to join me for a cigarette?" she asked. "I'm so sorry about what happened to you in those . . . places. They must have been *terrible*," and Peter smiled and nodded and, pantomiming desperation, did an about-face and dove for the men's room.

Inside the tiled room with its smell of wet paper towel and urinal cakes, Peter locked himself into a stall and, without unbuttoning or lowering his trousers, sat on the commode. He mopped his forehead with his palms; his body was running with sweat, his hair damp and coming loose in clotted waves from its pomade, and he feared he smelled bad. Peter hated this above all else. In the camps, they had all stunk. He leaned his forehead against the cool metal wall of the cubicle and closed his eyes. How many more minutes— fifteen, twenty?—and then this evening would be over and they could go home. Or at least back to the Larchmont house. Although Peter didn't know why he wanted that; it wasn't preferable, not really. What did it matter whether he was here performing like a trained seal or lying on the cot in the Loom Room, hands crossed behind his neck, staring into the dark? There was no place he wasn't without them, Masha and Vivi and Ginger, and no place where he could be with them, either. There was no respite from this grinding existence, no restful place anywhere anymore.

Peter must have dozed, his head leaning against the side of the stall, for he was startled when the men's room door clanked open and two men came in. Sol's voice, which Peter would by now have recognized anywhere, and a fellow Peter thought was Sol's fishing partner Dutch, a confusing name because the man wasn't Dutch at all. In fact, he had told Peter when the three were out on Sol's boat, Dutch's family were Jews from Romania, and he didn't know what had happened to them, they hadn't been close, but he thought they probably— *zzzzht!* and Dutch had made a cutting gesture across his throat.

"How much you think you pulled in tonight, Solly?" Dutch asked, as flies were being unzipped, and Sol said something unclear. "Wow," said Dutch, "that's some haul," and there was the sound of a healthy stream hitting porcelain.

"I didn't know that about the kid," Dutch continued, "that he'd been in more than one camp. I thought he was just in hiding and then at, you know, that really bad one." Sol said something else lost in the urinal's flush, and then Dutch said, "Gee, that's too bad. Still, thank God he has you, huh, Solly? It's a real *mitzvah*, you helping him out like that."

"He's family," Sol said.

"How's he working out at the law firm?" Dutch asked.

"He's not," Sol said. "He's cleaning tables at some restaurant in the train station," and a faucet ran.

"Huh? Why?" Dutch said.

"He's no good," said Sol. "No ambition. He'll never make anything of himself. Soft—his own father said so."

"Huh," Dutch said. Then, cautiously: "Is he a *faygele*?"

"No," Sol said. "He had a family over there, wife and two kids. Cutest little twin girls you ever wanted to see. But they didn't make it. He wasn't man enough to save them."

"Gee," Dutch said again, "that's too bad," and then the taps squeaked off, the paper towel dispenser cranked, the door opened and wheezed shut.

Peter waited until he was sure they had gone. Then he emerged from the stall and washed his hands and face. He finger-combed his shining hair back into place and looked at himself dispassionately in the mirror. If there had been some gesture big enough to express the violence of emotion within him at that moment, he gladly would have made it. Instead, he straightened the jacket of his tuxedo, gathered himself, and went out.

III.
GRAND CENTRAL TERMINAL
Friday, September 21, 1945

 6

The next day, a Friday, Peter was in the Oyster Bar kitchen eating a hamburger before the lunch rush when Leo, the manager, came in. This was a rare foray; Leo was usually back in his office or surveying the front of the house—Peter had seen little of him since the day he'd been hired. Leo was in his early fifties, bald but with a beard as long as a rabbi's, bristling with vitality as if to make up for the lack of hair on his head. He was also cross-eyed, so that on the occasions he had addressed Peter, Peter had a hard time meeting his gaze and settled for focusing on the bridge of the manager's nose. The other staff had

various nicknames for him, calling Leo "Chrome Dome" or sometimes "the Generalissimo," but Peter liked him. Leo had been kind
to Peter since the June afternoon Peter, killing time between when
the train from Larchmont had disgorged him and his language class
on the Lower East Side, had wandered into the Oyster Bar and tim-
idly asked, after ordering a chicken salad sandwich, whether Leo
could use any help. Leo had rolled his crossed eyes and said, *Kid,
what do I look like, the classifieds?* But then he had noticed the tattoo
on Peter's arm and his expression had softened to sorrow and he had
said, *Okay, I don't need a cook right now, but I guess I could use a busboy.
Why don't we start you off there and see how you do.* Peter wished he
hadn't gotten the job out of pity; he would have very much liked to
show what he was capable of—like the night after closing when he
had made crêpes for the staff, adding the seltzer that was his secret
ingredient for laciness of the batter; how they had all applauded
when Peter had flipped the large, thin pancakes in the pan! Still, for
all its humbleness, Peter was grateful for this job—so much better
than being an errand boy in Cousin Sol's office until he finished pol-
ishing his English, when the busywork would have calcified to clerk-
ing and, eventually, the dreaded practice of law.

Now Leo once again looked mournful. He came in, glared around
over his bushy beard, and said, raising his voice to be heard above the
sizzling grills and churning dishwasher, "Where's the kid?"

"You mean Pretty Boy?" said Big Al, one of the cooks. "He over
there by the walk-in, eating us out of house and home, as usual."
He wiped sweat from his forehead and winked at Peter. Big Al was
another one Peter liked, although at first Peter had been fascinated
and a little wary of the cook, the first Negro Peter had ever seen in
person, outside the cinema. But Big Al, too, had been in Europe
during the war, fighting in the Battle of the Bulge, and he, like

Peter, was a refugee in exile. *I'm from Atlanta*, Big Al had said, *and don't let nobody tell you the South ain't a different country from up here, boy, because it surely is. And I ain't never going back. I guess after what I been through, I got the right to be treated like a real man.* Big Al teased Peter mercilessly about his looks, which Peter knew from the Adlon was a sign of acceptance, and what Big Al called Peter's double life. *Lookit you, Prince Valiant!* Big Al had chortled one morning, holding up the society pages a diner had left on a table; to Peter's chagrin, there was a photo of him and Sol at one of Sol's fund-raisers, this time at the Pierre. *You some sort of secret agent? I knew you was hiding something! Why you slumming here when you could be dating Miss Lana Turner? Where your penguin suit at?* But in a quieter moment, when Peter explained about being the front man for Cousin Sol's admirable causes, Big Al had looked thoughtful, then sad. *I get it*, he said. *You and me, we alike, boy. Me to white men and you to the Nazis— and now even to your own people—we both niggers.*

"Yo, Goldilocks," Big Al called now, "Mr. Leo wants you," and Peter jumped up from the onion crate on which he had been sitting, cramming the last chunk of meat into his mouth. No matter how little appetite Peter had nowadays, he could not resist hamburgers, which was lucky as Big Al cranked out an assembly line of patties for him throughout the day—*After what them Nazis did to you, boy, you ain't got no more meat on you than a chicken wing! We got to fatten you up some.*

Leo spotted Peter in the corner and beckoned to him. "Kid," he said, "come with me," and he led Peter out of the steamy kitchen and through the rear of the restaurant to his tiny office. It was hot in this room, too, Leo's black wire fan riffling his pinup girl calendar, hiding and revealing Miss September 1945 in an endless game of peekaboo but doing little to stir the stuffy air.

Leo sat on the edge of his desk and looked sadly at Peter, who clasped his hands and fought the urge to stand at attention. He wished he had at least had the chance to remove his apron, stained with ketchup and Thousand Island dressing.

"Kid," Leo said, "I gotta let you go."

For a minute Peter didn't comprehend this. He processed and reprocessed the translation—*Let you go? Let go?*—and all the while what flashed through his mind was an image of his daughter's hand—Ginger's, not Vivi's—splayed like a star and winking white in the winter sun on the Grunewald freight yard platform.

"Pardon me," Peter said finally. "I am not sure I understand."

Leo gestured at Peter's arm. "It's that," he said. "The customers don't like it. It makes them uneasy."

"*Ach,*" Peter said, instantly amending it to "Ah." He remembered the way the woman—his mother's *Doppelgänger*—had eyed his tattoo yesterday and rolled his sleeve down to hide it, the green mark like the bite of a very small animal trap on his skin.

"I am sorry, Leo," he said. "I am not yet on shift, but—I will be more careful. I will keep my shirt like this—you see?"

Leo shook his head. "I wish it were that easy, kid," he said, "but this just isn't the place for you. If it had only been that lady yesterday—but this isn't the first time I've had this complaint. A lot of our customers have said it disturbs their appetite. To think of— you know—while they're eating."

Peter's ears grew hot as if Leo had boxed them—as the Adlon's head chef had been fond of doing to clumsy inferiors. He stood trying to think what to say. His first impulse was to laugh, to point out to Leo the irony of people being put off their meals by the images of people who had died of starvation. Then he felt very, very tired. How weary he was of all of it, the long faces like the one Leo now wore, the expressions of sympathy when there was no way anyone who hadn't been there could understand; of the fore-fingers loop-de-looping ears to signify Peter's sorry mental state; of the pity, curiosity, revulsion. He was tired of understanding why the Americans were revolted. How well he understood.

"I see," he said stiffly to Leo. "I will go now. I will not make more trouble for you."

"Aw, don't be that way, kid," Leo said. "I'd keep you on if I could—as a cook, even, where people wouldn't have to see your—arm. But then I'd have to let somebody else go to make room, and who would you want that to be? Big Al? Frankie? Lou?"

Peter shook his head. He took off his dirty apron and rolled it neatly into an oblong, setting it on Leo's desk.

"You'll make out all right, kid," Leo said earnestly. "You're a hard worker. I know you're a good cook. And you're one of the lucky ones—right? You survived everything those Nazi *momzers* threw at you and more. *Puh puh puh.*" He pantomimed spitting on the carpet. "You'll do good for yourself, I know it. It just can't be here."

Peter nodded and Leo walked him to the door. He put a palm on Peter's shoulder and handed him an envelope.

"Take care, kid," he said.

Peter stepped out of the Oyster Bar onto the main concourse. He rolled his shirtsleeves up again, undid his tie, popped open the top button of his shirt. Now he knew what seeing his mother's *Doppel-*

gänger yesterday had meant: meet one's mother's ghost, lose a job. Or maybe it meant they were catching up to him, his loved ones, even now, even here.

He opened the envelope Leo had handed him, more for something to do than out of any real curiosity, and drew out five crisp bills. Tens. Fifty dollars—that was, what was the slang for it? A lot of *simoleons*. At least, it would have been a great deal of money to a refugee not already bankrolled by Cousin Sol. Blood money, Peter thought, tucking it back in his pocket; a way for Leo to salve his conscience over *letting Peter go*. That was all right, though; whatever made Leo feel better was fine with Peter. He would miss Leo a little, and Big Al and the other cooks and servers and the job itself; it had been pleasant employment, certainly not as challenging as working on the line at the Adlon and far less demanding than Peter's duties at Terezín, first as cook when he arrived in 1943, then, once he was reassigned, as grave digger, road-layer, and, finally, pallbearer, driving around and around the streets of the camp every day to pick up the dead—each weighing less than one of the Oyster Bar's bus tubs—and loading them into the four-wheeled wagon and carting them to the crematorium. And that itself had been easier than Peter's labor at Auschwitz—although to be fair, Peter had been transported to the latter camp on New Year's Day 1945, only twenty-six days before liberation, when the SS were already as panicked and disorganized as ants whose hill had been kicked apart. So Peter had been spared the worst of it. As Sol's tailor and doctor and friends and Leo and so many others in this new country had pointed out, Peter was lucky.

He looked around the concourse, wondering what to do now. It was just before one, hours before his language class would start. Peter could go to Cousin Sol's office on Madison Avenue and confess what had happened—but he wouldn't. He could go to the Larchmont house and—what would he do there? Peter pictured the immaculate rooms slumbering in the afternoon heat, the pool as undisturbed as a sleeping eye; Ines moving about the kitchen, clattering cutlery and crockery as she prepared the evening meal. Peter alone would be out of place. No, he wouldn't go there.

He stepped out onto the concourse, drifting from column to column of light falling from the high semicircular windows. It was funny, that phrase he heard so often from Cousin Sol and others, that had been the title of the camps themselves from which people like Peter, if they were lucky, were plucked: Displaced Persons. You wouldn't think such a thing would be so bothersome, to be displaced—although when you stopped to think about it, you realized the discomfort; if a bone were out of joint, it would hurt to walk on it, wouldn't it? It would ache all the time. Peter navigated the circumference of the great room, sticking to the sides so as not to get in the way of these purposeful Americans in their clicking and clacking shoes, their hats and ties and lipsticks, each in such a determined hurry to get exactly where he knew he needed to go, and Peter felt like part of a toy his girls had been fond of, a cognitive gift his mother had given them for their first birthday. It was a board from which different shapes had been cut, square and circle and rectangle and wedge, with accompanying blocks that matched each; Vivi, ever patient and methodical, had quickly grown expert at putting the right piece into its counterpart space, but what Peter remembered now was Ginger banging and banging and banging a star against a square opening, increasingly red faced and frustrated as she tried, without success, to make it fit.

He passed a newspaper kiosk—averting his eyes—a shoeshine man kneeling before a bench with his brushes, vendors of sausages and bagels and pastries. It struck Peter every time, what a pity it was that he had so little appetite now that at any hour of day or night he could step up and, with the right money, buy whatever he wanted; only five months ago, one of Peter's bunk mates at Auschwitz had in fact died of enthusiasm for food—devouring an entire chocolate bar provided by a well-meaning liberator, which proved too rich for the man's starved stomach. Near a stairway leading downward, a violinist was playing something sad and sweet Peter recognized—Dvořák, the *New World Symphony*, the second movement. Despite his better instincts, Peter let himself be drawn over. He feared music now, though once he had loved it—anything classical especially, a preference about which Masha, who favored popular ballads and imported jazz, had teased him endlessly. *My stodgy burgher,* she had said, kissing his neck. *My hopelessly old-fashioned husband* . . . It had been his mother's doing, Peter's love of Brahms and Beethoven and Bach; Riva had whistled all these to him when he was a baby, dandling Peter on her lap, while he grabbed at her pursed lips and her long coils of hair—*When I married your father,* Riva often said, *I could sit on my braids*—and finally whistled back. Music had been Peter's language before language, and he had taught it to Ginger and Vivi, too, bouncing a twin on each knee and whistling snatches from their favorite, *Peter and the Wolf,* which even Masha liked because Prokofiev was so modern, the girls clamoring always for the part they thought had been written specially for him, their very own father! *Sing Peter, Papa, sing you, sing YOU!* How they had loved the tune of the triumphant boy, the child hero who captured the forest beast and put him in the zoo, never realizing that in the end, the wolf would come for them instead.

The violinist—a *schnorrer,* Cousin Sol would have said, a beggar—

glanced up, and Peter realized he was crying and jingling the change in his pockets. He took out the coins—all of them—tossed them in the musician's red-lined case, and fled. Away. Away, away. He didn't have to stay here, with Sol's philanthropy and Esther's solicitousness, on this precipitous edge of the continent where Peter was always in danger of tipping, slipping back into his memories; why, a good cook could go anywhere! He dashed across the concourse toward the ticket windows, feeling a sudden insane rise in spirits. He could go west, to a cowboy camp where he would stir beans in an iron cauldron over a fire. He could go to Montana, Idaho, the places where Cousin Sol went fly-fishing, and become a private chef in a rich man's camp there. He could go even to Hollywood—why not?—all the way across the country, and flip burgers in a luncheonette, behind a counter at which more stars would be discovered. How Masha would love that, she who had been so entranced by that magic land known as Los Angeles that every morning at breakfast she read Peter snippets from her movie magazines, such as, *Listen, Petel, it says here you can reach out your window in California and pick a lemon right off your own tree! Can you imagine? . . . Petel, did you know that in California it never snows?* Masha who had so adored all American actresses that she had insisted on naming the girls Vivian and Ginger . . . Blindly, Peter blundered into a woman at the end of the ticket line and said, gasping, *"Entschuldigung Sie!"*

The woman, a pretty blonde in red lipstick, stared at him. She was wearing a thick coat far too warm for the terminal and carrying a carpetbag, and Peter thought at first she, too, must be a refugee. But no, look at her hair, bobbed like an American starlet's. He had been right earlier, when he had left the Oyster Bar. They had caught up with him. He was seeing ghosts everywhere.

He took his place at the end of the line, head down and perspiring. The mad euphoria faded like a light going out, as Peter had known it would. He shuffled forward, mopping his forehead with one of Esther's monogrammed handkerchiefs, and when he reached the ticket window at last he took the envelope Leo had given him, sweat-damp now, and pushed it across the counter to the startled vendor girl there and said, in English this time, "Surprise me."

8

When Peter had the ticket in hand, he walked back out onto the concourse in the direction of the specific set of tracks toward which the salesgirl had pointed him. *Sir, I don't understand—you mean, you want me to choose?* she had asked, and Peter had replied, *Yes, anywhere, the destination does not matter, as long as the train departs very soon.* At the turnstiles, he presented his ticket to the uniformed worker stationed there, and the man examined it and handed it back to Peter and told him to have a nice day. Peter assured him he would. He descended down, down, down an escalator, reminding him of the long, long throat of the Zoo Station U-Bahn in Berlin before it was bombed, and finally emerged with other travelers onto the platform.

There they all stood, some reading newspapers, others peering along the tracks to watch for the train. A trapped bird flapped overhead, seeking a way out, the sound of its wings echoing. Here was another thing that was funny: given Peter's deportation to Terezín on the freight car and his second journey to Auschwitz, you'd expect him to be afraid of trains. But he wasn't. In fact, until now he hadn't given this mode of transport a second thought, and maybe that was because American railroads seemed so different from European ones, this platform not at all like the one on which he had stood with his wife and girls on that frigid day in the winter of 1942, in the Grunewald freight yard in Berlin, after spending two very cramped nights in the synagogue on Levetzowstraβe. That had been the first time his twins had been in a synagogue, since Peter was, like his father and much to his mother's disappointment, nonobservant, and Masha was, of course, a Gentile. His girls, Vivian and Ginger, had been unimpressed by their introduction to the house of organized religion, which for them had consisted of dozing on Masha's and Peter's laps, squeezed onto the long wooden benches with three hundred other people, in a room so cold that despite all the bodies they could see their breath. It was cold the morning they left the synagogue, too, a fine, sunny, freezing dawn that had drawn lace on the windows when they departed; a cold like ice water poured through their coats as they walked to Grunewald, and that chattered his daughters' teeth and reddened their small noses as they stood on the platform, so that Masha, who feared pneumonia above all after Peter's mother had died from it, said, *Petel, I need you to find Vivi a scarf. She's lost hers somewhere and she's shaking,* and Peter had said, *It's not too late. You can still go. Take the girls home and contact my father's friend for the papers. You're Aryan and you know the girls can pass,* and Masha, stooping to pull Vivi's collar up over her face, her long blond hair swinging, said, *Don't start that again, Petel. We're staying with you. Now would you just go find something warm to cover Vivi's head?* and Peter said, *All right, Frau General, I'll be right back.* Still holding Ginger's hand, he turned to scan the crowd for anyplace he might steal a scarf, and he spotted an elderly woman nearby, as bulky with furs as a raccoon. Surely she didn't need that head scarf more than Vivi, did she? His father would have taken it, Peter was sure; would have slid it from the old lady's head without a second's debate. *Don't be so soft, boy, the world will eat you alive!* But what if the old lady had spores in her lungs, like Peter's mother, and his snatching the shawl was her death warrant? Peter dropped Ginger's hand and was sidling toward the old woman nonetheless when the Nazis started them all moving, shoving them forward with truncheons and clubs, and there was mass confusion, shouting and screaming and heaving and pushing, and Peter was trying to shoulder his way back to his girls when he caught just a glimpse of Ginger's hand winking white in the winter sunlight as she reached for him, calling *Papa!* and then his family was gone. Peter was pushed onto one train and they onto another, and it was not until after the war, first in Cousin Sol's study when the man hung up the telephone and said heavily, *I'm sorry but I have it on good authority*, and then in the Red Cross office where Peter checked and checked and rechecked the lists, that while he, the lucky one, had gone to Terezín, a work camp, Masha and Ginger and Vivian had gone straight to Auschwitz.

The train was entering the station now, a vibration Peter felt in his stomach and feet. He studied the tracks. Was it only in the subway that there was a third rail that would electrocute you? If so, and there was no such thing here, was this train moving fast enough? No matter; if Peter jumped quickly and the engine rolled over him, it would crush him with its weight. He tensed his legs. Looked at the train, approaching. Looked at the rails, the litter-strewn cinders between them, chose his spot. Now. Now. Do it now. Sweat drenched his body; his thigh muscles trembled, as they had when he and his family took a cable car to the top of the Zug-spitze and his girls had gamboled along the Alpine peaks like little goats in their summer frocks and Masha had beckoned to him, laughing, calling, *Come on!* but Peter's legs had completely locked, and that night, lying beside Masha in their room at the hotel, his muscles ached so that he could not move them at all.

The train chuffed past inches from his face and stopped. Peter squeezed his eyes shut and more tears leaked out. People moved around him to get on, at first politely and then jostling and pushing as the train's departure grew nearer. "What's the holdup, pal?" they said, and, "Boy, that one's more than a little happy." It was too late. Peter could wait for the next train and the one after that; he could stand on this platform as a thousand trains came and went, but he would not be able to jump and join his loved ones because he was, as his father had said, soft; because he was, as Cousin Sol had pointed out, too weak, too passive and indecisive to be of good to anyone, let alone his family.

"Allllll abooooard!" the conductor called, and a man bumped Peter as he sprinted past, saying, "Hey, buddy, some of us have a train to catch, you know?" Peter apologized, in English. He opened his eyes and wiped his face. Then, as he had done all his life, he let the movement of others carry him; borne by strangers' momentum, he stepped forward onto the train.

~~~

ACKNOWLEDGMENTS

I once again thank the Holocaust survivors who granted me the tremen-dous privilege of recording their testimonies for the Steven Spielberg *Survivors of the Shoah* Visual History Foundation. I am also very much

JENNA BLUM

indebted to my *Grand Central* sisters, particularly Kristina McMorris, who originated this anthology; Cindy Hwang and the team at Berkley/Penguin Random House for bringing our novellas out into the world; and my superagent, Stéphanie Abou, who makes all things possible.

76

The Branch of Hazel

SARAH McCOY

September 21, 1945

A baby cried. It echoed down the marble portico and up, up, to the vast ceiling of painted constellations. The titanic blue canopy, less like the airy skies over the Ardennes and more like the ocean. Weighted and one fault line from crushing her.

Cata's breasts went wet with the sound of the child. She was glad she'd worn her winter coat despite the tepid weather of this New York. She'd given birth to a son the December before. A lifetime ago, a world away. He'd been taken in, adopted, by good people in Munich. A barren couple, the schoolteacher of her youngest brother. She was told they loved him. Of course, she thought, who wouldn't love a boy like that? He was cherub-cheeked with large feet and hands that made the Lebensborn doctors nod with appreciation. He was perfect. Just like his mother, the nurses had said.

Cata was ashamed now of the pride she'd derived from that compliment. She'd called him Yann and wondered if his new parents had given him a different name or kept the old. He would never know hers. The paternity papers had been burned.

The baby wailed again. This time, it ricocheted like a shot, making Cata's arms tremble, elbow to fingertip. She shoved her hands into her wool pockets. In the left were two passports. In the right a garnet hatpin, fletched like an arrow but sharp as a syringe. She stabbed it, judiciously, into her hip. Just deep enough to quell the trembling but not enough to cause a stain. Neat and tidy, an efficient wound. She was skittish. An unbecoming trait. There were tricks to mask one's true nature. The Program mothers had taught her. The prick burned a comforting pain and her body hardened like a clay pot in a kiln.

A train pulled into the station, drowning out the sound of the baby. Its engine hissed; wheels screeched against the metal rails, then sighed to a stop. Its billow of steam made the station even balmier than the Indian summer day.

Cata's head spun at the heat and the hatpin still inserted. She removed it and made her way to the line of ticket windows.

In her mind, she practiced again while waiting her turn. *Boston, Massachusetts.* It did not roll off the tongue easily—not her tongue, at least. Too practiced in the Germanic way. While she understood English and French perfectly, her elocution was infantile at best. She should've studied more as a schoolgirl. Too late. The American accent was an altogether foreign lilt, the words soft as moldering vegetables in her mouth. The consonants fell out without comprehension. So she'd guarded her voice on the sea voyage. Listening carefully to the Americans: the elite eating goose pâté and cured sausages in the vaulted dining room; the steerage passengers smoking cigarettes, backs to the wind, passing time; the waiters and porters who brought her tea and interpreted her silence as wealth; the children playing ball games on deck; and most especially the governesses, huddling together like wild daisies, eyes open and unblinking on their charges.

From them, she learned the most useful vernacular: going *bonkers* was not the same as *bunkers*, in German or English. *Horsing around* was behaving foolishly. *Swell* was a positive quality. *Giggle water* was alcohol and put to the same use here as it was in the Lebensborn Program: three glugs in bedtime milk for restless children; no more or they might not wake up on schedule. All the American governesses wanted *nine-to-fiver* employment and a *Doris Day* haircut when they arrived in port. *Horsefeathers* was used at various occasions, so Cata still wasn't sure its exact meaning. And then there were the hushed discussions of the war: *A-bomb, Japs, home front, rations,* and most notably what they would call her if she dared speak a word, *Nazi, Jerry,* German.

She penned all of these useful and offensive words in her journal and practiced them in a whisper alone in her ship's bunk each night. She had the basics down: *yes, no, thank you, pardon, please.* Those five had ushered her through Ellis Island security alongside her Luxembourg papers and an extra coat of lipstick.

The Program had not accepted her on her righteousness and intelligence, but on her smile and ability to fit in. She might've been naïve once but not anymore. Those who survived had the faces of doves and the cunning of serpents. She'd learned well and seen the proof in her roommates at Steinhöring. Hazel the dove. Brigette the serpent. At their memory, she winced and her eyes welled.

Dear Hazel. *I'm sorry, I'm sorry.* Her hands trembled again so she took up the hatpin to prick and prick and prick.

The ticket line moved forward, but she was busy allowing the slow sting to spread. A man, thin as a sapling, stumbled into her back and the needle plunged deeper than before. She gasped.

"*Entschuldigung Sie,*" the man stuttered, quickly and no louder than a lamb's bleat.

It would've gone unnoticed. The apology unknown to those

around them, and so mistaken for an incoherent mumble. The utterance of a walking ghost. Nothing more. Only it wasn't nothing to Cata. It was the language and land for which she'd given children, sworn oaths, sacrificed and killed.

He nodded apologies. He wore a busboy uniform with shirtsleeves cuffed to his elbows, an inky thread of numbers exposed. There was no mistaking. The tattoo seemed to rise off his skin like a line of black ants marching toward her. She stared hard at it, unable to peel her eyes away. A Jew from Germany—here?

Seeing her gaze, he crossed his arms, covering the markings, and took a deferential step back.

Cata pulled the hatpin from her flesh and felt the blood ooze hot through her stockings. Flames of guilt blistering her back. She wanted to turn and speak to him—in their language. To say all the things she'd been thinking ever since she'd learned the details of the Jewish camps. She'd been ignorant of those truths. Perhaps unconsciously, perhaps not. In a way, she felt as culpable as the Nazi officers she'd bedded and borne a daughter and son.

Nein, she would bite her tongue and leave this man to make his way in peace—to have a new beginning without any reminders of war and suffering. Leave the past behind. Take the fastest train into the future. Wasn't that what they were all doing here at the station?

"Whereto, miss?" asked the man behind the barred ticket window.

It was her cue. She'd practiced the proper response for weeks on the ship. Mass-ah-choo-sitz, she visualized it spelled out in phonetic syllables on her journal page. She didn't stumble if she said it slowly, but the slower she spoke, the more foreign she sounded. She wiped a sweat bead from her brow before it streaked her rouge.

"Massachu-setts." She hurried through the beginning and

broke it in two, flipping her bob between. It seemed to work. The man's gaze remained fixed to his receipts.

"Amherst, Springfield, Salem, Boston?"

To her relief, she was able to reply in perfect impersonation, "Baw-stin."

He looked up then and gave a crooked smile when he saw her. "Aw, yeah? I got a brudda up d-air. He's a caw-pentah. You goin' to see family or friends?"

She nodded. "Yes."

Mildred, called Milly, was a cousin, twice removed. She'd married a wealthy mercantile and moved to Boston a decade before.

You cannot come home to Luxembourg, Cata's mother had penned when the war ended. *It's too dangerous. Your brothers are young and still in school. Your father could lose his business.*

Cata had been banished, in essence. So she'd written the one family member removed from all connections to the Kutter family name.

Milly had consented to give her lodging and keep her heritage a secret if she financed her own way to Massachusetts and agreed to work as the family's governess. She had her hands full with three girls: ages eight, six and two. She was expecting her fourth child that winter. A boy, she hoped. Lebensborn Program mothers earned special privileges and honorary cards for their male offspring. Milly wanted to please her husband. Cata understood.

While she wasn't enthusiastic about the idea of playing the hired nursemaid to her distant cousin, she was in no position to debate the one charity offered. She had to leave Germany immediately. So she emptied her savings and sold off everything of value: jewelry from SS officers, nightgowns made of French lace, silk stockings, feather hats, fur wraps, her favorite pair of T-strap shoes dusted in gold sparkle, ivory-handled hairbrushes, perfumes and soaps, even her lavender talc power, half used. All for pennies on the dollar. Better to get solid coin for her journey, she decided, than hold on to the items merely to have them confiscated if arrested. She brought only what she wore and a small handbag containing toiletries, a change of underthings, pajamas, a card stack of photographs and a handful of personal effects. Everything else she sold, right down to the length of her hair. The bob was more American, she told herself as her traditional blond braids were lopped off.

In total, she was able to amass enough to pay for the Steinhöring Home's gardener to drive her to the coast in his covered produce truck, single-room passage on an America-bound steamship, one night's boarding at a women's hotel in New York City and this train ticket from Grand Central to the Boston depot. She was on the final leg and could not afford a careless mistake now.

The ticket booth man cocked his head as if waiting for her to go on. Instead, she silently counted out crisp American bills, tousled her blond hair and angled her chin down with a grin. He winked, took the payment and stamped her receipt.

"If you come back this way—stop in and say hello." He tapped on the counter. "This's my booth. I'll be here." He slid her ticket under the bar but kept his fingers there so hers were forced to touch his.

Amis or Jerries, she thought, all the same. Men were men.

"Thank you," she said and strolled off knowing full well that his eyes were on the sway of her hips with every step.

She nodded gingerly as she passed the Jewish man, but he kept his stare to the burnished floor.

A violin began to play somewhere, a slow, sad melody that didn't bounce off the walls like the child's cry but pooled in the station's enclaves like dew in a tombstone's etching.

Cata made a beeline for the Main Concourse where the song was lost in the scramble of people zigzagging this way and that, looking up to the train schedule and down to their luggage; porters and conductors tapping watches; children holding their parent's hands; soldiers in uniforms everywhere. Fleshly specters, pointing cloaked fingers, *Nazi*. She could hear the collective whisper in the rhythmic panting of the train engine, *Nazi, Nazi, Nazi*. She checked her ticket and the rail board then found her track.

Get on, get on, she told herself. Inside she'd be safe. Inside she'd be on her way.

On the platform between her and her train was a lonesome, young girl, standing straight as a quill amid the flurry. She surveyed the crowd then paused on Cata. Her eyes were bluer and clearer than any child born to the Lebensborn Program—bluer than Cata's daughter's eyes. Cata could not look away. The girl cocked her head under her stare but did not smile, her jaw set hard with thought. Cata's stomach dipped. A mass of chills crawled down her back and she had the unnerving feeling that the girl saw her. Saw everything — Steinhöring, the officers, the babies and Hazel.

She quickly moved on, down the platform, though her ticket was for first class. She'd walk back up the entire length of carriages to avoid those piercing eyes and did just that.

Finding her roomette, she pulled the door's shade, put her bag away, took a seat and exhaled. Finally. The voices, music, whistles and cries of the station muted to a dull discord. Her hip tweaked from the stab. She shrugged off her wool coat and rubbed the spot.

"The needle is worn," Hazel had said when they came home from the marketplace that awful night.

Hazel had been working on a dirndl bodice and pushed the needle through the material too hard. It had gone straight into her arm. She'd never been very skilled at sewing. She held a rag to the wound, splotched with more blood than Cata imagined a prick to produce.

"Nothing worse than a dull tip." Brigette had snickered and set her wet mittens by the stove. "Did you miss us?" Without waiting for a reply, she'd gone on, "A bad January. I don't know how we're supposed to make good German stock on a diet of root vegetables. We need meat! And what I wouldn't give for a slice of Black Forest cake."

Cata moved aside Hazel's brown dirndl panels to set the grocery bag on the table. "We saw your friend Ovidia. She had new buttons carved with edelweiss. They'd match your dress. She said hello."

Brigette said after a tsk, "Poor thing. I can't imagine how she goes on—after giving birth to a deformity. The dishonor would've killed me."

Ovidia had been in the Program with them. A tender, quiet girl who liked to take her meals alone in the garden so she could sketch the summer flowers and winter birds. She'd wanted to be an artist, so they said. Her talents garnered praise in the *Bund Deutscher Mädel*, Hitler's League of German Maidens program, and had been her doom, too. The leaders of the BDM had recommended her to the Lebensborn Program for her aptitudes. Her parents were of earliest Germanic heritage and she was pretty enough. Though she'd never said as much, they could all see her heart was distant from the Fatherland's mission. Many took offense—other mothers and staff. Insolent, they called her. So when she gave birth to a Mongoloid boy the spring before and was discharged from the Program, there was little sympathy. She didn't go home to her family. Instead, she opened a market stall and sold materials and sewing bits to make a living. There were rumors that she stayed in the hopes of finding the son taken from her at the delivery bed, a blemish on the Steinhöring Home's record. That kind of word spread fast, right to the doors of Hitler's Eagle's Nest if they let it. A shame, Cata thought. Ovidia had always been kind to her and a friend to Hazel.

"She does sell the finest fabrics." Cata nodded to Hazel's sewing. "That's got to count for something."

"A waste of money." Brigette pulled a grimy cabbage head from the sack. "Much good a pretty dress will do if the Americans and Russians come. Just one more enticement to throw you on your back and have their way."

Two spindly carrots, an onion and four pockmarked potatoes: Cata lined them up on the table. They'd paid triple what the items were worth, but with so little to be had, even the farmers' children were crying with hunger pains.

"It's for when my family sees me," Hazel explained flatly.

"*If* your family sees you," corrected Brigette. "The Program is not permitting anyone to travel or visit. Besides, you had best take better care of yourself first. If word gets out that you're producing flawed children—well, look at Ovidia—you could be gone for good."

"I'll make us a delicious vegetable soup," Cata had said and pulled a dark loaf of bread from the bag, smiling widely. Change of subject.

Hazel had given birth to twins near Christmastime, a girl and a boy. The girl was round and pink. A true Aryan gem. The boy, however, was terribly inferior and growing worse with each passing day by refusing to eat. Hazel had gone to see him more often than was typically allowed postdelivery. Cata only saw her Yann when called upon to wet-nurse. The doctors had hoped Hazel's additional mothering might break the child's starvation. Sadly, it had not, and they'd moved the boy from the Program's nursery to a facility better suited to care for his ailments. Now the doctors were conducting further testing on the girl twin to ensure she did not carry a hidden deficiency as well.

Since the boy's removal, Hazel had withdrawn completely. Her eyes were dark from nights of crying in bed, and she'd lost such a substantial amount of weight that her milk had dried up already. Cata couldn't blame her. While Brigette was as blunt as a butter knife, her words cut true: the sorrow and disgrace could kill a woman.

Hazel came close and inhaled the bread deeply. "Rye and dandelion root," she whispered, then took a seat beside the potbelly stove.

After she said it, Cata could distinctly smell the toasted herbs. She set the loaf in the middle of the table like a vase of flowers. "Better looking than blooms to hungry eyes!" She put on her apron to skin vegetables for the soup.

"Stoke the fire, Hazel," instructed Brigette.

Hazel opened the stove door and pushed a handful of dry twigs within. The coals glowed wraithlike. The kindle ignited and flickered red tongues, burning bright against the ash.

"No good if you keep it open." Brigette flung the metal door closed, wiped the soot off her hand and grabbed Hazel's arm. "Time to be useful—cabbage." She crunched the crucifer on the table.

If they had to live three to a room, they had to find a way to get along. Cata bristled at being hustled along like a prisoner, no matter how many stars and crosses, ranks and honorariums Brigette had earned. "Let her be, Brig." Cata scraped her knife down the sides of the carrot. "She's not herself. Remember her boy . . ."

Hazel pulled a slimy leaf from the cabbage and held the rotten pulp in her hand.

Brigette huffed. "The health of the child depends on the health of the mother."

"The girl came out beautiful," Cata protested. "Have you seen her? I was in the nursery feeding Yann, and she was lying in her crib, fair as a peach."

"I don't visit the nurseries. Once I give birth, they belong to the Fatherland." Brigette unclothed a moldy cheese wedge and shaved away the furry green with a butcher's knife.

Cata placed the vegetable peelings in an empty pot for the broth and began on the potatoes. "One good baby makes up for the other."

With a *thunk*, Brigette cut the centerpiece bread where it laid. "I heard they feed arsenic to the flawed ones." She put the cheese on the bread heel and bit down with a smirk. Crumbs sprinkled her breast.

That crossed the line. "Wicked gossip. Don't believe it." Cata's hand slipped and the half-peeled tuber skittered across the table.

Brigette continued, undeterred. "It's true. They burn them alongside Jews from the camp. That's why I make *sure* all my offspring are perfect."

Hazel rose to stand, but her knees buckled and she fell, head smacking the tiles.

"Hazel!" Cata knelt and pulled her into her lap.

Brigette smoothed a hair back into her tight braid. "She needs a pill."

It was too much for any mother to bear. On top of that, Hazel was a gentle spirit. She wasn't like Brigette: hard and rusted bitter as iron. She wasn't like Cata, either: afraid and able to feign apathy when the truth was that Cata had cherished the kick and stretch of Yann within her. The truth was, she loved her children beyond oaths of allegiance and would do anything, even give them up, for their well-being.

She undid Hazel's dirndl bodice. "Breathe slowly."

"*Ja*," Hazel whispered with eyes rolled back to whites. "Peter."

It was the name of Hazel's fiancé who died at the beginning of the war. She hadn't been in the Program then. Hazel's firstborn son, Julius, was created of love, not duty. Cata had always been envious. She'd never known a man's touch that was hers alone to claim.

Hazel flapped an arm in the air. "Peter!"

Brigette handed Cata the pillbox. The doctors had given them out to the girls for pain of body and mind, and they worked better than any liquor or opium or drug Cata had ever known.

"Hush, hush now, dear." She cradled Hazel to her breast like Yann. "This will help." She put a tablet to Hazel's lips.

Hazel's eyes rolled to color and met Cata's. She swallowed then reached out wildly to the pillbox for another, accidentally knocking it sideways. The overturned tablets eddied like stars across the floor.

"Don't waste them all on her," said Brigette. She took up the cabbage and began to chop. "If she doesn't come to her senses, give her a good slap."

"Just one more then."

Hazel's face was wet. Chalky spit smeared the corners of her mouth. "Cata," she mumbled.

"She's returned," assured Cata. "Look, she's calm."

"Let's hope her second born doesn't inherit this lack of fortitude. Germany needs strong daughters, not feebleminded fools."

Cata had put Hazel to bed then, drawing the feather coverlet up to her chin against the January night. She had not known her roommate would never wake up. At dawn, they found her cold and blue as the winter morn.

"You killed her!" Brigette accused.

Distraught, Cata counted the pills in her mind. "Two, I gave her two, like you told me!"

"You poisoned her. A Lebensborn mother, a German."

"No, I—" Cata had begun to defend then realized she had never taken more than one pill at a time. She couldn't say with confidence that the double potency was safe.

"Murderer!" Brigette seethed and pulled her shawl from the hook. "I won't stay in a room with a dead woman and a murderess. Gestapo!"

Before Cata could think, Brigette was gone and she was alone, standing over Hazel, beautiful as an angel even in death.

"I'm sorry, Hazel," she'd wept. "I didn't mean . . ."

She heard a shout outside. The Gestapo were arresting women and children, old and young, for the most inconspicuous offenses. For murder, they might shoot her on the spot! So she'd thrown everything she owned in a laundry basket, including Hazel's passport papers. They were the only documents with her Garmisch address.

In Cata's frenzy and self-reproach, she'd sworn to write Hazel's family anonymously to explain what she could about her death, her children, the Program . . . Hazel was close to her younger sister, Elsie. She'd spoken of her often. Cata hadn't any sisters and could only imagine what it might be like to have a confidante so true. If no one else, Elsie should know what happened there.

As she left, she grabbed a hat with black netting to cover her face. She'd forgotten that Hazel had let her borrow the garnet hatpin the last time she'd worn it—a windy day—and so, added thievery to her list of crimes.

Until the Allies invaded, Cata worked and hid as a laundress, writing her parents as if she were still at the Lebensborn Program. The truth was worse than any lie imaginable. But even now, she wasn't certain of what exactly that was: the truth.

Germany's chaotic collapse was her open window and she hurled herself out. The gardener said Cata reminded him of the sixteen-year-old daughter he lost to influenza. He had always been caring to her. She used that to her advantage and compensated him handsomely for the 865-kilometer ride to the Port of Hamburg. Kindness was as scarce as food in Germany and more deserving of returns.

————

"Trouble! Trouble!" A paperboy held up an inky newspaper outside her train car window. "Re-education-ing da Axis yoot! Berlin opens up school but double-trouble schoolin' fascists!"

A man in a business suit threw coins in the kid's overturned cap, scooped up a paper and moved on without a word.

"Trouble in Berlin!" the boy continued. "Whattaya do wit Nazi kids?"

Cata shrank back from the glass and pulled the window blind down. She had an ache in her jaw. Her teeth were clenched. She sucked in the hollows of her cheeks for a good stretch, making her lips pucker like the beak of a tit bird.

The door of the roomette slid open. A man in dark glasses prominently gripped the door frame. Cata coughed and hid her face down to her lap. He turned his cheek sharply to her, and for a moment, she had the similar striking fear as when a high-ranking

SS officer made his way along the line of Program girls for selection. His features were impeccably groomed: his suit jacket lacked a single crease, collar and cuffs starched, fedora at just the right tilt, a gleaming wedding band on his left hand and a matching gold-knobbed cane in his right.

She rummaged in her coat pocket for her ticket. She had paid the higher tariff, but this man looked far above her station. Perhaps she was in the wrong carriage.

"Pardon." She groped in her wool pocket, but her nervous fingers could not decipher between the receipt and the passports, and she dared not chance the wrong.

"No pardon necessary," he said kindly and removed his hat. His salt-and-pepper hair had been pomaded back from his forehead. "Is this car thirteen?"

She ran through her numbers, *dreizehn*. "Yes."

"Lucky number thirteen. The building I live in doesn't have a thirteenth floor. They skip right over it to fourteen. But I wonder how those residents feel about living on a floor that, no matter what you name it, is still thirteen in the counting."

Cata nodded. She wasn't superstitious when it came to numbers. Other things—living things: owls, bats, black cats and snakes were bad omens; flowers with thorns should never be given to friends you want to keep; wheat had to be planted under a full moon; the smell of basil on the wind was a good soul passing; burnt hair was a vengeful ghost. Numbers, however, had never given her trouble.

The train hissed a steam whistle then lurched, and the man staggered to the seat across from her. He set his hat down on the side cushion, undid his jacket buttons and placed his cane between his knees, holding firm to the golden knob with both hands.

"It should be cooler in Boston. Rather warm in the city today, don't you agree?"

She thought he was referring to her wool coat. The lenses of his glasses, like two black eclipses, barreled down on her. *There are spies everywhere*, Brigette had told her once about their countrymen. *They have technology to know German and Jew, trusted and traitor.* Cata's knee trembled, but her pocket pin was out of reach. She turned to the window. The paperboy grew smaller and smaller as the train pulled back from the station.

The man sniffed the air. "Is that 4711 perfume you wear?"

It was. An SS naval officer had given it to her as a gift. While it was military issued to all seamen to combat the ship fetor, she'd thought the gesture sweet. Perfumes of any kind were limited. He could've just as easily taken it home to his wife.

"My mutter wore that. She was from Cologne," he said *in German*.

The quake moved up her leg to the junction in her hip where the earlier stab still pricked. She gulped hard, her throat dry. He had to be a spy, *polizei* or international bounty hunter ready to arrest and ship her back to Germany. Unless she used prudence.

"I am from Luxembourg," she replied in labored English. "I have papers," she added in German. It'd been so long since she'd dared her native tongue that it sounded off, wrong, more foreign than all her practiced English.

The man smiled and tilted his head oddly to the side. "Are you Jewish?"

"*Nein!*" She sat up straight. Her heels clicked against the floorboards.

He raised a hand of goodwill from his cane. "I only ask because no one carries papers in America. My mutter was a German Jew and carried papers until her dying day. She wore that perfume, too.

My father was an athlete—the pentathlon. He competed on the German team. I was born just outside of Frankfurt but immigrated with my parents to seek medical treatment for my blindness."

Only then did he remove his glasses, carefully folding the wires back and sliding them into the front pocket of his jacket. His eyes were the color of late-summer leaves, intact and clear except for their inability to make focal purchase.

She lifted a hand and waved so slowly that her 4711 did not waft an inch closer. His gaze vacillated in every direction but hers. She'd known many elderly afflicted with cataracts and weakened sight but had never before met an adult who'd never seen sunrise or sunset or a single color between.

"Were you born so?" she dared, feeling more confident with his handicap revealed.

Whoever heard of a blind spy? Implausible. Not in Germany, at least.

"No, but I was quite sickly as an infant and suffered from fits of epilepsy. I lost my sight during one of those before my first birthday."

A child of seizures. The daughter she'd borne had suffered from those. When the Lebensborn initiative was at the height of popularity with the "special" girls being chosen from Hitler's League of German Maidens, Cata had begun her duty as a Lebensborn mother in a smaller Program Home across the border from Luxembourg. There, she'd given birth to a baby girl before Yann in Steinhöring.

When the child was not yet three years old, there was an accident. She was in the pool during the children's exercise hour. Somehow she slipped or was pushed and hit her head against the concrete ledge. When they pulled her from the shallow pool, she had a seizure in the instructor's arms. Hours later, she lay in bed nibbling cherry gummies, groggy but otherwise fine. They'd all hoped the frightening episode had been a singular response to the head contusion; however, a couple weeks later, while in the middle of a lesson on how to properly comb her hair, she fell prostrate amid her peers and seized. After examination, the medical staff concluded that her brain had been permanently damaged by the accident. They couldn't have an epileptic child in the Program. It would appear as a blemish on the data reports and skew future statistics. Their ultimate goal was to create perfect Germans. Cata's daughter was no longer that, and so there was nothing to be done.

Luckily, one of the attending physicians took pity and offered to take the child into his household. Shortly thereafter, the second war began and the doctor left the country with his family for America. There were rumors his wife had a distant Jewish relation, and he could not endure being separated from her or their biological children. Cata's daughter had gone with them. It was the last she'd heard of her.

It had always irked Cata how nonchalantly the Program staff expunged the child from their records and the Fatherland. Now, looking back, she had smug satisfaction that her child had truly held the upper hand. She had not been forced to live through all that Cata had seen. In silent retaliation, she imagined her daughter dancing to the "Boogie Woogie Bugle Boy" and watching Bing Crosby on the silver screen. Those sweet bluebell eyes glinting merrily in the theater lights, free of fear, free of Germany. If only she could look into that face again. Cata was sure she'd recognize her, even all grown up to age seven.

Meeting this man, she suddenly worried after a child she'd attempted to put out of her mind and hadn't seen in years. Could a seizure have blinded her daughter, too? She hoped not. But even if it had, look at this man: the son of an athlete and a Jewess. No one of marked pedigree. Yet here, in America, he had exceeded his biological affliction and the genetic sum of his forbearers. Cata's heart lifted for her daughter—for herself, too.

She'd had four miscarriages before Yann. What none of the other Program girls had known was that Cata's own medical record included years of failure. She'd been moved to the larger clinic at Steinhöring to take part in the experimental SS fertility treatments. They had worked. It was yet another reason it would've been impossible not to love her son as her own—hard earned.

"Do you still . . . suffer?" she asked, realizing halfway into the question that her guard had lowered with her mind's wandering.

He shook his head. "My last epileptic compulsion occurred just before puberty, and I haven't had so much as a shudder again."

She was envious. Even now, she had to keep her hands balled in fists to fight off her nervous tremble. She gulped hard and quickly parroted the ticket booth man's question:

"Do you have family or friends in Baw-stin?"

His right eyebrow raised in amusement. Had she pronounced it incorrectly?

"Both," he replied and tapped his cane to the floor with a happy *click-click*. "My wife and son being the most significant of the lot. I come down to New York once a month for business."

A blind businessman.

"What ist your trade?" The verb slipped and she stretched her mouth to the corners in unseen reminding: *Izzz*.

He didn't notice. Not that it mattered. He'd already tagged her as German. Now she simply had to hide her criminality.

"Educational literature."

She frowned and was glad he couldn't see it. Literature was a pastime, a hobby, a means of lively conversation with her male companions: *A man likes a woman who can entertain his mind and body*, the more experienced Program girls had taught her. But a business?

"What about you—what is your trade?" he asked.

"Children." To this, she could speak truth.

"Oh!" His eyes widened and swept back and forth over her head. "My apologies. I assumed a woman traveling alone was unmarried . . ." He stomped the cane again, this time in self-chastisement. "Old-fashioned assumption. It's a new age—women building fighter planes and running factories! My own wife spent much of the war working at the USO. I barely saw her—well, I never *see* her, but you know what I mean."

He smiled tenderly, and Cata could see that every thought of his wife was beautiful despite his lack of vision.

"So you've been blessed with children," he went on, still grinning. "My son is named Ralph. He turned sixteen last week—practically all grown up. How old are yours?"

"No," she formed the word carefully, her jaw hanging low and open in proper English. "I am to governess children in Baw-stin."

She draped the disguise over her identity once more and was oddly soothed by its shadow. The truth, too, burning bright. It was stuffy in the car. She lifted the shade slightly to open the window. "Do you mind?"

The incoming breeze lightly fingered his pomaded hair, but it remained steadfast. "Not at all. I enjoy fresh air." He inhaled deeply. "Thank God for weekends."

She readjusted her coat over her lap to keep her skirt from catching sail. The pocketed passports stuck up like miniature masts at her knees. Cata Kutter and Hazel Schmidt.

Click-clock, click-clock, the train wheels churned faster and faster. Their cadence echoed through the roomette. Suddenly, a whoosh of air: the cabin door pulled open again. The conductor with his metal ticket punch.

"Well, Mr. Krupper!" Her companion's presence surprised the conductor who quickly tilted his hat despite Mr. Krupper's inability to witness the salutation.

One of the League of German Maidens' courses had been the study of Germany's finest family lineages. Each of their dynasties had been sketched out like branches of a tree with the trunk being God himself. *Krupp* was distinctly German but not *Krupper*. That was Dutch. She thought he said his parents were German—or perhaps they simply lived in the Fatherland without blood ties.

"Is that you, Murphy?"

"Yes, sir. Are you headed home?"

"I am. Ruth made cottage pie and chocolate cake for dinner. We're celebrating Ralph's birthday tonight since I missed it while on business. How's Dorothy—happy for the kids to be back in school?"

"Oh yes, Mr. Krupper. Happy for life to get back to normal now that the war's over. Dottie was getting mighty tired of driving the Victory Speed every time she went to visit her mother in Philadelphia. Said she'd rather shoot a rifle and help lick the Jerries quick rather than driving at thirty-five miles per hour anymore. I had her stick to rationing rubber. I've seen her play catch—her aim would've proven as much an enemy as the bloody Nazis!" He thumped the doorway with a fist.

Mr. Krupper laughed and stomped his cane.

Cata cringed.

Acknowledging her with a demure nod, Murphy apologized.

"It's the fighting Irish in my Dottie," though she sensed more pride than regret. "Ticket, miss?"

With steadier hands, she recognized the feel of the thin voucher from the stiff passports and presented it.

Murphy studied the ticket, *click-clicked* and handed it back while Mr. Krupper pulled his own from his jacket vest. Murphy took it dutifully, and Cata was glad to see it was business as usual for the conductor. She had passed inspection. It was the American that produced a frown.

"Mr. Krupper, you're in the wrong train car."

Both of Mr. Krupper's eyebrows rose. "Am I? Is this thirteen?"

"Yes, but the porter has put your luggage in car *three*, per your ticket for a first-class roomette."

"Isn't this first class?"

"Well," Murphy looked to Cata, smiled weakly then turned his body so that he stood between them, his back walling her prying eyes from the conversation. "There's first class and then there's *first* first class," he said, lowering his voice to a deferential whisper. "You being one of our VIP passengers."

Mr. Krupper grinned. "How considerate of you, Murphy, but I really am quite fine where I sit."

Murphy cleared his throat. Cata dug her painted fingernails into her palm for lack of hatpin. Could he tell from her faded wool coat that she wasn't of the first first class or was it the bags under her eyes? She hadn't slept more than three hours a night on the boat. She eyed her shoes. She'd been sure to shine them with a little margarine wrapped up from the hotel's breakfast table. No scuffs. No hanging threads on her hem, either. Her makeup and hair had been done with extra care. She looked respectable enough to afford her seating. So why was this Murphy treating her like the plague? Damn the perfume—the stink must've given her away to him, too.

She drove her index finger into her palm as deep as she could without breaking the skin.

"Of course you may stay here if you like, but your things are way up in train car three. It might be easier if . . ."

"If I'm at the head of the train so as not to slow people down de-boarding," said Mr. Krupper. The forced grin remained.

"No, no," Murphy defended. "It isn't that at all."

A deafening silence settled despite the open window and rumble of steel wheels.

Murphy cleared his throat again, shuffled his feet a little then stood up tall. "As soon as I'm finished taking tickets on this carriage, I'd be happy to escort you to your private roomette, Mr. Krupper. I think you'll be far more comfortable there. Please, sir, allow me?"

Mr. Krupper simply nodded. Once.

Cata had unconsciously released her talons, leaving a seam of purple half-moons.

"I shall return shortly," said Murphy with an air of professionalism usurping his earlier geniality. "Good day, miss."

Cata kept her eyes to her T-straps. So it *was* similar in America. Discrimination. Even for a man who was obviously of the very *first* first class. She thought the reality might make her feel less ashamed of the Lebensborn Program and its strict codes of perfection, but instead, it made her sad. She hurt for Mr. Krupper. Though she'd only met him this hour, his heart was perceptibly kind and genuine. Regardless of his outward visage, physical insufficiency or financial sufficiency, he was a man due respect based on character alone. She couldn't say the same for herself.

As soon as the door closed, Mr. Krupper addressed her. "I'm sorry about all of that."

"It is fine," she assured. "You are a rich man. You deserve the best."

Mr. Krupper shook his head and said with a tsk, "Nonsense. I am a blind man but I am not blind." He held a finger straight up then pointed it precisely out the window. "Can you see the wind's direction?"

She looked outside. Between the train's movement and the foreign landscape, she could not.

Mr. Krupper continued, "I cannot see which way the tree leaves blow or feel the needle pull of a compass in hand. Yet I know it is from the northeast today."

"How?"

"Aw, that is the secret. When one is lacking in one area, he is amplified in others. It's a law of life. As definitive as seedtime and harvest. To every heat wave there is a cold front. To every drought there is a coming flood." He sighed and smiled. "So many people believe that *this* minute is all there is to the story, when in truth it is so much larger and freer than that. It is the wind sweeping up to the stars and bubbling down through the fathoms, round and through the planet regardless of our temporal lives."

She was fascinated and slightly frightened of Mr. Krupper. Already, she'd been misled into believing one charismatic man's rhetoric, and look where that had gotten her. Hitler was dead and she was a criminal in exile. She thought of all of the officers she'd slept with. All of them were certainly dead or exiled as well.

"How do I know it is *truly* northeast wind? Where is the evidence?" she countered.

"I have faith in—"

She scoffed reflexively before he'd finished. *Faith?* She had no faith left.

He remained still for a full minute. Even the wind through the window seemed to quiet its whistle. Then Mr. Krupper cocked his head to the side like a bird on a branch watching a dog below try to climb its tree.

"Do you believe in God, Miss . . . ?"

"No," she answered hastily.

"Mm. I got the impression you might not."

She straightened her shoulders. Her parents had been Roman Catholic but hadn't asserted their religious beliefs. The eldest of her siblings, Cata had set the example by being enrolled in the League of German Maidens starting at the age of ten. Her education and moral curriculum had been strict and in keeping with the Hitler Youth doctrine, which superseded the Roman Catholic Church. She'd never made First Holy Communion and couldn't recall her church baptism, though her mother swore she'd had one as a baby.

Cata had always thought her parents foolish for praying to a big spirit man in the sky and believing that priests swinging smoke pots held the only telephones to reach him. As unseen and unreal as St. Nicholas and Père Fouettard handing out gifts and punishments at the Yuletide. All were regular men in costumes. No more or less powerful. No more or less worthy.

"Do you," she countered, "believe?"

"Yes," he said with equal haste.

His absolute response needled her deeper than the hatpin in her flesh.

"May I speak . . ." Her English was failing her. "*Ehrlich?*" Frankly.

"Please do," he replied.

She gulped. It was a risk. This talk. This sharing of true self.

Like the pills she'd administered to Hazel, she wasn't sure of the potency or the effect. But it was too late now to simply shut up. That would be more suspicious than pursuing this semirealistic charade of atheist German governess.

"Do you believe God made you blind? And if so, how can you love someone who would leave you to so much pain?"

It was a question that had been rolling around her mind far before this meeting. She'd wanted to ask it of someone—her daughter, her son, herself. She hadn't realized how long it had been lingering until she spoke it aloud.

Mr. Krupper smiled, sadly, as if he pitied her, though he was the one blighted with God's disfavor.

"The world is rooted in pain, and we, born to it, are perpetually suffering. Warring, hating and killing each other on partialities when our souls are all made of the same material. Who's to say your vision isn't the affliction and I—I see heaven's wonders every minute?" He raised an eyebrow with an almost flirtatious charm.

He is blind and *mad*, she thought but didn't entirely believe. Then it dawned on her. "You say you are in the business of disseminating educational literature, but you speak like a priest. No robes, so perhaps you are a Protestant man of God, *ja?*"

He grinned and nodded as if bowing to a game of chess. "Bravo, new friend. You've proven my assertion. You are able to see the unseen. You *do* have faith! You just don't realize it." He winked. "I am a publisher of braille books. Bibles are our bestsellers."

"Br-ill?" The wind swept through, stealing the sound of his correct pronunciation.

"Braille," he repeated. "It's a means for the sightless to read with our fingers." He lifted his left hand and smoothed his thumb from pinky to pointer. His wedding band glimmered gold across her face.

"Read with fingers?" She'd never heard of such a thing nor could she fathom how one might go about it. What next would she discover in this America—children tasting strawberries through their ears and hearing toy rattles through their noses?

"Each letter is a series of raised dots that form words and sentences," he explained. "Just like writing only through touch. It's been very successful and well embraced. We have a whole library at the Perkins School, in fact."

"A school and library for *blind* people?"

In Luxembourg, Germany, and what she had seen in most of Europe, the blind were shut away to be treated more like family pets than members: spoon-fed their meals and walked at various hours until they expired, darkness to darkness. That was if they were lucky and too poor to go to a sanitarium. Families of wealth usually opted for professional care. But then again, she'd never met an adult blinded since childhood, and the only libraries she'd been into were part of the Hitler Youth Movement. They had a small one at the Steinhöring Home. It had been intentionally stocked only with whimsical adventure novels, entertainment for the officers and erotica that helped some of the shier men come to mood. A library for the sightless? Inconceivable. The Program hadn't allowed for blind flesh, never mind blind books. But she was far from Steinhöring now, far from Germany and doing all that she could to propel herself far from all Nazi connections.

"Yes," Mr. Krupper nodded. "The Perkins School is quite prominent in Boston. Charles Dickens embossed copies of his books on the school's printing press. And Helen Keller was a star pupil."

She knew of Charles Dickens's work, of course, but he wasn't blind—or at least she didn't think he'd been. She had no idea who this Helen woman might be, but if she was prominent in Boston, Cata thought it best to be familiar.

"How very *modern*," she replied.

It was the word a governess on the ship used to describe her benefactress's European dishwasher with electric drying coils. Cata could tell from the other women's reactions that they were clueless but didn't want to appear as such, so they'd all parroted the word back: *modern, yes, so very modern.* She used it now to similar effect.

"You should come over to the school sometime with your wards. The library is open to all, Monday through Friday. We welcome visitors, even those with sight!" He gave a chuckle.

Cata smiled at his good nature, though she failed to see the humor in what he'd said. She couldn't imagine her cousin Milly allowing her children to coalesce with the disabled. If it were her daughter or son, she surely wouldn't. But that was just the point. That was the old Cata and the old ways. She needed to be an altogether different woman here in deeds, in thoughts and, most significantly, in name. She placed her palm over the passport pocket.

Mr. Krupper turned to the open window and inhaled deeply. "It's the smell of the sea."

Cata followed his example and breathed in. It was hard to distinguish after her voyage. She'd grown accustomed to the briny tang that stuck to everything as stubbornly as the salt. She'd tried to cover it up with her 4711 perfume, and look where that got her. Now, she closed her eyes to concentrate, and immediately, there it was. Wet, cold and invigorating. She could feel the smell and taste the brackish blue. She could see Mr. Krupper's ocean though it was far from sight.

"That's how I know for certain that it blows from the northeast."

She opened her eyes and he was staring directly at her without a blink.

"So that is the trick." Another conversational phrase from her journal: *the trick*.

She'd received that one from a steerage passenger telling his buddies about the competitive nature of selling Coney Island hot dogs. *The trick* was different in America. In Europe, any *trick* was dishonest guile, but here, *the trick* was a fleck of wisdom that gave an individual the upper hand. She could certainly use every bit of that.

The door slid open. Murphy returned.

"All right now, Mr. Krupper, we got you all set up in car three. I had the porter bring over a cold Coca-Cola, too."

Mr. Krupper shook his head. "Totally unnecessary, but I'll enjoy it nonetheless."

Murphy helped him stand against the train's sway and began to lead him out, but Mr. Krupper pulled back, searching his inner jacket pocket until he found his calling card. He extended it slightly too far to the left of Cata's shoulder.

"Should you need anything in Boston or if you have any troubles, please don't hesitate to call. My wife is a most delicious cook, and she loves to host new friends in the city. We'd be delighted to show you around."

An invitation to see the city from a blind man. Cata took the card. This was an unusual land, to be certain.

"Thank you, Mr. Krupper."

He nodded. "A pleasure to meet you Miss . . ." His smile deflated, and he pursed his lips. "I'm sorry, I don't think I caught your name."

Here it was. The moment she'd successfully avoided for weeks, months—nearly a year, in fact. Since she left the Lebensborn Program and hid in the steamy washroom basement disguised as a laundress. The last person to speak her true identity had been Hazel. Even the gardener had called her by his dead daughter's name. And the Ellis Island inspector had dubbed her Kate Kutter. It was more American, he said.

"Name?"

Mr. Krupper smiled. "In English or German? Nayme. Nah-meh. The same, *ja*?"

She nodded quickly, smoothing his card between her thumb and forefinger. Wrong or right. Death or life. Lie or truth. *Choose*, she told herself. *Choose*.

"Hazel," she said, and the name gave her strength. "Hazel Schmidt."

"Hazel," he repeated. "One of my favorite names—it has a lyrical quality."

The train shuddered to the right, pushing Murphy against the wall and taking Mr. Krupper with him. The steam horn blew and hissed the smell of burning coal.

Murphy found his footing. "We'd best get you seated before the next track change."

The men left, leaving Cata, now Hazel, alone in the car, just as she'd wanted from the beginning. However, the vacancy was not a comfort now. She closed her eyes and let herself be in Mr. Krupper's world. The vibration of the seat and floorboards tickled uncomfortably from finger and toe tips to core. The round thump and screech of the train wheels. The taste and smell of engine oil mingling with the ripe crops in the harvest fields they passed.

For a moment, she was transported home but not to the home she'd fled—further back to the home of her childhood and her first train ride alongside her parents. It was late summer, as she remembered. A nip was already in the shadows. Only one of her brothers had yet to be born. Not yet a year old, they'd left him in Luxembourg with her *oma*.

They were traveling to Amsterdam for a wedding. A friend of her mother's? A colleague of her father's? A distant relation? She couldn't remember nor did it matter. All that did was that she was going to a place where no one but her parents knew her. A land of magical windmills and flowering fairy pastures, a dreamscape where she could lose herself in adventures previously known only in storybooks. She'd overheard her parents discussing it all— how very much the bride and groom had paid for the pomp and flair of the extravagant nuptials officiated by a giant windmill. Her father had called it an absurd waste and sentimentalist crud. Her mother had simply deemed it heretical: *Only weddings in a holy church are legitimate.* But they'd still gone, paying their respects and drinking the mulled wine called Bridal Tears until her father stopped grumbling and smiled wide at the unmarried women tying ribbons to the Wish Tree.

Cata's mother had bought her a set of red painted clogs so that she could dance the night away. She argued she didn't want her wearing out her good shoes. Those clogs were her most prized possession at the time. Cata couldn't remember where they'd gone after the trip. Vanished into memory.

With eyes still closed, she pulled the two passports from her coat pocket. *Paper and ink, that's all*, she thought. Man-made titles and photographs bound together. Both would burn if set to a flame. Both would rot if left under a summer cloudburst. The natural world knew no difference. Here or there. Two women. Two names. The passports would be equal in Mr. Krupper's hands. They might as well have been the same.

She opened her eyes. Cata Kutter. She ripped the passport into fourths then flung the pieces out the open window. The shreds tattered in the wind like gunshots, and she did not watch to see where they fell. Instead, she closed the pane and slid her new life back into her pocket.

Only then, in the stillness and certainty of the beginning of her beginning, did she see Mr. Krupper's fedora left on the bench.

She picked it up. The stylish felt brim was soft as velvet, but less yielding. She missed luxuries like this. A man's beautiful hat free of military insignia. Something in her stomach fluttered and she beat it down, unwilling to taint an honorable crown with even innocent ardor. Mr. Krupper had been a gentleman and a friend to her when there was every reason to be less. She would rise to his example. She vowed to make Hazel proud and live her life as a eulogy to a worthier calling. She would love her cousin's children just as she hoped her own and all the Lebensborn children would be loved, though not of flesh and blood, imperfect and perfect.

She left the roomette and made her way down the narrow corridor and across carriages to car number three at the front of the train. The shade was up. Inside sat Mr. Krupper with face turned into the sunshine, a small silver tray beside him with a bottle of cola uncapped and fizzing at the glass rim.

She knocked. He turned toward the sound. "Come in."

"Mr. Krupper, it izz—"

"Hazel," he greeted.

In his American voice, her name did, indeed, sound lyrical. "You left your hat." She held it out to him and he reached into the air just where she'd extended.

"It seems I did. So kind of you. I am in your debt."

"Debt? *Nein*, no. It was my happiness to assist you." She cleared her throat and turned to exit.

"Hazel," he said again. "My mother used to read me fable stories from *die Brüder Grimm*."

She was quite familiar. Hitler had championed the Brothers Grimm tales as part of his approved literary canon. Joseph Goebbels had proclaimed the stories excellent didactic tools. At the Lebensborn Program, the children were read them at bedtime and rest time and playtime.

"'The Hazel Branch' was my favorite," said Mr. Krupper.

Yes, she knew it, though not as well as the others. It was usually skipped due to its brevity and its evocation of the Christ-child, which was not popular with the party. Jesus was Hitler's competition in the hearts of many. She wasn't surprised Mr. Krupper favored the story, given his Protestant faith.

"In the strawberry patch, the green hazel branch protected the Holy Mother from the fatal adder's bite. *As the hazel-bush has been my protection this time, it shall in future protect others also*," he recited. "A tale of life and substance and a reminder. Evil may crawl the earth, but we are ensured more miracle branches than snakes." Carefully, using two hands, he placed the fedora snugly back on his head. "Thank you." He nodded. "I am quite certain our paths will cross again, Ms. Hazel Schmidt."

Though she didn't see how or why, she believed.

ACKNOWLEDGMENTS

Infinite thanks to my readers! From cities across the globe, Amsterdam to Santa Cruz, you championed *The Baker's Daughter*. Audiences at each book event pleaded for more. I was deeply humbled and moved to pick up my pen and venture back to these characters and their story world.

Most significantly, thank you to the Lebensborn children who have come forth bravely to share. While Hazel and Cata are fictionalized, they are inspired by the tangible evidence and emotional truths of these men and women's courageous lives. Let historical shames and fears never silence us. Every life story is worthy and honorable by virtue of God's greater design.

Last but not least, I bow in gratitude to my brilliant *Grand Central* sisters in this collection: Melanie Benjamin, Jenna Blum, Amanda Hodgkinson, Pam Jenoff, Sarah Jio, Kristina McMorris, Alyson Richman, Erika Robuck, Karen White and Kristin Hannah. An extra shout of praise to Kristina McMorris (aka my Ladybug 2), who spearheaded this WWII anthology from dream to the book we now hold in hand. I'm privileged to stand beside all of these sublime authoresses and blessed to call them truest friends. The *GC* band of sisters will bring down the house with our boogie-woogie bugles and maracas. I'll be sure to bring the alpenhorns.

The Kissing Room

Melanie Benjamin

The Kissing Room.

How embarrassing! She'd had to go to the information desk, right next to the USO booth, which was crowded with eager servicemen, to ask where it was. "Please, can you tell me how to get to the Kissing Room?" Marjorie had asked, unable to prevent a slow, rosy blush from burning her cheeks, even as she was very aware of how pretty she looked, because of it.

"Way on the other side of the concourse." The bored gentleman had pointed to a distant corner. "It's close to the platform where the *Twentieth Century* arrives. You can't miss it. It's where everyone waits."

"All right," Marjorie replied, unsure. She was not from the city, or at least, she wasn't from this city. She was a proud Philadelphian, but even so, was quite cognizant of how it paled in significance to New York. Still, she was no rube, and she made herself stride purposefully into the mass of people headed in that direction, forcing herself not to stop and gape at the enormous concourse, the ceiling so high up, cavernous yet crowded with shoeshine stations, newsstands, restaurants and bars, and people, so many people! Her parents took her and her sister into Manhattan every Christmas to see a show and do some shopping. But they always detrained at Penn Station, not Grand Central.

Today, for the first time, she had come into the city alone, no longer the baby of the family, petted and cosseted by her parents and tolerated by her older sister. She had not relied on her father to buy her ticket and tip the porter; she had not blindly followed along as her parents determined the schedule to be followed, never varying: first, a taxi to the Empire State Building to gape at it (although never, ever to take the elevator to the top); then, a stroll down Fifth Avenue to window-shop; then, a matinee at Radio City Music Hall; finally, dinner at an Automat, not because it was the only thing they could afford, but simply because it was fun and novel. Marjorie and her sister, Paulina, never tired of ordering little dishes, putting the nickels into the slots, the plates or bowls full of steaming, yet somehow tasteless, food appearing as if by magic: baked beans and macaroni and cheese and limp green beans.

After this heavy, hot meal, her feet burning as if she had walked on hot coals instead of hard city pavement, her eyes scratchy and red, as if they simply couldn't take in one more astounding image, Marjorie usually found herself nodding off on the train home, until her mother gently shook her just as they pulled into the station.

But that was then, back when she was a child. Now eighteen, Marjorie Konigsberg was in the city as an adult, as a woman. With a precious business card in her hand and an appointment to keep. In "the Kissing Room."

Swept up in a crowd, Marjorie found herself pulled toward the other end of the concourse, where the throng divided and branched off as people hurried to different train platforms. Marjorie turned away from them then and spied a large corner room, somewhat awkwardly splaying off the main concourse, all pink marble and high-backed wooden benches and cigarette haze, full of expectant people. Women, men, small children, old ladies with ugly flowered hats; all sat patiently or impatiently, reading magazines or looking at the clock as if they could will it to move faster. In one corner of the room was an elevator, almost as if it were an afterthought. It was small and looked out of place.

"Excuse me, is this the . . . I mean to say, could this be the—Kissing Room?" Marjorie whispered to a woman seated on the corner of a bench, a crumpled, damp paper bag in her hands.

The woman stared at Marjorie as if she didn't know what to say, and Marjorie felt that blush creeping over her cheeks again. She was about to turn, perhaps even run away, when the woman nodded briskly, then opened up her paper bag and peered inside before closing it again and rolling down the top, as if to prevent whatever was inside from escaping.

Marjorie whispered a thank-you, then walked about the room for a few minutes, calming herself. She was in the right place, and she had forty-five minutes to spare. She was in her prettiest outfit, a graduation present from her mother; it was a black-and-white-checked wool suit, nipped in at the waist so fiercely that she could scarcely draw breath, with a slight peplum. She wore new black pumps that pinched her toes but made her legs look endless. She had carefully, and stealthily, applied pancake foundation and crème rouge and a bit of mascara in the bathroom this morning, managing to hide her face from her parents as she hurried off to work.

Or so they thought.

Instead of going to her part-time job of watching Mrs. Samson's "two little angels," as that lady referred to them with absolutely no irony, Marjorie had taken the train from Narberth to the 30th Street Station in Philadelphia, where she changed to a Pennsylvania Railroad train to Penn Station, and from there she'd taken a cab to Grand Central. Ella May, her best friend who was sworn to secrecy, had agreed to watch the two little angels for the day while their mother, a new war widow, cleaned houses.

With any luck, Marjorie would be home for dinner, and her parents wouldn't be the wiser. With any luck, the Samson angels would not rat on her to their mother, who cleaned Marjorie's own house.

With any luck, Marjorie would sweep in the door with a movie contract in her hand. An MGM contract, to be specific.

She reached into her handbag and pulled out the card, holding it with gloved fingers, somewhat at arm's length because she was farsighted yet refused to wear glasses. Still, she could make out the cherished words.

Abe Holmes, Talent Scout. MGM Studios, Culver City, California.

And scribbled underneath, in her own handwriting, *September 21st, 12:30, Grand Central. Screen test at 1:30.*

This was it; this was her ticket to the future. She knew it in her bones. Her young, tender, hopeful bones that felt pliant and supple; she bent slightly backward in front of the polished metal facade of a cigarette machine just to see how willowy she was, how young and pretty, a starlet already. No. A movie star.

Exactly like Vivien Leigh, her absolute idol. She even resembled the star of her favorite movie of all time, *Gone with the Wind*. Vivien Leigh was just a tad more slender, her lips just a bit thinner, her cheekbones just slightly higher. (Marjorie had spent quite a lot of time locked in the bathroom with fan magazines, in the study of this matter.) But they shared the same glossy black hair, creamy white skin, green eyes, and Marjorie could say with more than a little satisfaction that her eyes were larger, more innocent looking.

Perfect for the movies.

There was a hum in the room now; the quiet, expectant air vanished, chased away by chatter and laughter and anticipatory rustlings. A train must have just arrived, for rumpled, exhausted-looking people carrying traveling bags or small suitcases were stumbling into the room, eyes blinking wearily, most just standing there, waiting to be claimed like lost luggage. And they were; now there were cries and embraces and more than a few tears. Marjorie stopped to watch, to witness, to learn. She was an actress, after all, and Mr. Carson had always told her how an actress had to stop and listen, and absorb. An actress was an observer, he had always said. You can't become a character if you have nothing to build on.

So Marjorie watched, a benevolent, slightly superior smile on her face lending her an air of one who seemed unclaimed herself, although she didn't know that. She only knew that she suddenly felt so very kind, so very indulgent toward the entire world; she hoped that each reunion was a happy one, for everyone in the Kissing Room deserved to be as joyful as she was this autumn day in New York, her entire future ahead of her.

Although, from the way the defeated-looking woman with the paper bag greeted the defeated-looking man in uniform who simply stood before her with no word or movement of greeting—with barely a nod, her gaze downcast—Marjorie felt that not every reunion was going to be happy. But that, too, was something to pay attention to. Even with the war over, not everyone was happy. There were bad things to be endured, sadness, wickedness even. And these were things of which Marjorie had little knowledge. She did long to follow this tired, silent couple out of the station into the street, to wherever they were headed, so that she might learn something of their tired, silent lives.

Naturally, Marjorie did not do this. She only checked the time again—half an hour left now!—and took out her compact to powder her nose. She noticed that one or two couples did not leave the Kissing Room with the masses, but instead went to that elevator, spoke quickly to the operator who asked each a question that Marjorie could not make out, and were whisked away to some mysterious destination.

She wondered where it led, that elevator. But wondering led to frowning, and that would not do; she snapped her compact shut and continued to pace around the room. She was so full of energy, so nervous yet excited; she had to get rid of it all now, before Mr. Holmes arrived. Movie stars did not *pace*.

Mr. Carson—Doug, he had insisted Marjorie call him after graduation—was the one who had taught her about movement. About stillness, gracefulness, repose; how to make an audience lean toward you, instead of the other way around. And Marjorie was grateful; she had already rehearsed her first Academy Award acceptance speech, in which she would thank her high school drama teacher for "all he taught me, back home in Narberth, Pennsylvania, the town that will always have my heart."

Mr. Carson had shown up midway through Marjorie's junior year, after the previous drama teacher, Mr. Blanchard, had been drafted. Of course, everyone expected some old doddering teacher brought out of retirement; the high school was overrun with that type, now that the war was on. But Mr. Carson was neither old nor doddering; he was young, very young in spite of his receding hairline, the only physical flaw that Marjorie and all her girlfriends who hung around backstage during lunchtime, dreamily reading scenes from plays, could detect.

No, this new drama teacher (well, to be perfectly honest, the new English teacher who directed the Drama Club after school) was about thirty, in peak physical condition with a dancer's grace-ful yet athletic build. He did not even wear glasses. He didn't have a harelip, or a limp, or a lazy eye, or terrible teeth, or any number of physical defects that would qualify him as 4-F, which he must have been. He was simply perfect, and young, and male, and out of uniform, and therefore so exotic and rare as to resemble a prized exhibit in a zoo. Even the athletes—the dumb Blutos who nor-mally would never set foot inside the auditorium except to get their letters at the end of the year—were intrigued by him.

"I hear he's related to Roosevelt. That's how he's not in uniform."

"I hear he's got a bad ticker. Rheumatic fever or something. He'll probably keel over in the middle of a class."

"I hear he's on the lam. He's running from the draft board. He'll be gone by Monday."

"No, dears, it's none of those things," Miss Turnberry, the librarian, whispered to Marjorie and her friends one afternoon. Miss Turnberry was writing down a request for the latest Drama Guild script, although she reminded them all that there was little chance of the Lower Merion High School Library actually order-ing it. "The school board sets our budget, you know. We can't only order plays for you girls." But she smiled sympathetically, her gray, watery eyes blinking kindly. Miss Turnberry was not old; Marjo-rie's mother had guessed her to be about thirty-two. But Miss Turnberry was still a miss, not a missus, and she didn't even have any tragic wartime love story as an excuse. She had not been engaged only to lose her fiancé to a bullet or torpedo. She had remained firmly Miss Turnberry, unchanged and unloved since the first day she had become librarian, long before the war. Unloved, that is, in the acceptable way, by a man. She was very much loved by the serious young girls who spent their time either in the library or the auditorium, dreaming big dreams, not getting too caught up in boys and crushes and popularity, if only because they were so certain these things would come later, in their time. After the big dreams were reality, and they were in no danger of turning into the next Miss Turnberry.

"So what is it? Why isn't Mr. Carson in uniform?" Marjorie asked as the girls draped themselves about Miss Turnberry's desk one afternoon in 1944. Drama Club—the first Drama Club of Mr. Carson's tenure—was about to commence. They would be auditioning for the winter play, *Dulcy*. Normally Marjorie, a junior, wouldn't have a chance of landing the lead role, originated by another one of her idols, Lynn Fontanne. But with a new director, perhaps one not given to the archaic class system of awarding the leading roles only to seniors, she just might have a chance.

"He's the only surviving son," Miss Turnberry said with a sad shake of her neat head, her hair pulled back into a stern knot, no poofs or rolls or even a part. It was simply scraped back from her forehead. Miss Turnberry did not wear glasses, for which Marjorie was happy, as that would be too sad and predictable. But she could use some powder and rouge, and during Marjorie's entire reign at Lower Merion High School, she looked for an opportunity to introduce the notion of cosmetics and a youthful hairstyle to the librarian, whom she did love. But no opportunity ever arose.

"An only surviving son," Miss Turnberry repeated, for emphasis. "He lost one brother at Pearl Harbor, another at Midway. His parents petitioned the draft board. That's why he's not in uniform."

Marjorie's big eyes filled with tears. During the Drama Club meeting, she was unable to look at Mr. Carson, young, sole-surviving Mr. Carson, without her eyes brimming all over again.

Needless to say, she did not get the role of Dulcy; she simply wasn't in the mood for comedy, not after Miss Turnberry's woeful tale.

But that was the last time she auditioned for Mr. Carson and was not rewarded with a leading role or a show-stealing supporting part. It was quickly established that Marjorie Konigsberg was Mr. Carson's favorite, and while there were some grumblings from the seniors, for the most part the rest of her peers surrendered to the inevitable. There was always a teacher's pet, and there was nothing to be done about it.

Of course, Marjorie fell in love with Mr. Carson. All her friends did. They all read aloud romantic scenes from plays in the privacy of their bedrooms, pretending that Mr. Carson was reading with them, and Marjorie only felt herself superior in that she chose Shaw's *Caesar and Cleopatra* instead of Shakespeare's *Romeo and Juliet*, the obvious choice.

But for some reason, none of these crushes ever lasted; after a mad period of a few weeks, during which the girl would manufacture excuses to see Mr. Carson after rehearsal for a bit of advice; during which test scores inevitably suffered and appetites waned, she would somehow find herself uninterested. It would happen gradually, no abrupt wrenching of the heart or denouncement or declaration. Just soon enough, the girl in question would find herself more interested in one of her classmates, unformed and pimpled as they were, but still emanating that strange, masculine attraction that was so puzzling—they smelled, after all!—yet so thrilling.

Even Marjorie felt her attraction to Mr. Carson waning, after a few weeks of close contact. She could never put her finger on it; she only felt her interest no longer held any physical thrill of having him accidentally lean too close, or carelessly drape his arm over her shoulder while giving her stage direction, no longer a violent, shocking jolt to her system.

She wondered if the reason for her disinterest, at least in a romantic sense, had anything to do with what she overheard her parents whispering one evening before dinner. It was a rare occasion when Marjorie had managed to rouse herself from her daydreams of a different life, different parents, different friends, and different city, and come downstairs on time, for a change.

"It's a disease. He's a degenerate. That's why he's not in uniform. They can't allow that type in the service."

"Oh, Jonathan, you don't really know. Mr. Carson seems perfectly normal to me."

"No, Paula." And Marjorie heard her father's voice soften with fondness and dismissal, both; he often treated her mother like an infant, and as far as Marjorie could tell, her mother seemed to enjoy being treated so. "You're an innocent, my dear. He's definitely that way."

"Oh well, then we should be thankful, I suppose. Because of all the time he's been spending with Marjorie, filling her head with notions of being an actress. At least we don't have to worry about anything else."

"You would see the bright side of it, wouldn't you?" And Marjorie's father laughed, and Marjorie heard a loud kissing sound, and so she turned around and crept up the stairs in order to stomp back down them noisily, again preventing further disquieting action.

So Marjorie and Mr. Carson had settled into a friendly mentor-student relationship, which suited them both. Marjorie never did fall in love, real love, with a real boy her own age, during high school, and she did wonder about that. Was she lacking in some basic female quality? Or was she simply too focused on what came after, unlike most everyone else she knew who could only think ahead as far as the senior dance? She knew it would have been so easy to fall in love in wartime; even the plainest, most pitiable girls managed to find a soldier who was eager for her lipstick-sealed letters and pensively posed photograph. And sometimes Marjorie did feel a pang of regret, or of missing out on something—like now, for instance, in the Kissing Room, as she watched a trembling young woman fling herself into the arms of a private with a duffel bag slung over his shoulder, heard the muffled, tear-soaked cry of, "Oh, Doug!" and then nothing. Nothing but tremulous yearning, unchecked joy. Experiences and feelings that Marjorie had never had, except onstage.

It was onstage that Marjorie came to life; it was onstage that she was known as someone special, someone different. Offstage, in her own home where people ought to have known better, since they lived in such close proximity to her brilliance, she was just little Marjorie, spoiled daughter of a banker, annoying baby sister of a WAVE who had gotten her picture in the local paper simply because she had joined up. Offstage, in the hallways of Lower Merion High School, she was one of many pretty little coeds, expected to marry a returning soldier someday sooner rather than later, maybe after attending a year or so of junior college so she would have something to contribute to dinner parties other than her meat loaf.

But onstage, underneath a mask of makeup with her hair pinned up inside a hot wig, wearing a threadbare, stained costume that still turned her into someone else entirely; onstage, beneath bright lights that nourished her, fed her, made her blossom and grow and expand . . .

"You're the most promising student I've ever seen," Mr. Carson said, almost reluctantly, one day after rehearsal for *Susan and God*.

"You have to work on your voice, for it's too small. You have to project better. But your face—you can't hide a thing with that face, and that's your ticket."

Marjorie had blushed, of course; she had always hated the way every emotion and thought could be read on her traitorous face. She'd never been able to keep anything from her parents or her sister, who had the best poker face in the world, everyone in the family agreed. But not Marjorie; no one dared tell her a secret or asked her to hide something as a child. One too many birthday presents had been revealed, one too many surprises spoiled.

But Mr. Carson said her face was her fortune! Mr. Carson said she had talent, real talent! Encouraged for the first time in her life by someone who really understood her dreams and didn't dismiss them as childish notions that should have been outgrown long ago, Marjorie worked hard. Harder than she had ever worked at anything in her life, to her own astonishment. When Mr. Carson gave her books to study, she pored over them, not quite understanding them all—Stanislavski seemed to speak in a language she could not share, for instance—but reading them, nonetheless, practically memorizing them. And when, after graduation, Mr. Carson encouraged her to go to acting school, she nearly fainted to hear the unspoken dreams finally articulated out loud. And she asked him to talk to her parents, who disapproved of any kind of career in the arts. They weren't keen on careers for their daughters at all, but had allowed Paulina to enroll in nursing school, and then the WAVES, because of the war.

"No, Marjorie, I'm not getting involved between a student and her parents," Mr. Carson replied one afternoon right after graduation; only the underclassmen still had class, but Marjorie and her fellow graduates had decided, grandly, to visit the "dear old place" for old times' sake.

The two of them were hanging out in Mr. Carson's dingy little office off the wings of the auditorium stage; after a year and a half it still seemed impersonal, as if he could vanish and no one would ever know he'd been there. There were no photos, no framed diplomas or certificates, not even a pile of old playbills. No, there was only his coat and his hat and his battered briefcase, and a copy of the last play they'd done together, the last one they would do together, *You Can't Take It with You.* Surprisingly, she had not played Alice, the lead; he had given her a smaller, flashier role as Essie, the ballet-dancing older sister, and she had simply stolen the show with it.

But now the end of the school year loomed, and Mr. Carson seemed unaccountably glum.

"I've learned my lesson, unfortunately, in the past," he admitted, leaning against the front of his desk but balancing lightly upon the balls of his feet, as if he might suddenly leap into the air upon the slightest whim. He played with the end of the scarf he used as a belt, just like Fred Astaire; Marjorie loved that about him, thought it dashing and original (though even she had to admit that Fred Astaire had done it first).

"But my parents won't hear of me becoming an actress. They won't! But if you put in a good word for me, perhaps I can get them to at least give me a few months. I've looked into schools, and the American Academy of Dramatic Arts seems perfect—of course, if I could even get in." Marjorie tried to look doubtful about this, but she simply could not hide a sly smile.

"Of course you'd get in," Mr. Carson said, knowing that was what she wanted to hear. "But I can't risk it, Marjorie. Although

really, I don't know why I shouldn't. I'm going to be replaced anyway. Now that the boys will be coming home, I'll be the first to get
the boot for some returning war hero."

"Oh no, that's nonsense!" Now it was Marjorie's line. "Of course
they'll keep you! Why, look at the quality of the plays we've put on
since you've been here! And we even got reviewed by the local
paper! That never happened before."

"That's kind of you, but it doesn't matter. Not in a high school.
I know I'm the low man on the totem pole."

"Well, the war isn't really over, not yet, Mr. Carson. There's still
Japan," Marjorie said, although she couldn't quite sell it. Everyone
knew it would all be over by the end of the summer. This graduation, unlike previous grim, stoic years, had been a truly joyous
event with tears overflowing, because this time they were tears of
happiness, cried freely by mothers who no longer feared their sons
would trade their graduation caps for combat gear. Oh, sure, the
war with Japan was still on, but by the time these boys finished boot
camp, it would all be over. Europe was won, Germany defeated.
The graduating class of 1945 was spared; the roll of honor in the
school courtyard would have few new names added to it now.

"You're sweet, Marjorie. And please, call me Doug, for God's
sake. I hate this Mr. Carson stuff, with all of you." And Mr. Carson
leaned toward her, to brush her hair off her shoulder. For a brief
moment, Marjorie tried to summon up the old crush, but she
couldn't; she only smiled and shook her hair back, and accepted the
compliment when Mr. Carson—Doug—told her she looked much
better with it up. Then he returned to the subject of her future.

"At least try out for some of the little theaters, a community
playhouse or something. Do that, for me? If your parents won't let
you go to New York, surely they would let you still perform here.

You're good, Marjorie. I don't usually encourage students like this. Hell, half the time I can barely suffer through watching them onstage myself, let alone inflict them upon others. Cigarette?" He offered her one from the box on his desk.

Marjorie laughed and accepted it, delighted by the surprisingly intimate, catty turn of the conversation. "Even Susan Taggart?" Susan Taggart was the closest thing Marjorie had to a rival; she had played Alice in *You Can't Take It with You*. Woodenly, Marjorie couldn't help but think.

"Especially Susan Taggart. She 'ran the gamut of emotions, from A to B'—to quote Dorothy Parker on Katharine Hepburn."

"Oh, I've never heard that before!" Marjorie inhaled, quite sophisticatedly, she thought; then she laughed, and felt as if she was at the beginning of this wonderful new career, a career made up of opening night parties full of witty banter, exactly like this. She wondered how she might continue to see Mr. Carson—Doug—during the summer, as a sort of preparation for the next step.

But Mr. Carson, true to his prediction, was gone by the end of the month; gone from Narberth, gone from her life without a word of farewell. Nobody knew where he went, although there were rumors, of course. Dark, dangerous, spiteful rumors. Marjorie was sad, naturally, but not quite heartbroken. Merely melancholy and a little bit piqued that he didn't get to see her in her debut with the Narberth Community Playhouse, not quite the Walnut Street Theater in Philadelphia, where all the big plays tried out before Broadway, but still semiprofessional. One of the leads had understudied Fredric March once, on Broadway.

Mr. Carson, the one person in her life who could have truly appreciated it, was not there to see her performance as Tweeny in *The Admirable Crichton*, a real coup for a newcomer. However, her parents were there on opening night, supportive in their own way, praising her performance while somehow tempering the importance of the achievement. ("Yes, dear, you did well in this nice little play. We're very proud of you, although it's not quite the same as your sister getting her nursing degree, now, is it?")

But nothing, not even her parents' backhanded compliments, could dull the luster of her first real opening night, in a play with adults playing adult parts, no teenagers donning gray wigs and doddering around in their misguided attempts to indicate age. This was the real thing; she was part of a troupe, part of a club, and her curtain call had been received with a nice little burst of applause, indicating her success in the role. And she had been invited to the opening night party! She, only eighteen, had been asked to "come along, ingénue," to the home of the actor playing Crichton (he who had understudied Fredric March). She was just about to ask her parents if she could go, when a complete stranger came up to her and interrupted the family conversation.

"Hey. Good job, kiddo." And he handed her a business card.

Abe Holmes, Talent Scout. MGM Studios, Culver City, California.

"Excuse me?" Marjorie's father had said, his bushy eyebrows raised nearly to his hairline. He moved instinctively nearer his daughter. "I don't believe we've met."

"Abe. Abe Holmes. I'm a talent scout for MGM. Sister here has the goods, I think." He jerked his thumb toward Marjorie.

Her heart beating wildly, her legs suddenly trembling, Marjorie could only stare at the business card.

"The goods?" Marjorie's father repeated, incredulously. "Now see here, Mr. Holmes. This is my daughter you're talking about. I don't like your tone of voice."

"Sorry." And Mr. Holmes did appear to be contrite. He removed his hat, looked down at his shoes meekly, then shook hands with Mr. and Mrs. Konigsberg before turning to Marjorie. She peered up at him; he didn't look much like a talent scout, although she really had no idea how one should look. Mr. Holmes looked like a banker; like her father, in fact, in a boring gray suit, gray tie, white shirt. The only flashy thing about him was a gold ring with a ruby on the second finger of his left hand. Marjorie had never seen a ring on a man that wasn't a wedding or a class ring.

"Miss, uh, Miss Konigsberg." Mr. Holmes consulted the rolled-up program in his hand. "You did a very nice job in the part. I would like to talk to you, and your parents, of course, about making a screen test for MGM."

By now, the rest of the company was circled around Marjorie, her parents, and Mr. Holmes; Marjorie detected that the tide of good feeling toward her had already turned. Waves of hostility seemed to emanate from her cast mates like the heat from the footlights, still burning bright on the other side of the curtain. The actress who had played Lady Mary turned and ran off the stage, only to reappear in her costume from the first act, much finer and more flattering than the one she wore at the end.

"Well, I'm sorry, but this sounds like a con to me." Mr. Konigsberg barked a laugh, and Marjorie was seized with a desire to shove her father, who had never even raised his voice to her, into the orchestra pit. But she merely bit her lip and waited.

"I can understand that, sir," Mr. Holmes said, still so very respectful. "I assure you, however, that I do work for MGM. Please feel free to call the studio—the number's on the back—to confirm."

"Well, that would be a long-distance call," thrifty Mr. Konigsberg muttered, and Marjorie had to practically put her fist in her mouth, to prevent a scream.

"I would tell you to reverse the charges, but the boss wouldn't like that much," Mr. Holmes admitted with a rueful smile. He wasn't very handsome, Marjorie thought, finally conquering her excitement enough so that she was able to assess him coolly, like any other man. He was a little bit younger than her father, she decided; his hair wasn't gray, but it was thinning on top. His face was rather fleshy, with a bulbous nose and absurdly pink cheeks. But he oozed confidence; his eyes, particularly, seemed awfully penetrating, despite being rather small. He narrowed those eyes at her now, and she raised her chin and met his gaze, taking extra care to widen her already large eyes, and to smile in her best imitation of Vivien Leigh.

Mr. Holmes did not smile, but he did nod with what Marjorie felt to be appreciation.

"Say, I'd like to take you all out for a soda to talk about this. What do you say, sis—I mean, Miss Konigsberg?"

Marjorie inhaled, thankful he had addressed her and not her parents. For she knew the best way to handle her father; it was the way her mother always counseled handling a man. "Use the assumptive close, Marjorie. Don't ask permission, just do what you want and let him think it was his idea."

So now Marjorie said, without a hint of hesitation, "I think that would be grand, don't you, Mother? Let's go to Shubert's. You love their sundaes, Dad; I just know you were going to suggest it yourself. Now, if you'll give me a moment, I'll go change and grab my coat." And she pivoted, slowly, gracefully, and walked unhurriedly away, scattering the little circle of her fellow actors, whom she had previously held in such awe. Now, with the appearance of one business card, all that had changed; they looked small and ordinary. Destined to spend their lives with the Narberth Players. She must remember to come visit once in a while, for it would do them all good to see how successful one of their own had become.

Marjorie took her time changing out of her costume, blotting her face with a handkerchief in order to tone down her stage makeup, reapplying her lipstick in a more natural shade, not that fire-engine red she had been told to use. She powdered her face all over again, sprayed some perfume on her neck, wrists, and under her arms, then donned her street clothes, which fortunately were rather nice—a ruffled blouse, flared wool skirt, and vest in a deep emerald green that matched her eyes.

And then she joined her parents and Mr. Holmes, willing herself not to speculate about the conversation they must have had in her absence. In his own car, Mr. Holmes followed the Konigsbergs to Shubert's, a bustling ice-cream shop with shiny metal counters, bright red stools, polished black-and-white floors. It was corny, it was small town, but it was the perfect setting for a young, big-eyed aspiring movie star.

They ordered, Marjorie and her mother on one side of the booth, Mr. Holmes and her father on the other. And they listened to Mr. Holmes's practiced speech; he was sent out a couple of times a year, even to the sticks like this—Mr. Konigsberg bristled at that—to see beauty pageants and local plays. MGM was sure that now, with the war over (VJ day had happened a month ago), there would be a big surge in popularity for the movies, and they needed stars. Some of the older ones—well, you all know whom I'm talking about, Kate Hepburn and Dietrich and even Garbo—who were big prior to the war were washed up now, kaput. The studio needed young, pretty things, new faces, to match the new, jubilant mood. And it was his job, Abe Holmes, happy family man who hated to leave his wife and daughter to traipse all over the country but a job's a job, don't you know that, sir?—it was his job to find these new faces and bring them either to New York or Hollywood for a screen test. All expenses paid, of course; any train fare or hotel stay would be reimbursed. It was all completely legit, on the up-and-up; why, Ava Gardner had been discovered this way, you know the story, right, sis—I mean, Miss Konigsberg?

All three adults had then turned to Marjorie, who had smiled demurely, cast her gaze down, and sipped her milkshake before nodding. Of course she knew how Ava Gardner had been discovered, her picture in some photographer's window, and then a screen test in New York. And now, she was married to Mickey Rooney! Or was it Artie Shaw? Marjorie was a bit confused. But Ava Gardner was prominently featured in the fan magazines and appeared on her way to stardom, and she had been screen-tested right in New York, just as Mr. Holmes was suggesting for her, Marjorie Konigsberg!

"Of course, the name will have to go," Mr. Holmes said now, with a remarkable lack of tact considering the company. "Konigsberg. What is that? Jewish?"

"German," Mr. Konigsberg replied icily.

"Marjorie's okay, maybe. Kind of long. But we'll let the publicity department deal with all that. First, we have to screen-test you. Now let me see, I'll be in New York in a week. I have to swing through a few more of these towns first. So how about the twenty-first? Early afternoon, say?"

"Mr. Holmes, I'm sure we appreciate your interest. But we need time to discuss this. I have to say, I'm not at all impressed by Hollywood; it's not a place for a proper young woman. We have more realistic plans for Marjorie, as I'm sure you do for your own daughter. Now, let me pay for the ice cream, and we'll be in touch."

"I understand, I do. The truth is, I have a whole lineup of girls ready to be tested, so it's no skin off my nose if Miss Konigsberg decides otherwise. I do think she'd test well, though." Mr. Holmes turned those penetrating little eyes on Marjorie again, and again she met the gaze head-on.

"Would I have to prepare a scene for you?" Marjorie asked, once more taking the tactic of assuming her parents would say yes.

"No, don't bother. It's mostly about how well you photograph. We have plenty of acting teachers on the lot. That's the least of it, to tell the truth."

Marjorie felt her excitement sour a bit; she was an actress already and did not take kindly to having her talent denigrated in this way. Yes, she understood that the movies were more about how you looked than how you acted; that was why she loved Vivien Leigh so, because she was a real actress first, a great beauty second. But to have it put forth so bluntly did diminish the sacred splendor of this moment, when she—just like Ava Gardner!—was being "discovered." As if she were some new, important country!

"I can prepare one anyway. I've got several memorized, naturally, for auditions," Marjorie murmured, and Mr. Holmes merely shrugged.

"Suit yourself."

A few more pleasantries were exchanged, Mr. Holmes shared a photograph of his wife and child, grumbled a bit about having to take an early train to Baltimore, then they parted. Mr. Holmes shook Marjorie's hand firmly, bending down to peer into her face before grunting and nodding once more.

On the brief car ride home, the Konigsbergs did not discuss the events of the evening; as adept as they were at handling each other, Mr. and Mrs. Konigsberg were even more adept at handling their daughter and knew better than to interrupt her certain reverie with anything so dreadful as practical words and plans. This tactic continued for two days until one night at dinner, Mr. Konigsberg casually revealed that he had indeed telephoned the number on the back of the card, and discovered that an Abe Holmes did work for MGM studios in Culver City, California.

"So that's all square anyway," he said while passing the lamb chops to Marjorie. "The man's legit, if crude. I'll give him that."

"He did seem rather forward," Mrs. Konigsberg chimed in supportively. "Not what I would call refined."

"I don't see what that has to do with any of this," Marjorie said primly.

"Well, it's the heart of the matter, Marjorie. Do you really want to do business with a man that rough around the edges? Certainly not. But of course, the whole idea is preposterous anyway; I don't know why we're even discussing the man. It's out of the question, this screen test. Marjorie, I know you'll pout, but you'll thank me later. It's best to get these silly notions out of your head now. You're young, you're sensible, you'll recover."

Marjorie did not pout. She did not cry or storm off to her room; she simply bit her lip, looked thoughtful, ate little, and left the room quietly. She caught her parents exchanging glances over her head several times, but no further mention of the "whole idea" was made.

But it consumed her every waking moment and her dreams, so vivid that they seemed like movies themselves, even to the point of a director shouting "Cut!" right before she woke up. She must get to Grand Central on the twenty-first. Another chance like this would not come her way; she'd never heard of a movie scout coming to Narberth before. And her ties here were already cut; there was little chance she'd get another part at the Narberth Players, given how hostile they all were to her now. Subsequent performances had been trials, as no one spoke to her backstage, and onstage, every trick in the book was pulled out, from simple upstaging to discovering vicious pins in inconvenient places in her costume.

Plus, she was eighteen. Next year she would be nineteen. How old, how dreary and unexciting, nineteen was to eighteen! *An eighteen-year-old new discovery.* She could just read it in the fan magazines. Nineteen simply wouldn't be the same; it would be too late. No, this was her chance, her every dream and desire come true, and she was not going to let her parents ruin it for her.

And then, joy of joys! Her stupid sister Paulina telegrammed with the news that she was marrying a sailor, some hick from Nevada that nobody knew, and that they were in such a hurry to be wed they weren't coming home to Philadelphia first, and then the entire household blew up. It exploded, just like the photo she'd seen in *Life* of the bomb that was dropped on Hiroshima; a giant mushroom cloud hung over the Konigsbergs' nice white colonial home, a looming gaseous mass of tears and recriminations and shouting and long-distance phone calls made through gritted teeth. And Marjorie's "whole idea" was forgotten by all—except, of course, by Marjorie. Who managed to sneak in her own long-distance call—waiting feverishly for the operator to ring back that the call had been put through, terrified that someone else would answer the phone before she could—to Mr. Holmes's secretary, confirming her appointment and being given the instruction to meet him in the Kissing Room at Grand Central at the appointed hour.

And here she was, waiting for Mr. Holmes, waiting for her future, her ascending star to the Hollywood heavens, just like—

Marjorie stopped her pacing. She gaped. She stared. For walking briskly into the Kissing Room was a couple, both wearing dark glasses, both avoiding eye contact with anyone, especially with each other. But they were together; the man, tall, thin, with dark hair and a prominent nose, had his arm around the woman's waist. She was tall as well, with golden brown hair and blushing red cheeks like a milkmaid. Marjorie could not help herself; she gasped as she recognized this hurrying, bashful-looking woman as Ingrid Bergman. She gasped again when she recognized the man holding on to her, so tightly, as if afraid she might bolt, as Gregory Peck.

Two movie stars! Right here, in the Kissing Room, in Grand Central, where Marjorie Konigsberg was to meet Abe Holmes, talent scout for MGM, and be screen-tested herself. She couldn't quite believe her luck; it was a sign, a blessing, an absolution of the guilt she felt in lying to her parents. She had an urge to rush up to the couple, now standing before that mysterious elevator sharing a nervous glance, and confess that she, too, was like them. She, Marjorie Konigsberg, was on her way to a screen test, and would see them in Hollywood soon. But the elevator opened and Gregory Peck practically shoved Ingrid Bergman into it before following her, and Marjorie heard the elevator operator ask a question that was given a muttered answer before the door shut, and the light went on above it indicating it was rising.

Oh, where did that elevator go? Marjorie had an impulse to press the button and find out for herself, but it was too late; it was nearly twelve thirty, and Abe Holmes would be here any minute, and it was time to check her reflection one final time. She pulled out her compact, ran her tongue across her teeth, smiled, looked pouty, looked radiant, looked sad, looked mysterious, all in quick succession. Satisfied, she snapped her compact shut and quickly surveyed the room, looking for the most fetching seat on which to array herself. Deciding upon a corner—the very corner where the paper bag lady had sat—Marjorie took her seat carefully, smoothing her skirt, placing her handbag discreetly by her side, and choosing a far-off spot on which to focus, dreamily, as if she had more pressing, ethereal notions in her head than a mere screen test.

"Well, the kid decided to meet me after all," a voice boomed down at her.

Taking a deep breath, Marjorie raised her head slowly and met Mr. Holmes's appreciative, penetrating gaze. She realized she had forgotten what he had looked like; in her dreams and fantasies, she had only seen that business card, and a mysterious voice behind a giant camera, and bright lights, screaming fans, a bouquet of flowers from Mr. Carson—or maybe Gregory Peck!—with a card that said, *I always knew you had talent. What I didn't know was how much.*

"Why, of course. I telephoned your secretary. Did she not tell you?"

"Sure, sure. Still, you never know. Your parents were pretty slick, I have to say. I didn't think they'd let you."

"I'm eighteen, Mr. Holmes." Marjorie kept her voice low, modulated, slightly amused. "I make my own decisions now."

"Hmm." Mr. Holmes snorted a laugh. "I think we should drink to that."

"Well," Marjorie consulted the clock. "It's nearly time for the test, isn't it? I don't think we have time."

"Don't worry about that. They wait for me, not the other way around. Let's go."

Mr. Holmes gestured for her to stand, and she did; he then made his way to that mysterious elevator, and she followed, her heart pounding.

"Oh! I just saw Ingrid Bergman!" She couldn't help herself; she knew she sounded ridiculously juvenile and starstruck but she simply had to tell someone. "She was with that new actor, Gregory Peck. They went into this elevator, too!"

"You don't say." Mr. Holmes, shifting his suitcase from one hand to the other, looked amused. "Not my problem—neither one of them is at MGM—but still interesting. She's married, of course. I don't know about him."

"Goodness!" Marjorie gasped. "But you don't think they were— well, they got into this elevator, that's all. Does it go up to some studio? Where I'll have my screen test?" That made sense, of course; if the two stars had made use of this elevator, and she was, too, apparently—Mr. Holmes had just pushed the button—then it must have something to do with the movies, with the studio.

Mr. Holmes didn't answer; he turned to her, looked her up and down as if realizing, for the first time, she had a body attached to her face (her fortune!), and grinned. Mr. Holmes grinning was a sight that made Marjorie's stomach sour; his teeth, which she had not noticed before, were yellowed with tobacco and coffee. And his lips were slightly liver colored.

Marjorie turned away right as the elevator arrived. It opened, and Mr. Holmes ushered her into it; the red-capped elevator boy closed the door.

"Reservations?" he inquired, without making eye contact.

"Yes. Holmes. MGM."

"Very good, sir."

Marjorie relaxed, only now realizing that she had been tense. But there had been something in the way Mr. Holmes looked at her that had set her nerves on alert. Everything was all right, though; obviously they were just going up to wherever the screen test would take place.

The elevator bell dinged, and the boy opened the door. Mr. Holmes gestured for Marjorie to step out first.

"Will I have time to freshen up my makeup and hair?" she inquired, too focused to take much notice of her surroundings.

"We have hair and makeup; don't worry about that. They'll fix you up for the camera."

"Oh good," she said, and followed him as he made his way through a crowded, lobbylike room full of couches and potted palms, a pianist playing in some far-off corner, a bar in another corner, intimate little seating arrangements —and a front desk, just like a hotel. And then she realized this *was* a hotel; a fancy script *B* was emblazoned upon every door and desk, even the ashtrays and matchbooks on the tables.

"Nice, isn't it? You ever been to the Biltmore before?" Mr. Holmes asked, strolling unhurriedly, as if he was a tour guide and not an important Hollywood talent scout, to the front desk. He even pointed out the famous gold clock hanging from the ceiling. Marjorie was completely befuddled. That elevator led to a hotel lobby? The Biltmore Hotel?

"I just want to drop my bags," Mr. Holmes explained; he must have sensed the questions bursting out of her, making her perspire so that her blouse started to cling to her, her hair to frizz slightly at her hairline. She knew her nose must be as shiny as the mirror behind the desk.

The clerk, an older man with a neat mustache, cast a look her way. He raised an eyebrow but did not say a word as he filled out a registration form, taking Mr. Holmes's information.

"One key or two?" he finally inquired with another look at Marjorie.

"One."

"Very well, sir," the clerk replied, barely concealing a smirk.

Marjorie's body suddenly felt all wrong; her legs were strange and wobbly, having no connection to her torso; her neck seemed to grow, and her head was large and hovering over the rest of her. She looked down at her gloved hands; they seemed yards and yards away. Her throat was parched, and she heard herself whispering for a glass of water, please.

"What? What'd you say?" Mr. Holmes pocketed his room key and turned to her, taking her by the arm and ushering her away from the desk.

"Water? Could I please have some water?"

"Sure, sure. There's plenty of time, just like I said. We can sit and have a drink and talk about the test. I have some pointers for you. I tell you, kid, you have what it takes. I guarantee it. But every little trick helps, and I've been doing this a long time. A long time. I've seen some real talented girls just wilt on set. We don't want that to happen to you, do we?"

"N-no, of course not," Marjorie managed to whisper, her throat still so dry she marveled at the sound of her own voice.

"Of course not. Now, let me drop my bag." Mr. Holmes moved toward a bank of elevators opposite the front desk.

"I'll . . . I'll just wait here," Marjorie stammered, looking about for a place to sit. But to her wavering eyes it seemed that despite the hundreds of couches, there were no empty seats.

"Sure, sure. But I worry about you. You look a little peaked. I don't want to lose you. Come on up with me for a second. I'll dump my bag in my room and we'll come right down and get you something to drink. Maybe to eat, too; you don't look like you've eaten in a while."

And because Marjorie simply did not know if she could stand

on her own, if she would not crumple to the floor from fear and nerves and hope and longing and a devastating feeling of being overcome by something larger than herself for the first time in her life, she nodded. And allowed herself to be propelled toward the elevator. But not before catching the disapproving eye of the clerk who had signed Mr. Holmes in.

Mr. Holmes kept a firm grip on her elbow, and she was both nauseated and grateful for it; without his grasp, she knew she would fall to the floor, as her legs no longer seemed to have any bones at all. He gave the elevator boy the number of the floor, and Marjorie realized, too late, that she hadn't heard it, and that perhaps it would be necessary for her to remember it, at some future, awful time.

But the door opened and they got out and Marjorie had no idea what floor she was on, but then remembered that the door numbers would easily tell her this, and so she concentrated on the numbers as they walked—well, Mr. Holmes walked; she was fairly dragged—down an endless carpeted hall, black dial-less telephones on polished tables at intervals, bright lights in sconces. *1124, 1126, 1128, 1130.*

1132.

Mr. Holmes pulled out the heavy gold key, inserted it, and opened the door. He walked inside first, without hesitation; he walked inside like a man who had walked inside many hotel rooms, not even noticing his surroundings, throwing his hat on a chair without even looking to see where the chair was. From the doorway, where Marjorie had stopped, frozen like a dog who had reached the end of its leash, the corner of a bed, covered in a white bedspread, could be seen.

"C'mon in, kid," Mr. Holmes called. She could no longer see

him; he no longer had a grip on her. And so she wondered why she remained where he had left her, poised on the threshold of a hotel room, and not already running toward the elevator.

"I don't think so," Marjorie Konigsberg managed to whisper. But still, she did not leave.

"What?" Mr. Holmes reappeared, his jacket off, his tie loosened. He had a glass of water in his hand.

"I said, I don't think so," Marjorie murmured, looking down at the plush, slightly dirty carpet.

"Here's some water." Mr. Holmes thrust the glass in her hand. He took a step back. He did not touch her.

"Thank you." Marjorie gulped the water, but her throat was now so constricted it nearly came back up again. She slowed down, taking little sips. Not meeting Mr. Holmes's amused gaze.

She handed him the glass, and their hands touched. His was warm and clammy; she could feel the heat even inside her glove, a wet spot where the sweat penetrated. Mr. Holmes took the glass and sat it on a small table just inside the door. Then he took Marjorie's hand, which she had been unable to make behave properly; it simply hung in the air still, an awkward, lifeless thing. He removed her glove, and intertwined his fingers with hers, sending a deep, bone-rattling shudder through her body.

"Now, c'mon. Be nice. I have a lot I can teach you. And we have plenty of time before the test."

"But—but there *is* a test?" Marjorie felt desperate and exhausted, both, like an animal with one leg caught in a trap, uncertain whether to gnaw it off or simply give up.

"Yes, of course. There's a test. What, you think I'd pull a con like that? Giving out my business card with MGM on it? Nobody could get away with that. There's a test. There's always a test. And you'll be swell. All you need to do is relax a bit. Now, let me help you relax."

Marjorie took a step backward, even as her hand was still claimed by Abe Holmes. Talent Scout. MGM Studios. Culver City, California.

She took a step backward. She hesitated. She thought of her parents. She thought of Mr. Carson, who had picked her out first. She thought of Ingrid Bergman and Ava Gardner and Vivien Leigh.

She thought of Miss Turnberry. Of her sister Paulina, and her bandy-legged (for he must be bandy-legged, surely, as well as dull) sailor from Nevada.

Marjorie closed her eyes and made a decision. She took another step. Forward or backward? Only time would tell.

Meanwhile, down in the Kissing Room, no director had yelled "Cut!" An endless montage of reunions was played out, with each muffled announcement of an arriving train. Tearful and happy, successful and tense, alternately boring and overly dramatic. Actors and players all, some more natural than others.

And another girl arrived in her best outfit, wearing too much makeup that didn't disguise how young and unformed she was; clutching a well-worn business card inscribed with words Marjorie could recite by heart, along with any number of soliloquies and acceptance speeches and love scenes from Shakespeare:

Abe Holmes, Talent Scout. MGM Studios, Culver City, California.

I'll Be Seeing You

SARAH JIO

For the great-uncles I never knew, Terrence and Lawrence Ruff—both war heroes who lost their lives in World War II. And to my dear grandmother, Antoinette Mitchell, who mourned the loss of her dear brothers every day thereafter.

I told Sam not to come to the station. We said our good-byes last night on Bleecker Street. He'd kissed my cheek softly and begged me to stay, begged me not to make the journey. Why couldn't I start a life with him? he asked. Here. Now. The war's over, he said. It's a new world. We aren't the people we used to be. No one is. And that's the truth. In some ways, the two years I'd spent working as a nurse in New York City had felt like a lifetime. I'd come to the city as a wide-eyed eighteen-year-old. I was scared and uncertain. Now, I hardly recognize that girl. I don't want to go home to Seattle, and yet, last night I looked up at Sam on the sidewalk—hair slightly disheveled, big brown Clark Gable eyes fixed on me—and I knew I had to face my past.

After all, I made a promise.

Sam stands beside me at the station. His hand is on my waist, and he pulls me toward him. I think of the way he held me last night, cradled me in his arms. I think of what he said about us spending the rest of our lives together, how he'd make me his wife, how we'd start a family. Of course, I want that, too. But my hands feel sweaty, and my knees faint. Would Sam still feel the same if he knew the truth?

A rogue tear spills onto my cheek. Sam whisks it away tenderly with his wrist and I take a deep breath. "Don't you have one of the handkerchiefs I embroidered for you?"

He places his hand on his forehead. "I keep forgetting to put them in my pocket. Guess I'm not in the habit quite yet." He tucks a wisp of my hair behind my ear. "Darling, please don't cry. You'll sort things out in Seattle and come back. And we'll be married and we'll start our life together."

"Yes," I say, forcing a smile.

"What you need is rest," he says. "You look pale. You've been working so hard. The train ride will be good for you. You can sleep."

I had been working hard, yes. With all the men returning home, there'd been loads of patients to tend to at the clinic, and paperwork. I hate paperwork. Yesterday, I couldn't hold down my lunch. Three of the other girls had been out with the flu. I guess that's the price you pay for living in such cramped quarters in the city.

"I'll rest," I say, reassuring Sam. I don't tell him that my mind will likely keep me awake, that I'll be thinking about what I should do, or not do. That our future hinges on this cross-country journey of mine.

"I'll wait for you," he says, searching my eyes. I love him, I do. And for a split second, I consider tearing my ticket in half and starting life over, right here. I'd tell him everything, and he'd forgive me. He'd understand. We'd handle it together. But then I remember the promise I'd made. And it all comes rushing back. And I know I can't give myself to him entirely until I do what I need to do.

An attractive woman about my age saunters by. She wears a chic black-and-white-checked suit that reveals the soft curves of her breasts. She approaches the information desk. "Excuse me, sir," she says in a shy voice, cheeks flushed. "Please, can you tell me how to get to the Kissing Room?"

I smile to myself, realizing that her journey will be a lot different from the lonely one I have ahead of me. And then I think of the first time I kissed Sam, at a speakeasy in Brooklyn. Against my better judgment, I'd been talked into going out with a group of girls from the clinic. My friend Elaine had insisted I wear her red dress with fire-engine red lipstick to match. Sam was at the bar when I walked into the club. Like a beacon of light in the fog, his face shone bright through the dim, smoky room. He smiled; I smiled back. Then he stood up and walked toward me. We talked all night.

I close my eyes tightly as I feel Sam's hand on my chin, turning me toward him. "I don't know what you think you must face in Seattle," he says, bringing each of my hands to his lips and kissing them lightly, "but please, don't let it cloud your love for me."

I nod, wiping away another tear. It isn't fair. None of this is fair. Sam. Handsome, kind, good—he'd been relegated to a desk job during the war because of a childhood leg injury that prevented him from being able to run. But that didn't stop him from sweeping me off my feet, even though, given my past, I'd tried very hard not to let him. And now he'd given me his heart, and I'd all but taken it.

"Don't cry, baby," he whispers in my ear. "I have something that will cheer you up." He reaches into the pocket of his coat and pulls out a blue box from Tiffany and Co., then places it in my hands. "Go on," he says, grinning. "Open it."

I untie the ribbon with trembling hands and lift the lid of the box. Through tears, I see a silver chain. A necklace. I lift it into my hands, and a diamond ring dangles from it. It sparkles under the lights in the station, and I gasp. "Sam, what is this? You're not . . ."

His smile is cautious, tentative. He lowers onto one knee.

"Rose, I know you told me you weren't ready to get engaged, but I couldn't send you across the country without you knowing how I feel about you, really. I want to be with you, forever. I want to marry you, and have a family with you. You know I want that with all my heart."

I'm too choked up to say anything. His words are beautiful and real, and they're piercing my heart in a way I could have never expected.

"You don't have to give me an answer," he says, standing up. "Just wear the necklace, and think of me. When you come back, you can decide whether you want to put the ring on your finger or not." He smiles, a nervous, boyish smile. "But I really hope you do."

He's so handsome standing beside me. I reach up and caress his cheek. A tear streams down my own, and I long for a handkerchief to mop up the mascara that must now stain my eyelids. "Thank you," I say. "I wish I could give you an answer right now but I—"

He places his finger to my lips and shakes his head. "I don't need you to tell me now. Go. Do what you need to do. But come back to me. Please come back to me." He searches my eyes again. "Because, Rose, I don't know what I'd do if you didn't."

I hear a whistle in the distance, the shuffle of footsteps. There's hugging, kissing, commotion all around. I reach for my bag. "I better go," I say.

Sam kisses me once more. And I close my eyes, and know the life we'd have together would be beautiful. I can see it play out like a movie in my mind: There'd be laughter and love and so much passion. And yet, there would also be a shadow hanging over us . . .

"Good-bye, my darling," he says as I take a step closer to the train. Another whistle sounds, and I know I must board or risk being left at the station.

"Good-bye, Sam," I say. Walking away from him is like fighting gravity.

"Will you wear it?" he asks suddenly. "The necklace?"

I smile and nod as I step onto the platform. "Of course I will."

I hand my ticket to the conductor and walk inside the train. The sleeping car, where I have a tiny compartment with a bed, is several cars behind. Right now I just want to sit, so I tuck my bag beside me and sink into a seat lined with scratchy red fabric. I look out the window and there Sam stands. I smile at him through the glass and clutch the necklace in my hand.

If only he knew that I'm already wearing someone else's ring around my neck.

Three years prior
Seattle

"Don't look now, but someone has eyes for you," my best friend, Elsa, says.

It's late. The sun has set, and Mama will be worried if I don't come home soon. But Seattle is so gorgeous in the month of July, temperate in a way that you can leave your cardigan at home and never worry about catching a chill. There's music playing on the lawn in the distance. Jazz, the kind I love to dance to. I like the way my feet feel dangling over the dock into the cool, glacial water of Lake Washington.

"Oh stop," I say. "No one is looking at me. Besides, there isn't anyone here I'd even *want* to look at. If I meet another boy from Seattle Prep, I think I may be sick."

Elsa and I had been invited to a party thrown by our much wealthier friend, Mary, who lives in the Windermere neighborhood, where people reside behind fancy iron gates and employ cooks and housekeepers and dog walkers and other sorts of staff who buzz around you and meet your every need. To her credit, Mary doesn't behave like a spoiled child; she never has. It's why we're friends, I suppose. She's turning eighteen, and her parents have thrown her a lavish party, with dancing and music, ice sculptures, and champagne passed around by waiters in white suits.

Mary is not beautiful. She has a plain face, and her thin brown hair is a constant target of her mother's anxiety. (I once overheard Mary's mother complain that she'd never find a boyfriend if she didn't change the way she wore her hair.) But what she lacks in beauty she makes up for in generosity and kindness. She saw to it that Anna, a poor friend of Elsa's, was able to buy new dresses for school last year; books, too. Mary didn't swoop in and write a check in a showy way; she'd simply whispered to the shopkeeper to put the charges on her account, then smiled at Anna and discreetly told her not to worry.

"Hello, you two," Mary chirps to us. She's wearing a navy dress that looks a little too big for her thin frame. I imagine her mother, already tipsy in her low-cut designer dress, disapproved of her daughter's plain wardrobe selection. "Having fun?"

"It's a divine party," Elsa says.

Mary looks to her right and smiles to herself, then turns back to us. "I see you've met Louis and his friends."

Elsa smiles. "No, we haven't," she says. "But I was just telling Rose that she has an admirer."

I turn around, finally, and catch a glimpse of the men on the lawn. There are five, maybe six. They must have come to the party late, because I hadn't seen them when we arrived. All are in uniform. They're tall, clean-cut. One smiles in our direction, but his eyes are entirely fixed on me. He's a few years older, at least. He looks restless, wise.

"That's Louis," Mary whispers. "Isn't he a dreamboat?"

"Well, yes," I say honestly, a little dumbfounded. "How do you know him?"

"Our fathers are in banking together," she says. "I grew up with him."

"Are you . . . I mean, do you—?"

"Am I in love with him?" She giggles. "Rose, he's like a brother to me."

I smile.

"Come on, let me introduce you," Mary says, suddenly. "He's here with his friends before shipping off to Europe. He's a part of the Second Armored Division."

My eyes widen with interest. "You mean, he's going to war?" Boys from school had already shipped off, left for Europe. I guess I'd somehow accepted that. But now? I feel a flutter in my heart, like when you spot a beautiful butterfly in your garden and you know that, in three seconds, it will fly away.

Mary nods, and I think I see a flash of emotion in her eyes, but it vanishes. "Of course he's going to war, silly," she says. "He doesn't wear the uniform for kicks. Come on, let me introduce you. Trust me, you're going to like him."

"Louis," she says. "There's someone I'd like you to meet. This is my friend, Rose."

He takes a step toward us. He's even taller up close, and I feel a little quivery in his presence. "Hello," he says, looking directly at me. I take his hand in mine. It's strong, solid, and also tender. I let go reluctantly.

Elsa's talking to one of the other men, but I don't hear what she's saying. I barely notice Mary standing there, either. The periphery is all a blur.

"Some night," he says.

I smile. "Yeah."

A waiter approaches with a tray of champagne flutes, and Louis selects two. "Cheers," he says, handing me a glass.

"I really don't drink," I say, smiling. "And my mother will murder me if she detects alcohol on my breath when I get home tonight."

He smiles, producing a pack of peppermint gum. "Try this," he says.

I nod and tuck the stick of gum into my purse.

Louis grins again. "Surely she wouldn't fault you for having a drink with a soldier who's about to go to war?"

I answer with a smile and then take a long sip from one of the flutes, letting the pink bubbles fizz in my mouth.

"Walk with me," he says. "It's a beautiful night."

I don't see Mary. She must have weaved her way back to the lawn, where people are dancing. Elsa's still talking to one of the other soldiers. She grins at me, an encouraging "go walking with him" grin.

"Okay," I say. "But I really shouldn't go far. I have to be home soon."

Louis takes my hand, and as we pass the buffet table, he swipes a bottle of champagne and tucks it, nose down, in his back pocket.

"You're something," I say with a laugh.

"Can you blame a guy for wanting to drink champagne with a beautiful woman before shipping out to the unknown?"

My heart seizes for a moment, for this stranger, for his uncertain future. And I smile. "So you're saying it's my civic duty, then?"

"Yes, ma'am."

"Well, then," I say, holding out my empty champagne glass, "when you put it in those terms."

He pops the cork and pours more bubbly into my glass.

"Where to?" Louis asks. We're standing on a little vista of the lawn that looks out to the lake. "Want to walk along the beach?"

"Alright," I say, as he takes my hand again. We wend our way along the gravel path, which deposits us onto a sandy beach. Soft gray waves splash onto the sandy shore, near the charred remnants of a campfire someone had enjoyed earlier.

"Here," Louis says, pointing to a large piece of driftwood wedged into the rocks. "Let's sit."

I take a seat beside him and spread my yellow dress over my legs. "So you grew up with Mary?"

"Yes," Louis says. "I spent many happy days of my childhood right here, swimming along this shore. Mary's like a sister to me."

Louis tops off my glass. I think about setting it down, but instead I take another sip.

"You mean, you never thought of her as anything more?"

Louis shakes his head. "I mean, when I was thirteen or fourteen, maybe the thought crossed my mind. And there was this one time when we were on her dad's boat." He laughs to himself. "But no, I could never love her that way."

"Well," I say. I feel light, airy; the champagne has gone to my head. "And what if she loves you?"

Louis shakes his head. There's a seriousness to his expression, a look of warning, as though I may have crossed a line, a boundary. "No, I would never lead her on," he says. "I respect her too much to do that. Mary and I have been friends our whole lives, and I intend for our friendship to remain the same."

"Well, of course it will," I say.

His smile returns. "And you? Are you seeing anyone?"

I shake my head.

"Why not? You're beautiful."

"Lots of my friends are getting married," I say with a sigh. "I don't know, I guess I haven't met the right person. Don't they say you know when you meet the person you're supposed to spend the rest of your life with?"

He grins. "Like a bell goes off in your head or something?"

Just then, the dinner bell sounds on the lawn above us. Mary's parents have used it at parties before, but now it sends goose bumps down my spine. Our eyes meet, and I quickly look away.

"So you believe in love at first sight, then?" Louis asks.

"I don't know what I believe," I say. "I guess mostly I'm just afraid of making the wrong choice. That or being left behind."

"Left behind?"

"Remember in school when kids would line up to form teams? Well, I was always the last to be chosen. I was small. I couldn't throw a ball to save my life. But it hurt. It hurt to be the last chosen, or not chosen at all."

Louis smiles. "I can't imagine anyone not choosing you."

I feel his gaze on my cheek, but I don't let my eyes meet his.

"Let's get out of here," he says.

"And where do you suggest we go?"

"I'll take you dancing, downtown. At the Cabana Club."

I imagine the way he'd lead me out to the dance floor. Just the two of us, on the eve of the unknown. His unknown, and mine, too. But we'd dance. I'd let him hold me close. My heart races, and then I remember Mama. "But it's getting late," I say.

"Do it for me," he says. "On my last night. Just let me dance with you."

I smile and take his hand. I'd beg for Mama's forgiveness later.

Three years later

I feel a tap on my shoulder, and I open my eyes, startled. And I remember where I am: on the train, en route to Seattle. Yes, of course. I pat around my lap for Sam's ring, but my fingers can't find it. *Did it slip from my grasp while I dozed off?* My heart beats faster. My vision is blurry, but it comes into focus. There's an older woman standing in the aisle. She's tall and thin, with short gray hair and kind eyes, about Mama's age. "Excuse me, miss?"

I sit up in my seat, and nod. "Yes?"

"I'm so sorry to wake you, but I believe you're sitting in my seat."

"Oh dear," I mutter, reaching for my bag. "I apologize. I sat down for just a moment, and . . . well, I must have dozed off. I have a sleeping car down the way. I'll just collect my things and let you have your seat."

"It's really alright," she says. "I just got on at the last station, and when I saw you sleeping, I hated to wake you, so I spent the last hour in the dining car."

"I didn't realize I was so tired," I say, shaking my head.

"Must have a lot on your mind, honey."

"I do," I say.

She sits down in the empty seat beside me. "My name is Grace," she says.

"I'm Rose."

"Want to talk about the burden you're carrying?"

"I wouldn't know where to begin," I say honestly.

She hands me the necklace with Sam's ring attached. It might as well weigh a thousand pounds, because it carries the heavy weight of my heart. "You could start by telling me about the man who gave you this."

"Yes," I say, nodding. And I realize that I want to talk. And I want to tell her about my big secret. "But first I have to tell you about someone else."

Three years prior

The Cabana Club is smoky and dimly lit when we arrive shortly after nine thirty. It's busier than usual, and I wonder how many women, like me, are here with soldiers about to leave for war.

Louis says something to the hostess at the podium in the entry-way, and she lifts a telephone up. "Why don't you call your mother," he says. "Just so she doesn't worry."

I smile. "Thank you." But instead of dialing Mama, I ring up my neighbor, Miss Privett. I can't bear to take on Mama right now. Miss Privett, who is a dear, could pass along the message to Mama and let her know I was safe but would be out late.

"There," I say, walking back to Louis who waits near the coat closet. "All set."

I follow him into the club, and we find an empty booth that we both squeeze into. It's intimate, and we're closer than we were on the beach. A waiter appears, and Louis orders martinis for us both.

"I've never had a martini," I say, grinning.

"You'll like them," he says. "They're strong, but in a good way." He grins. "So, tell me about you."

"What do you want to know?" I watch as a man in the booth across from us lights a cigarette for an attractive blond. And, for a split second, I feel like an outsider. I feel like I used to, someone looking from the outside in. The awkward schoolgirl with knobby knees and pigtails, a smattering of freckles across her nose. But I see the way Louis looks at me now. He's the handsomest man I've ever seen outside of the movie theaters, and somehow, out of all the women in the world, he wants to be sitting here with me right now. My heart races.

"Well, I'd like to know what you want in life, when this damn war is behind us."

"Oh, I don't know," I say vaguely. "I suppose I want the same things that every woman wants. Happiness. A family. Security."

He looks amused. "Really?"

"Why do you act so surprised?"

"I don't know, I guess I pegged you as a different sort, more of a free spirit."

My eyes narrow. "I don't know what you mean by that, but I—"

"Don't get sore," he says with a smile. "Maybe I'm seeing something in you that you don't even see in yourself yet."

"Like what?" I ask, cautiously. For a moment, I feel annoyed. Louis is a stranger, by all accounts. It seems presumptuous, and a little rude, that he spends one hour with me and thinks he can size me up.

"Well," he says, pointing out to the dance floor, where a gaggle of blonds make eyes with the men across the room, "for starters, you're not like most girls."

"Oh, I'm not, am I?"

"Not at all," he continues. "I think you want different things, deep down."

"And what do I want, my wise and all-knowing friend?" I smirk. "Please be good enough to tell me."

Louis looks thoughtful. "I think you're wound differently than most women," he says. "I think you'd rather go off and see the world than be stuck in a kitchen with an apron tied around your waist."

I feel tears sting my eyes, and I look away.

"Oh," he says with concern. "I'm sorry. I didn't mean to upset you."

I shake my head quickly. "You didn't upset me. You just . . . well, you just read my mind." I sigh. "You're right. I hate it, but you're right. Marriage frightens me more than anything else. I suppose it has something to do with my own parents. My mother married the first man who proposed, and he turned out to be a con artist who strung her along, milking her bank account until there was nothing left, and then he was gone."

"I'm so sorry," Louis says solemnly. He pats the pocket of his shirt. "Darn, I wish I had a handkerchief to offer."

I smile through tears for many reasons. For the eve of war. For the fact that his words have struck a chord. His words have unearthed a memory etched on my heart. I was sixteen, at Pike Place Market, when I watched, perhaps, the single truest expression of love in my lifetime. One I haven't been able to forget. It was simple, really, and yet profound in its own right: Beside a produce stand, an elderly man tenderly offered his wife a handkerchief when she, for unexplained reasons, began to weep. For me, forever, it was the epitome of true love.

"What are you thinking about?" Louis asks, tilting his head to the right.

"Just a memory," I say. I want to tell him about the exchange at the market. But I take a deep breath, remembering my mother and the brand of epic love she never could have. "Yes, my mother." I nod. "She still won't blame him. She waited for him, all those years, after he left with the money she'd inherited from her parents. Every last penny. He left her—he left *us*—with nothing, and yet she'd make his favorite biscuits every night for years in hopes that it would be the night he'd come home." I shake my head. "I don't know. I don't think I could ever be that devoted to someone."

"You don't have to," Louis says. "Marriage doesn't have to be like that."

"But doesn't it always end up in unhappiness, one way or another?" I shake my head to myself. "Have you seen the way Mary's parents hate each other? And Elsa's?" I chew on the edge of my lip. "I'd rather die than live like that."

"We don't have to," Louis says. His words make my heart race. *Did he just say "we"?* He takes my hand before I can catch my breath or venture a response. "We can live by our own rules. We can create our own beautiful, perfect marriage, better than any marriage that ever was before."

I swallow hard. "What are you saying? We don't even know each other."

He smiles and points to his heart. "But we do." And I know. The bell sounded. And now a choir is singing in my ears. Louis presses his lips against mine. And I am certain: This must be love.

———

It's late, but we know the justice of the peace's office will be open. Thousands of Seattle's finest men will be shipping out in the morning, and when there are men shipping out, there will be marriages. Mass marriages.

Louis and I stand in line together, amid dozens of couples like us.

Kissing, crying, holding each other tightly. And when it's our turn to sign the certificate and exchange vows, we do so without hesitation.

"I can't believe we just did that," I say as we walk out of the office, hand in hand.

"I can," Louis says, smiling. "I just married my dream girl."

I smile as he takes me in his arms again. The lights of the Olympic Hotel shine in the distance. I feel warm and light from the drinks at the Cabana Club. "And now, I'm taking my wife to the fanciest hotel in town."

My wife.

I squeal with delight as he takes my hand and we walk together to the hotel.

———

I open my eyes the next morning, and my head hurts. I rub my forehead and squint as sunlight streams through the gauzy silk curtains that hang over the windows. The memory of last night slowly seeps in. Champagne. The Cabana Club. Louis's passionate kisses. Martinis. The justice of the peace. My eyes shoot open. I look to my right. Where's Louis? I hear whistling coming from somewhere. The bathroom? And then he appears around the corner.

"Oh, good morning, darling," Louis says. I pull the sheet higher above my nude body. He's buttoning up the shirt of his uniform; his hair is still damp from the shower. "Finally decided to wake up, did you?" He lies on the bed beside me and props himself up on his elbow.

"Did we really—"

He smiles. "We did." He points to the large ring on my left finger—his class ring, gold with a red stone. A man's ring. "Hello, Mrs. Hathaway."

I feel panicked for a moment, and even though I'm trying to

conceal my emotions, I know that Louis can tell. "What is it?" he asks. "Please don't tell me you think you made a mistake, because . . . I can't go off to war thinking that my wife doesn't want . . ."

"No," I say quickly. "No, it's just so sudden. Of course I'm happy." I force a smile. "I just married the handsomest man in Seattle."

His smile returns. He kisses my lips and then my neck. He pulls me to him, and I don't resist. He is my husband.

———————

"Promise to write me?" Louis pleads.

"Of course I will," I say. "Write me as soon as you're in Europe so I know you made it safe."

He kisses my hand. "You've made me the happiest man in the world." His words make me think that I didn't make a mistake last night. They make me think our night, our meeting, was all fate. Meant to be. Of course it was. It has to be.

"Have I?"

"You have. You have given me the greatest gift. The gift of love."

"And so have you," I say.

I hear the ferry horn sound, and I remember bits and pieces of what Louis said last night about his impending journey. Louis and his comrades will take the ferry to Bremerton, then board a naval ship that will take them to their next destination, somewhere in the Pacific, before eventually making it to Europe.

Soft music plays in the ferry terminal, and I recognize the song immediately: "I'll Be Seeing You," the very song that played last night on the lawn at Mary's house.

Tears sting my eyes, and Louis takes me in his arms for a final embrace. "It won't be long until we're together again," he whispers. "And we'll have such a life together. It will be the stuff they write stories about."

I nod. I want that, too. I just hope he's right.

Three years later

Grace smiles at me. I'm relieved to see that after hearing my story, she doesn't judge me. "So you're a war bride?"

I nod. "But I never told anyone. Not a single soul, even my best friend at home."

"Why not?"

"I guess it was partly because I didn't believe it, even myself. It happened so fast. It was easy to just pretend it never happened and go on with my life."

"Did you write each other like you said you would?"

"We did at first," I say. "But then the letters tapered off, especially after I met Sam. I just felt so guilty. Believe me, I sat down and confessed everything in letters to Louis a hundred times, but I never mailed them. It didn't seem right to have him get that news on a battlefield somewhere." I shake my head. "That's why I'm going to Seattle. To tell him—everything."

"And what do you want from him, honey?"

I sigh. "Forgiveness. And, well, closure, I guess. I hope that he wants to move on, too."

"And is that what you really want? To move on?"

"I think so," I say. "I have a wonderful man waiting for me in New York."

"Honey," Grace says. "Don't you see?"

"See what?"

"There may always be a man waiting for you," she says. "But you can't hinge life's most important decisions on which man is waiting for you." She places her hand on her heart. "You have to do what your heart wants. I wish I'd learned that lesson for myself a long time ago, before I wasted half my life doing what someone else wanted me to do."

I blink back tears. "I don't even know that I can trust my own heart," I say.

"Oh, but you can," she says. "Love is a funny thing. We think we know what we want, and we're so often easily confused and distracted. But if we consulted our hearts more, it wouldn't be that way."

"I just wish it were easier," I say.

"But it is," she says. "You just have to teach yourself to see. The details of true love are so faint that sometimes we fail to see them unless we stop and look more closely. They're there; you just have to really want to see them."

"I don't know," I say, discouraged. "I feel sad and worried every time I close my eyes and see Sam's face, and Louis's."

"What you have here is the gift of time," Grace continues. "An entire train ride to just sit back and listen. Your heart is trying to tell you what the right choice is; you just need to remember how to listen to it."

I look out the window and let the *clickety-clack* of the train wheels soothe the anxious voices inside my head, the ones telling me that I'll never be loved, never be happy. And for a moment, all is quiet. And Grace is right; my heart has a lot to say. And I'm finally listening.

———

"Morning," I say to Grace. I find her in the dining car hunched over a poached egg and a plate of toast.

"Good morning," she says. "Sleep well?"

"Like a log," I say. "I had the strangest dream. Sam and Louis were each driving in separate cars on the highway and they collided. They each died."

"How telling," Grace says after taking a sip of coffee.

I look out the window at the lonely, dry Midwest terrain and shake my head. "I have no idea what this dream could mean."

Grace nods. "I think it speaks more to you. I think you're afraid of ending up alone like your mother." She places her hand on my arm. "Don't fear that, honey, okay?"

"What about you?" I ask. "Were you ever happy in love?"

Grace looks thoughtful for a moment. She takes another sip of her coffee, then sets the cup down on its saucer. "I met a man many years ago, yes. I married him because I thought I should." She lifts her arm up and tucks a lock of hair behind her ear, which is when I think I see a faint shadow—a bruise?—beneath the cuff of her sleeve. "I did a lot of things back then because I thought I should." She shakes her head. "I married Bill because I had no reason not to. He was handsome, rich, everything. And then we had children, and I had no way out, even when he started hitting me."

"I'm so sorry," I whisper. "Here I am going on about my frivolous problems, and yours are so much more important."

"Well," Grace says, "I'm done with that life. I finally got up the courage to leave him, to move on with my life. I only wish I'd had the guts to leave him years ago. I thought staying and suffering was the honorable thing to do. It wasn't. I may not have many years left, but I'm going to live them to the fullest." The waiter comes to the table, and I order a cup of coffee, before Grace turns to me again. "I recognized myself in you the first time I saw you yesterday. You have the look of a woman who is in conflict with herself. It's as if you believe there's a life you should live, but then there's the life you desperately want to live."

"And if you're right," I say, "what do I do?"

"I think you have to do what I did. I think you have to walk through the fire, do the thing that scares you the most. Let your heart break. Then get up again."

"I wish I were that brave," I say.

"You are," Grace replies. "You just don't know it yet."

———

Another day passes, and I'm no closer to reaching a decision on the mess that is my life. We passed through Idaho this morning. Seattle is closer now. I find Grace in her seat with a book, and I slump into the seat next to hers.

"We'll be in Seattle tomorrow," she says.

"I know," I say. "I'm not sure if I want to get there, or if I'd rather stay on this train forever. There's something pretty comforting about being stuck in limbo, you know?"

"I do," Grace says. "I was stuck there for thirty-five years of my marriage. But I can tell you, with it all behind me, I'm so happy to be off that train."

I nod. "And what about your future? Do you think you'll ever marry again?"

"No," she says swiftly before her lips turn upward into a sly smile. "But I may have a lover."

I giggle at the thought of this woman, my own mother's age, dreaming about things like this, and I admire her free spirit. I envy it, even.

"But I can tell you, any man who takes me out again must adhere to strict criteria," she says.

I grin. "Criteria?"

"Yes," she says with conviction, as if she's thought this over carefully, for years. "He must be a gentleman, through and through. No alcohol. I don't like who men turn into when they drink. He must hold my chair out for me at the table. He must make me laugh, and love books, and not be seasick on boats. Because I want him to take me sailing. And when I sneeze, he will say, 'Bless you,' and offer me his handkerchief."

"I second that," I say with a smile. "Do you think you'll ever find this Mr. Perfect?"

"I'm certain I will," she says.

"How can you be so sure?"

"Because I believe in pots of gold at the end of rainbows. And I've traveled a very long way in my life. I've weathered a lot of storms. And there will be a charming end. And I know he's waiting."

I smile. "But you won't marry him."

"I won't marry him." She grins. "But we'll have a marvelous time together."

———

It's day five. My legs are stiff from sitting, and I'm eager to step out on land again. The station is near; I can feel the damp Seattle air all around me. Evergreens line the train track, and when they give way to the familiar Seattle skyline, my heart begins to race.

Louis will be there soon. He'd written months ago to plan this day, our reunion. My mind and my heart are a jumble of emotion. What will I say? What will I do when I see him?

I turn to Grace and give her a nervous smile. She squeezes my hand. "You already know your decision," she says. "Trust in that."

"Do I?"

"You do," she says. "You may get sidetracked, but it will be clear to you."

"I hope you're right," I say as I open my compact and dab a dusting of powder on my nose, then line my lips with red lipstick.

Grace smiles calmly. It's as if she can read my mind. "When you see him, you'll know what to say."

"And what about you?" I ask. "Where will you go from here?"

"Well," she says. "I will see my sister, and then I'm not sure. I've always wanted to go to Canada. Maybe I will."

"You should then," I say. "Will you write me?"

"Yes," she says, pulling out a piece of paper from inside her purse and writing her address on it. "Send me a note when you're settled, wherever you decide to settle, and I will write you there."

I nod and slip the paper into my purse.

"Next stop, Seattle, Washington," the conductor says from the front of the train car.

It's been a long journey. In some ways, it's felt like a lifetime. I am not the same woman I was at Grand Central Terminal. I am in the possession of two men's rings, and yet I have only one heart to give. King Street Station is ahead. I'll step out onto the platform and Louis will be waiting. I smile to myself, thinking of the first night we met, the way his eyes searched my face. The way he'd gotten down on one knee and asked me the question that would forever change my life. I'd said yes, even though I had no idea the trajectory it would send me on. I don't regret it anymore. Louis was meant to be a part of my life; I know that now.

The train slows to a crawl, and then stops. "This is it," I say to Grace.

"Good luck, honey," she says, embracing me. "Remember, whatever happens, you are in control of your own destiny. You, and no one else."

I'd like to believe her. I would. But my life feels out of control, like a runaway train. I don't know where I'm heading, where I came from, what peril lies around the next corner.

"Trust me," Grace says. "We women are strong like that. We can face the worst and still carry on. When you learn how to tap into that kind of strength, well, you realize you can get through anything"—she winks at me—"even a tough decision."

I nod as she reaches for her suitcase and steps into the aisle. "I'll look forward to hearing the next installment of your journey in your letter."

I smile. "Good-bye, Grace."

"Good-bye, Rose."

And then she is gone. And I am alone again. I look out the window to the King Street Station. Strangers bustle by. I scan the crowd, but don't see Louis. Not yet.

"Time to disembark, ma'am," the conductor says.

"Yes, uh, I was just leaving," I say. But I want to tell him, "I'm not ready to leave. I'd like to stay on the train a bit longer. I'd like to hear nothing else but the *clickety-clack* of the wheels and my own thoughts churning in my head. I want to stay on this train until I know what to do."

But I may never know what to do, and that unsettling feeling haunts me as I step off the train onto the platform. It feels good to be on land again. I have to steady myself as I walk a few paces then set my suitcase down. I look right, then left. Louis must be here somewhere. Of course, he might be late. I'd find a bench and wait a while. He'd come, just like he'd written.

I walk a few paces to a bench beside the ticket counter and sit down. A minute passes, then five, then ten. I watch the old clock tick by on the wall overhead. And then I hear an announcement on the loudspeaker, and my name. "Paging Miss Rose Wellington. Paging Miss Rose Wellington. Please come to the ticket counter for a message."

I leap to my feet. A message? For me? Surely it's from Louis, explaining that he's late, and would be here soon. He'd gotten stuck in traffic. Or maybe his car had broken down. I remember how handsome he is, those eyes. I could imagine a life with Louis. A good one. My heart begins to beat faster. I take a deep breath and walk to the counter.

"I'm Rose Wellington," I say to the man behind the glass. "You have a message for me?"

The man eyes me through his spectacles and then nonchalantly passes a small envelope with my name typewritten on the front. "Telegram arrived for you earlier," he says.

I nod and take it into my hands. My heart races as I eye my name on the front of the envelope. Only two people knew I would be on this train, arriving in Seattle. Sam and Louis. I swallow hard and tear the flap open, which is when I hear my name. His voice.

"Rose?"

I turn around to face Louis. He looks handsomer than before, something I didn't think could be possible. There's a patch of gray forming at his temples. (I remember him telling me that the men in his family gray in their early twenties.) He looks distinguished, wiser than before.

I run to him and wrap my arms around his neck. He quickly peels them away and looks at his feet.

"Louis? What is it?" My heart beats faster now. His eyes dart around and then return to my face. They are distant, conflicted.

And I know it then, to him, the love we shared is gone. The well has gone dry. I take a step back. "Oh, I see."

"I wanted to tell you," he says. "I tried to tell you, so many times in letters, but I couldn't get the courage up to say it. I didn't want to break your heart."

I think of Sam. I think of how I'd carried on with him while Louis was at war, while he was presumably being true to me. Loving me. I don't deserve to be angry. I don't deserve to feel slighted. I brought this on myself. Perhaps he could feel it in my letters. Perhaps he knew I was only giving him half of my heart. And yet, now, as I stand here and see him before me, I want to give him everything I have, every piece of me, every fiber of my being. I want to try again. And yet, he no longer wants to accept it. He no longer wants me.

I look ahead and see a familiar face in the crowd. "Rose!" Mary exclaims, rushing toward us. She's smiling, and I smile back. In this moment of deep pain, it's comforting to see a familiar face. She's changed, too. Her former schoolgirl awkwardness has vanished. She's blossomed into a stylish, beautiful woman. She wears makeup now, and her hair is short, curled chicly against her head. I imagine her mother must be satisfied. Mary gives me a hug, then looks at Louis tentatively. "Good, so you talked? You told her? I'm glad to have that behind us."

I look at her, confused. "What do you mean?"

"Mary," Louis says, "I haven't told her yet. Can you please give us some time?"

"Oh," she says. "Yes, of course. I . . ." She turns and walks deeper into the station, leaving us alone again.

Louis rubs his forehead. "I didn't mean for it to happen that way. I wanted to tell you earlier. Listen, Rose, I don't even know how it happened. I mean, she was like a sister to me my whole life, and then I came home last month, and she, well, I realized it was something more. And it had been for a very long time, I was just too thickheaded to see it."

"Oh," I say again. I feel like someone has just taken a bucket of icy water and dumped it over my head. I feel shocked and jittery. The warmth has been sucked out of me. "Of course. Well, I—"

"Please don't be angry with us," he says. "It would break Mary's heart. She's been so worried about how you would take the news of our engagement."

"Your engagement," I mutter. The words actually hurt as they cross my lips.

"Well, I can't expect you to forgive me, or us, right now," he says. "But I hope you'll find it in your heart to do so one day. That's all I ask. That, and I'll need you to sign these papers for the divorce." He pulls a thin stack of folded papers from his jacket pocket and hands them to me.

Divorce. The word pierces my heart in a way I could have never expected. "Oh, that's right," I say. "We're married."

I reach for a pen in my purse and scrawl my signature on the last page. "Here," I say, handing them back.

"I guess this is good-bye, then," Louis says.

I nod and pick up my suitcase, then hand him the necklace with his class ring on it. "Good-bye, Louis."

"Don't go like this," he says.

"There's nothing more to say." And I walk away, to the far corner of the station, where I find a seat and bury my head in my hands.

I could have never seen this coming. Not in a thousand years. *Now what? Do I try to make a life here? Return to New York? Do I try to salvage what I once had with Sam? Would it be fair to him?* I think for a long while about the man I left behind in New York, the man who desperately loves me. I'd only spent one night with Louis. Ours had been a whirl-wind courtship, furthered by letters and the angst of war. Had it even been real? What I had with Sam, on the other hand, *was* real. Solid. Lasting. How foolish that I didn't see that. And now I sit in a train station alone.

I walk outside and gaze up at the cloudy Seattle sky, then study the buildings that line the hilly streets that lead down to Puget Sound. Oh, Seattle, I shall always love you, but there is nothing here for me now, not anymore. Mama, yes. I'd write to her. I'd tell her about Sam; she'd love him, of course. We'd have her come visit New York after we were married. I'd take her to see the Statue of Liberty. Elsa would be sad to have missed me, but she's busy with her husband and kids now, twin boys. I smile to myself. I'd go home to New York. I'd go home to Sam.

My Sam.

I run to the ticket counter. The next train to New York leaves in an hour. I buy a ticket.

"Excuse me, miss," the man behind the counter says. "Weren't you just on the train coming from New York?"

"Yes," I say.

"And you're going back? So soon?"

I nod and smile. "Apparently sometimes you have to travel across the country to come to your senses."

He shrugs and turns back to his work at the counter, which is when I remember the telegram. I'd been so distracted by seeing Louis that I'd forgotten about it entirely. I lift the envelope out of my purse and stare at it again. He'd probably tried to reach me to give me the news in New York, and they'd forwarded it to me in Seattle. Did I even want to read it? Did I even want to relive the pain of his rejection? I consider throwing it in the garbage can ahead, but I decide to lift the flap instead, and when I read the first few words, my mouth falls open:

WESTERN UNION

Dear Rose,

I am Sam Gearhart's sister, Jane. He told me about you before he proposed. He said he met a wonderful girl and that I would love you. Sadly, the night you left on the train, his cab was struck by a truck and Sam died. I am heartbroken, as I'm sure you are. I am so very sorry.

"No!" I scream, before letting out a deep, guttural cry. "No, not Sam. Not Sam." The telegram slips from my hands and I fall to my knees.

One year later

Mama pulls out her handkerchief and dabs it to her eyes. "Are you sure you're ready to return to New York? I imagine it will be awfully emotional for you." She doesn't want to see me go. And I don't really even want to go. All I know is that it's time. Sam's sister, Jane, has offered to give me some of Sam's belongings, and I miss the energy of the city. Maybe I'll even take night classes and pursue my dream of writing a novel.

"Please, Mama," I say. "Don't cry. I'll be fine. I'll call you every Sunday. I'll write."

She nods. "Yes," she says. "I know you will be. You're a grown woman now. No sense in me fretting about you."

"That's right," I say with a smile. I have to be strong for both of us. I kiss her cheek and step onto the train. I think of Grace and our long cross-country conversations as I head to the dining car and order a club sandwich and a Coca-Cola. I remember how confused I was, how uncertain. I pull out the stationery set in my purse and write her a letter.

Dear Grace,

I'm sorry it has taken me so long to write you. I hope you still remember me. I was in a terrible place then, and you listened. You encouraged me. In many ways, it was you who made me believe that I could handle whatever was coming. And there were storms coming. Louis fell in love with another woman, a friend of mine, in fact. And then, I received a telegram telling me that Sam was killed in a car accident. I didn't think my heart could take the pain. It was so deep, so raw. But I thought of you a lot this past year. I thought of what you said about inner strength. And because of you, I've found mine. And you were right. Once I learned to tap into that strength, I knew I could weather any storm. And I got through this one. So thank you, Grace. Thank you for passing along that wisdom, for believing in me, and most of all, for being a friend to a stranger on a train, who so desperately needed to talk to someone.

Please write soon. I'm on the train now, returning to New York for Chapter Two of my journey. Wish you were here sitting beside me.

With love,
Rose
P.S. I hope you found your pot of gold.

"Excuse me," a man says just as I finish tucking the letter into an envelope.

I look up, and a man with light brown hair stands beside my table. About my age, he wears a tan suit. His blue eyes are friendly, familiar somehow, and when they meet mine, my cheeks flush a little.

"Sorry to interrupt," he says, "but do you mind if I share your table? There's hardly a free seat on this train."

I smile. "Of course."

"I'm Graham," he says, offering his hand.

"Rose," I say.

We talk a little as we eat, and then Graham smiles. He pulls out a handkerchief from his jacket pocket and offers it to me. "You have a little ketchup on the corner of your mouth."

I smile, flushed, and look for a napkin, but the waiter has already taken mine. "Thank you," I say, dabbing his handkerchief to my mouth. I fold it into a square and hand it back to him. I smile, remembering the way the old man at the market in Seattle gave his wife his handkerchief so lovingly.

"My grandfather said a man should never leave home without a belt, a wallet, and a handkerchief."

"I think I would have liked your grandfather," I say.

"You would have," he says. "He passed away last year. But before that, he and my grandmother would have lunch at the market every day. He called it a date."

"Pike Place Market?"

"Yes," he says. "I miss him. Grandma does, too. And I figure, if I can be one ounce of the man he was, I'll be doing something right, you know?"

I watch Graham tuck his handkerchief back into his pocket, and I think of Grace's words. "The details of true love are so faint that sometimes we fail to see them unless we stop and look more closely. They're there; you just have to really want to see them."

I smile to myself.

"What is it?" Graham asks.

"I just realized something, that's all," I say. "Something I've been waiting a long time to figure out."

Graham looks at me quizzically. "I'll Be Seeing You" begins playing through the speakers overhead. Bing Crosby's voice grabs my heart, as it always does. I think of Louis. I think of Sam. I think of their roles in my journey, a journey that has brought me to this train, to this seat, to this moment. The ghosts of my past will always be with me, just as they are with all of us. We take a part of everything, everyone we encounter, with us on our path. Perhaps that's what makes life so rich, so full. A map, starred and circled and drawn with the paths we've taken, for better or for worse.

And now I am here, sitting across a table in the dining car of a train with a man who has just offered me his handkerchief.

"This is going to sound crazy," Graham says, rubbing the faint shadow of stubble on his chin, "but when this train arrives in New York, would you like to have dinner with me?"

"I'd love to," I say. My eyes meet his and I'm unable to look away. And something moves inside of me. And somehow I *know*.

I'll Walk Alone

Erika Robuck

For my grandmother, Marie Hernan

I see myself everywhere. In the furtive glance, the anxious carriage, the downcast eyes, the flinching at the simplest human touch. The body cannot help but anticipate when it has suffered prior hurts.

That young girl over there, handling the mop at the top of the ramp leading to the Lower Concourse of Grand Central Terminal, I don't care for the way she won't look into the eyes of the porter who whispers in her ear. He hisses at her while scanning the crowd, her thin arm pinched between his fingers. And I judge her and think: *At least mine never does that in public.*

We all have to convince ourselves that we're better than someone else.

Then there are the others—reverse reflections like those in mirrors at circus fun houses.

They are a studious pair, a young man and woman, clutching books to their chests, both wearing thick glasses and clothes that announce their poor origin—practical brown wool trimmed in coarse thread. They sit at the bottom of the west stairs on the Main Concourse, unaware of the travelers hurrying past them or the hard, cold marble underneath them. They have eyes only for each other. He opens his book and begins reading to her, his cheeks blazing red. She stares at him from inches away, her thin hands like butterflies, brushing errant wisps of hair off her forehead, eyes wide with ardor for this simple boy. Love makes them beautiful.

I am suddenly ashamed of my scarlet lipstick, waved black hair, the green satin dress I've worn because he likes how it sets off my eyes. I was surprised when he bought such a dress for me. Only for special occasions, he said.

As I pass the young lovers I hear the young man's voice. It is bolder than I would have anticipated, as if reading the words of another gives him power.

"Mon enfant, ma soeur, Songe à la douceur, D'aller là-bas vivre ensemble!"

I do not speak French, but I feel the emotion behind what he reads to her. I somehow know they have chosen to read to each other from those exact books in this precise spot for their shared pleasure.

"Mama," says the child at my hand. "Mama."

He has been saying this to me for some time, but I've been too distracted to pay attention. When I look down, I see that my three-year-old son is staring at me. This sweet little person always knows how to recall me from my thoughts back to the present, to attend to the moment. "I'm hungry."

I didn't tell Timmy why we were coming today. I plan to do so just before we see his father for the first time since Timmy was five months old. My son knows about the man from whom he came in vague ways. On the side table there is a photograph of Mitch in uniform, handsome and stern; a line of dress shirts and pleated pants hangs in the closet next to my clothes; a framed, folded flag from his father's military burial hangs on the wall opposite the door to our apartment. It is the last thing we see before we leave, and the first thing that captures our eyes when we walk in the door. Mitch says the flag is a sign of valor and strength, a perfect representation of his father. I stand up straight when I walk by it.

I lead Timmy past a great flag hanging between the departure signs in the Main Concourse, stopping for a moment to direct his attention to it. I think how different this flag looks unrolled, open, gently swaying over the commuters. It is more like an invitation than a command. I glance once more at the lovers at the bottom of the stairs where he continues to read and she continues to watch, and I'm hot with envy.

The round Tiffany clock in the center of the vast room shows one o'clock. One hour until his train arrives. No wonder Timmy's hungry. The poor thing won't get a nap today, either. A sheen of sweat dampens my forehead, and I reach up to dab it with my handkerchief, making a silent plea to God that Timmy doesn't have a tantrum on Mitch's first day home. I look down at the hand-kerchief monogrammed with our initials, MJM, now streaked with my makeup. Mitch gave me the handkerchief when we were courting. He said it was fate that our initials were the same.

I wish I remembered to feed Timmy lunch at home, because now we'll have to go to the lower level. Underground spaces make it hard for me to breathe. I always take the bus in the city because I can't bear to go hurtling under streets and buildings in a metal sub-way car. At least the ceiling isn't too low under Grand Central, and the Oyster Bar is well lit.

As we move to the lower-level stairs, I catch the melancholy sound of a violin playing in the distance. The strains remind me of some-thing I've sung in Moody's Jazz Club, on the roof of my friend Sheilah's apartment building, where I've spent so many magical nights while her war-broken husband stayed with our two boys. I feel pulled toward the sound, but I know I must continue in the opposite direction.

As we step onto the lower level, I can't help but notice the clocks facing me. Clocks are everywhere in Grand Central. Fifty-five minutes left, they say. Mitch will be home soon. Fifty-three minutes. A moment in a long life . . .

I think of Mitch's letters filled with news of USO shows, singers and beauties of the highest caliber. He told me that when Dinah Shore sang "I'll Walk Alone," there wasn't a dry eye among the men, and how proud he was to have a wife like me waiting for him, walking alone until he returned from the war.

I pass the mirror outside of the Oyster Bar and stop to check my face and arrange my bangs over my forehead. My eyes are dull with exhaustion from the sleepless nights of this week. I finished my last night at the club just two days ago, and I've spent the others worrying over Mitch's return. My skin is pale beneath the makeup. I reach in my purse and pull out a compact, pressing powder on my forehead and nose even though it's rude to do so in public. No one seems to notice me.

There are many rouged, primped, set women wandering around the station today. We are our own army of wives and girlfriends, sisters and mothers, walking alone, bravely carrying on while our men rid the world of evil. Some of us hold photos in our pockets, others trinkets and flowers. I have a letter he sent me when the war ended. It is worn and the paper is soft from frequent handling. Mitch has always been convincing in his correspondence, but this note tops all the others. I cling to its words of love and tenderness, apology for past wrongs, and promises of a better future. I think that if I read it enough, I might believe it.

Before walking into the Oyster Bar, I place the compact back in my purse. My hand brushes against the wine cork my mother sent with her last letter. I lift it out and read the name stamped on it:

Louis M. Martini, Since 1933. After my father's death she moved with her spinster sister to a vineyard in Napa Valley. It was always her dream. She says California is the new promised land, where the weather is never harsh. She writes how the work is harder than she anticipated, but how pleasing it is to look over the rows of grapevines from her tiny cabin, watching the sun set over the abundant vegetation at the day's end. I wonder if she is lonely or content. It is hard to read between the lines of her letters. She writes that she wishes she had more room so we could visit. We both know I can't afford the trip, but fantasy has its value. The truth that we'll probably never see each other again is too harsh to look straight in the eye.

"Pudding." Timmy has pulled his hand out of mine and stands at the dessert case just inside the restaurant. Why not let him eat pudding? I don't know if his father will approve once he's home. I guide Timmy to the counter section, looking for two empty seats together, but the place is packed. There is an energy in the bar, a frantic mingling of noise and motion. I snake around the counter, inhaling the briny smell of the oysters, listening to the slosh of ice being poured over their rough shells, shouts from the shuckers to the waitresses. There are no seats to be found.

I turn back, planning to take Timmy to a hot dog stand outside the station, when a man grabs my arm, causing me to start. For one panicked moment I think it's Mitch, off the train early and angry that we weren't there to meet him. The man has blond hair instead of Mitch's brown, however, and I breathe. He is dressed in a crisp business suit.

"Hey, aren't you . . ." His voice trails off.

I don't recognize him, but it occurs to me that he might have seen me at the club, and a new terror arises in my heart. What if some man approaches me when I'm with Mitch?

"I don't think so," I say, looking down and pulling out of his grip.

I walk away, still holding Timmy's hand, and end up near a back corner. I am leaning on the counter by the kitchen to catch my breath when a hand reaches for mine. I flinch, but I see that it is a woman, probably in her midfifties, with lines around her pale blue eyes, and graying strawberry blonde hair. There are seats open on either side of her, and she slides over so Timmy and I can sit together. I remove his coat, lay it on the stool, and place him on top of it, kissing his head before I sit.

The woman returns her gaze to the crossword puzzle in the folded newspaper in her hand. Without looking at me she says, "Something one is bound to do out of duty, ten letters."

I'm only half listening to her as the waitress approaches us. She is frail and unkempt. I wonder how long it takes her to wash the oyster smell out of her hands and hair each night, or if she bothers. Perhaps she is used to it. When she sees my son, with his round, teddy bear eyes and crew cut hair, she becomes a different woman. A smile lights her face.

"You look like a little soldier, a brave little soldier."

I run my hand over his stubble, and feel an ache as I remember watching his soft chestnut ringlets fall to the floor of the barber shop yesterday. His father wouldn't like to see his son looking so cherubic.

A word rises into my consciousness. "Obligation." I turn to the woman at my side. "The word is 'obligation.'"

She uses the eraser of her pencil to count out the spaces, and her eyes widen. "That's it."

I order a chocolate pudding for Timmy and an old-fashioned for myself. The waitress doesn't judge me for my midday drink, and I'm glad for it. I feel so jittery, I'm afraid I'll get sick.

Seated across from us are another set of lovers—a soldier and a young woman who is as primped and pressed as I am but altogether different. She is fair with brown eyes. She wears a pale blue dress with sleeves that puff at the top, and a matching headband. Light radiates from her, and her beau is basking in it. She reaches up and runs her hand over his face. I can't hear them over the din, but I think she must be saying, "It is you. You're back to me. All of you." And he must be saying, "Thank God," while a parade of the men he has watched die marches through his mind. He'll hide this darkness to protect her.

I wonder if I will be so lucky.

The waitress brings my drink. I notice my hand trembling as I reach for it, and catch the sideways glance of the woman with the crossword. I take a healthy nip and set the glass down harder than I intend. My eyes dart to her and back to my drink.

She speaks without looking at me. "Nervy."

"Excuse me?" I say.

"You're nervy. Coming or going?"

"Waiting."

"Ah. Boy's father coming home on the two o'clock?"

I look at her, but she continues to study her crossword puzzle. "Eight letters. Faithful practice."

"Yes, he is." I reach up and even out my bangs.

"Monogamy," she says.

The song restarts in my head. "I'll Walk Alone."

I've never dallied with anyone these years he has been away, though there have been plenty of chances. But I haven't been faith-

ful to his ideal. I'm a performer, a lounge singer. We bear the
weight of the audience's projections. Our songs touch their hearts
and make them think we are singing only for them. Mitch doesn't
like people falling in love with me over their martinis, but I do. It's
a temporary respite from their cares, and I like to help people. So
does Sheilah.

I met Sheilah at the Red Cross. She had her hair set so pretty
and wore a polka-dot dress and shiny shoes, all dolled up just to
roll bandages. I thought she looked like a movie star, and felt
ashamed of my kerchief and worn dress, just a step up from the
housedresses my mother used to put on. Timmy was just about a
year old, and toddling all over the place.

Sheilah smiled kindly at me and winked. "Hey, doll, mind
watching my piles while I grab some smokes?"

I shook my head.

"Thanks!"

When she walked next door to the corner mart, all eyes were
on her. I wondered if she wore stockings or if she'd drawn lines on
the back of her legs. She was back in a flash and placed her cigarette
in a shiny ebony holder. I never saw anyone look so glamorous
while rolling bandages.

We chatted, talking about the weather and war, and she told
me that her handsome husband lost a hand in the fighting, and she
was glad because he was home with her. He had been a sniper, but
the enemy cut him down quick. She laughed when she said this,
like it was a joke. The ladies near us glanced at us and shuffled farther down the table.

Sheilah told me my voice sounded deep and pleasing like warm,
drippy honey. I laughed and told her that I used to sing in a big band
in my hometown of Spencertown, New York, but I didn't have

much chance now with the baby, and my husband gone. When she mentioned the flower stall where her husband often bought her bouquets, I realized how close we lived to each other. It was the same place where Mitch bought flowers for me, though the thought didn't warm my heart.

"We'll have you and your little one to dinner sometime," she said. "We love babies, but I don't think I can have any since it hasn't happened so far."

I couldn't believe how frankly she spoke, and with such nonchalance. She carried on in a way I had never seen a woman do. There was something different about her than almost every other woman I'd known, but I couldn't figure out what it was.

I was mentioning that my husband was still overseas when she interrupted me and said, "Why do you hide that gorgeous porcelain skin?" She reached up and made a motion to brush the bangs out of my face, causing me to flinch. I moved my bangs back into place.

"Such a jumpy thing!" she said. As soon as the words tumbled out of her mouth, her gaze clouded. She was quiet for a whole minute without taking her eyes off me. Her look seemed to touch my skin, and the scar on my forehead tingled. I hoped she hadn't seen it. She arranged a smile on her lips.

"We'll have to have you over sometime," she said.

————

Moody's was on the roof of Sheilah's apartment building, which was the first reason I fell in love with it. Living in a city like New York after having grown up in the Hudson River Valley, I felt the continual oppression of stone and brick, cramped rooms, tight corridors, creaky elevators. With so many people and dwellings crammed onto one island, one is bound to feel claustrophobic.

I took the steps slowly, swallowing gulps of fresh night air and gazing heavenward. Waiters in black shirts scurried over the rooftop, and a heavy, melancholy sound at odds with the energy of the place issued from the upright piano in the corner. The bartender, a slender man with a long nose and eyes twinkling from the reflected lights of the hanging strands, stared at me without bothering to hide it. I looked away, wondering where Sheilah was. The kindly old Irish woman next door was sitting in my apartment with Timmy while he slept. It was the first time I'd left him alone, and though I trusted her, it had been so hard to walk out of the building without him. Sheilah had told me to meet her at nine o'clock. I half hoped she'd stand me up so I could get back to him.

When the piano song ended, applause rose from the tables, and the hanging lights went off, dropping darkness over us like a blanket. Distant car horns rose on the breeze, and the stronger stars, those that could be seen over the glow of the city lights, flickered overhead.

A large, raucous group spilled from the top of the stairs onto the roof. A half-dozen women and a man or two pushed past me and seeped into the chairs around the midnight blue–covered tables. The waiters lit candles, and the hanging lights around the stage went on one section at a time, until the rooftop was ablaze. The silver stage curtain trembled from the wind gusts and motion. I took a seat near the table by the stairs. In moments, a waiter jotted down my order and vanished as the curtain parted.

The piano player had returned, but he didn't have the same hangdog look as before, and I could see why. The gorgeous blonde accompanying him wore a red satin gown and shook her hip to his musical introduction. When she turned and began to sing, I saw that it was Sheilah. Her pretty, open face and soprano voice were magnetic, and it was only her and each one of us, in our own place, listening to her sing.

I realized then that what made her stand out from other people was her happiness. I knew almost no one who was purely happy. Sitting in this rooftop bar was the closest I'd been to happiness in a long time, but it still didn't permeate me the way it did Sheilah. By the time her set had finished and flowers rained down on the stage, she had made me believe I might be happy again someday. It was all I could do not to sing.

———

Within a month of seeing Sheilah's performance, I began singing at Moody's. Over the years I'd been dressing more plainly so Mitch wouldn't have to worry about other men ogling me. I'd only kept the green satin dress he'd bought me to wear out for his birthday, but because it reminded me of him, I didn't want to wear it. I started performing in Sheilah's borrowed dresses, padding my brassiere to fill out her tops, using her lipstick, allowing her to set my hair. My neighbor let Timmy sleep at her house on the nights I worked, and after Sheilah had baby Andrew, her husband kept both boys. I performed only a couple of times a week, making just enough for extra pocket money, but it brought me more joy than I'd ever known.

It is this life I will miss the most.

Sheilah is a light, the best friend I've ever had. She has never judged me or pushed me for details, but always seems to understand that this was just a gig and that it would all end once Mitch came home. Two weeks ago was the first and only time she spoke any words out loud that showed me she understood about him.

I stayed the night on their couch after a great show at the club.

Timmy slept on his little blankets in Andrew's room. When the baby fussed, Sheilah brought him out to sit in the darkness with me and nurse him. The light from the street lamp lit her like a modern Madonna with long fingernails and makeup. She didn't look at me. Once he'd latched on, she began whispering.

"I didn't ever think I'd get a little gift like this," she said. "I have a baby. I can't believe it. I hope I do right by him."

"You will," I said.

"You'll help me?" she asked.

"Of course."

We sat in silence until the clock chimed the two o'clock hour. Once its sound was extinguished by the night shadows, she continued. "You are always welcome here," she said.

"I know," I replied.

"No, I mean if you need to get away from . . . anything."

She looked at me. I could see she wanted to say more, but I understood what she meant and didn't want to talk about it.

I had a hard time sleeping that night.

———————

The Oyster Bar waitress is back and chatty, but my simple responses send her to another patron. How can she not see that a storm is brewing inside me? When I close my eyes it's as if I'm in a small boat on a big sea, but when I open them, the room is steady around me. People laugh and suck oysters from their shells. Timmy eats his pudding and hums a little song. I pick up the melody of "All Through the Night," and I'm in a fresh panic. What if Mitch is suspicious of how Timmy knows that song? But no, that is ridiculous. I can simply say we hear it on the radio, which is true. I blot my forehead again with my handkerchief.

"You remind me of my Lorraine, my daughter." The woman is speaking to me. I look at her, seemingly so interested in her crossword puzzle, and am somehow certain that she is acutely aware of me and of my tension. "Dark hair like you. Green eyes. A wife."

She says the last word with ice in her voice, and looks at me.

Her blue eyes are moist and filmy. Her cheekbones are high, and her hair is styled neatly. She wears a navy blue dress with a white lace collar, and has a smear of pink on her lips. She was pretty once.

But I think again about how she said *wife*. It sounded like a dare.

The little island of pleasure where my relationship with Mitch began is a place I often go in my mind. It is a still shore in a vast and chaotic sea, and it seems far away.

I met him at a blueberry festival. All was blue that day—my dress, the sky, the fruit, pies, farmers' dungarees, the berry-stained fingers of children, Mitch's eyes. I saw him, a handsome stranger looking tense and lost, searching the midway for someone. He studied all of the passersby but clearly couldn't find the object of his search.

I stood with my mother at our pie stand. I noticed him because I had never seen him before, and when he caught me watching him, his face softened. He stood there like a man struck, and I glanced away, hoping my mother didn't notice his open admiration. I made busywork of arranging our pies in neat rows until I sensed that he was near. I looked up and he was right before me, grinning at me with only the table between us. I found my voice and tried to sound calm, though I felt jumpy. Growing up in a small town made outsiders captivating and dangerous.

"Would you like a slice of pie?" I said.

He shook his head no, and his expression was so funny that I laughed. I glanced back and saw my mother whispering with her sister. My father wasn't with us. He didn't like mixing in town.

"I'd like a walk with you by the river," he said.

"I don't even know you."

"I'm sorry. I can't believe I just said that," he said. "Hey, you don't happen to know Bobby Miller, do you? He's my cousin. My name's Mitch."

The faintest trace of a New York accent hung about his perfectly formed lips, and I had to blink and look away. I'd gone to school with Bobby my whole life, and easily picked him out of the crowd buzzing around the soda pop counter.

"There," I said, pointing toward Bobby's group. He looked at them, and then back at me.

"Thanks," he said. Awkwardness settled between us, and he seemed to be thinking whether or not he should say more. He finally spoke again. "I know this is forward, but could I have a dance with you later?"

As much as I yearned to agree, I couldn't. "I'm singing. They don't let us offstage."

"Then afterward? I bet the river is pretty by moonlight. We could take a walk."

Bobby caught sight of him. "Mitch!"

"You'll consider it?" he asked.

My mother was at my side with her hand on my arm. "Would you like a slice of pie, young man?" She must have sensed the energy buzzing between us, and wanted to protect me.

"No thank you, ma'am, though I'm sure it's delicious. I don't want to eat before I go on the rides."

"Smart," she said.

"But I'll come back when I'm finished and get some. If there's any left. I'm sure it's selling better than all of the other stands, with flaky crust like that."

And in an instant, she was won over. I think I even saw her blush. He nodded to her and didn't look at me. I couldn't help but stare as he walked away.

"I wonder who that nice young man is," she'd said. "Seems like a catch, Mary Josephine."

———————

I wish I could whisper to my younger self, "Run, Josie. As fast as you can."

But my mother's blessing and encouragement all through that afternoon felt like fate to me. She had never approved of a boy so quickly. I should have seen the strength of his charm and been wary, but I was just as snowed as everyone else about Mitch.

Timmy's spoon clinks against the inside of his empty glass dish. Chocolate outlines his lips in a sloppy smile. I grab my napkin and dab it into the water the waitress has placed before me without asking to refill my old-fashioned. As I clean his face, I can't believe I finished my drink so quickly. I crave another, but I'm already afraid Mitch will have something to say about the smell of booze on my breath.

Timmy's face is perfect enough to be a sculpture. He still has the rounded slopes of his baby profile, though his hands have grown knuckles where dimples used to be, and he's less afraid of venturing away from me. He used to cling to me like a little koala, and some days I felt like I'd never be free of sticky fingers grabbing my hair, but seemingly overnight I long for him to wish to be picked up and held close. I long for the days, about to end, when it was just the two of us in our little apartment.

I've grown soft over the years. I no longer stiffen when walking around corners. I don't worry if I leave my stockings lying over the chair, or if the sofa cushions are piled on the floor. I have become a woman who plays the radio too loud, wears her hair loose more days than not, and who sometimes serves dessert first just for the fun of it, not that there's been much dessert during the war years—often just half a biscuit with blueberry jam from my parents' farm.

The farm is gone now. When my father died last year, my mother sold the already failing land, the wooden farmhouse where I grew up, the rights to the paths in the woods that wound down to the river where I'd escape my father's temper. I could hear my father's voice yelling at my mother for some minor farm failing that was of great magnitude to him, until the bend in the path, when the rush of the water silenced him. When I'd creep home after spending hours away, my mother's eyes would be puffy and red, and my father would be off in the field. She'd stand over her canning and tell me to behave so I didn't upset my father when he returned, and that the burden of the farm was too much for him. Then she'd mumble about the golden vineyards she'd read about in Napa Valley.

I love my mother, and I miss her. I hope her vineyard gives her everything she didn't have all those years in New York.

I focus on my own life now. I think of the way I tidied and straightened the apartment this week. How Timmy has been curious and watchful as I instruct him in new ways to live in the space. He hasn't adjusted well to our new rules, and I know it's my fault. I shouldn't have waited so long to acknowledge that Mitch would be home, but God forgive me, I never believed he'd come back.

Until recently, the stoic telegram bearers were a daily sight. I think of how they had the worst job in the world. When the knock would come, we'd peer out our doors, hold our breath, rush to comfort the newly bereaved. But the knock never came for me.

It pains me to allow such terrible thoughts, but I had already planned the stories I'd tell Timmy about his brave, handsome father after he died. I'd conceal the nights I lay awake with eyes wide open, afraid to go to sleep because Mitch might hurt me; the way I learned to keep my gaze straight ahead and down so I didn't make eye contact with another man in Mitch's presence; the times when his anger couldn't be contained. Timmy would only hear about the better attributes of his father so he'd never know he came from anything but goodness.

But we'll never have that conversation now. Timmy will get to know his father himself.

———

Whenever I think of Mitch, I think of flowers. Flowers were his form of apology. Bouquets he hoped would brighten my eyes after he'd hurt me. After he hit me with the iron in the head, I received two dozen scarlet roses. I was lucky the iron had cooled, and all that remained was an ugly white slash across my forehead.

It began with plans for an evening out. Before going with him to the movies to see *Rebecca* I thought I'd surprise him by tinting my hair red. He'd been mooning over the lead actress Joan Fontaine in the theater posters, and I thought he'd like to see a change in me. He hadn't hit me in so long, I'd dropped my vigilance. My speech had become loose. I'd expressed on several occasions how I wished I could sing onstage again, and didn't heed the warning look on his face.

"You know I don't want them looking at you," he said.

"I only have eyes for you," I teased. He didn't smile.

I told him I'd meet him after my appointment at the beauty parlor at the corner diner for a quick bite before the picture. When I walked in, a group of young men whistled. I wish I hadn't smiled. Mitch misinterpreted it as flirtation.

"What did you do to your hair?" he hissed.

"I thought you'd like it. I wanted it to look like Joan Fontaine's."

"You look like a harlot. And you drew attention like one, too."

My shoulders tensed. I knew I'd made a terrible error. I clenched my sweating hands together in my lap to contain their trembling and prayed his anger would pass.

"We're going home," he said.

That old, familiar dread filled my stomach, but I obeyed without a word.

"Hussy," he said as he closed the door to the apartment. He pushed me forward, and I almost hit the frame holding his father's flag across from the front door. I caught myself with my hands and ran toward the bedroom. He followed, yelling hateful words at me, throwing me on the bed. I climbed over the side and tried to run out the door, but he picked up the iron and threw it at my face, clipping the side of my forehead and drawing blood. It spit on the white wall, and he was horror-struck.

"Oh, Josie, I'm sorry. I'm so sorry."

He lunged for the iron, and I thought he'd kill me with it, but he pushed it into my hands. "Hit me with it. I'm so sorry. Hit me."

He begged me to hit him, but I could only crumple to the floor and cry.

He grabbed a towel and pressed it to my forehead, whispering apologies, sobbing with me, begging for my forgiveness.

I gave him words of forgiveness, but I didn't mean them. The red roses that lay on the table the next day didn't soothe the pain. Their red reminded me of my blood. The roses were like my husband, pleasing and smooth to behold but thorny, dangerous.

It was his charm that made it impossible not to believe him. Weeks, months would pass with such kindness, tenderness, and ease. Our lives would fill with light. I told myself this was the true Mitch, not the monster. Helping to suppress the monster became our shared mission. When the atmosphere would inevitably begin to grow dark, I made myself believe that it was my fault for smiling when men noticed me. I thought of my own vanity and how I enjoyed being watched as a performer.

In truth, I didn't feel worthy of Mitch or anyone then, and something inside me still doesn't. I have ugly chicken pox scars on my chin and close to my left ear. The pox scars on my torso could be a constellation. That's what Mitch said the first time he traced them, when he said my body was like the night sky, and he kissed me from one end to the other.

Later he called me deformed, a mutant, lucky to have a guy like him who was willing to overlook my imperfections. His words spoke to the demon that whispered such things in my ear. At first, his voice sounded like my father's, but over the years it became Mitch's.

———

I'm tapping my fingernail on the counter when the woman places her hand on mine. My instinct is to pull away, but she is too strong.

"How much longer?" she says.

I glance at the clock. "Thirty-five minutes."

She stares at me for a moment with a furrowed brow. Then she nods as if she has decided something.

"You're just like my Lorraine." She has said this before, but it sounds different this time. She chokes on the name. I look into her pale eyes. Her mouth is pursed. It is clear that she is trying not to cry. I know I can't pull away from her. She looks up to keep the tears in place, and the futility of the gesture as the salt water starts a path through her blush stirs me with pity. I pass her my napkin and she pulls her hand away and presses it to her cheek. "God rest her soul."

We live in a world of loss. Tears among strangers are common. That her daughter has been lost is no surprise. I think she must have been killed in the war.

"Was she a field nurse?" I say.

"No, but she lived in a war."

"In Europe?"

"At home."

I don't know what she means.

"Like you," she says.

Understanding begins to form in my mind, like clouds merging in a dark sky. My teeth are suddenly chattering, though I am not cold. Timmy tugs my arm, but I cannot look at him. I'm afraid he'll see my shame. Am I so obvious? Do I wear my fear so prominently? I spend a lot of time in nightclubs with liars and actresses, and living with Mitch has made me one as well. I transform my face into stone.

"I don't know what you mean," I say, hating myself.

"You do," she says. "The way you flinch, the lock of hair you keep moving to cover the scar on your forehead, your nerves. You don't fool me."

I stand quickly. Timmy looks at me with wide eyes.

"I have to go," I say.

"Please," she says. "Please let me talk to you."

"No!" My voice is louder than I intend, and the couple across from us looks over. They stare for only a moment before they turn back to each other. "No. There's nothing to talk about."

"Please. You don't understand."

I don't know what she can mean. All I can take in is that the clock says I only have thirty more minutes before he arrives. I look up at the ceiling, the archways made of brick, and the weight of the stone above presses down on me. I have to get out of here.

"Come on, Timmy."

I'm hurrying with putting on his coat, and my elbow knocks his glass dish to the floor, where it shatters. I could cry over this broken glass.

"Stay there," I say to Timmy with a trembling voice, setting him back on the stool so he doesn't get hurt.

The waitress arrives in moments with a towel.

"I'm sorry," I say.

"Don't fret over it," she says. I crouch on the floor with her and carefully pick up the broken pieces. A busboy sweeps the rest into a filthy dustpan and disappears.

"I'll have my check," I say to the waitress as I sink onto my stool.

"Miss," says the woman, as persistent as a mosquito. I want to swat her away, but when I look at her, I see her pain and suddenly wonder if I am her reflection. Does she see herself in me? She seems to be trembling as much as I am.

"Lorraine was a girl like you," she says. "Tall, dark haired, pretty as a summer's day, but always with a storm in her eyes. At least, once she married Harry. My lively girl became quiet. Sullen. She grew jumpy and snapped at me. She became secretive and started showing up for Sunday dinners with strange bruises and stranger stories of how she got them. Then she stopped coming. I think the hiding wore her out."

I have the urge to run from this woman again, this stranger. But my curiosity about her daughter keeps me in place. I sense her story doesn't end well, and like some form of self-punishment, I have to hear it from her lips.

"Harry was a major in the army," she says. "He worked under my husband, and was the pride of his hometown, the brightest in his class, the handsomest man. Harry used to bring *me* flowers and visit me when no one was home. He'd ask me about my needle-work and the sewing circle at church with what seemed like real interest. I never would have guessed what a monster he was."

It is as if she's telling my own story to me, and it hurts to hear it. I've been training myself these past few months, knowing he'd eventually come home, hating myself for wishing he wouldn't, and rereading the promises in his letters, praying he'll be different— that my love for him will change him. I don't want to hear the rest of this woman's story, but the waitress hasn't yet brought the check. I put my hands in my lap and squeeze them together.

"One night, Lorraine was dropped off at my house in a car I didn't recognize. She came in smelling of alcohol and cigarettes, mascara running down her face, and wearing a purple welt around her pretty blue eye. She was drunk and started shouting about how Harry had punched her, and her friend came to help but grew afraid and dropped her off at my house. During her incoherent tirade Harry stepped out of my drawing room with his hands in his pockets, wearing a look of sadness that nearly broke my heart. Lorraine's eyes widened, as much as they could, and she backed up until her head hit the wall.

"'Didn't I tell you?' he said to me. 'Her drinking has gotten so out of hand, Mom. And her friend is another man. I'm sure he did this to her, and now she's accusing me. It kills me.'

"And do you know, I believed him?" The woman seems to coil within herself. Her breathing becomes labored, and I worry that she'll faint. I am moved to reach for her hand again, and she takes mine.

"Why didn't I look at his knuckles?" she says, her voice high from emotion. "I would have seen the broken skin, the swollen ridges."

"You don't have to tell me any more," I say, worried for her heart, worried for mine. We could be sitting in a confessional if it weren't for the people around us.

"She's dead," she says. My breath stops. All other sound leaves the room and we are alone. "He killed her, just a month after that night. My baby girl came to me for help, and I took his side. She died knowing that I didn't believe her. Even though he's in prison now, it's too late. I'll never be free from my own prison."

Prison. The word triggers a memory of the worst kind, the one I try so hard to forget but that hovers at the rim of my consciousness always, because it has to do with my son, the night he was born early. Mitch begged me to report him to the police so he could die in prison for almost killing us.

I shake my head, but the memory persists.

When I became pregnant, Mitch acted like a changed man. He doted on me, treated me with tenderness, took me for walks in Central Park. At night, he held me close to him and whispered promises about what a good father he'd be, and how he'd treat his son with such love.

His son, it was always a son. He never considered he might have a daughter. As the months passed and I grew used to having a husband who didn't hurt me or say hateful things, I began to lower my guard, speak my mind, provoke him further than I ever had. Part of it was the pregnancy. I felt out of sorts and got frequent headaches, which left me irritable, but part of it was the different man Mitch seemed to have become. I was foolish.

One morning, when I was fighting a particularly bad headache that left me nauseous, he was humming in the kitchen when I woke up. He'd taken to addressing my stomach as Timmy—named after his deceased brother, and without any consideration for what name I might like.

"How's Timmy this morning?" he asked.

I was so sick of being thought of as nothing more than a vessel for Mitch's child, whom he refused to acknowledge could be anything but a son, that I snapped at him.

"It could be a girl, you know," I said.

"But it's not," Mitch replied. "I can tell by the way you're carrying him. The old lady next door said so."

"That's another thing," I said. "You never even asked me about baby names. What if I don't want him to be named after your dead brother?"

Mitch slammed his coffee cup on the counter, and I wished with all my heart that I'd never said such a thing. He stood with his back toward me, clutching the edge of the counter and breathing deeply. I stood slowly and wrapped my arms around my stomach.

"I'm sorry," I said. "I shouldn't have said that. My head hurts and I don't know what I'm saying."

He stood in the kitchen for a moment more before turning and walking out of the room, brushing me hard with his shoulder as he passed. I closed my eyes, still clutching my stomach, waiting for the blows, but I only heard him in the hallway grabbing his keys and slamming the door.

I sank in my chair, trembling, and thanked God that he hadn't exploded. It took me a while to calm down, but I began to feel hopeful. He had been able to hold his temper.

He stayed away all day. I wanted to make everything perfect for that night, so I found the most becoming frock I could to cover my eight-month-pregnant figure, set my hair, and applied lipstick and perfume. I baked a potato casserole and let it brown in the oven. Just as I was about to set the table, I heard a knock at the door.

My heart pounded, but I knew it couldn't be Mitch. He would let himself in with his key. I passed the flag in the hall, pulled my shoulders back, and opened the door to find the building super. I had forgotten that he said he'd come by at five o'clock to fix the leaky faucet in the bathroom. He was a large man of Eastern European descent and had a strong jawline and large, square shoulders. He wasn't yet in his forties and had a cheeky, devilish glint in his eyes. Mitch didn't care for him.

I showed the super inside and he started for the bathroom, where he'd fixed the leaky faucet a half-dozen times over the years.

He looked me over and inhaled. "Ah, smells so good. Your husband's a lucky man."

I smiled and allowed him to get to work while I cooked. The super hummed in the bathroom. I fantasized how nice it would be to have a husband I didn't fear—a lighthearted man who sang songs while fixing leaky faucets, and whose compliments lit a fire inside me. Then guilt caused me to suppress such imaginings. I fetched the plates and utensils and set the table. As I turned to go back to the kitchen to get the water glasses, I ran into Mitch.

When I saw his face I shrank back toward the dining table. His clothing was wrinkled. Dark circles hung heavy under his eyes. He reeked of booze.

"All done, Mrs. Miller." I heard the super's voice as he walked down the hall. "It's simple to fix. I bet your husband could do it next time, no trouble. Not that I mind. Oh, hello."

The super had reached us and extended a hand when he saw my husband. Mitch stared at it like he didn't know what to do with it, while his face burned red. The super looked from him to me and back.

"I guess I'll just be going."

He must have known I was in some kind of trouble by the glance of pity he gave me. He hesitated at the door and looked like he wanted to say something, but I hurried past Mitch. "That will be all, thank you."

I nearly shoved him out the door and closed it before I lost my courage. I wished I could have fled.

Mitch didn't wait for me to return to the dining table. He crossed the room and clenched my arm, squeezing it with his clammy hand. He put his mouth up to my ear and started his accusations through clenched teeth.

Did you dress up and put on perfume for that man? How many times has he been here when I was out? Do you show off your cooking to tempt him? Do you always sit around making fun of my lack of handyman skills when I'm not here?

I denied his accusations and cried in a string of incoherent words, pleading with him to let my arm go, terror rising in my heart that he'd hurt the baby and kill me, half wishing he would do it quickly so the horror would end. I pulled out of his grip and thought he'd leave me alone when suddenly he said, "Is the baby his?"

It didn't matter how preposterous the accusation was. In Mitch's inebriated state, in his misreading of the situation, and on the heels of our morning quarrel, he'd lost all sense.

I suddenly felt as if a great wave pushed me from behind, and I was sent forward with terrible force into the wall. When my stomach hit the door frame of our bedroom, I felt a searing pain and became soaked in blood and water. I collapsed to the floor, clutching my stomach, horrified to feel the terrible tightening and knowing my baby might be dead. I fended Mitch off with my fists when he approached in tears, and he let me pummel him until the pain once again doubled me over. He ran to the bedroom, wrapped me in a quilt, and carried me down the stairs and out the front door, where he shouted for a taxi.

Timmy was born a month early that night, small but perfect. Mitch came to me after the delivery and stayed with me all night, begging my forgiveness, whispering promises in my ear, telling me to report him so he'd have to spend time in jail, and ultimately collapsing on the bed, spent, sober, and more sorry than he'd ever been in his life. At dawn, as a shaft of light spilled over the room, I opened my eyes and saw him on his knees, praying. He thanked God for sparing Timmy and me and vowed he would never, never hurt us again.

And he didn't.

———

I feel as if I'll get sick.

"I'm sorry about your daughter," I say to the woman.

She takes my other hand. I look at her and see that she has a new light in her eyes.

"You are my chance," she says. "A chance to atone. I tell you this because I know now that waiting even one more day will be too late. I couldn't help my girl, but I can help you. You must flee him."

"That's impossible."

"You are good at convincing yourself of things," she says. "Of lies."

Anger rises in me, and I snatch my hands from hers. She is a woman. She knows that I have no real choices, especially with a child. How can I give my boy a life with no father, take him away from the man to whom he rightfully belongs? And Timmy could soften him. So many children of difficult parents want to do right by their own kids. I know I have. I know Mitch wants to.

Mitch isn't her son-in-law. Lorraine's story isn't mine.

"I see you trying to make my story separate from yours, but it isn't," she says.

"You don't know me," I say. "You don't know my husband. Besides, I have no money. I've packed nothing. We have a son. I have nowhere to go."

"Truly? You have nowhere? You could stay with me if you had to. Everyone has somewhere to go."

I know Sheilah said I'd be welcome, but then what? I can't stay in her tiny apartment just blocks away from Mitch. He'd find me. I don't have my clothing or belongings. I've saved a little money, but it won't last. And then there is Timmy. What kind of woman takes a child from his father? No court in this world would be on my side, particularly against a veteran of the war.

Timmy crawls into my lap and starts sucking his thumb. He's

so tired. I wish I could curl up with him and sleep this awful day away. And the ones that will follow.

Nine minutes.

"I have to go," I say. "I'm sorry. About it all."

She turns her head away from me, her shoulders stooped. She feels defeated, and I can't give her reassurance.

I reach into my pocket, drop a whole dollar on the counter, and stand up with Timmy in my arms. His weight adds more burden than I think I can bear, but I am able to make it to the doors of the Oyster Bar. I catch the face of the clock staring at me.

Seven minutes.

My chest is so tight, I can't breathe, and I'm afraid I'll faint. I place Timmy's feet on the floor and lean against the wall until I'm steady. Then I take Timmy's hand and we climb the ramp to the Main Concourse.

———

I lift my face to the constellations on the ceiling. I'm breathing better up here. The air stirs more freely. I walk toward the stairs where the young lovers sat, but they are gone. Of all the difficulty of this day so far, their disappearance is what threatens to unmoor me. I return my gaze to the grand ceiling. I wonder why they have painted it teal instead of blue or navy, but somehow, it seems perfect. It is like the sky before a summer storm, or the reflection of stars in a Caribbean sea.

The night we first met I went with Mitch for a walk by the river. The stars seemed to rise from their reflections on its meandering surface, becoming the fireflies that winked through the night. He lifted his hand to cup one of them and held it for me to see. When he opened his hands, it flew to my dress, and he reached to brush it away. As it flew off, he allowed his hand to rest heavily on my collarbone, and after a moment, he kissed me with his hand still there.

Then there were the walks after my singing nights. All through the rest of that summer, he watched me sing on Friday nights. Young lovers would dance to my songs. He and I couldn't hold each other while I was onstage, so I'd look into his eyes, and he would gaze at me so intently that I felt spellbound. How I wish I had understood that his look was of obsession, not love. He wished to hold me not to share himself with me, but to keep me for himself alone.

"I can't wait until we're married," he'd say, squeezing me into his side on the bench by the river. The branches of the willow hung over us like black vines in the night, the hiss of its trembling leaves around us. "You can take care of me. I've always wanted someone to watch over me."

My heart would burn with pity for him when he said this. I knew he'd lost his mother and brother and had a cruel father, a military man he respected and feared. I mistook his meaning. I thought he meant I was to take care of him with love. I didn't know that he meant I was to give up my life to wait for him, wait on him, be ever ready to respond to his wishes and whims . . .

On our wedding night, he clung to me, trembling. "I finally have you where I want you." That was the first night I heard the warning in his words. Why hadn't I heard it before? Was I so desperate to escape my youth, my father's shadow? I wish I knew then that they were nothing compared to what I was in for.

———

A new surge of panic engulfs me as a throng of soldiers pours forth from the lower terminal. My goodness, are they early?

People fill the space around us. Perfume and aftershave, sweat and heat. Greetings, tears, kisses, embraces.

The woman is suddenly at my side, whispering in my ear. "You must go. Now," she says.

"But the boy? His father . . ."

"That's why you must. Do you want to raise one like him?"

There. The essence of the question. I touch the scar on my forehead and feel something new rise inside me. If not for myself, then I must leave for Timmy.

"Here," she says, thrusting a paper at me. I look down and see a bank envelope.

"It's not much, but it's what I came to the city today to collect. A payment on my late husband's inheritance. It's yours. Take it. It will get you somewhere that isn't here, though not much farther." She sees my hesitation and shoves it in my purse. "Now!"

I don't think. I lift my boy and start through the crowds, keeping my eyes fixed at the top of the staircase leading to Vanderbilt Avenue. I push through the people. They are nothing to me. I have strength I didn't know existed.

Four minutes.

I climb the steps, clutching Timmy to me, feeling the weight of Mitch's letter in my pocket like a sack of rocks. I stop for a moment at the top of the stairs, throw the letter into the wastebasket, and turn to look down over the concourse.

One minute.

The woman is still there, smiling at me through her tears. She waves me on, but not before I see him.

Mitch.

My breath catches. His face has a new openness to it. His eyes are full of joy and longing. His gaze darts over faces in the crowd;

he is excited, anxious. His hair is newly cut, and I imagine running my fingers over it, feeling its softness. I think of his strong hands tracing my scars, kissing each along the constellation on me. I feel my courage failing. My arms tremble under Timmy's weight.

And then he sees me. His face glows. "Josie!" He rushes through the masses. And I notice what he holds in his hand: a bouquet of red roses.

I tear my gaze from his and run.

PUSH says the sign on the door, and I turn with Timmy still in my arms and back out, running into a man who is pushing in, and nearly falling back into Grand Central Terminal.

I am out. I run forward. The steam from the manholes parts like a curtain and I rush to the curb.

Waiting in the cab line, I think I'll be sick. I turn and watch the doors with wild eyes. My God, he'll come through any moment now!

I dash to the corner where the taxis pull in and grab the door of one still rolling. I thrust Timmy in before it stops and jump in after him. I give the startled driver the address of Sheilah's apartment building, but a large truck pulls up beside us, blocking our way.

I look toward the door, frantic, but only strangers move in and out. While the cabbie presses his horn, I reach in my purse where the woman shoved the bank envelope and see it contains sixty dollars—a small fortune to me. There is also a bank slip with her name: Mary Hagerty. Next to it rests the cork my mother sent me.

The promised land.

I turn back to the doors, and Mitch appears, his face like a bull. He looks right and left, and then spots us.

"Drive, please!" I beg.

The driver yells curse words out the window but begins to inch around the delivery truck. Mitch runs toward the taxi, wearing a look of pleading confusion that gives his face vulnerability. A rush of doubt washes over me. Maybe I'm supposed to stay. Maybe it will be different this time.

My eyes return to the bouquet he holds.

"Go!" I shout, and the taxi lurches forward. I pull Timmy close to my side. He must be so confused, but he doesn't say a word.

As we leave Grand Central Terminal, I don't want to look back, but I can't help myself. I can no longer make out Mitch's features through the dirty window. All I can see is the steam rising from the manholes, the crush of pedestrians bound for work and home and new horizons. I wonder where I will lay my head this night or the night after. I wonder what I will tell Timmy.

But I know I've done the right thing. My last glimpse of Grand Central becomes the end of one story and the beginning of another.

And on the dirty sidewalk in front of the station lies a bouquet of red roses.

The Reunion

Kristina McMorris

In honor of the female pilots of World War II, whose extraordinary feats, sacrifices, and bravery should never be forgotten.

For an entire year Virginia Collier had avoided this trip. Tomorrow would mark a year to the day, in fact, since the life she'd known had ended.

But the clerk in the ticket booth would not know this. He stared back, impatience and puzzlement creasing his brow. It was Virginia's turn to approach the counter, yet her strappy heels had melded with the marble tiles of Grand Central.

"Miss?" he said, and expelled a sigh. A presumption of incompetence.

Virginia had grown well accustomed to enduring that sound from a slew of male Army pilots, even after General Hap Arnold himself had pinned shiny silver wings onto her starched white blouse. A pretty dame like her couldn't possibly have the brains, let alone the gumption, to operate something more complex than a pop-up toaster. If they did not say this to her face, it blared in their snickers, their mutterings, and, yes, irritated sighs, until her butter-smooth landings of any aircraft from P-38s to B-24s silenced their derision, or at least reduced it to a low-level hum.

"Come on, lady," came a gruff voice in her queue. "Are you buying a ticket, or ain't ya?" Grumbles of agreement arose from other suited men. They had trains to catch. They had lives to live.

A woman touched Virginia's sleeve from behind. She wore a black dress and matching hat with netting. Wrinkles crowded her eyes as if accumulated from the wiping of countless tears, further hinting to her rank as a wartime widow. "Don't you pay them any mind," she said. "I'm in no hurry." In her voice lay a depth of understanding, a message that the hammer of grief had once shattered her own compass, too, leaving her lost and alone in a world that kept on spinning.

"Miss," the clerk repeated. Before he could spout an ultimatum, Virginia salvaged her strength and stepped forward with her travel bag. She produced a thin stack of dollar bills from her pocketbook and traded them for a voucher.

"Thank you," she said, and the man grunted. She started away before turning toward the widow to nod in gratitude, but the woman was already at the counter, occupied with her own journey.

Overhead the destination board shuffled its letters. Friday afternoon marked the start of the weekend bustle. The long arms of the four-faced clock ticked in unison toward departure time.

Gripping her ticket, Virginia ventured through the main concourse and descended the terminal stairs. She snaked through the dim stretch of tunnels and located her platform. The cool underground air prickled her skin, a warning. Yet she proceeded to weave through the crowd as if stitching a patchwork of strangers: a porter lugging a monstrous trunk, a mother soothing a crying infant, a couple meeting in an ardent embrace. Now a month past war's end, Virginia had prepared herself for the sight of such reunions, but not for the lone soldier emerging from the train ahead. Eagerly he scanned the teeming platform with crimson roses at the ready.

The memory of a similar bouquet, a similar serviceman, slammed into Virginia. A punch to the chest. All at once, she again saw the burst of flames and smelled the gaseous smoke. She heard the agonizing screams that had plagued her dreams for months.

"All aboard!"

The conductor's voice yanked her back to the station. She strained to regain her composure, masking the anger and sorrow festering within. Her locomotive would soon be leaving, yet doubt spiked over her ability to board.

One step at a time. This was the advice offered by her instructor in a kind, grandfatherly tone just moments before Virginia's first flight. Between shallow breaths, she had muttered regrets for thinking a college socialite like herself was fit for such an adventure. But once they had gone airborne, in a turquoise sky wispy with clouds, a fresh wave of emotion overtook her. It was peace and freedom and danger all rolled into one. It was the thrill of truly living. She'd had no inkling the world could look so beautiful, its problems seem so small, from a simple change of view—one she had experienced only by taking a risk.

Emboldened by the thought, she squared herself with the train and finally entered the coach.

Inside, cigarette smoke hung in a veil of gray. Anxiety and excitement further thickened the air. Uniforms of all military branches adorned the space, clean-shaven veterans heading for home. They were the perfect models of a thousand propaganda ads. It would take days, even weeks, before their loved ones would sense the wounds that went unseen.

Virginia stored her luggage and settled by the last available window seat. She noted several fellows, most aged around her twenty-five years, tossing smiles in her direction. She did not return the gestures. Rather, she held her purse to her lap, firm as a shield, keenly aware of the missive inside. For on that page were the last words she'd received from the man she had planned to marry. Words engraved in her mind from countless readings.

She angled toward the window to hide the emotion welling in

her eyes. She pulled a long breath, let it out. A glimpse of her reflection reminded her of the extra effort she had devoted to her appearance: the navy belted dress and cream sweater, the rouge and lipstick, the smoothing lotion in her platinum blond hair. As if a polished look could reassemble the shambles of her life.

The transport suddenly creaked, its muscles being stretched. With a shudder, the wheels began to churn. Each rotation would bring Virginia closer to a collision with her past.

She bridled the impulse to escape as standing passengers located their seats. Chatter continued among those not engrossed in their books and periodicals. It was difficult to recall which topics had filled daily papers before the outbreak of war.

In the row ahead, twin girls with double braids broke into an argument, battling over a Hershey bar.

"Good gracious," snapped a woman in a beige brimmed hat, presumably their mother. She reached across the aisle to confiscate the candy. "How is it you two are best of friends or worst of enemies, and never in between?"

The comment sent a shiver up Virginia's spine, for the same could have been said of her relationship with Millie Bennett. At one time, they, too, were like sisters, as close as twins. Who would have imagined the price they would pay for interweaving the strands of their lives?

If only they had stayed enemies. If only they had never met.

If only.

Avenger Field had served as their training center in Sweetwater, Texas. Every barracks had been divided into two living quarters for six women each with a latrine to share. Although extensive

flight experience was a prerequisite, the program was to be a gru-
eling one as they learned to "fly the Army way."

And yet, on move-in day in February 1943, Virginia's roommates chirped with all the zeal of spring nestlings. Introductions
looped and overlapped: *Where are you from? Are you married, have a
steady? Is he serving? Where's he stationed?*

Can you believe we're actually here?

It was quite surreal to be surrounded by an entire group of
female pilots. Often deemed an oddity elsewhere, their common
passion instantly bonded them all—save for Millie.

Like her appearance, her clipped two-word answers set her
apart from the others. She had arrived in roughened trousers and
a plaid cotton shirt. Her reddish brown hair was bound in a pony-
tail, loose with stragglers, completing her look of a day spent in the
fields. Her features were pleasant enough, sun tinted and dusted
with freckles, but the set of her jaw and dark, hooded eyes defined
her bearing with an edge.

"Well, I'll be," exclaimed the gal named Lucy, her drawl thick
as molasses. Everyone in the room was in the midst of unpacking.
"I know why Virginia struck me as familiar. She's that model I've
seen in the magazines!"

Begrudgingly, Virginia looked up from her half-emptied trunk
to find herself pinned by a circle of gazes.

"Really? Is it true?" a couple of the girls asked in near unison.

Before Virginia could respond, Lucy flipped open a copy of
Good Housekeeping and skipped past the usual advertisements that
featured sketches of apron-clad wives. "Lookee, right here," she
said. Ladies clustered around her, oohing and aahing over the
Kodak Film ad in which Virginia had been photographed wearing
a frilly dress and propping a parasol.

Virginia attempted to wave this off. "It's just a silly picture," she insisted, and not out of false modesty. She wished to be known for greater skills than striking dainty poses. She had accepted the job only to afford flight lessons in secret, for she knew better than to ask her parents.

Although the couple was reasonably supportive of women's independence, her father, as an esteemed surgeon, had pieced together too many broken bodies to approve of his only daughter buzzing through the sky. Virginia had little choice but to sign the permission form on his behalf. Eventually, when she was accepted into the elite training detachment that ultimately formed the WASP, or Women Airforce Service Pilots, she did her best to stress the high points: *Graduates will be hired as pilots but still as civilians. Don't you see? By ferrying military planes in the States, I'll be doing my bit for the war effort.* Her parents did not share her enthusiasm, but denying her entry would have been unpatriotic. And that was one thing the Colliers were not.

"Honestly, it's nothing," Virginia told the girls who were still fixated on the magazine. She resumed her unpacking as their questions rolled in about Hollywood and starlets and glamorous things of which Virginia had no knowledge.

"I agree, it's nothin'," Millie interjected, standing off by her cot. "Nothing that'll be useful, anyhow, if you're a serious pilot." She muttered this as if to herself, though loud enough to plunge the room into silence.

Stunned, Virginia had to work to find her voice. An array of retorts formed in her head, but by then Millie had walked out of the barracks.

Lucy jumped in, overly cheery. "I don't know about you ladies, but I'm rightly famished."

Virginia replied with a smile, one that wasn't entirely feigned. Her father had taught her that acts of success ultimately trumped boasts to the effect. Thus, in that instant, she set her sights on topping that self-righteous Bennett girl in every evaluation.

The goal proved more challenging than anticipated.

As it turned out, Millie could hold her own in any aircraft the instructors threw her way. Skill-wise, she and Virginia were a relative match. "Not bad," Virginia said to her once in passing, after Millie sailed through her flight on an AT-6. Millie paused for a beat, clearly surprised by the compliment. Her lips had just curved upward when Virginia added, "For a farm girl, that is."

It was a petty jab Virginia immediately regretted. But before she could say as much, Millie glared with disdain and marched away, leaving a solid barricade in her wake.

In the months that followed, whether in the barracks, mess hall, or classroom, even waiting on the flight line, the two made a point of avoiding all contact. A running joke, Virginia heard, was that the temperature fell ten degrees whenever they inhabited the same area. Not to say Millie was overly chummy with the others. Although in cordial fashion, she invariably declined invites for any group outings: evenings at a picture show, Sunday suppers with local residents, formal dances with eager Army cadets. Evidently she preferred to stay in the barracks, alone, writing letters home or scribbling in her diary.

Then, at the start of the fifth month, it happened: Millie Bennett failed a check.

On a regular basis, the women were tested on their ability to fly a wide range of Army aircraft. The first failure earned a warning. A second one sent the pilot packing that very day. The thought that Millie might soon "wash out" gave Virginia a sense of satisfaction.

Hours later, at lights-out, this was the feeling that carried Virginia off to sleep.

It seemed mere seconds had passed when her eyes snapped open to a room draped in darkness. Unsure what had woken her, she listened closely, hearing only the soft rush of her roommates' breaths. She rolled onto her side, adjusted her pillow, and noticed Millie's cot stood empty.

Just then, a sound came from the latrine, like the clearing of a person's throat. No doubt it was a similar noise that had disturbed Virginia's rest.

Could Millie not manage to be quieter?

With a grumble, Virginia flipped the other way. She closed her eyes before another sound reached out. This time it resembled a wheeze.

Perhaps Millie suffered from asthma, an affliction Virginia recalled from a classmate in grade school. Instinct took hold and launched Virginia to her feet. She hurried into the restroom, where the glaring light forced her to squint. Through the dots in her vision she found Millie seated on the floor. The girl was hunched in a ball, forehead on the knees of her nightdress.

Virginia knelt in a panic. "Are you having trouble breathing? Should I go fetch someone?"

Slowly Millie raised her head. Tears streaked her face. Her breaths indeed were short but solely from sobbing. "It's too much," she said in a whisper. "I can't . . . do it anymore . . ."

Virginia surveyed the books on the floor, the manuals they had been tasked with cramming. Atop the pile was Millie's diary, splayed open, exposing her private words. But those words were not recordings of her life. Instead, they were centered on aircrafts, from facts and formulas to sketches of instruments.

Suddenly Virginia realized: all those evenings when the other girls hit the town, Millie had stayed to study.

With a single month until graduation, every trainee was feeling the pressure. Of their initial class, only two-thirds remained. It was not unusual to see a pilot shedding tears from nerves or dread. Yet somehow the sight of Millie breaking down melted Virginia's heart, and with it her defenses. The truth of the matter was, Virginia could barely remember what had prompted their grudge from the start.

Millie wiped her cheeks with the back of her hand. She released a calming exhale.

In the silence, Virginia settled at Millie's side and picked up a manual. The pages were dog-eared, the margins filled with notes. "Jeez, Millie, why didn't you just tell me you needed help?"

A dry laugh shot from Millie's mouth.

Virginia leveled a smile at the obvious. "Fair enough," she said. "Why not another girl, then? You've seen plenty of us quizzing each other."

Millie reclined against the wall. Following a pause, she said, "I guess, where I come from, asking for help doesn't come easy."

Virginia gave a nod. She could understand allowing pride the upper hand. It was the reason she herself had not dared, before now, to attempt a truce.

"Where is that, anyway?" Virginia inquired.

"Where's what?"

"Your hometown." How strange that in all these months—the two of them sleeping, eating, breathing just a few yards apart—Virginia did not know even this much.

Before speaking, Millie appeared to gauge the sincerity of the question. "Dover, Ohio. Not far from Alliance." She added pointedly, "Where I don't live on a farm."

Virginia grinned, not fighting it this time. "Yes, well. I suppose we're both guilty of jumping to conclusions about each other. Wouldn't you say?"

Millie did not answer, though her chin raised and lowered just enough to pass for agreement.

Virginia ran her fingertips over the manual in her hand, the wrinkles and curled edges. Her own manuals had fared no better. "You know, Millie, if it's any consolation, I'm personally thankful we didn't start off on the right foot."

Millie narrowed her eyes, dubious. "Why's that?"

"Because, more than anything else, trying to keep up with you has made me a better pilot." And that was the honest-to-goodness truth.

Millie digested this for a moment, and an air of confidence seeped back into her eyes. She shrugged and said, "You're not too bad yourself." But then clarified: "For a brainless model, that is."

Virginia's smile dropped, along with her jaw, and for the first time at Avenger Field she heard Millie laugh. It was an infectious sound that caused Virginia to giggle, cut short by her recollection of the other women sleeping.

"Shhh," Virginia said, not to stop their conversation, but to resume it in a hush. As if meeting for the first time, she wondered about the path that had led the girl here. "So, tell me, Millie Bennett, whatever made you want to fly?"

At the sheer mention of the topic, like a flame to a wick, Millie's face gained a glow. Her standard edge continued to soften. "There was this barnstormer," she said. "He'd swoop over our town and burp the throttle. Folks—mostly kids—would race to the field where he'd landed. My brothers and me would all line up to pay for a ride. I was ten the first time Pop let me go up. And, well . . . I guess you could say, part of me never came down." She seemed to catch her own sentimentality and pulled back a little. "After that, I saved every penny I could from working at my dad's general store. When I was old enough, I hired the same barnstormer for lessons. Never thought I'd be flying for the military, though—not till Pearl Harbor, when my cousin went down with the USS *California*."

Virginia covered her mouth, taken aback. "Oh, Millie . . . that's terrible. I'm so sorry."

The memory of the tragedy played across Millie's face. The cause of her initial attitude, her resentment toward leisurely pilots, at last gained clarity.

"What about you?" Millie asked, either curious or diverting. "When'd you get the itch to fly?"

Virginia had to collect her thoughts. The impetus behind her own journey paled in comparison. "It actually never occurred to me until my third year at Cornell," she admitted, recalling the scene. "I was in the library, preparing for an exam, when I overheard a girl at the next table. She was going on and on about how the government was charging college students just forty dollars for flight lessons. But the guy she was with, he told her not to be a dimwit. That gals are meant to be stewardesses, not pilots."

Long before then, Virginia had been intrigued by articles about Amelia Earhart's feats, though no more than the next person. If anything, the woman's mysterious disappearance had served as a deterrent against following her lead. But in that moment, hearing of yet another way in which females were expected to behave, which careers were too ambitious, and how foolish it was to want for more, Virginia felt an inner fuse spark to life. Her brother, even at nine years her junior, was already viewed as a future doctor or leader by any number of guests at her family's regular dinner parties. Virginia, on the other hand, like one of the art pieces in her parents' Manhattan home, was a collectible to be auctioned. *My, what a lovely face. What exceptional poise. No doubt a fine husband will snatch her right up!*

Virginia's jaw would clench behind her smile. She had already surrendered her aspirations of an Engineering degree, despite her fascination with how things worked, and settled for the more "practical" major of Home Economics. One could say she'd been in training for the role of a professional housewife, destined to marry a man who, like the boy in the library, believed she was there to serve, never steer.

"I signed up for lessons the very next day," she said to Millie. "Of course, that was after I marched over and told that fellow what he could do with his theory." It had not been her most articulate speech, but the guy's stunned expression was ample reward.

At this, Millie smiled in approval and a comfortable silence drifted in. There it remained, pleasant as a summer breeze, until Virginia refocused.

"All right. Enough of this chitchat."

Millie scrunched her brow as Virginia snatched up more books from the floor and said, "We have plenty of work to do. So, where should we start?"

"Next stop: Alliance!"

At the conductor's announcement, Virginia bristled in her seat. Her vision sharpened, snapping her free of her memories and a haze from the overnight stretch. Not even the train's rhythmic rocking had eased her restlessness. She pulled out her powder compact and touched up her makeup, attempting to conceal the dark patches beneath her eyes.

Through the window, clouds sieved early afternoon rays, producing a mix of yellow and gray. Small clusters of buildings transformed the rural landscape. She felt the wheels begin to slow.

Clickety-clack . . .

Clickety-clack . . .

Once more she was twelve years old, riding the Thunderbolt in Coney Island. Her roller-coaster cart had plodded up the steep incline, and her stomach became a bundle of knots. With her first crush seated beside her, however—a daredevil of a boy named Neal Langtree—she had disguised her fear with a brave face. Same as now.

She retrieved her travel bag from the rack above.

Clickety-clack . . .

Clickety . . . clack . . .

The locomotive came to a stop and released a heavy sigh, as if having held its breath since leaving New York. When Virginia disembarked, a young boy in overalls a size too small rushed by in a flurry.

"Auntie!" He threw his arms around a woman from the next train car. Her hat and cape distinguished her as a member of the Army Nurse Corps. A trio of adults caught up and showered her with adoration, their pride for her service shining bright on their faces.

The sight gnawed at Virginia—not from envy as it might have in the past, back when she yearned for equal credit; accolades for herself had come to mean little. Rather she felt a rise of resentment on behalf of those whose sacrifice would never receive due honors. No flags. No parades. No name etched on a plaque.

Shoving down the thought, she resumed her mission. With guidance from a ticket clerk, she confirmed the bus number that would take her to Dover.

Too soon for her to reconsider, the bus rolled up with a shriek of its brakes. She climbed on board, paid her fare, and nearly fell into her seat as the vehicle rumbled onward. The bus was no more than half full, the windows wide open, but still humidity clung to the air, thick and warm as winter fur.

Virginia shed her sweater, tucked it into her luggage. Perspiration slid down her back.

Close to an hour trudged by as riders stepped on, stepped off. Virginia's eyelids grew heavy until another steely shriek alerted her of the impending stop, the one she had been waiting for. She had a mere instant to decide. If she stayed on, the bus would swing her back to the station. Easy as pie, she could hop on a train and return to her parents' home. She could uphold her façade of normalcy, like Greta Garbo performing on cue. A marionette, hanging by a single string.

She's still not herself, she'd heard her mother whisper, just a week earlier. Late one evening, from the hallway outside of Virginia's room, the observation had slipped under the door, a frustrated, helpless rasp.

Now, now, Virginia's father had replied quietly, a professional tone honed for next of kin. *Everybody heals at their own pace. She'll find her way. She just needs time.*

But—if we were firmer, pressed her to talk about it. Perhaps if we urged her to go and see Millie . . . The rest trailed away, and Virginia, cocooned in her coverlet, had envisioned her father ushering his wife off to their room for the night.

The suggestion was far from a new concept to Virginia. Yet hearing it aloud had affirmed the idea, and after that night she could not stamp it out. She spoke to no one of her travel plans, leaving only a note on her pillow stating her destination.

There was no need to explain.

The stocky driver now opened the bus door. Virginia could already picture the look of anticipation on her mother's face upon Virginia's return. The curiosity. The hope.

She gathered her things and hastened outside. The transport drove away, spouting a puff of acrid gray smoke.

A mix of shops and houses lined the street. Nearby, clusters of trees ran along the Tuscarawas River.

Aided by a map, she navigated her way through the town. The Bennett family's address burned in her pocket. How many hours had young Millie spent on these streets, waiting for a barnstormer to zoom overhead?

Many blocks and several turns later, green grass filled a wide stretch. A park, Virginia assumed, with its scattering of trees. But upon her approach, she realized what she had found. Her heart hammered in her chest. The map quivered in her hand.

In a town of this size, there would be but one cemetery.

One resting place for Millie.

Virginia had intended to come here. Of course she always had. Yet she had envisioned paying a visit to Millie's father first. It was best, she had been taught, to start with the most challenging task. Only now was it clear: Ranking one above the other was ludicrous. Both confrontations filled her with an equal level of dread.

In the distance, an elderly woman stood before a grave, whispering prayers into a rosary. A caretaker was on his knees pulling weeds by their roots. Off in another row, a young boy in a sailor shirt placed a little flag at the base of a headstone, a woman behind him fixed with a pensive look.

One step at a time.

Virginia set down her travel bag, its weight suddenly that of a boulder. She pushed the map into her purse, and her fingers brushed the envelope encasing Taz's letter. His voice echoed in her mind, boosting her courage, prodding her onward.

She moved with slow, deliberate steps while reading the names on the markers. The air continued to thicken, each inhale like breathing underwater. For the span of a year, she had been drowning.

And then she saw it: *Mildred Anne Bennett.*

The formality of Millie's full name solidified reality.

Virginia's pulse stalled, skipping several beats, but then returned with a vengeance and pounded in her ears. She fought to keep her knees from buckling. This time, Taz was not here to catch her.

The caretaker was tidying around Millie's grave. He glanced over his shoulder and issued a polite nod. He was twisting back to his work when he stopped.

"Virginia?" he said in a husky tone, and her thoughts spun.

"How—did you—?"

"I've seen you in the photo. Of you and Millie . . . from her valuables."

The obvious struck then. This man was not a groundskeeper, but Millie Bennett's father. Virginia scrambled to recall the speech she had prepared for this day, for this moment.

Wistfully, he rose to his feet. He had kind eyes and a small paunch and his hair was salt-and-peppered. "My Millie, she wrote so much about you. I'd always hoped to make your acquaintance one day." He wiped his palms on his pants and extended a hand.

When she did not meet his greeting—because physically she could not bring herself to—he stared, not understanding.

But soon he would.

With the deepest of breaths, Virginia gathered her words. At last, she let them spill free.

———

The day Virginia and Millie graduated, after six months at Avenger Field, had been a bittersweet celebration. It was certainly a thrill, being congratulated in person by the director of the program, legendary pilot Jacqueline Cochran. But the question of where Virginia and Millie would be sent was an unsettling one. More aptly, the possibility they might not be stationed together.

Their first study session in the latrine had served as the initial thread connecting them, but thereafter, it was understanding and admiration, laughter and late-night talks, that wove a braid thicker than a seaman's rope. And always there was the shared love of flying.

While Virginia had taught Millie insider tips for cramming details from a textbook, Millie helped Virginia to trust her instincts in the air, to know when to follow her gut. They were a perfect complement, in many ways as different as two people could be, but where it mattered they were one and the same.

Their relationship had done such a swift about-face, Lucy often teased, "Mercy, my neck is aching from the whiplash." Of course, that did not stop the woman from rejoicing over news that all three of them, along with a few others in the group, were to be stationed together in North Carolina.

Unfortunately, upon arriving at Camp Davis, they discovered the base had been dubbed "Wolf Swamp," and for good reason. Surrounded by thousands of airmen, the two dozen female pilots were clearly viewed as lambs in a pen. Their presence, to most, served one of two purposes: a broad to belittle, or a skirt to date. Yet ever gradually, with their completion of advanced training, the girls earned respect by allowing their aviation skills to silence the snipes. Millie's sharp tongue further helped in that area.

As for courting, some of the gals relished their expanse of options. Especially after half a year spent at Avenger Field, known as "Cochran's Convent" for its strict regulations on romance. Those rules had suited Virginia just fine, as any distractions held no appeal. Her transfer to Camp Davis had not changed this. She was there to fly, not to land a mate. There was a real war on, after all. Real soldiers, sailors, and airmen losing their lives. And for that fact, she took great pride in her duty.

Granted, it was taxing work, ferrying aircrafts back and forth between factories and bases, from one coast to the other. It was not unusual for any of them to be assigned a single flight that multiplied into ten before finally returning to their post. Whenever Millie and Virginia had a chance to catch up, they were never short on tales, but typically nodded off on their cots before finishing a full recount.

With a schedule like that, who had time for a steady?

This was the explanation Virginia gave every time she declined a date. Most fellows accepted her answer and went on their way. But not Nick Tazzara, better known as "Taz." On a clear April morning right after breakfast, he approached her outside the mess hall and, for the third time, invited her to a night of swing dancing at the Officers' Club. Despite his dark, handsome looks and emanating charm, she responded with her standard brush-off.

"So, I'll try again some other day," he said, unfazed.

"I suppose you can," she said, walking away with Millie. "But the answer will be the same."

"Well, then . . . I'd better get creative with my asking."

She wasn't sure what that entailed until the next evening. Fresh from a flight, she returned to the barracks to find a white four-petal flower on her pillow. Scribed on a note tied to the twig was her name on one side and *Taz* on the other. One of the girls recognized the gift as a dogwood, the official state flower of Virginia. The sentiment teetered between sweet and corny, but at least he was resourceful. Who knew where he was able to locate such a specific variety.

The following day a second dogwood lay on her pillow, this time with *Dear* on the front of the card, and on the back, simply *me*. Its recipient and sender evident, there was apparently no need for specifics. But to Virginia, his addressing her as *Dear* struck as much too familiar. How many other girls had he successfully baited with this approach?

At the discovery of a third flower, Virginia warily picked up the card to review both sides: *date* and *please*. Nothing more. His literacy level appeared no higher than that of Tarzan, and his note the next evening only upheld the notion.

"*Allow* and *1930*?" she read aloud. "What on earth am I supposed to allow at nineteen thirty hours?" She groaned, tossing the note aside, exhausted from the workday. "The guy acts like he was just *born* in 1930."

"You know what's funny." Millie paused while hanging laundered clothes in her locker. "He sorta reminds me of this boy I knew in third grade. Sometimes he got his words all mixed up. Course that was after he got kicked in the head by a goat."

Virginia couldn't imagine the Army allowing a man with brain damage to fly their expensive contraptions. Then again, she had heard Taz was a test pilot. Anyone willing to serve as a guinea pig had to be short a few marbles.

"Mixed up . . ." Lucy repeated. "That's it!"

Virginia raised a brow at her friend, who was finishing a cross-word on her cot. It was Lucy's usual way of relaxing, as she'd claimed her mama insisted an idle mind left room for the devil's work.

"Let me see those notes again," Lucy said, shuffling over. "All of them together. From the start till now."

The only thing Virginia wanted to do was bathe and collapse on her mattress, but she knew better than to resist Lucy's persistence. Once Virginia had handed over the cards, Lucy began to write on a piece of paper. She tilted her head, then erased and scribbled some more. "I knew it," she said to herself. "It's a scramble of sorts. Lookee here."

Though reluctant, Virginia followed Millie in peeking over Lucy's shoulder.

Dear Virginia
Please allow me date 1930

Taz

"You gotta admit," Millie said, "the fella did come through on the creative front."

Virginia rolled her eyes. "Too bad he's not coherent."

"Or . . ." Lucy added, "maybe he's just not done yet."

And she was right.

Every evening, more girls in the barracks circled around to read the additional clues. By Saturday, Virginia deciphered a request for *the pleasure of a date on Sunday at 1930.*

Pressure mounted for her to accept, even from Millie, who volunteered to take Virginia's flight if she were assigned to an overnighter, or find someone else who would. Given all of Taz's efforts, coupled with Virginia's upbringing, it seemed discourteous not to appease the airman with a single outing. Besides, his name was not among those listed on the wall by the phone, a *Do Not Date* compilation from fellow women pilots.

And so, when Sunday evening arrived, Virginia opted to wear basic trousers, a cotton blouse and cardigan, and the lightest swipe of lipstick. "Just because I'm going doesn't mean I'm getting dolled up," she told Lucy, who had urged her to at least don a dress for the occasion.

Millie laughed. "Looks like my stubbornness *and* fashion sense are rubbing off."

Waiting outside, Virginia could feel a throng of stares behind her, unsubtle spies in the windows of her barracks. She regarded her watch. He was seven minutes late. Three more and the date was off. Already this was turning out to be a huge mistake.

Just then, Taz strode up in his khakis, his Army-issue duffel in hand.

"Sorry I kept you waiting. Had to snag a few supplies for the show."

"The show?"

"Uh-huh." He did not elaborate, merely offered his elbow. "Shall we?"

She had every right to be agitated. But how could she be, given the smile that lit up his eyes, a rather mischievous but genuine glimmer. Not to mention his air of familiarity. While this might have been off-putting from another stranger, something about his words, his tone, the way he angled his arm in waiting made her far more comfortable than it should have.

Against her better judgment, Virginia accepted.

They zigzagged through the base, making small talk, with no hints of their destination or what "supplies" filled his bag. Compared to her usual dates back in New York, this one promised to be wonderfully adventurous—not that she would say so. It would be wrong to lead him on. She would only be joining him for one evening.

They continued past the airstrip and into the field, ending at a long line of trees. Taz dropped his bag, out of which he unpacked a pair of Army blankets for a picnic on the grass. There was no champagne or wine, no stuffed olives or caviar. He had brought beers and Reuben sandwiches and Twinkies for dessert—which just so happened to be her favorite childhood treat. Everything about the meal broke the mold of expectation. It was free of pretention and . . . perfect.

"I thought you said there'd be a show," she reminded him, once they had settled on their respective blankets.

"Oh, there will be." He handed her a bottle that he clinked with his own, and they traded smiles before downing a few swallows.

As the sun slid away, purple and pink streaked an orange sky. In the distance appeared the silhouette of a B-17. Its four engines thrummed as it approached for landing.

"Just look at that," Taz murmured, his gaze on the sleek bird. He straightened, attention rapt, as one would respond to the tuning sounds of an orchestra minutes before a concert.

That's when it dawned on Virginia that the show, in fact, had commenced.

"Amazing, isn't it?" he said. "That a big chunk of metal like that can even get off the ground, let alone soar through the sky?"

The awe in his voice revived memories of Virginia's first flight, the adrenaline rush, the splendor of it all. Though her love of flying had not tapered since that day, she'd begun to take for granted the miracle of the feat.

Together they grazed on their sandwiches and watched aircrafts rolling in. Raised in Connecticut, the only son of an engineer, Taz explained that this had been his favorite pastime with his late father.

Virginia warmed from knowing he wanted to share it with her—but then wondered how many other girls he had escorted to this place, softening them up with the exact same story. Perhaps the flower deliveries and scrambled invitation, too, were not as unique as she had assumed.

"So, I take it this is your usual spot for a date," she said.

He crinkled his brow, deciphering the implication, and shook his head. "I come here all the time, but it's the first time with anyone else." The mischief in his eyes had slipped away, leaving inarguable sincerity.

Still, she remained cautious.

"What made you think I wasn't hoping for a fancy night on the town?" she asked.

He angled a glance at her clothing—reminding Virginia of her casual appearance—and shrugged. "Whenever I'd seen you around . . . you just seemed like someone who'd enjoy being here."

She pondered this, and nodded. A good guess.

They spent the rest of the evening enjoying takeoffs and landings of night training flights and learning about each other's lives. To fend off the cooling air, he draped her with his blanket, forcing them to sit close together on hers. And she was glad for it.

When it came time to leave, Taz held her hand and walked her back. So tender was his grip she dreaded pulling away. There was no good-night kiss before they parted, only his invitation for another date. Virginia agreed, this time without reservation. Then she disappeared into her barracks, where Millie awaited with a full interrogation.

Soon after, a second date followed, and a third and a fourth, until Virginia lost track of the total. Beyond plane gazing, they ate at local diners, caught picture shows in town, and even kicked up their heels now and then. There were times Virginia sensed a smidge of jealousy from Millie, an understandable reaction. But inviting her to join on occasion seemed to remedy the issue.

Their work schedules stayed rigorous, of course, often one of them coming when the other was going. But as a result, every minute Virginia and Taz shared, every kiss and embrace, was cherished tenfold.

Then, in September, Taz learned he would be sent to Arizona to test new aircraft models and would not return for a good two months. While Virginia knew the war effort had to take priority, the idea of their extended separation caused a sinking in her chest.

On what was to be their last day together, she had been assigned to tow a target behind a P-40, giving ground troops the opportunity for shooting practice. However, her claim of feeling ill succeeded in keeping her day open.

Stealthily, as not to be seen, she made her way to the trees by the airfield. She arrived at their usual spot right on time, but Taz was nowhere in sight. An A-24 roared its engine and sped off the airstrip.

Could Taz have been ordered to take an earlier flight? Had he left without a chance to inform her of the change? Her throat tightened, trapping a breath in her lungs.

Something white fell from above and brushed her cheek. She snapped her head up and discovered a hand sprinkling petals. From a dogwood, no doubt. She spun around to face Taz with a laugh of relief.

"You're a goof," she said, giving him a light shove.

He kept her palms on the chest of his uniform, his heartbeat pronounced beneath. "But you love me anyway," he said, and she affirmed this by pressing her lips to his.

She was determined to savor the moment, to not think about how much she would miss this, or dwell on her fear that one of his test flights could go terribly wrong.

When they drew apart, he whispered, "Follow me."

She smiled, aware he did not have to ask, and trailed him deeper into the cluster of trees. In a small clearing were several blankets, as he typically laid out, but this time with a bottle of wine and a bouquet of dogwoods displayed in a vase.

"My, my, Lieutenant," she said. "If I'd known this was such a lavish event, I would have worn a nicer dress." She knelt down to admire the flowers and noticed several cards dangling. "Love notes, too, I see. You must really be worried I'll step out on you while you're away." She lifted the first two cards to read: *Virginia* and *Me*.

The clues rang as familiar until reaching the last one: *Marry*.

She mentally reversed the order of the words and swung toward Taz, now down on a knee beside her. Her pulse skittered and goose bumps rose on her skin. She stared into his eyes, seeking confirmation that the proposal was real.

"I love you so much, V." Gingerly he grasped her hand. "When I come back in two months, will you do me the honor of—"

"Yes," she said, even before he could finish.

He heaved a sigh and scooped her into his arms. She closed her eyes, absorbing the warmth of his breath on her cheek. In a flash the whole world made sense. Every detail had found a place, oddly even the flaws. She would not have thought it possible to feel so complete. But already she could see her future built with this man. Her fiancé. Her groom.

She held him closer than ever. Soon Taz was kissing her neck, then the slope leading to her shoulder. Her mind started to drift, blurring at the edges—until a noise sliced through the haze.

A siren.

The warning of a crash.

Instantly sobered, she and Taz snapped their attention toward the base. Trees obstructed the view. They gathered themselves, exchanging worried looks, and hurried into the open. At the far end of the airstrip, a plane had angled into a ditch. Orange fire sprouted from the engine. Ground crewmen raced to reach the P-40, its tow target strewn behind.

A P-40 . . . a Warhawk . . . the type of aircraft Virginia was supposed to have flown today.

The assignment Millie had taken in her stead.

"No," Virginia breathed, imagining, comprehending. "No, no, no . . ." She scrambled down the tarmac, yelling over and over, "Millie! Millie!"

Virginia vaguely heard Taz calling her own name, but she did not slow, did not answer. She had to reach Millie first. Why wasn't the girl bailing out?

The siren continued to blare. Officers shouted orders. Panic seized every inch of the area. Virginia was halfway to the aircraft when a fiery burst exploded, devouring the enclosed cockpit. She could hear a woman's screams. Were they her own or Millie's? Were they both?

From behind, someone's arms enwrapped her—it was Taz—preventing her from lunging forward. Even from here she could feel the heat of the flames.

Servicemen worked frantically to extinguish the fire. Virginia struggled to free herself as tears stung her eyes. Every second became an infinite stretch of terror, a nightmare from which she could not wake. The stench of smoke and gasoline invaded her nose, her mouth, her lungs, but it was the thought of her friend trapped and burning that curdled Virginia's stomach. She strained to hear Millie, the scantest sound of hope.

But there was nothing.

Oh, God, there was nothing.

"Millie!" Virginia tried again to break free, yet Taz held her tighter.

"She's gone, V," he said hoarsely by her ear. "She's gone . . ."

The ground crew's expressions, of shock and sadness and resignation, served as a maddening testament.

Slabs of guilt piled on Virginia as if dropped from the sky. When her knees gave way, she collapsed in Taz's arms. Despite the support and comfort he offered in that moment, and then from afar in the weeks that followed, she rejected such undeserved tokens. For on that day, on that tarmac, her soul had retreated into itself, and there it remained as fellow WASPs wept and hugged. They cursed the engine fire and faulty latch that had sealed Millie's end. They even took up a collection, wanting to contribute to the transfer of her remains. After all, they were mere civilians, warranting not a single benefit from the military.

No one actually asked Virginia if she would care to be the escort. It was assumed. And why wouldn't she?

"It's time to go, honey," Lucy said to Virginia, who sat in the barracks, staring at Millie's vacant cot. All of Millie's possessions sat in a suitcase, ready for the trip. How many times at Avenger Field had Virginia wished the "farm girl" would simply pack her things and go? Yet now, there was nothing she would not give to have Millie back, if only for a day, an hour, a minute.

"Sugar?" Lucy stepped closer. "If you don't leave soon, you'll miss the train to Ohio. Millie's family . . . they'll be waiting."

Virginia attempted to move but failed. It was as though she had just ferried an aircraft from one of the factories in the northern states. In open-air cockpits, she would wear wool from head to toe, underclothing included. Still, the cold would sneak into her bones. Often, after landing on base, her suit had been so frozen she could not stand without help.

A similar, debilitating chill set in as she imagined meeting Millie's father. She pictured him at the station, placing a trembling hand on the lid of the casket. As a widower, he had already lost so much. How could Virginia look him in the eye? What right would she have to console him?

"I can't go," she managed to say, her jaw tight as a vice. "I just can't . . ."

Lucy presumed grief alone rendered Virginia incapable of making the trek. Always the compassionate sort, the woman patted Virginia's shoulder and volunteered to serve as the escort. Virginia did not argue, and by the next morning she herself departed on a train as well, but bound for Manhattan. She left behind her job as a WASP and most of her belongings. Even her shiny silver wings. Nothing seemed valuable enough to pack.

The memories, however, followed her home.

They stalked her in hallways and lurked in corners. They loomed in the spaces between words. No matter how many times Virginia reviewed the tragedy, there was no logic to be found. There was only sorrow and anger and guilt. Plans for a simple picnic had led to her dearest friend's death. Sure, Millie had been quick to agree to fill in for the flight, perhaps suspecting the intended proposal. But that did not change the fact that she was never meant to be on that plane.

Was it any wonder, then, that Virginia could not follow through with the engagement? One injustice did not warrant a second. Had she conceded to Taz's appeals, he would have been marrying a ghost. For though Virginia's body had escaped ruin, her soul remained trapped in that cockpit. Her zest for life had burned to ashes. She yearned to explain this to Taz, but there were no words for such a notion. This was the reason, once back with her family, she did not answer his letters or calls. Nor did she so much as venture downstairs when he appeared at her home during his furlough in December, and then again in March.

From the haven of her bedroom, she caught her mother's apology. "I'm afraid she's just not up for a visit today."

"Did you tell her it's me?" Taz asked, and the plea in his tone wrung Virginia's heart.

"I'm sorry for your troubles, Lieutenant, coming all this way. Perhaps another day would be better."

At the heavy pause, Virginia moved to her door, hand on the knob, torn by her longing to walk through. But the mere sight of him, she knew, would bring them together. And that reunion would signify officially moving on, or, even worse, picking up from where they left off. As if Millie's death was so easily brushed aside.

"Please, then," Taz said, a drop in his voice, "give this to her for me."

"Of course," her mother said, and seconds later Virginia heard the front door close.

What he left was a letter, his final effort. A letter Virginia had since read a hundred times over. Although brief, it conveyed love and hope and the sadness of parting. The same emotions that had brought her to Ohio, to see Millie's father, to face Millie's grave.

————————

By the time Virginia finished her confession, tears poured from her eyes. An unstoppable stream, Mr. Bennett gazed at his daughter's grave. He had listened without interruption, and only now did he speak.

"So, you're saying it should've been you on that plane," he said, not looking up.

Virginia tried to say yes but only edged out a nod.

He took in a breath, pondering, hands hitched on the hips of his trousers. Finally he met her gaze. "I'd like you to come with me," he said. "Family's gathering for supper, and I think you ought to be there."

It was not a question. It was a ruling already made.

The thought of repeating the admission to more of Millie's loved ones caused anxiety to ball in Virginia's throat. But she swallowed hard, forcing it down, and yielded her agreement.

She trailed the man through the cemetery, clutching her purse to her middle. She hazarded a glance back at Millie's grave, but just once from a distance. When she went to pick up her travel bag, Mr. Bennett assumed the duty, and Virginia was in no place to object. She dried her cheeks with her palm, aware she must look a fright, but her appearance mattered little.

They walked in silence through a neighborhood of modest, weathered houses. Before long, he turned at a slate blue two-storied home. He led her onto a porch that hosted a planter box and a faded gray rocking chair.

"Wait here," he said, and disappeared inside.

The minutes that followed passed with all the speed of slogging through mud. Behind the rooftop, the sun slinked downward. Sheets on the clothesline gained an eerie glow.

Virginia was struck by an urge to flee, but penance required she stay.

Mr. Bennett returned and held the screen door open. "Come in," he said.

Girding herself, Virginia proceeded into the entry. Bread and roasted meat scented the air. She turned toward a mingling of voices and discovered a small crowd in the living room. The conversations halted. All eyes trained on her, Virginia became the target of a firing squad and now recognized the appeal of a blindfold.

An elderly woman in a floral apron took steps forward. She did not rest until a foot away from Virginia. Behind her glasses, her eyes glimmered with moisture and her lower lip shook. "I'm Bess," she said. "Millie's grandmother."

Again, the wringing returned to Virginia's heart. It was no secret how close Millie had been to the woman. Virginia gripped her purse tighter, uncertain how much Mr. Bennett had shared with the group.

But then Bess laid her hands over Virginia's, and her mouth curved up at the corners. "We're just so pleased you could join us—on such a special occasion. Millie would be tickled."

A special occasion . . .

Naturally, for the anniversary of Millie's passing, they had gathered in remembrance. A framed photograph of Millie stared from the brick mantel over the fireplace. Virginia should not have chosen today, of all days, for a visit.

Bess declared to the group: "Well, don't be shy, all. Come meet Millie's most cherished friend in the world."

Virginia swiftly angled toward Mr. Bennett, seeking a cue of how to respond. Was this to be a means of atonement?

He offered a nod, a signal for her to oblige.

And so she did. One by one she exchanged introductions with relatives and friends. They were brothers and cousins and schoolmates of Millie's. Each of them filed past with sheer kindness in their greetings, shaking her hand, some giving hugs. It was clear they did not know better.

"Tommy," Bess called out while removing her apron. "Bring a chair down from the attic for Virginia. And you place it right next to mine."

A tingling of panic rose in Virginia. How could she sit at their table, share a meal with those she had inadvertently wronged? She had accomplished what she'd come for. It was time to depart for the bus. A motel in Alliance would suffice until the morning train.

She scanned the room for Mr. Bennett. Not seeing him, she embarked on a search for her luggage and found it in the entry closet.

"You're not leaving yet, I hope." The comment turned her to Mr. Bennett, who had just descended the stairs.

She was not proud of slipping out, but staying felt grossly inappropriate. "Mr. Bennett, I'm grateful for the invitation. But . . . under the circumstances . . ."

After a pause, he released a sigh and looked down at the photograph in his hand. "At least take this with you. I know my Millie would've wanted you to have it." He handed her a snapshot of his daughter on graduation day. At Avenger Field, she posed in her uniform beside the propeller of a P-51 Mustang. Virginia had never seen Millie beam so brightly, and the memory again summoned tears to Virginia's eyes.

"This here picture isn't meant to make things worse," Mr. Bennett explained. "It's to remind you that she passed away doing a job she loved more than anything in life. And from what I gathered, she never would've had that without you."

Indeed, there was truth in his claim. Nonetheless, it did not bear the power to dissolve Virginia's guilt.

"Let me just say this," he added. "When my wife died, me and the kids spent a good chunk of time—me most of all—wondering if there's something we could've done different. But in the end, we learned the Lord makes those choices, not us. It'd be flat-out wrong to think otherwise. And it'd be a real disservice to Millie if we wasted our lives dwelling on her passing. Especially knowing she's at peace with her mother now."

For a long moment, Virginia stood there, absorbing the message. A father's genuine tribute. A stranger's gift of redemption.

"Time for supper!" Bess announced, and the herd headed into the dining room.

Mr. Bennett gazed at Virginia, awaiting her decision.

She glanced at her travel bag, then back at Millie's photo. The light in the girl's eyes projected a look of hope that Virginia could not deny. "Sir," she said finally, "I'd love to stay, if that's still all right."

A smile widened the man's lips. "We'd like that a lot."

Around the table, and in chairs lining the dining room walls, the guests settled in their seats. Once the blessing was given and plates filled with food, stories about Millie began to flow.

They were tales from her childhood, of "losing" her shoes in the creek when she preferred to go barefoot, and sneaking taffy from her father's store, betrayed by her blue-stained teeth. Gradually they moved on to her teenage years, which few in town thought she would reach on account of her daring antics. She was fearless and fun, but also loyal and kind. Taking the fall for her younger brother, when the teacher raised a rod in punishment for a prank, served as one of many examples.

Virginia had only intended to listen, but ultimately, with coaxing from Bess, she found herself describing a night involving a tad too much whiskey. Somehow Millie, Lucy, and Virginia had landed on a nightclub stage, belting out what was surely a ghastly version of "Straighten Up and Fly Right."

By the end of the evening, everyone in the room had laughed, more than half had dried their eyes. The pain was still there—how could it not be? But there was happiness, too, as Millie's limited number of years on this earth did not reflect the fullness of her life.

Best of all—perhaps from Bess's smile that perfectly matched Millie's, or from the regalement of so many tales, or maybe from all that love for a single person in one room—for those few hours around the table, it felt as if Millie herself was there.

At the family's insistence, Virginia agreed to stay overnight; the last bus for the day was long gone. But sleep, despite her exhaustion, did not come readily. She tossed and turned in the guest bed, the house now dark and still, until she realized what was left to do.

With a flashlight from a kitchen drawer, Virginia tiptoed out of the house and made her way back to Millie's grave. It was a moment for them alone. There Virginia sat, the cool grass beneath her, a milky moon shining down, and she whispered, "I miss you, Millie Bennett. I miss you so very much."

Yet even as she said this, pressing Millie's photo to her chest, she understood that her friend would never truly be far away.

————————

"We're sure glad you came," Mr. Bennett said the next morning as Virginia's bus rolled up. "Promise you'll keep in touch, now."

"I will," she said with a smile. It was a promise she planned to keep.

Once seated on the bus, she waved good-bye through the window and watched Millie's hometown shrink from view. Although a single night could not entirely heal a wound, the rawness had notably lessened.

She opened her purse to deposit change left from her fare, and again she spotted Taz's letter. For the first time in months, she felt a desire—no, a need—to unfold the page. She ran her fingers over his words, hearing Taz speak them in her mind.

My dearest V,

I'm truly sorry for all you've gone through. If I knew how to stop you from hurting, I would do it in an instant. I can only tell you I love you. Please remember, no matter where our lives lead, you'll always have a place in my heart.

Yours always,
Taz

After all this time, he had every right to have moved on. Virginia had shut him out. Perhaps part of her, though irrationally, had even blamed him for the loss. Logic told her to let him be, that he deserved a girl who wasn't tainted by tragedy. A clearheaded girl who, quite possibly, was already in his life.

And yet, at the train station, instead of a ticket bound for New York, Virginia could purchase a trip headed south, back to Camp Davis, where Taz was stationed. Assuming he had not been transferred . . .

No, it was foolish. Traveling all that way with so many factors unknown. Virginia shook off the idea. Writing a letter would be sensible. Or reaching him by phone. Even a telegram would be wiser. She hadn't the faintest notion what she would say on paper, much less in person.

But then, through the thought, another voice interrupted, familiar and strong.

Trust your instincts, she heard Millie say. And only then did it occur to Virginia that maybe, all along, the advice was intended for more than flying.

Tin Town

Amanda Hodgkinson

Over seventy thousand British "GI brides" emigrated to the U.S. in the 1940s. The war brides, some of them as young as seventeen, left their homes and families behind knowing they might never see them again, and travelled to America in the brave pursuit of love. My short story "Tin Town" is humbly dedicated to these women.

I didn't look out of the window of the taxi when Mother told me to. Just like I hadn't wanted to look earlier in the day when we stood on the deck of a ship carrying thousands of American servicemen home after the war, and had the first glimpse of the New York coastline rising like a hazy grey mist on the horizon.

Mother sat beside me in the taxi, her head angled upwards, staring wide-eyed at the city, holding her hat as if she feared it might be blown away. Mrs. Lewis sat on the other side of me. She, too, urged me to look at the sights. She wanted me to see all the people walking the wide pavements. "I mean the *sidewalk*," she corrected herself. She pointed out big motor cars and advertising billboards, the sky-high buildings, so tall they hid the sun, throwing shadows over the streets, all the metal fire escape balconies like jumbled birdcages hanging from their walls. I kept my head down and pretended not to be interested.

"Spoilsport," Mrs. Lewis said, jogging my shoulder in a familiar way. The way I knew, from growing up with five cousins, four of them boys, that siblings treated each other.

"Don't look then," she said, sticking her tongue out. "Suit yourself."

Mrs. Lewis was often childish. She had been our travelling companion on the ship, sharing a cabin with us, spreading her clothes everywhere, washing her smalls in front of us and hanging them to dry over the bunks. Mrs. Lewis claimed us as family because she and Mother were both war brides. She was plain faced and had thick ginger hair, pin curled and worn in a low side parting. She wore far too much makeup, I thought. Her cheeks were pink and dusted with powder, her mascara-thick lashes black as tar. My cousin Susan had once read me a magazine article that said nice women should always strive for a natural beauty. Obviously Mrs. Lewis didn't know this. She was very talkative, too, something else Susan's magazine said a lady should never be. Mother insisted we make allowances for Mrs. Lewis. She'd grown up poor in a crowded tenement building, an east-end waif not quite seventeen and expecting a baby when she wasn't much more than a child herself.

"Cheerio for good, old London town," Mrs. Lewis said gaily as the taxi took us on towards the train station. "So long and ta-ta for now. Molly, for goodness' sake, I can't believe your feet are that interesting. Look around you. Say hello to your new life. Say hello to New York."

I didn't want to see New York. I didn't want anything new. I wanted old. Every time I thought about how far we were from the farm, I felt my heart kick in panic, thumping my ribs like a rabbit caught in a poacher's sack. Home was miles away now. Weeks away. Ship and train and bus journeys away. No, I would not look out of the window.

"Let her alone, Betty," said Mother, patting my hand. "I expect Jack will show us around when we've got over the journey."

Mrs. Lewis announced that this was a historic moment. A very important day for us all. The day we finally put England behind us and began living in America. She could imagine herself in years to come, she said, as a very old lady, remembering all of this perfectly.

I thought that when I was old I would remember our farm and the bedroom I shared with Susan, right up in the eaves of the house where swallows nested under the thatch. I would remember nights curled in Susan's bed and the magazines she read. *Stitchcraft* and *Screenland* and *Woman's Own*, the last having a weekly romance story that she liked to read out loud to me.

I pulled my father's wristwatch from my satchel. It was set on English time so I knew it was late afternoon back in the village. Clarkie would be having a tea break at the tannery, sitting on a barrel in the factory yard by the river, smoking a cigarette. Uncle Roger would be ploughing acres that had, until the end of the war this year, been home to a USAAF airfield and three thousand American airmen. I imagined the now abandoned control tower, the Nissen huts and empty hangars. With the men and their planes gone, Uncle Roger would be working a quiet day, seagulls chasing the tractor as he returned the wartime airfield to farmland. Aunt Marion might be peeling spuds in the farmhouse kitchen with Grandma, or collecting the eggs since Mother wasn't there to do it anymore. Susan was probably out walking, pushing the ancient Silver Cross pram Clarkie had bought secondhand from the vicar's wife.

I pressed my father's watch to my ear to hear its steady ticking, as if I could hang on to the English afternoon a little longer that way. I could picture Susan clearly. Her silky head scarf fluttering around her defiant face, her good tweed coat, brought out of its mothballs for the slight chill in the air on this late September day. I imagined the oak trees towering over the lane into the village, the crunch of acorns under the pram's wheels. This was the lane where, when I was little, my father used to sit me up on the cart horse with him and we'd try and touch the curved ceiling of green leaves above our heads.

There was a footpath leading off the lane which led to a ruined farm cottage where holly bushes grew over a running stream. It had been my father and Clarkie's childhood haunt. Father had

shown my mother this secret place when they were courting, pro-
posing to her by the stream. Growing up I often played there, taking a few dolls with me for company.

When the taxi stopped at the train station, I reluctantly slipped
the watch into my schoolbag and got out of the car, helping Mrs.
Lewis take the suitcases while Mother paid the driver.

"This is not just any station," Mother said. We looked up at the
majestic building and its stone columns, tall and straight as woodland pines. Mother smiled at us. I knew she was trying to hide her
nervousness. She had a small book open in her gloved hand, a
guidebook Jack had sent. Her fingers trembled as she read from it.
"This is Grand Central Terminal," she said. "Isn't it just splendid?"

And it was. I had never seen so many people, nor a building so
elegant and fine. The three of us in our dowdy, war-rationed
clothes, all creased from too much time at sea, stood in what
Mother said was the grand concourse. The marble floors gleamed
under our travel-weary feet. Gigantic chandeliers of electric lights
glowed golden as Christmas. The glass ticket booths had queues
that merged into the thick shuffle of travellers. Railwaymen
chalked up information boards. Cigarette smoke hung in thick
clouds, and all around were voices echoing, trains being announced,
exclamations, and chatter. How Jack was going to find us here in
such noise and bustle, I had no idea.

I stared up at a ceiling as high and heavenly as Ely Cathedral
which I had once visited with Mother and Jack on a rare day out. If
all the bustling crowds had stopped still for a moment and sung
hymns together, their voices rising to the roof, then surely God
would have heard us. Maybe Clarkie and Susan might have heard
the sound, too, drifting on the wind across the ocean.

I had loved singing hymns in our village church, standing beside

Susan in the family pew. Susan was tone-deaf and only ever pretended to sing, opening and closing her mouth like a fish, trying to make me laugh. I thought of the overgrown churchyard, its ivy-covered stone walls and rickety wooden gate. The grass had been left to grow tall there during the war so it could be scythed and cut for hay, my father's gravestone hidden in a feathery green meadow.

The farther I got from home, it seemed the more I thought of it. Just then, all the bustle and movement of people rushing back and forth in the station reminded me of summer ants in our farmhouse kitchen, how they dashed around the sugar bowl, and Grandma in her jet-black mourning dress, like a giant queen ant herself, going at the little blighters with the flyswat.

I felt so homesick that I began to cry. I hurriedly wiped my face with my sleeve. I was nearly twelve years old. I never cried. Never. I had to be strong for Mother.

"I'm dying for a decent cup of tea," said Mrs. Lewis, yawning and rubbing her back. "I'm gasping. I'd even drink coffee if that's all there is."

Mother said we had to stand by the four-faced clock. That was where Jack was going to meet us. We huddled together while all around us were reunions. Soldiers and airmen came and went. They swaggered and joked, and Mrs. Lewis said they were heroes, thanks be to God and bless the memory of the ones who hadn't come back. She stared at a group of young women near us. I thought Mother might tell her it was rude to gawp, but I couldn't take my eyes off them, either. Bright as butterflies, the women had jauntily angled hats, patterned dresses, fur collars and satin coat linings, high heels, and seamed stockings. They danced into the outstretched arms of returning soldiers who lifted them up and waltzed them away. Even in their finery, none of the women were as beautiful as my mother. In her flat lace-up brogues and her dull brown felt hat with its pheasant feathers quite broken, Mother was still the prettiest English rose in the whole of New York.

"What on earth will Jimmy think when he sees me?" Mrs. Lewis wailed. "I've not changed my clothes in days. I'd say the porters here are better dressed than me."

"Jimmy will think you are blooming," said Mother, who was always kind. "You'll dazzle him, Betty. You'll see."

Mrs. Lewis was what Grandma would call *down at heel*. On the ship, Mother had darned and mended Betty Lewis's clothes, yet she still looked shabby. She was heavy with child and waddled when she walked, leaning backwards with her hand pressing into the small of her back. In her grey swing coat with its big shoulder pads and her round straw hat perched on her curls, Mrs. Lewis looked like a hand-bell, swinging back and forth.

I hoped I might be as kindhearted as Mother one day. And that I might begin to look like her and gain in prettiness. Mrs. Lewis had pointed out I must take after my father with my boyish freckles and fawn-coloured hair cut in a short bob. Mother had promised I could grow my hair once we were settled in New York. We would have a dog, too, because we'd had to leave my father's old sheepdog behind. Jack had a house out in a place called Woodside-Winfield, and it had a garden front and back. Plenty of space, Jack said, for a family dog. According to his letters, which Mother read parts of to me, I was going to make a whole heap of friends when I started school. I'd learn to love baseball and I'd spend my Saturday mornings at the movies. Jack was going to buy me pretzels and egg creams and take me to the corner candy store. He would get me Kewpie dolls and paper dolls to play with. I told Mother I'd rather watch cricket on the village green, and even though I loved the idea of paper dolls, I insisted I was too old for that kind of thing. It was cruel of me to be so rough with their dreams, but Mother said nothing. She folded the letter away and her smile went with it, tucked back into the envelope, placed into the bundle of correspondence tied with a ribbon. She suggested we think of a name for the dog when we got it.

"Imagine if our husbands don't come?" said Mrs. Lewis. Her brown eyes were glassy with tears. "What will we do?"

She'd been asking that question since we met her. On the long boat journey, lying seasick in our bunks, Mrs. Lewis had cried most days worrying about whether her Jimmy would be here to meet her.

"Now, Betty," said Mother. "Jimmy has probably been counting the days until he sees you. You're his wife. He's going to be a father, after all."

"That's the problem." Mrs. Lewis put her hand on her belly and lowered her voice. "It wasn't planned, you know. This was a mistake."

"Jimmy has responsibilities," soothed my mother. "He'll honour them, I'm sure."

"If he doesn't, I'll have to go back to London. I couldn't stand that. Think of the sorry looks I'd get in the neighbourhood. 'Poor cow,' they'll say. 'On her own with a kid, rejected by her GI husband . . .'"

I thought I would go home under any kind of circumstances, even if it hadn't been the happiest of homes we'd left behind. After my father died, Uncle Roger found it difficult to run the farm without him. Then there had been the upset with Susan. I had caused that. But still, the farm was home. It was all I had ever known, and I missed it terribly.

"We're at the mercy of our husbands," said Mrs. Lewis. "Look at you, Irene. You say Jack loves you, but what if he's changed his mind since you last saw him? You've come all this way trusting a wedding ring bought in a hurry. You've got a one-way ticket to New York, a suitcase, and a few dollars in your purse, that's all."

Mother said she also had me. Her daughter. I stood a little straighter and linked arms with Mother, glad we were briefly united against Mrs. Lewis and her constant complaining.

"Not much to start a new life on though, is it," Mrs. Lewis replied. "And what if your Jack gets fed up with Molly and wants to send her back? What will you do then? This is their country, not ours."

Grandma had voiced the same concerns when Mother first announced we were emigrating. In the late spring of this year we'd been to London to have medical examinations and an interview at the embassy for our visas, and Grandma had said she would not let Jack adopt me. Mother could marry her Yank and live in America if she wanted but she could not take me with her.

"Well, it's very decent of him to have Molly," Mrs. Lewis continued. "Because after all, it's a lot to ask of a man, to take on a child that is not his."

"That's enough now, Betty," said Mother firmly. "Jack loves Molly like a daughter."

I wanted to tell Betty Lewis to shut up. To point out her red lipstick was cheap looking and her eyes were too bulgy to be pretty. I hated her for saying what I was most afraid of. That Jack only put up with me because of Mother.

When the arguments at home began over whether I was going to America with Mother, Grandma had shocked everybody by saying the Yanks were oversexed.

"No need for vulgarities, Ma," said Uncle Roger, coughing over his cup of tea. We were all scarlet with embarrassment, but Grandma was not going to be stopped. Major Jack Williamson would want a big family. Bigger, even, than the village vicar's family of twelve—his valiant apostles no less—and everybody knew his wife had gone weak as a bolted lettuce with the strain and had troubles remembering her own name. Mother had better know what she was letting herself in for.

Uncle Roger stomped out the back door, slamming it behind him. Mother went upstairs. Grandma sat by the range and rustled her black skirts while I stood there unable to move, since it was me being discussed.

"She is staying here," Grandma said, banging her walking stick on the table. "We've already lost Susan. We're not losing Molly."

———

Mrs. Lewis reached in her handbag and pulled out a bag of barley sugars. I knew she'd been saving them. She pushed them into my hand. "I'm sorry," she said. "My nerves are all shot to pieces." Her voice was husky and full of tears. "It's just . . . it's just that I might never go back to London. I probably won't see my mum and dad ever again. They'll never be able to afford the crossing over here, will they. They won't even get to see their grandchild."

"You keep them," I told her. I felt sorry for her. She was as home-sick as I was. "I bet Jimmy will be mad keen to see you," I added.

"Thanks," she replied with a watery smile. "I don't know about that. Surprised more like. The last time I saw Jimmy we danced all night. I used to love dancing. Now all I want to do is put my feet up. I'm gasping for a cup of tea. Irene, can we go and get a pot of tea and a bun somewhere? I can't go on my own. I just can't. I think I'd get lost in this crowd."

Mother looked doubtful.

"I don't want to miss Jack . . ."

"Molly could stay with the suitcases," Mrs. Lewis said. She thrust a photograph of a man in uniform into my hand. I'd seen this picture of Jimmy a thousand times already. "You could watch out for Jimmy, couldn't you, Molly? We'd be ever so quick."

"I'm not sure," said Mother. "This is an awfully big station . . ."

"I'll be fine," I told her. I was happy to think of some time without Mrs. Lewis's shrill voice in my ear. Mother took one of the identity tags off our suitcase and tied it to a button on my coat.

"You have to stand right here and not move."

"I will," I promised. "And if I see Jack or Mr. Lewis, I'll call out to them."

I sat down on the suitcase watching them walk away. I took a small teddy bear from my satchel and hugged it. We hadn't seen Jack for five months. He'd gone back to America in April, just before the end of the war. Would I even recognise him without his uniform? And if I saw him and didn't call out, perhaps he'd look straight past me. He'd be searching for Mother, after all, not me. As Grandma said, I was an English farmer's daughter, not a New York lawyer's child.

Up till now I had still imagined something might happen on our journey, something unforeseen that would mean we could go back home. Now I wondered whether Jack might be caught in some dark accident on his way to the railway station; a flood or a motorcar crash or whatever kind of disasters befell people in big cities like New York. Surely, if he didn't come to get us, Mother and I would have to go back to England.

I imagined myself returning to our village, walking over to Clarkie's cottage. He and Susan would be sitting in the front garden on deck chairs with the sound of birdsong in the hedgerow. I'd be the returning traveller, describing the storms I'd seen in the Atlantic, the Statue of Liberty, the biggest train station in the world.

"I reckon you've seen enough for a lifetime," Clarkie might say, giving a low whistle of admiration. "Best you sit down and take your shoes off. Rest your feet, my girl. You won't want to be going anywhere for a while."

I put the teddy back in my bag and decided that when Jack came I would hide. I would hide and he'd leave, thinking we weren't here. Then I'd tell Mother I hadn't seen him. It was awful to imagine lying to her, but if Jack didn't come to claim us, we would go back to the farm. Just me and Mother together, sharing our memories of Father.

———————

When Father was alive we had two heavy horses that pulled the hay cart and he taught me to jump from the back of one to the other. The horses' haunches were broad enough, he liked to say, for a family of three to picnic on. I loved him so much I couldn't admit I didn't want to do it. I was no good at acrobatics. I have always been a clumsy sort of kid. Grandma used to tease me saying I'd never be a ballerina. I scrambled on my knees from one slippery horse's back to the other, clutching at the leather harnesses, hoping I wouldn't fall.

"G'arn, Molly, my little tuppenny bit," my father liked to yell, pushing his soft cap back on his head, his summer-tanned face creased with smiles.

Everybody loved my father and his games. Stepping from one horse to the other was one of his many tricks which made hay making memorable. He stood on their backs like a circus performer. Mother said the horses' hooves were too big. She worried I might get hurt. My father said that would never happen.

"Molly is like me," he liked to say. "Fearless."

I wasn't fearless, but I always pretended to be. I was six years old when Father died in the winter of 1940, and I had to carry on pretending to be fearless for Mother's sake. After the funeral, she began going out for long walks, coming back in the dark, raindrops sparkling in her hair, lichen and moss on her clothes, a stony look in her eyes. Grandma and I watched her come through the kitchen, going upstairs to her room. It was as if she had forgotten me. Grandma said grief was wearing Mother out.

"But you're my little apple dumpling," Grandma told me, holding me on her lap, her hands wrapped round me. "Don't you worry. I'll look after you. They can put me in my grave and I'd still be here watching over you, my darling girl."

I wanted to get off Grandma's lap when she talked about graves, but she held me fast and it was comforting, in a way, to be pinned in her embrace. To feel her greedy love for me.

Uncle Roger and Aunt Marion were silent after Father's death, as if it were a secret, but Grandma talked to everybody: the grocer's delivery boy, the vicar's wife who bought eggs from us and always expected a glass of sherry at the kitchen table, the coal man, the milk lorry driver, anybody who came to the farm. She said God knew no pity. Her big shoulders shook and she wept lavish tears. What a poor little mite I was with my mother fading away, and she at her great age doing what she could. "Irene is a wraith," she exclaimed. "A ghost. My Roger's working himself into the ground now he's got to run the farm alone, and what's the point when a bomb might fall on us at any moment? This blessed war will be the end of us."

Grandma was wrong about Mother becoming a ghost. Mother was turning to stone. If I climbed into bed with her and watched her pretending to be asleep with her eyes open staring at the ceiling, she looked like she had been carved from marble. Like the tomb in the village church where we did brass rubbings with our schoolteacher. It was a memorial carved in stone, a noblewoman from the sixteenth century wearing long robes, her hands in a praying position, pointing to heaven. That's who Mother reminded me of. The stone woman in the church. I knew she spent hours sitting by Father's grey granite headstone. Mother's face had a greyish tint to it. I wanted to hug her so badly in those early months after his death, but I was afraid to touch her in case she turned me to stone, too.

My grandmother was neither stony nor shadowy. She had limbs like suet dumplings, softly fleshy. She sat by the stove all day because her legs gave her trouble. After the funeral it was Grandma who was in charge of grieving. The rest of us were dry-eyed, as if there were only so many gallons of salty tears to go around for Father, and Grandma had them all for herself.

Everybody knew my father, Robert, had been her favourite son. Susan had told me often enough when we lay in our room at night. After he died, my other cousins avoided me, but all that year Susan let me curl up against her at night and we'd talk about what she'd do when the war ended. Susan was sixteen in 1941 and had left school the year before. She was kind to me, perhaps because she had four brothers and would have preferred sisters. She adored my mother, who was an expert dressmaker and often jazzed up Susan's clothes for her with ribbons and furbelows.

Susan wanted to fall in love and marry a bank clerk or a man who sold insurance, someone who wore a suit and had a job in an office. While she worked in our fields, hoeing and pulling weeds, she dreamed of fox furs, pink satin, and cocktail parties. She smoked Grey's Cigarettes that she bought in town because she said smoking gave a woman a certain elegance, opening the window in our room, leaning out, wafting the smoke away.

In the autumn of that year, German planes flew over the coast, heading inland. We heard them every night for a week, and in the next village, boys picked up pieces of shrapnel. Aunt Marion gave a ruling. The whole family, including Uncle Roger who worked until after nightfall, had to be indoors by six o'clock in the evening. Only Mother ignored my aunt's curfew, going out in Father's old coat and her red Tam o' Shanter hat. Grandma begged her not to. She said Mother made herself an easy target for the Germans. I tried hard not to think of her so clearly visible, standing for hours by the village lake, looking across its deep waters.

Susan watched the sky for planes from our room, leaning out of the window with a cigarette, her hand cupped over it to hide its glowing tip. The sun was setting, pouring gold light across her brown curls. I sat on the bed doing a jigsaw puzzle. A hunting scene of men in red coats on horses galloping with hounds across a wooded landscape.

"Grandma called him a gift," Susan said. "Your father, I mean. She was fifty when he was born." She blew a smoke ring. "Dreadful to think of a woman of that age, you know, doing it. Grandpa was ten years older than her. He died when your father was twelve. That was the year I was born. Everybody called your dad a miracle child. The last fruit from an old tree. Who knows what my poor old pa thought when your golden-haired father came along."

Grandma had told me Uncle Roger had always been in awe of his younger brother. That he had always doted on him. My uncle was as reserved as my father had been outgoing. As strict with his family as Father had been happy-go-lucky. I'd heard our farmworkers saying Uncle Roger blamed Clarkie for Father's accident.

"Poor Clarkie," said Susan, her cheeks darkening. "Your father's death wasn't his fault."

I carried on with the jigsaw. I liked to talk about Father, but I never mentioned how he'd died. I had begun to suffer from nightmares, and thinking about it made them worse.

"Sorry, Molly," said Susan, closing the window. She sat beside me, putting a piece of jigsaw in place. "Why don't we sneak out and go see Clarkie? We can go after tea."

"How is Irene?" asked Clarkie when we knocked on his door. He squinted across the dusk-dimmed fields and woodland in the direction of the farm, as if he hoped he might be able to see her. I told him I thought Mother was turning to stone. He said it wasn't that at all. Her heart was broken and that was worse than shattering every single bone in your body because there was no plaster cast or sling you could put on a damaged heart.

We had glasses of milk in his kitchen and Clarkie talked to Susan about the German planes. Clarkie was twenty-six back then, a year younger than my father would have been. He had been born with a funny leg and had a limp which stopped him doing military service. He said his leg put women off and that was why he was still a bachelor. I couldn't see why it would put anybody off. He was marvellous. A great one for jokes and acting the silly goat. He liked to ride his bicycle downhill with his arms folded. Only when he was thoughtful did his mouth in repose fall to slackness, giving him a disappointed look.

"What Clarkie needs is a wife," I once heard Mother say to Susan. "He needs somebody to care for. He's a romantic soul and that's half the trouble."

I thought how nice it would be to live with him. I thought my mother should marry Clarkie.

"You have to look after her," Clarkie told me, walking us home in the dark that night. "She needs you to be strong for her. You've got to look after Irene."

I remember I put a hand to my seven-year-old chest and felt the beating of my heart. It had a hurried, frail rhythm. Nobody had ever asked if it had been broken by Father's death. They just told me to look after Mother.

By the time Mrs. Lewis and Mother returned from their quest to find a decent cup of tea in the station, neither Jack nor Jimmy had come to find us and I had sat in a daydream hardly noticing the noise of the travellers around me.

"There's all sorts of shops," said Mrs. Lewis. She was puffing with the exertion of walking. "You wouldn't believe the café, Molly. Fresh fruit in big baskets. A cheese shop, too. They even had a bit of Stilton on sale. And there's an oyster bar, though I can't be doing with shellfish in my condition. Couldn't get a proper cup of tea but the waiter was awfully nice, wasn't he, Irene?"

"He was," agreed Mother. "Any sign of Jack?" I shook my head, and she handed me a brown paper bag. "I've bought you pretzels, Molly. So you can tell Jack you've tried them."

I thanked her and turned my face away. How could I accept her kindnesses when I was plotting to hide from Jack?

"We thought you two could sit in the waiting room," said Mother, picking up our suitcase. "That way Betty can rest her feet. I'll stay here."

"No," I said hurriedly. "I can stay here. You go and sit down. I'll look out for Jack."

Mother smiled and said I was a very good girl. Jack would be proud of me.

I wanted to tell her I loved her and didn't mean to do her any harm. So that later, when I explained how Jack hadn't come after all, she would not think badly of me.

Mother leaned towards me and kissed my cheek. "Poor Betty is not feeling too well. I think she'd be better off sitting down."

I didn't tell Mother I loved her. The lies I planned stopped me, turning me silent and unable to watch her walking away.

Three years after Father died, when our tiny village was buzzing with the arrival of three thousand American airmen on the newly built airfield that bordered our farm, Mother stopped turning to stone. In the middle of summer in 1943 I heard her laughing again. Her eyes shone as if they had sunlight caught in them. I believed I had finally mended her broken heart. She began wearing lipstick and had her hair done in a permanent wave. She took up dressmaking once more, unpicking some of Susan's old dresses and making me skirts and pinafores.

Earlier in the year we'd heard the first American trucks arriving. Susan was eighteen and working part-time in the local pub. That was a compromise between her and her parents, who had refused to let her get a job in the ammunitions factory in town. Susan desperately wanted to do her bit for the war effort, but Uncle Roger said working on the farm *was* doing her bit.

We watched lorries trundle past for days. Each one of the corrugated iron buildings that had been erected was marked U.S. ARMY AIR FORCES in huge lettering. Big brown tents were put up, a whole rippling sea of them. At school, a boy brought in something amazing. He showed it to the whole class. A juicy-looking orange. He had been given it by an American airman, he announced.

When I told Susan, she said we should go and ask if we could have some fruit. On the airfield there were sweet cooking smells and the odour of petrol. Swing and Big Band music played through loudspeakers. In her best cotton dress, the blue one with tiny white daisies, Susan danced me along the concrete paths between the temporary buildings. She said the Americans were going to kick Hitler's backside, and we stuck our hands in the air, holding up two fingers like Churchill had just done, making his "V for victory" sign.

The airfield was vast. A whole bustling American town built on our farm's fields. There was a tent with a sign hanging off it saying *Sleep Lagoon* where pilots could rest before air missions. They had a fire department, a corrugated iron parachute store, a dentist surgery, a base infirmary, even a metal-roofed cinema where we village children would be invited to watch Walt Disney films over the years. We watched some GIs putting up a sign. A painted wooden board. It said *Welcome to Tin Town.*

"You ladies thinking of becoming pilots?" asked an airman. Susan and I were looking up at a huge B17 bomber plane. The man smiled. His face was all brightness in the last glow of afternoon sun. He was very tall. His uniform buttons were polished. His eyes were deep blue and full of kindness.

"We're just having a look round," said Susan politely.

"That's okay. Are you from the village?"

"We live at Swan farm," said Susan, pointing. "Over there. This is my father's land."

"Oh, is it?" He took off his hat, turning it over and over in his hands. "Well," he said. "I hope he doesn't mind too much us being here?"

"Not at all," answered Susan. "It's all for the war effort, isn't it." She asked him whether we could buy some oranges.

"Oranges? Sure, I can get you a couple of oranges. And tell me, over on your farm, do you have chickens?"

Susan looked confused. All farms had chickens.

"We've got lots," I said. I liked this tall American and his soft way of smiling.

"We only get powdered eggs," he told us. "I figured some of these farms round here must have hens."

"Do you want fresh eggs?" I asked, eager to please. "My mother looks after our chickens and they lay all year round. We can get you eggs."

We arranged that I would take him a dozen every other day. He told us to wait outside a corrugated iron hut and he came out a minute later with a brown paper bag filled with oranges. I wanted to jump up and down with glee. Mother loved fruit and we had so little during the war. I imagined sharing an orange with her, the happiness it might bring her, its sweetness delighting us both.

"And you won't forget about the eggs? You bring them to the building over there, you see? Ask for me, Major Jack Williamson."

"We'll do that," said Susan.

"That's great. So, are you two sisters?"

"We're cousins," said Susan. She held out her hand. "Miss Susan Marks. Pleased to meet you."

"Delighted to make your acquaintance, miss. And what's your name, kiddo?"

I saluted him. "Molly Marks," I said. He laughed and saluted me back. I thought of him as a friend after that.

"And how about you, Major Molly Marks? Does your father farm round here, too?"

I blushed and looked at Susan. Everybody in the village knew about Father. I had never had to tell anybody what had happened. I didn't know what to say.

"We should go now," said Susan. "Thank you for the oranges." She grasped my hand, leading me away.

"Don't forget the eggs," Jack called after us.

———————

All summer either Mother or I took eggs to the officers. I liked the Americans. They gave us wonderful things; dried fruits and oranges, chewing gum, parachute silk, ice cream and fruitcakes. Everybody liked the Americans. Even grumpy Uncle Roger. Some of the men had farming backgrounds and discussed tractors and combine harvesters with him. By then he'd sold our farm horses and had a tractor bought on lend-lease, sent all the way from Pennsylvania. It arrived at Ipswich docks in pieces, and his airmen friends helped him put it together.

When Jack Williamson called at the farm to offer Susan an invitation to a dance on the airfield, Aunt Marion got out the best china and we had tea in the dining room.

"Oh no," said my mother, smiling, when Jack suggested she come to the dance, too. My heart seemed to slow, she was so beautiful then. I wished Father could have seen her. She put an arm around my shoulders and said she could not go dancing, thank you.

Uncle Roger refused to let Susan go to a dance unaccompanied. Aunt Marion and Grandma cajoled him. Jack Williamson was an officer. Top brass, really. In civilian life he was a New York lawyer. A gentleman. When Mother agreed to chaperone Susan, my uncle relented. Mother invited Clarkie to make up the foursome and I was pleased. I didn't like to think of her sitting alone while Susan danced all night with American airmen.

Mother kissed me good-night before she and Susan left to walk over to Tin Town. She wore the pearls Father had given her as a gift when I was born. She put her arms around me and said she had let me down by falling into her own sadness these past few years. "But I love you very much, darling. More than you know. I'm better now. We're going to be happy again, you'll see."

I had managed to mend her broken heart by being a loyal daughter. By following her around and refusing to let her turn completely to stone. I was proud of saving Mother, bringing her back to us.

On the landing upstairs was a sash window and a tall-backed chair where Grandma liked to sit. That night I climbed on the chair and watched Tin Town across the fields. The sound of jazz music floated in the summer night. There were voices, too, sudden bursts of laughter and the occasional noise of jeeps and motorbikes. I imagined Susan dancing with Jack. I hoped she would marry him and that Mother and Clarkie would get married, too, so we could live in his cottage and be happy.

When I called at Clarkie's cottage that summer, there were often American servicemen sitting in the cramped little parlour. Jack Williamson and his friends, smoking and chatting, Clarkie sharing his homemade blackberry wine with them. Mother and Susan, who was suddenly very grown up and had lost interest in doing jigsaws with me, sometimes spent the afternoons with them.

Susan took to wearing trousers and men's shirts tied tight at the waist. She put her hair up in victory rolls and bought herself a red lipstick.

"Jack Williamson was engaged to a girl in New York but he's broken it off," she whispered to me one night. "He's fallen in love, Molly. Head over heels, drunk on love. It's crazy and romantic and

I can barely breathe because I think I am in love, too. Promise not to tell anybody, won't you?"

I crossed my heart and swore an oath, feeling giddy with excitement, promising I would not breathe a word, not even to Mother.

In July I won a prize at school for best composition. I wrote a story about a family who had lived in the ruined cottage by the stream. The vicar published it in the parish news and Jack and Clarkie took Susan, Mother, and me to visit Ely Cathedral to celebrate. Grandma knitted me a lacy yellow cardigan as a gift. I was ten years old, and Mother and I had just started being able to talk about Father again, sharing memories of him.

We sat on the grass, eating sandwiches in the shade of the cathedral.

"Do you remember the picnics we had at the ruined cottage?" I asked her. "And the Christmas roses Daddy used to pick there for you?"

"Those were good times," she said, her cheek against mine. "Such good times. We're going to be happy like that again, I promise you."

I wasn't the only person who stood waiting at the station clock. People were forever meeting and going away in merry groups. There was a soldier with only one leg, shifting his weight back and forth on his crutches. He had been waiting as long as I had. There was also an old woman who wore no hat or gloves and held a handkerchief in her hands that she twisted over and over. She had wide black eyes, dark as a well and full of emptiness.

When trains arrived at the different platforms in the station, the main concourse filled up with people. They poured forwards like factory workers heading homewards, filling the hall with the sound of their marching feet, the chatter of their voices, all of them with somewhere to go, hurrying to get there. I saw how the old woman and the wounded soldier looked around then, as if they expected to see somebody they knew. If Jack came at such a moment, it would be very easy to hide. I could step into the flow and be lost. I opened the bag of pretzels. I hadn't realised how hungry I was. I had eaten almost all of them when I saw a girl in a yellow dress. It was the same yellow as my favourite cardigan, and the colour filled me with thoughts of the farm. A porter in a red cap brushed past her, and the girl stumbled, dropping her suitcase. It sprang open and she blushed hotly as she bent to retrieve her things. I felt sorry for her. I would be mortified if I dropped our suitcase and all our belongings were spread out for strangers to stare at. She was older than me but still young. She wore a hat with a circle of flowers and looked like she might be from the country, though I wasn't sure why I thought that. Maybe it was her hair that reminded me of ripe barley fields, or perhaps I recognised the bewildered look in her eyes. As if she, too, knew what it was like to be far from home. I dusted crumbs off my coat, straightened my Sunday-best beret, and went towards her. As I did so, I saw an airman in uniform standing under the clock. I didn't need to look at the photograph Mrs. Lewis had given me. It was Jimmy. I wasn't sure whether to go to him or run back to Mother. The girl by then was being helped by the same porter. I ran to the waiting rooms.

"He's here!" I cried when I saw Mother. "Jimmy's here!"

Mrs. Lewis stood up, swaying as if she had a fever, as if she might faint.

"I can't go. I don't want to see him."

"Of course you do," said Mother. "He's waiting."

"I can't."

"You're expecting a baby . . ." Mother began saying. "He's your husband . . ."

Mrs. Lewis began to cry. She was mumbling about babies and fathers and the night she had gone dancing because she'd been lonely just after Jimmy had been posted abroad. I didn't know why she was saying any of it. Jimmy was there, waiting for her. Mother asked if she loved him, and Mrs. Lewis said she'd come halfway across the world for him and would do it all over again if she had to.

"Well then, go to him," Mother urged her.

"Hurry!" I blurted out, grabbing her hand. "He's waiting for you with a Mickey Mouse doll and a bunch of flowers."

"Flowers?"

"Roses," I volunteered. "Yellow ones."

"Go to him," said Mother again.

Mrs. Lewis dried her eyes and said she had better smarten herself up a bit first. She re-applied her lipstick and mascara and powdered her nose. Then we walked to where Jimmy stood, waiting. Mrs. Lewis saw Jimmy and her face lifted into a smile. I knew she was forgetting everything that had gone before. Us, her home back in bombed-out London town. We were all gone into the past already. She gave a small cry as Jimmy bent to kiss her on the lips. Her ginger hair untidily fanned her face, and he moved it away tenderly with his fingers. I realised she was not plain at all. Standing beside her Jimmy, Mrs. Lewis was unexpectedly beautiful.

─────────

"I was sixteen when I had you," said Mother. We stood staring after the Lewises, as if we could still see them walking away. "Just a child myself. Your father and I enjoyed life. Picnicking and ice-skating, swimming in the lake. We rode our bicycles all over the county. At village dances people used to love to watch us together. Your father would have wanted us to be happy again. When Jack comes we'll be all right, you'll see."

"I want to go home," I told Mother. But I knew what I wanted was already gone. I wanted home as it was before the war, when Father stood on the backs of horses and the farm was the centre of our world.

"We can't go back," sighed Mother, and she turned her head away. I was sure she was thinking of Father. Of what happened and how we lost him.

We were skating on the lake on a winter's afternoon. Clarkie was there. He and Father were racing around the edge of the lake. Mother and I were turning small circles, holding hands. There were patterns in the ice, curling leaves and feathers that bloomed under our feet. Winter's magic, Mother called them. We heard a yell and on the far bank Clarkie went through the ice. The water was shallow. It was only out in the centre that it became deep and black. He stood, knee deep, swearing and cursing. My father hauled him out and the two of them were laughing by the time they reached us.

Mother insisted we get home before Clarkie caught a chill. It was getting dark and he realised he'd dropped his hat. Father went back for it. Clarkie told him not to bother. It was a worn-out old hat. Father laughed. Worn-out or not, he'd get it back. He made it sound like a quest. A lark. A dare. He skated straight across the lake in fine style, my fearless father, a lovely inky figure against the turquoise sky. Out he went, out to the deep waters where the ice was too thin.

Mother rubbed her forehead as if she, too, were remembering. "Endings hurt," she said. "But they give us new beginnings."

"Everything changes," she added softly. She dug in her handbag for her address book and told me to stay by the clock. She was going to phone Jack's office to see if he was on his way.

I knew it would break her heart if he didn't come. She walked away, promising she would be back in the wink of an eye, an expression Clarkie liked to use.

I had really believed Mother might marry Clarkie. Just before Christmas in 1944 I told him so. Jack's squadron had been flying a dangerous mission. All night we'd heard the planes going over, and the next morning Mother and Susan went to church and prayed for the airmen to return safely. I called to see Clarkie. There'd been a deep snowfall and I trudged across white fields, the air glittering with frost.

We sat in his living room and he made me a cup of cocoa and toasted bread in front of the fire. We talked about the mission the Americans were flying over the French coast. Clarkie said my father would have admired them for their bravery.

"He would have liked Jack Williamson. Do you like him, Molly?"

"He's very nice," I said. I was bursting to tell Clarkie that Susan loved Jack. I considered his cottage, the oily green wallpaper and dark cupboards. The cooking range in the kitchen covered in grease and used pans. I imagined Mother and me cleaning the place up.

"And would you ever want to get married?" I asked.

"Goodness, Molly, you ask some funny questions. Marry who?"

"Mother. She likes you, I know she does. She says you're our best friend."

Clarkie buttered some toast for me, handing it to me on a plate.

"Any man worth his salt would want to marry Irene," he said. "When your father first brought her home I admit I'd never felt so jealous in all my life. But it wouldn't be me. Not me." He poked the fire in the grate. "I did everything I could trying to save your father. You know that, don't you?"

"I do. We could live here with you, Clarkie. I'd like that."

"People have to be in love to get married. Do you understand that, Molly? You can't choose who to love. You'll understand that when you're older. Irene should marry again. You're right. She deserves to be happy. You both do."

When I got home Mother and Susan were full of smiles. Jack's squadron had come back safely. I felt sorry Clarkie was going to stay a bachelor. He thought he wasn't good enough for Mother, but I'd make him realise he was.

On Boxing Day, I got up early and went out, trudging through snowy lanes and along the footpath to the ruined cottage where bloodred holly berries sparkled in hoarfrost, and the stream that ran under them was frozen grey. I picked Christmas roses to take to Clarkie. I thought he could offer them to Mother as a gift. I was crouched down, picking the white flowers, when I heard voices. A man and a woman stood in the shelter of the cottage walls. I crept up on them, startled to find people in my secret place. It was Mother and Jack. Mother had his flying jacket around her shoulders.

"When you come," Jack was saying, "I'll show you Times Square and we'll eat strawberry shortcake at Toffenetti's."

He bent and put his arms around her, kissing her on the lips.

Afterwards I heard her laugh. She sounded happy. Her happiness was not to do with me. I crouched in the snow and knew it had been Jack, not me, who had mended her broken heart.

I dropped the Christmas roses and followed the frozen stream to where it ran into the lake. I had not been there since Father died, but this was the quickest way to Clarkie's. I ran down the side of a beet field and stopped outside his cottage. The blackout curtains were drawn and smoke curled from the chimney. I slammed the front door open. Clarkie sat on the hearthrug in front of the coal fire. Susan sat between his legs, her back leaning against his chest. He had his arms around her. They didn't move when they saw me. Susan told me to come in and warm myself.

I found Uncle Roger in the barn. He stood with an oil can and a rag in his hand. A hurricane lamp hung from a beam, flaring yellow light across the tractor's engine box. He listened to me, and when I'd finished, he wiped his hands on the rag.

"Susan's there now, you say?"

"She's lying on the rug with him," I said, still breathless from running. "In front of the fire."

I was glad to hear him say he hated Clarkie. Glad to see he believed we had been betrayed by my mother and Susan.

Uncle Roger went to Clarkie's cottage and threatened him with a shotgun. Susan stood between them, so Clarkie told me afterwards. Uncle Roger said Susan should get on home or consider herself disowned.

Susan never did go home. She and Clarkie married in town. Mother and Jack announced they were getting married, too, and Jack's mother sent a blue wool coat over from America for me to wear to the wedding. It arrived along with a letter, saying she was looking forward to meeting us when the war was over. At Mother and Jack's wedding I made my face hard and pulled petals off the silk violets I carried. In the pub gardens afterwards, Jack told me grown-ups were hard to understand sometimes. He said there was nothing wrong with crying. That I didn't need to be tough all the time.

"I'm not crying," I insisted, wiping my nose with my sleeve.

"Of course you're not," he said and handed me his handkerchief.

When Susan had her son she named him Robert. My uncle refused to see him. Mother was preparing to go to America. Grandma had finally given Mother and Jack her blessing. She'd decided there would be opportunities in America for a smart girl like me.

A week before we left, Susan brought Robert over to the farm for the first time. Grandma, Mother, Aunt Marion, and Susan's brothers all took turns holding him. I was allowed to bottle-feed him, and he drank like a hungry lamb, bubbling milk down his chin.

"An absolute darling!" exclaimed Grandma.

Grandma said Susan and Clarkie should have a big family, and Aunt Marion said she thought Susan had enough to be going on with for the time being.

"Clarkie's a good man," Susan told them. "He's a good father."

Aunt Marion and Grandma agreed, as if they had both forgotten they were meant to be angry.

When we heard Uncle Roger drive his tractor into the yard, a defiant look came into Susan's eyes.

"I'd better be going," she said.

After she left, Grandma and I stood at the upstairs window and watched her walk briskly back across the fields with her son in her arms.

The wounded soldier by the clock had a young, hopeful face. His clothes were neat, and if I didn't look I could pretend his leg wasn't missing. I was glad when a couple came to meet him. That he had family to go to. He nodded to me when he left. The old woman with the black eyes stared at me, too, twisting her thin hands together. I decided to find Mother. I walked up and down the telephone queues, but she wasn't there and she wasn't in the waiting rooms. I went along the wooden benches and dragged our suitcase down the ramp to the lower levels. I returned to the main concourse and climbed the stairs, standing on the balcony so I could see across the hall. An awful panic began to grip me. Several trains must have arrived at once because the concourse was suddenly packed with people.

"You're lost, aren't you?" said a voice. It was the black-eyed old woman. "My son is in the navy. He's coming back soon, you see? I got a slice of my Good Luck lemon pie waiting in the refrigerator for him. But who are you waiting for, dear? Do you want me to ask a porter to help you? I know them all. I come here every day to wait. You're awfully young to be on your own . . ."

She gripped my elbow and offered to take me home. I could have her son's room until he came back. The bed was all made up with a blue satin comforter. She showed me a telegram from the War Department and explained they must have made a mistake. Her son couldn't have drowned. He was a terrific swimmer.

"I'll look after you, dear," she said. "I'll take good care of you."

There was a roaring in my ears; panic was washing over me. I tried to pull my arm free from this woman offering me kindnesses I didn't want. I searched the crowds again looking for Mother, and instead I saw Jack. Tall and unmistakable, standing by the clock, his hat in his hands, turning it over and over.

"He's here!" I cried, struggling free of the woman's grip, pushing her away. I picked up our suitcase and tried to fight my way down the stairs. Jack was the first person I had seen in all the weeks we had been travelling who knew me and our farm and the people I loved. Seeing him was like seeing home again.

"Jack!" I yelled, all ideas of hiding from him gone from my head. "Jack, Jack, it's me!"

———————

Mother and I left the farmhouse in the dark. We'd said our good-byes the night before and promised we'd write when we arrived in America. Grandma made us a picnic to take on our journey. "You take care," she said and hugged me so hard I couldn't breathe. She gave me a small, worn-out teddy bear. "It was your father's when he was a child. You keep it."

Mother had put out my travelling clothes on Susan's empty bed. A pinafore dress and my favourite yellow cardigan. The navy blue coat with a velvet Peter Pan collar, a pair of gloves, and my Sunday-best beret.

We tiptoed past the sheepdogs dozing in the farmyard. Up the grassy track in the August moonlight we went, silver light splashing us, moths dancing, the dew soaking my socks and sandals. I stopped and looked up at the thatched farmhouse that had been my home forever. A figure stood at the landing window. It was Grandma. She lifted her hand and sank down very suddenly, onto the chair that was always there.

I knew then, that even when I was a very old lady, I would never forget the shape Grandma made in the window. How she had waved me on my way and then dropped into the chair, as if broken by our leaving.

Mother was already farther ahead, striding out in the darkness. I ran after her, asking her to wait.

"Grandma . . ." I said.

"Don't look back," Mother whispered, walking fast. "Don't look back."

———

Mother stood by the big clock with Jack. I cried out to them both, and somehow, in the noise and commotion of the train station, they heard me. They heard me and all I could think as they wrapped their arms around me was that I belonged with them.

"I was going to hide," I said. I needed them to know I was sorry. I had got so many things wrong.

"Darling girl, we'd have found you," said Jack, picking up our suitcase. He had a way of speaking that put sunshine in my mother's eyes. I felt it, too, the warmth of his words. "Are you ready, Molly?"

Mother looked at me anxiously.

"Yes," I said, letting her take my hand. Yes, I was ready to go.

~~~

ACKNOWLEDGMENTS

I would like to thank Roger Watts for his generosity in showing me around a World War II American airfield in the tiny village of Rattlesden in Suffolk, England. During the war the airfield was used by the United States Army 8th Air Force 322nd and 447th Bomb Group. As we stood in the original control tower and looked out over what is now farmland, Roger's ability to bring that extraordinary past to life, in the form of personal and historical anecdotes, was invaluable to me.

Strand of Pearls

PAM JENOFF

In loving memory of my grandparents, especially Bubby Fayge, whose courageous real-life journey from China to America inspired this tale.

Ella stepped onto the platform, still feeling the gentle rocking of the train under her feet. She adjusted her hat as she tried to gain her bearings. It was Mama's hat, actually, the one that she had insisted Ella would need, made by the lone Jewish haberdasher in the Hongkou District. It felt old-fashioned now and too stuffy, just like her dress, its hem a good inch longer than those worn by the New York women who swirled sleekly past her.

She moved back against the wall to free herself from the current of travelers that surged this way and that. Plumes of cigarette smoke rose to a pillowlike cloud above. The crowd did not bother her; Ella had grown accustomed to the crush of humanity in the Shanghai market, and had learned how to surf the tide of bodies, which pressed together until they seemed to be part of her. More than once she had emerged with strange impressions on her arm, left by bags and belongings not her own.

Ella leaned against the cool, rough wall, savoring the plainness that allowed her to just fade into the backdrop. It was a luxury she'd seldom had in China, where no matter how ordinary she had felt, her wheat blonde hair and pale blue eyes had still caused her to stand out. But she had learned well on the train to avoid drawing the unwanted attention of a woman traveling alone. Here she could just watch the parade of travelers passing through Grand

Central Terminal at midafternoon. There were soldiers everywhere. Though the heaviness of the war had lifted from their faces, the pain and hardship were still fresh enough that their eyes danced with appreciation at everything ordinary around them. A man in a bowler hat rushed past, nearly colliding with an old woman who hobbled across the platform. Ella had always marveled at the fearlessness of elderly travelers who battled the crowds on the Shanghai buses, stooped women, their faces as jowly and hanging as those of Shar-Peis.

Ella started forward once more, trying to make her strides long and confident to match the pace of the crowd. She passed double doors that led to a hotel lobby. *The Biltmore Room*, the sign beside the doors read. On the other side, a couple was locked in a tight embrace, oblivious to the crowds around them. Ella tried to avert her eyes, but she found herself drawn to the place where the pair's lips met, wondering what it might feel like. Looking away, she saw another couple standing close with a young girl of three or four at their feet. Suddenly it seemed as if everywhere she looked there were people together. Only she was alone.

Alone, that was, until she found Papa. What would it be like to see him again? Ella had searched a hundred times during her journey for the right words that would abate any awkwardness and make them something more than strangers. She had been just twelve when he left, lifting her one last time to press her cheek against his scratchy beard, which smelled sweetly of pipe smoke, before starting jauntily aboard the ship. Four years later, his image had grown shadowy in her mind, and the low roll of his laughter had faded. But now here she was in the very same city, just kilometers, maybe even blocks, away.

Reaching the main concourse, Ella gazed upward at the high,

vaulted ceiling. She stopped, breathing in the deliciousness of the open space, a stark contrast to the claustrophobia of the rocking ship and the train and the city of her youth. Two rounded staircases rose to meet on the balcony above. Over the ticket windows, a large poster of Ingrid Bergman, stunning even in nun's garb, advertised showtimes for *The Bells of St. Mary's* in the Grand Central Theatre. (A cinema in a train station—who could imagine such a thing?) Sprawling signs ringed the perimeter of the station, touting different trains: the *Owl*, the *Merchants Limited*. The dizzying choice of destinations made her weary. She had traveled for weeks; now she just wanted to rest.

By the clock in the center of the concourse stood a girl in a blue beret, seemingly also alone. She could not have been more than twelve years old, and Ella considered asking whether she needed help, before realizing that she had none to give her. The girl's light eyes and freckles reminded Ella of her brother back home. "But why are you leaving?" Joseph had asked plaintively. Now five, he had been too young to remember when their father had gone.

She cleared the image of her brother from her mind and looked toward the clock once more. This time she noticed the girl was nibbling from a bag of snacks. She had no look of being lost, after all. Ella wished she could say the same for herself. Again, she glanced around the concourse, searching for the best way out of the station. Spotting the information kiosk, she took a step toward it. As she did, something bumped into her from behind. "Oh!" she cried as the half-broken clasp on her valise opened, sending the contents sprawling. Hurriedly, she knelt to pick them up, embarrassed to see her nightgown and underthings exposed. But people kept moving around her, not noticing.

"I'm so sorry," a deep voice said from above. "Let me." The

accent was strange, not like the Americans she had heard. She looked up, clutching a silk slip to her breast. A young man with dark eyes stood over her. His hair beneath his cap was dark, too, but feathered with a fine gray, as if it had snowed only on him.

Ella swept her belongings quickly back into the suitcase before the man could touch them. "I've got it. Thank you, though." The words tumbled out crude and unclear.

"You speak English?"

"Some. French would be better." Life in Shanghai had been a cacophony of languages—Chinese she had learned to understand on the street, French at school, Yiddish at home, or Russian if the adults did not want her and Joseph to know what they were saying. She had studied English on her own in the years since Papa had left, but it was mainly from books, and the opportunities to practice speaking had been few.

"English," the man pronounced decisively. "You need to practice." The note of condescension in his voice made her bristle. He reached for her valise. "At least let me carry it for you. That looks heavy." Ella smiled inwardly. The small, rounded suitcase was only a fraction of what she would have brought if Mama had her way.

She noticed then the red color of the man's cap. "You're a porter." He carried bags not for kindness, but for money.

He nodded, gesturing with his head toward the handful of brown-skinned men in caps like his clustered by the kiosk. "Something of an odd duck among the group, but they don't seem to mind me."

"I'm afraid I don't have enough money to pay you," she said, as he lifted her suitcase.

He waved his hand. "I'm finished working."

"Your shift . . ." She fumbled for the right word. "Is it over?"

He shook his head. "Done for good. Today was my last day."

"Oh." He did not look distressed, as he surely would have if he had been fired. But who would give up a job here willingly?

He stood the valise upright. Then he straightened, a good head taller than her now. "Where to?"

Ella faltered. She had Papa's address, of course, copied from the back of one of his letters onto a scrap of paper. But she was not sure how to get there—and she wasn't quite ready to go just yet. "No one here to meet you?" the man pressed. She shrugged. "Let me buy you a drink," he offered. "To apologize for bumping into you."

Ella glanced at the tall clock that stood in the middle of the station. It was nearly four and she needed to get to Papa. She had no idea how far it was to where he lived, and she did not want to arrive unannounced at dinnertime. Today was Friday—did Papa still observe the Sabbath, either on his own or with other Jews? There were compromises that had to be made during their years in China, food that was less than kosher when nothing else could be had during the war. But surely some things remained.

Not waiting for a response, the man picked up her valise. He started walking briskly through the waiting room with its neat rows of wood benches toward the elegant restaurant at the end of the concourse, leaving her no choice but to follow. "Wait!" Glimpsing the potted palms and fine white linens on the tables, Ella's stomach jumped. She had not envisioned anything so grand, and she did not want the man to spend his hard-earned money on her.

But he led her past the restaurant and out the double doors of the station to a metal cart that gave off a savory smell. "Two hot dogs and two sodas, please," he said to the vendor, fishing coins from his pocket.

"I'm . . ." Ella started to protest that she was not hungry, then stopped as her stomach grumbled. She'd spent a nickel on a buttered roll for breakfast, but that was several hours ago, and she had no idea what Papa might have for their supper. The vendor handed her a napkin-wrapped frankfurter, warm through the bun. "Thank you." She looked at it uncertainly.

But David bit into his without hesitation. "You learn not to be so fussy in the camps," he said matter-of-factly as he chewed.

"You're Jewish?" He nodded, then passed her a soda. "Me, too." Here, it did not seem awkward or dangerous to acknowledge.

His thin lips lifted to a smile that seemed to reach his eyes. "That's a fine coincidence." Finding other Jews seemed to mean something now, after so many had been lost. "I'm David Mandl."

"Ella."

"Like Ella Fitzgerald," he said.

She cocked her head. "I don't know who that is."

"Really? She's a wonderful singer. Very famous."

"Oh." Ella was suddenly mindful of her unkempt hair and the smell that lingered despite her attempt to wash up in the toilet on the train. She had taken a room for a single night in San Francisco. The hard, narrow bed with its clean sheets and real pillow had seemed like heaven. But that was six days ago, and all of the freshness had worn off. The yellow silk of her dress was gray with soot, the clutch of flowers that sat atop the hat like eggs in a robin's nest now crumpled.

David led her to a bench, then brushed at it with a napkin before gesturing for her to sit down. Ella perched on the edge and took a small bite of hot dog, delighting in the rich, salty flavor that filled her mouth. Willing herself to eat slowly, she tilted her head upward. The warm air was pleasant, late summer trying to hang on a bit longer than it should. An odd fog swirled above, obscuring the tops of the buildings along the wide expanse of 42nd Street. She could just make out the now-tattered yellow ribbons that hung from the fire escape ladders on the other side.

They sat beside one another, not speaking as they ate. Buses and taxis filled the street before them, their engines gurgling noisily as they inched forward. Ella studied David out of the corner of her eye. He was not handsome in a classic way: his nose was crooked, as though someone had twisted the end a few degrees to the right, and his chin was a bit too pronounced. But it all came together in a way she rather liked. He gazed out at the street with wide, unblinking eyes, as if trying to memorize the scene before him. Though the gray in his hair and deep lines by his eyes suggested he was older than she, Ella could not tell by how much. The fingers he drummed against his knee with his left hand were unusually long.

"I'm from Prague," he said, turning toward her and picking up the conversation. "Have you been?"

She stared straight ahead, embarrassed to be caught looking at him. "No." Ella's family had left Odessa before she was born, fleeing east to escape the hatred and violence toward Jews that had always been present but seemed to worsen in times of famine and hardship. "I grew up in China." They had spent her earliest years in Harbin, and Mama often told stories of watching as the harbor village rose to a bustling city right around them. But after the Japanese came, they moved to Shanghai and opened a small bakery. Ella could not remember life very well before the overcrowded, polluted city.

His eyes widened. "Well, that's unusual." A flash of something crossed over his face—recrimination, maybe, at her having escaped the suffering. She had seen it in the eyes of the Jews that had come to Shanghai from Europe, weary, stoop-shouldered travelers. They lived in the cramped ghetto apartments, cluttering the once pleasant streets, and had no money to buy bread or cakes. "That must have been hard."

She did not know how to answer. Life in China had been different than other places, she assumed, but it was all she had ever known. There had been better days, with governesses and studies at *l'école*. But then war had broken out and the government shut down the bakery, and the bombing raids came almost nightly. Mama kept things bright, though, with homeschooling and games and small treats—routines and rituals that connected the days like a strand of pearls. "And you came all of this way yourself?" he asked.

She nodded. The visa window had been a narrow one: Chinese citizens above the age of eighteen only. Mama's Russian passport had kept her from coming, and Joseph was too young. Ella was the only one who could pass. "You go," Mama had said over her protestations. "It will make it easier for us if you are settled."

"How old are you?" David's questions came rapid-fire now, like a journalist or policeman interrogating a suspect.

How old? In other circumstances, the question would have been routine. "Nineteen," Ella replied, a beat too quickly.

She looked reflexively over her shoulder and smelled the burning incense in the back of the shop where the man had made her papers. The forgery had been a good one, worth the precious gold coin Mama had paid for it. The immigration officer in San Francisco had scarcely looked at the documents before stamping her passport and handing it back. "You don't look Chinese," he had quipped instead, laughing at his own joke. The trick had worked, but her secret was still there, lingering, waiting to be discovered.

Ella watched David's face, wondering if he believed her. Though her hair was rolled in the grown-up way Mama had shown her, Ella was undeniably petite, and her thin, sparrowlike frame made it difficult to pass for her actual age, much less three years older.

"Nineteen," he repeated evenly. There was a part of her that wanted to trust him and tell him the truth. Secrets shared were so much less of a burden. But she did not dare. "You look younger." She blushed, silently pleased at what otherwise would have been a compliment. He was looking at her admiringly, and for the first time, she did not mind the attention. Then her stomach twisted. Looking younger meant she could not pass for the age on her papers, and that she would not be able to stay. She held her breath, wondering if he would push the matter.

When he did not, she changed the subject. "Where do you live now?"

"Home?" He cocked his head. "I'm not sure where that is anymore. I've been staying at the Y while I earn my way. It's a community center," he added, before she could ask. "They have a dormitory with a lot of beds. I teach drawing classes at night there to earn my keep. I'm an artist." So that explained the elegant fingers and keen, observant gaze. "Or at least I was. I studied painting at Charles University. My work was beginning to be shown in the major galleries," he added, in a frank way that kept him from sounding too boastful.

"After the war started, I spent two years sleeping in the forest, helping the underground document what the Germans were doing and trying to get word out to the west. Then I came back to find everything I knew gone." A chill ran through Ella. "Later, I was arrested as a political prisoner. I was lucky," he said, though the way he pronounced the word suggested anything but. "I survived the camps because I was strong enough to work." There was a thinness about him still that spoke volumes about the starvation he had endured. A deep, pale line ran from the collar of his shirt to his ear, and she wondered if there were other scars, ones she could not see.

Ella raised the glass bottle of soda, cool beneath her palm. She took a sip, and the unfamiliar fizz tickled her nose deliciously, causing her to sneeze. Sticky cola spilled over the rim onto her chin. David extended a napkin. Then, seeing that her hands were not free, he dabbed at her mouth in a way that was both too familiar and just right.

"I'm twenty-four now. I was just a boy when the war started." She nodded. Six years was a lifetime. They had grown up knowing war instead of school and dances and the usual things. But life happened alongside the fighting. How might her own world have been different if the war had not been?

"Were you glad to come to America?" he asked, steering the conversation back to her. Ella considered the question. She had not wanted to come alone. It was not just the length or danger of the journey, but Papa's temper, which was as quick and unpredictable as his laugh. Mama had a way of defusing his anger and cajoling him into a better mood, and she had shielded Ella from blows on more than one occasion. Ella did not relish facing Papa's wrath on her own, and the awful memories, which had faded with the years, had come back into sharp focus during the long nights crossing on the ocean liner.

She had not liked their confining life in China, either, though. Jobs for women had been scarce and prospects for marriage still scarcer. Like Tom Schwartzer, whom Mama was always pushing Ella to invite around. Anywhere else he would have been considered ugly and awkward, but in Shanghai's Jewish community he was a prize. So Ella had welcomed the chance to leave. But saying farewell to Mama and Joseph on the pier had been heartbreaking. Ella had not considered whether or not she could do it—she was a practical sort, putting one foot in front of the other, peeling her brother from around her legs and trying not to hear his cries as she boarded.

Those first few minutes on the deck of the ship had been the hardest. However, when land slipped from sight and only the wind blowing her hair remained, Ella felt free in a way she never quite had before. Guilt enveloped her then—how could she feel good leaving those she loved behind?

"I had to come for my mother and Joseph—he's five." There was a note of defensiveness to her voice.

"And what about you? What do you want for yourself?" Ella had not thought about it much. Just the doing, of getting here and finding Papa so they could bring the others over and finally be together as a family, was enough. "Each of us must find his or her own path. It's like this book I just read." He reached into his coat and pulled out a book with *The Fountainhead* emblazoned upon the cover. "Would you like to read it? I'm finished."

Ella eyed the book. She had managed to fit just one in her bag, a Mark Twain novel that a missionary had left behind at the bakery years earlier. She had reread it on her journey until the binding had fallen apart. At the train station in San Francisco, she'd looked longingly at the bookseller's stand, not daring to spend the money. She desperately wanted to take David's book, but she would have no way to return it, and she hardly knew him well enough to accept a gift. "Are you sure?"

He nodded. "It will be good for your English. You should try listening to the radio as well. Some of the programs are a bit fast to follow, but something simple like *Little Orphan Annie*, or soap operas like *The Guiding Light*. The women seem to like those." Which women? she wanted to ask. But it was none of her business. He held out the book to her. "Here."

"Oh." She noticed then the gold band on his right ring finger. "You're married." Disappointment tugged at her.

"Yes. That is, I was." There was a slight shake to his voice. "I had been away for months with the underground. One day, I came back to find my wife and son, Emil—he was two—gone." His tone was even and unemotional, as though telling a story reported in the newspaper, not his own. Ella felt guilty for having spoken to David of another child, her brother Joseph, but she had not known about his son. "I searched for them without success until I was arrested. After the war, I returned to Prague, hoping that they had gone back and were looking for me. I learned that Ava had been taken to Auschwitz and died there. But Emil, I could not find. Ava never would have let him go, so I can only assume . . ."

"I'm sorry . . ." Ella fumbled, unable to grasp the magnitude of his grief, vaster than anything she had ever encountered. Her guilt rose again. There were two types of Jews, it seemed—those who had suffered in Europe and those who had not.

David cleared his throat. "Thank you. There's nothing to be done. It's surreal, though, to go from that to this." He gestured with his hand at the scene around them where passersby milled, eating peanuts and other snacks with post-rationing abandon, making their way toward leisurely weekend plans. "People here, they didn't know."

"In China, either," she hastened to add. News of the war had come to Shanghai first at a trickle, bits about Hitler's march across Czechoslovakia and Poland. Later, as the refugees came, news poured in, but it was still fragmented. Everyone knew of someone who had been arrested, but not personally, and so the stories took on the air of a novel. It had been easy to try and, if not dismiss the rumors, at least limit them somehow. To claim that those taken were political activists, troublemakers—not like us. Like trying to say someone who died from illness had gotten sick because they had not taken care of themselves, an attempt to distance and deny.

One day there was word of a transport of Jewish children that were coming to Shanghai, escaping without their parents from the situation that was undeniably worsening. The principal, Madam Boudreau, made preparations, squeezing extra desks into each class-room. On the morning the children were scheduled to arrive, the students went down to the harbor with welcome signs and bal-loons and waited for hours. Ella had felt giddy imagining the new friends who might arrive, and the adventures they might share. But the ship did not come that day or the next. Eventually the desks were moved or used to stack books.

Only later would they learn the true extent of the devastation, villages burned to the ground, innocent women and children slaughtered. No one outside of Europe seemed to have known how far spread the killing had been. There had been signs, though, hadn't there, in China, as well as here? Even the Jews had not wanted to admit such things could possibly be in the era of radio and movies and cars.

David held up his hand. "I should take my ring off. I just wasn't ready."

"There's no rush," she chimed in quickly.

"I lost others: my mother, my sister." David ticked them off methodically on his fingers, his grief a faucet that, once opened, could not be easily shut again. He paused expectantly, waiting for her to share her own losses. But Ella had nothing to offer. She lost no one in the war, a notion that would surely be inconceivable to him. It might have been her family, too, if they had fled Stalin's Russia west instead of east. Many times over the years, Ella had gazed longingly at the fashion magazines and wished that she had been in Paris or Milan. But exile to strange, dusty Asia had proven a gift, the difference between life and death.

He blinked, clearing the sadness from his eyes. "You are going to family?"

"Yes," she said quickly, grateful to have something to answer this time. "My father." She handed him the piece of paper with the address.

"Hmm . . . Brooklyn. That's lucky—you can take the bus straight from here." Ella exhaled slightly. "Where does he work?"

She looked down, fidgeting with her cuffs. "I'm not sure." An element of uncertainty crept into her voice. Papa did not know she was coming. They had always planned it, of course—he would go ahead and send for the others. In the beginning, his letters had been so bright, talking of plentiful work and full shelves in the grocery stores. But details of his actual life were vague. Papa had come to America when a group of visas had opened up for railway workers, claiming experience on the Trans-Manchurian line to Harbin. In reality, manual labor was foreign to him. He was a musician and a bootlegger, a vagabond who played lively tunes at bar mitzvahs and weddings, but had never been able to hold down a sensible job. The bakery in Shanghai was his in name only. It was Mama who got up before dawn to make the bread, then dress and sell it behind the counter.

Papa's correspondence had dwindled, and it had been more than six months since he had last written. Meanwhile, things were getting worse in Shanghai, the distinctions between the refugee Jews and those who were permanent residents mattering less and less. She realized this when the grocer from whom they had bought food for years would no longer serve her. Even though she had lived among the Chinese her whole life, they still considered her a foreigner—and a Jew first. So when she saw a notice of an additional quota of visas, she had registered for one, and boarded the ship less than a week later without writing. She hadn't the money for a phone call; she had thought about sending a telegram but decided against it. But that was okay, wasn't it? After all, she *was* family. She hesitated now, wondering.

Her back straightened. She did not, of course, intend to be a burden. She would get a job and earn her keep, though doing what, she wasn't exactly sure. Education in China still followed the old model, training women to be wives and mothers and not much else. But she knew how to do things from watching Mama— knitting and baking and taking care of children.

David handed the paper back to her. "I didn't have anyone here. They wanted to send me west right away, but I persuaded the man at customs to let me work in New York for a bit. He gave me papers to work for a few months, just enough to earn my fare. But my papers are about to expire and I've made enough, so I'm going."

Ella's heart seemed to skip a beat, though she was not sure why. "Where?"

"The Midwest, Missouri or Nebraska." Ella cocked her head— she had just come through the West, and could recall nothing but wide, desolate prairies stretching endlessly in either direction out the train window. "New York is too crowded. There's opportunity out west, though. Kansas City will be my first stop, and if not I'll keep going until I find the place. I'll know when it's right." He spoke with the confidence of a man who had nothing left to lose.

"What will you do?"

He shrugged. "I'm strong. I'll find work, and maybe someday I'll earn a living as an artist. Dreams are fine but you have to be willing to work for them."

"Will there be Jews?"

"That's an odd question coming from someone who has spent her whole life in China." The words sounded like a rebuke, and Ella's cheeks burned as though she had been slapped. She started to tell him that there were Jews in China. The community had been small, to be sure, when they lived in Harbin in the early years. It had been there, though, and had grown, especially once the refugees flooded Shanghai.

Ella looked up and saw the twinkle in David's eyes and knew that he had been teasing her. She chuckled. It was odd to laugh so easily with this near-stranger, but it felt good, too, after the weeks of solitude. Then he shrugged earnestly. "Someone has to be the first to go. If people knew us, maybe it would not be so easy to let these things happen." He was talking about the killing in Europe. She wanted to point out that people there had let the Nazis massacre their Jewish neighbors after living side by side for centuries.

"Anyway, other Jews don't matter so much to me. I'm not a religious man," he added. "I left God on that killing field at Birkenau. I believe in things I can see and touch, in the ability of man to make a difference for better or worse." His words unfurled like a wide landscape. Then the corners of his mouth fell. "Or maybe my not believing is a form of self-defense."

"I don't understand."

"If there is a God, he will surely demand an accounting from me. I was involved in political causes at great danger to my family."

"David, you were off fighting for what you believed in." It was suddenly as if he was in a deep hole, and she was trying with her words to reach him.

"I was selfish." He dropped his voice, as though not wanting the passersby to hear. "The night before I returned to the city, I was celebrating with the men over a small skirmish in which we had beaten some Germans. The next morning I came home to find everyone gone. The Gestapo had come looking for me and arrested all of the residents of our street. They shot a dozen men—whether they resisted or it was simply in reprisal for the dead Germans or refusing to disclose my whereabouts, I don't know. The destruction was fresh—you could still smell the blood through the smoke. If I had come a day earlier . . ." He buried his head in his hands. "It's my fault they are gone."

"No!" Ella searched for words to comfort him. "You couldn't have known." His family had died because they were Jews, and the Germans killed Jews. But the remorse would always be with him.

"I never should have left them," he lamented.

"The work you did . . . you had to try and help." David did not seem like one who could fight and kill. But he had stood up, in his own way. She placed her hand on his shoulder.

A moment later he looked up and cleared his throat. "I never told anyone that before," he mused. "I wonder why I'm telling you now." She saw then the deep lines in his cheeks, the way in which his features must have hardened over time. But there was a light in his eyes, and an undeniable energy about him.

"How do you do it?" she asked. "How do you keep going after all of the pain?"

"Because I'm alive. To lie down would be an affront to my family."

A young woman in a pilot's uniform strode past, neat and self-assured. "It must be nice to have purpose like that," Ella said wistfully. She admired, too, the woman's sleek bob with bangs beneath her cap.

"Purpose? You've just come halfway around the world by yourself. I'd say you have that."

She flushed slightly. "I . . ." A loud thudding sounded behind them, causing both to jump. Ella spun to see a pile of crates that had fallen from a delivery truck idling at the curb. When she turned back, David sat frozen, shoulders hunched defensively. She understood then all that he had suffered, and the damage that persisted despite his determination to press on. She wanted to put her arms around him, but she did not dare. "It's all right," she soothed.

His face relaxed. "There are some things," he said, "that are hard to let go. But I'm here now—a fresh start for all."

"Do you mind it much, being alone?" The question came out more intrusive than Ella intended, for she did not want to remind him of his pain. But she was curious; for her, solitude was an odd, temporary state, to be remedied when her family was back together. For David, it had become the norm.

"I suppose it might bother me, if I allowed myself to think about it." Ella had thought about it every night as she lay on the hard wood flat of the ship among five other girls, listening to the bow creak and the wake lap up against the wood. She imagined creeping into Mama's bed, pressing against her for comfort as she and Joseph so often had after Papa had left. "We are all alone," he added. Despite the warmth of the afternoon, Ella shivered. "I'm used to it now." Did he mean it, or was he simply determined not to get hurt again, or to love anyone if it meant losing them?

Her eyes traveled to a newspaper headline, a photo showing the destruction of Berlin after the Allied bombings. "So many suffered," David remarked.

She was surprised how charitable he could sound to those who had taken his family. "You don't hate them?"

"I hate those who killed my family and neighbors." He gestured widely toward the street, then lifted his arms toward the sky. "But hating an entire country is not going to bring back my family." There was an energy about him, a constant fluttering of the hands. She reached out and put her hand over his, the gesture so impulsive and bold it hardly seemed her own. Their eyes met. A second passed, then another. Ella saw the fear that if he stopped moving he might crumble like dust. She released him.

David continued, "It's going to be quite a job, though, rebuilding the world. Let's hope they get it right this time." He was referring of course to the Great War, not three decades earlier. Then the peacemakers had thought they were creating a new world order. What would make this time any different? "It's going to be a trick, with the Russians and all," he added.

Ella nodded. Trouble was emerging already between the Soviet Union and the West, squabbling over Eastern Europe like stray dogs fighting for a scrap of meat. "The communists, are they really so bad?"

He looked hurriedly in both directions. "Shh—people here, they need something to be afraid of, and now that Hitler is gone, well, that's it." Hitler had shot himself unceremoniously months earlier. Then the German army surrendered and the whole thing ended.

The war in the East had lingered on, though. Hearing of the destruction, especially the awful bombs that had been dropped, Ella felt a bit sad. She knew the Japanese were hated in America. But they had kept the Jews of Shanghai alive, albeit in deplorable conditions, and that was something. She was not sure who the enemy was anymore.

As she thought about it now, Ella's stomach hardened—what would happen to Mama and Joseph now that the Japanese no longer controlled Shanghai? China had always tolerated the Jews, but the political situation would be unstable at best.

"You'll do just fine," he said brightly, misreading the consternation on her face.

"I'm not worried about . . ." Then she stopped, accepting the encouragement he offered, which she had not known that she needed until just that moment.

"You've got a lucky feel about you," he added. *Luck.* It was not the first time he had mentioned it, though perhaps it was fitting that someone who professed to no longer believe in God should put so much stock into chance. "I should take you with me," he blurted. "That is, you could come along." She inhaled sharply, taken aback by the boldness of the suggestion from a man she just met. "There are lots of opportunities for women, too, I'm sure, if you weren't off to see your father."

He was joking, certainly. But there was something familiar about sitting here talking with David, as if she had known him for years. And it felt nice, after weeks of traveling alone, to know someone. He was going his way, though, and she hers, and there was nothing to be done about it. She would have liked to have invited him along to Papa's if she knew what it would be like there.

Across the station the clock chimed five. "Oh goodness," she said, standing up. Time had flown so much more quickly than she'd expected.

"If we had more time, we could see a film," he said, an unmistakable note of wistfulness to his voice. *If.*

"You could take the subway," he added, his tone practical now. She shuddered. The dark underground maze seemed scary and alien. "A bus, then. Right at the corner of Lexington. I can go with you if you'd like. My train doesn't leave for another few hours."

But she shook her head. She needed to meet Papa on her own. "I wouldn't want to take you out of your way."

A look of disappointment crossed his face. "Well then, Miss Ella." He brought his lips to her hand and then held it for a second, leaning in. She wondered if he might kiss her cheek—or more. But he let go of her hand and tipped his hat. "Good-bye."

Ella picked up her suitcase, which seemed to have grown heavier, and started walking toward the corner. When she turned back, David had disappeared.

Sadness filled her then, and she was seized with the urge to turn and run after him. Enough, she thought, brushing the notion away. Papa was waiting. Ella began walking once more. Ahead of her, a man pushed a pram down the street, while the woman at his side licked an ice-cream cone. So this was what life was to be like here. Ella's step grew light and confident, as if she were sailing down 42nd Street. She had made a friend already. She would not see David again, and she was sad to see him go. But he had surely found her interesting, and if she did that in just a few minutes, maybe there was a chance to make any life here that she wanted.

Forty minutes later, Ella climbed off at the stop the driver had indicated. Clearing from her throat the fumes the bus had belched before leaving, she set down her bag and paused to gather her bearings. The ramshackle neighborhood, with its run-down stoops, seemed worlds away from the gleaming city she had just left across the river. Laundry lines awash in white sheets were strung between the tenement buildings. How had Papa come to live here? She knew so little about his life—perhaps he lived in a boardinghouse just for men. He might not have a place for her.

Ella paused in front of a drugstore. She eyed the front window. A wall of penny candy, rows and rows of gum balls and taffies and licorice, danced before her eyes, taunting her. Joseph would have loved it. Outside a shoeshine boy sat on the ground, waiting for a customer. He reminded her of the barber they used to see on Chushan Road, cutting hair on the front steps of his house for change. Ella considered asking the boy for directions. Then, thinking better of it, she kept walking. The house numbers were going lower now, confirming that she was headed in the right direction. The neighborhood here was shabbier still, voices arguing loudly through a cracked window over a broadcast of a baseball game, the sound of something breaking. The stench of warm, rotting garbage rose from a sewer. A teenage boy sat idly on a dirty stoop, his socks improbably white below rolled jeans.

As she neared the address on the paper, her heartbeat quickened. It was a real house, with a freshly washed stoop and yellow flowers in the box outside the window. Papa really had done well here after all. But was he kinder now? She stood motionless, as if her feet were now cased in concrete. On the journey, which seemed as though it had taken years, Ella had pictured the reunion a thousand times. She had practiced the words she would say in her mind, how she would tell him about all that he had missed. Now that the reunion was actually here, she was not ready.

But there was nothing to be gained from waiting. Steeling herself, she walked to the house. She knocked on the door, then touched the silver mezuzah mounted on the door frame, not unlike theirs back home in Shanghai. From inside the house came the Sabbath smells like a nearly forgotten dream, baking challah and roast chicken mixing familiarly with stale pipe smoke. Her pulse quickened as she imagined stepping inside, a welcome daughter.

A woman appeared in the doorway, brushing back auburn hair from her face. Ella started. There had to be someone, she reminded herself. Papa would not have prepared such a delicious-smelling meal himself. Was she a cleaner, or a cook, perhaps? But the woman moved with an ease that suggested something else. "Yes?" Her voice was harried but not unkind.

Uneasiness tugged at Ella's stomach. "I'm looking for Jacob Saul." The woman had strawberry freckles. Her face was too small, features seeming to cluster in the center.

"Jack is still at work at the press," the woman replied. Ella cursed herself inwardly for not remembering the Americanized name from his later postcards. "Can I help you?" There was a note of possessiveness to her voice.

"I . . ." Ella stopped, noticing the pearl bracelet that swung around the woman's wrist. Papa had given the bracelet to her mother as a wedding gift, representing both her birthstone and her namesake. It was her most cherished possession.

But Mama had given it back to him on the dock that foggy day, much like this one, when he had left. "In case money gets short," she insisted.

"Until I can put it on your wrist again," Papa had corrected. Now it hung around another wrist, not pale and graceful like Mama's, but thick and sturdy.

"I'm Mrs. Saul," the woman added, before Ella had time to grasp the gold band on the woman's fourth finger.

A rock seemed to slam into Ella's chest, making it hard to breathe. No, she wanted to correct, Mrs. Saul was in Shanghai, dutifully waiting for Ella's husband to send for her.

Ella's mind reeled: Papa was married to someone else. How could that possibly be? Easy enough, she realized, when your wife was halfway around the world, and nobody knew about her—or the two children you shared.

"And you are . . . ?" Ella clenched her fists as her shock hardened to anger. The woman did not know about her. Of course not. She did not know about any of them. Ella opened her mouth to deliver the news that would shatter her world into tiny little pieces: *You aren't the first wife. None of this is real.*

Just then a little girl appeared from behind the woman's legs. "Mama?" The woman tried to shoo the girl from sight, but when she popped out again, she picked her up. The girl had curls the same shade as her mother's, with hazel eyes that were unmistakably Papa's. She was younger than Joseph, but she had to be at least two. As Ella did the math, her rage grew. Papa had scarcely waited a year after leaving them before he married again. Had they not mattered at all? Papa's letters had continued to come after that date, though with decreasing frequency, as he maintained the charade.

"Did you want something?" the woman pressed. The child watched Ella's face, curious.

Ella faltered. She could stay and confront Papa, insist that he take her in. The woman's expression, though worried, carried a kindness that said she would not turn her away. But Ella would be extra here, a reminder of a life nobody wanted. And there would be no place for Mama or Joseph.

Ella tried to think of an excuse that would have her standing on the woman's doorstep with a valise, but could not. "Nothing," she said finally.

Something registered in the woman's eyes. It was her voice, low and lyrical, so clearly like her father's. "You . . ."

Ella turned to walk away. "Wait . . ." The woman ran after her clumsily, bobbling the little girl. "He said he had been married once, but he never mentioned a child."

Children, Ella corrected silently. She waited for the woman to ask about her mother, but she did not. "My name is Alice," the woman added. "I lost my husband at Normandy during the war." She seemed to be asking Ella to understand. Ella wondered if Papa still had a temper. Had that changed, too, or did his new wife simply bear it as the price of having someone?

Ella debated whether to say more about who she was, or the distance she had come. This woman should know not just about Ella, but the little boy and the wife who waited faithfully. She did not want to know this woman, though, or to acknowledge that any of this was real.

The woman's eyes followed Ella's gaze to her wrist. She set down the child and took off the bracelet. "Here."

Ella hesitated. She would not accept pity or charity, especially not from this woman. But she would reclaim Mama's bracelet as payment for leaving her alone, and not destroying her world. Ella took the bracelet and slipped it in her pocket.

Her gaze traveled to the second floor of the house, where pale yellow curtains billowed behind an open window. There might be a bed, she thought—a bath, a place to lay her head, even just a cup of tea. Surely the woman would not refuse her husband's blood kin. But she did not offer and Ella was too proud to ask. She stepped from the porch.

"What should I tell him?"

Ella wavered: even if she did have an address to leave, or some idea where she would go, she did not want Papa coming after her with the half-truths and excuses that would be so far short of making things all right. Or perhaps he would not follow her, a rejection that would hurt worst of all, if she were to let it happen. She reached into her valise and pulled out the sweater. Navy blue and wool, Mama had knitted it bit by bit each late night, and had insisted that Ella fit it into her bag where space was so precious because she was sure that Papa needed it. The stitching alone would be a calling card, Mama's meticulous handiwork a rebuke.

"And ask him if he remembers the barber on Chushan Road." There were a thousand other memories racing through her head, but she did not want to share them. The woman nodded. Would she tell Papa and give him the sweater or pretend none of this ever happened? It did not matter now.

Ella walked down the steps. Though she could not look back, she felt the woman's eyes on her, watching to make sure she was really gone. Around the corner, she leaned against a low wall, shaking. She saw Papa walking merrily through the streets of Shanghai holding her hand and carrying Joseph—how could he have forgotten so easily the life they had shared? "America really changes a person," Mama had said with each letter they received from Papa. Because she so, so wanted to believe it. Partly it was true—Papa had found a job and a good place to live, in the house that had surely belonged to Alice and her dead first husband. But the rest, about the money he was saving for boat tickets and the life they would share, had all been a lie.

Ella's mind flashed back to when she was five and had gotten momentarily separated from her parents at the market, lured around the corner by the curious site of a monkey shelling peanuts. Standing perfectly still in the sea of tall bodies that milled around, Ella had felt alone for the first time in her life. Mama had found her quickly, of course, and scolded her for wandering off, but the shaken feeling had lingered for days.

Suddenly on this Brooklyn street corner, she was five again. *Abandoned.* How dare he? Others like David had traveled the world looking for their families, while Papa had cast his away so callously. For what? The woman had been plain, with none of Mama's boundless grace. But she had been there in front of him, more convenient than pining for the beautiful wife he'd left thousands of miles away. And Papa, more so than anything, had always been about easy. Ella thought of the little girl with the hazel eyes like Joseph's. Would she grow up not knowing that she had two half-siblings, her own blood?

Across the street, Ella spied a print shop. Through the glass front window, she caught a glimpse of a familiar graying head, bowed low over one of the presses. The solemn, hardworking man was a stranger to her now. America really had changed Papa, but it was too late for their family. How could he have done this? Her stomach pulled, torn equally by the desire to run into his arms and to slap him. But neither would change a thing. She turned.

She stood for a second on the curb, feeling more alone than she had since leaving China. The streets were dirty and dank. Buildings crowded in above her. It was everything she hated about Shanghai, but with none of the family and love to make it worthwhile.

What now? Her whole journey was premised on a lie. She did not belong here. But even if she had the money to return to China, she could not face her mother and brother, knowing that she had failed them. And she could not tell Mama the truth. Ella would figure out something else to save her mother's pride, lie and say that she had not been able to find Papa. Even telling Mama that he was dead would bring her less pain and shame than the reality that he had moved on and left her behind.

No, she could not go back. And she did not *want* to go back to China, she realized with newfound clarity. Though she had been born there, she had never quite fit in. She would stay and make a

PAM JENOFF

life here somehow and make good on the promise to bring Mama
and Joseph over. But she did not want to stay here in this city, no
less stifling than Shanghai, which would always belong to her
father and his new family.

Ella looked at the clock above a tobacco shop. It was after six. David
would surely be boarding his train soon. Her stomach fluttered as his
dark eyes and dancing hands appeared in her mind. He managed to
look bright, despite all he had lost. How could a man she had known
only an hour linger with her so? She had felt stronger with him, more
capable. Go west, he'd said. She was suddenly as alone as he. Ella
wanted to put her head down and give up. But if David would not
retreat in the face of such pain, she could not, either.

Ella began walking once more, passing the bus stop. She kept
going, turning this way and that, feeling for the towering sky-
scrapers of the city that loomed ahead, obscured by the fog. Ahead
stood the wide expanse of the Brooklyn Bridge.

Half an hour later, Ella reached the other side of the bridge and
kept walking down the unfamiliar street. She paused and set down
her valise, her feet aching. The fog broke then, and a faint beam of
late-day sunlight shone through, revealing a hint of the city.

Across the street sat a pawnshop. Ella's eyes traveled to the window as she fingered the roundness of the pearls in her pocket. She
did not want to part with Mama's bracelet. But food on the trip had
been more costly than she expected. She'd had just enough money
to get to Papa and not much more.

And even with money, she still would not know where she was
going. In the West, David had said, it was open. Anyone had a
chance. Once, as she was traveling to New York on the train, she
had glimpsed an animal—like a deer, only thinner and more lithe

(a gazelle, perhaps, if she was sure what that had been), leaping across the horizon. *Free*. What would that feel like?

Come with him, David had said. What if she had taken him up on it? It was madness to consider going after him. Maybe he had been joking after all, and liked it better now being alone. She might not even make the train.

Ella had nothing and would not know a soul—except him. She simply had nothing to lose. She could not be dependent on him, any more than her father. But she could go.

Rest, it appeared, would be another step away. She pulled the bracelet from her pocket and stepped toward the door of the shop.

ACKNOWLEDGMENTS

My gratitude as always goes first to my family—without them this amazing journey would be neither possible nor worthwhile. Deepest thanks to editor Cindy Hwang and everyone at Berkley, and agent Scott Hoffman at Folio for their time and attention to my work. And much love to the *Grand Central* sisters, especially Kris McMorris, for including me in the most exciting project of my writing career.

The Harvest Season

KAREN WHITE

To my nephew, First Lieutenant Gavin White. Your bravery in service to your country and your strength and determination in the face of adversity are an inspiration.

～ 1 ～

Journeys end in lovers meeting. Shakespeare's words tumbled with my own inside my head, pushing aside the panic that had been building since I'd left Mississippi. Like the tiny seeds inside a cotton boll, my guilt and worry would have to be plucked out before the panic could go away.

My heels clicked across the marble floor of New York's Grand Central Terminal as I jostled past servicemen and their stuffed duffel bags as they were embraced by a mother, a father. A lover. Cigarette smoke hovered thickly, stinging my eyes. I blinked, focusing instead on the feeling of the telegram I'd tucked into the wrist of my glove.

The paper had been folded and unfolded so many times that a hole had started to form at the center crease. There'd been no need to bring it with me; I'd memorized every word even though it had not been addressed to me. Will had sent it to Indianola to his father, letting him know that Will was finally coming home. A home I was afraid he wouldn't recognize.

SHIP ARRIVAL EXPECTED SEPT 19 WILL STAY
WITH FRIEND IN CITY IF EARLY STOP IF YOU

STILL PLAN TO COME TO NYC AND RETURN
HOME WITH ME MEET ME AT THE CLOCK ON
THE 21st AT 5 PM IN THE CENTER OF MAIN TER-
MINAL STOP LOVE WILL

I clutched my carpetbag in my gloved hands. The kid gloves
matched the smart tweed suit I wore—complete with silk stockings that I refused to feel guilty about—purchased four years
before at Bergdorf Goodman on my last trip to New York with my
mother. I'd never worn either the gloves or the suit, nor any of the
other beautiful things purchased on that trip. This one suit had
been a recent and furtive token from my mother. The rest of the
clothes had remained in a trunk in my closet in my girlhood bedroom at Oak Alley, folded neatly with tissue paper and tucked in
alongside the dreams of the places I'd once imagined wearing
them. Three years is a lifetime when each minute is measured by
all the things that have been lost.

I stopped near the information booth in the center of the main
terminal and looked at the round face of the brass clock that pro-
truded from the middle, an acorn perched incongruously at the
top. Ten more minutes to stop my hands from shaking.

I began to people-watch to distract my thoughts. Grand Central
was busier than I'd ever seen it on my yearly shopping and theater
trips with my mother, the war's end bringing an influx of soldiers
and sailors through the cavernous space where the voices of so
many people roiled and bounced against the arched ceilings and
stone walls. Strangers jostled each other as they hurried in myriad
directions toward the arched entranceways and ramps that lead to
the tracks. Men with red caps scurried after harried passengers,
clutching valises and hatboxes as they headed toward track num-

ber thirty-four where the elegant and luxurious *Twentieth Century Limited* waited.

It was darker inside the terminal, and not just from the fog that had closed around the city like a soft fist. The large arched windows on the east and west ends had been painted black to protect the city's icon from possible air attacks, and the paint hadn't yet been completely removed. I half expected the enormous American flag hanging beneath a row of half-moon windows to be frayed around the edges like the lives of so many of her citizens.

It was as if New York's Grande Dame was stained, her beauty hidden by the pall of war. Despite the joy of the war's end, people wore the strain of the past four years like battle scars. For Will and so many others, the long journey home was only just the beginning.

I set down my bag, the raw skin on my knuckles and palms burning even with my gloves to protect them. My hands had once been declared in the *Greenwood Commonwealth* to be the creamiest and softest in all of Sunflower County. But those hands and the girl I'd once been no longer existed. And I'd long grown past the need to lament their passing.

Clasping my hands neatly in front of me, I began to search the crowd in earnest, hoping to spot Will before he saw me. I had the advantage. He was well over six feet, and I was a good foot shorter. And he wouldn't be looking for me because he had no idea that I was there.

I watched as a well-to-do businessman in a suit and hat approached a young man in an Air Force uniform and offered his hand. The young man dropped his duffel and grabbed the older man in a bear hug, knocking the hat from his head. The businessman scrambled to pick it off the floor and replace it on his head, but not before I'd seen his smile and the dampness in his eyes.

Still smiling, I turned my head slightly to the right and stopped. Stopped breathing, and hearing, and seeing the people walking past me. Everything seemed a blur of color except for the single image of Will Claiborne walking toward me in his olive drab Army dress uniform, his First Lieutenant silver bars on his shoulders, his dark brown hair nearly hidden by his cap. Ribbons decorated the left breast of his jacket; a Bronze Star, a Silver Star, a European Theater ribbon. A Purple Heart.

But this wasn't Will Claiborne. The man approaching me was a new version of the boy I'd known since I was tall enough to climb the fence that separated our families' properties. It was as if his youthful face had been fired in an oven, removing all softness and replacing it with harsh angles and a pair of hazel eyes that burned as if still remembering the fire.

I had time to see all this, to study him, as I watched him move around the information booth in search of his father, then finally come to a stop only five feet away from me.

Clutching the handle of the carpetbag, I opened my mouth to speak. "Will."

The word was immediately absorbed into the jangling air around me, bounced between passersby before falling, unheard, to the floor.

He turned his back to me as if preparing to make another trip around the information booth. "Will," I shouted, louder this time, desperate to be heard because I didn't think I'd find the strength to say his name one more time.

His shoulders stiffened inside his jacket before he slowly turned toward me. "Ginny," he said, too soft for me to hear. But I remembered the sound of my name on his lips.

"Hello, Will."

I hadn't expected him to embrace me, or even to smile. But I hadn't expected the coldness that filtered into his eyes.

"Where's Tug?" he asked.

My carefully prepared words deserted me, my frayed nerves coming undone in the babble springing from my lips. "He couldn't come. That's why I'm here. Our train doesn't leave until six. Why don't we go get something to eat so I can explain. There's a terrific oyster restaurant . . ."

"Where's Tug?" he asked again as if I hadn't said a word.

My hands began to shake again. I stepped closer so I wouldn't have to shout. "Your daddy had a stroke in January. A bad one. Amos found him by the cotton shed when he didn't come for supper. He hadn't been doing so well after Johnny . . ." *Johnny.* There. I'd said his name in front of Will and I hadn't split down the middle. Will's eyes never changed. I continued. "After we heard about Johnny being killed in action."

"How bad?" he asked, his voice emotionless.

"He can't walk, or speak. But his mind is sharp. He knows what's going on, and can nod or shake his head. He wanted to be here to greet you so badly and make the trip back home with you. He couldn't, so he asked me." There was so much more I needed to tell him, but he needed time to absorb each blow. It's why I'd agreed to the trip. Despite the troubled waters that rippled between us, I owed him this one last kindness.

"Your mama and daddy let you come all this way by yourself?" His disbelief was belied by a grudging look of admiration.

"My daddy has no say in my life anymore. Mama offered to give me money for the tickets, but I told her I was paying for them myself." I took a deep breath. "I sold your engagement ring to upgrade our tickets for our first leg on the *Twentieth Century Lim-*

ited, and for my stay last night at the Biltmore. It was a splurge, but it's where Mama and I always stayed when we came." I blushed, realizing that some of the old Ginny remained, stubbornly clinging like a child to his mother's hem.

Will hoisted his duffel onto his back as if preparing to leave. "I'm sorry you wasted your time. I'd rather hitchhike all the way to Mississippi than spend five minutes in your company, much less two days on a train."

I touched his sleeve, the one with the three yellow bars lined up one after the other. One for each six-month period he'd spent in a combat zone, never once returning home. I could tell he wanted to jerk away, but I held on.

"I promised your mama and daddy that I would bring you back safe and sound. And if you decide to hitchhike, then I guess I'll just have to hitchhike right along beside you."

He looked down the length of me to my calfskin wedge-heeled sandals, his expression an odd mixture of anger and amusement. And uncertainty. The corner of his mouth lifted. "That's tempting enough to take you seriously."

There'd once been a time when I would have pouted or stamped my foot, but the desire was long gone, replaced by the need to show Will that I was a different girl than the one he'd left behind. Kneeling down in front of my carpetbag, I opened it and removed the paper-wrapped package that I'd carefully placed on top, right next to the folded letter I'd brought to give to Will. If I found the courage.

Standing again, I handed him the package. He unwrapped it slowly, revealing a dark blue bottle that had once contained sarsaparilla purchased at the state fair. "From Lucille?" he asked, his voice thick.

I smiled weakly. "She took it off her bottle tree and told me to give it to you if you gave me any trouble. It's supposed to help you focus on getting home as quickly as possible." I paused. "She said you can smell the Mississippi mud inside, which is guaranteed to make you homesick." I recalled the scent of the lye soap she used to scrub the floors that clung to her skin like a dress, and the tears slipping down her dark face as she'd handed me the bottle.

He stared hard at the blue bottle and smiled for the first time. He lifted the lip of the bottle to his nose and sniffed. "I think she might be right about the Mississippi mud." Carefully, he wrapped the bottle and handed it back to me to repack. "Can I see the train tickets?"

With relief, I twisted open the clasp on my pocketbook and slid out the tickets, hesitating only a moment before handing them to Will. "I've already worked out the train schedule for the next two legs of the trip once we reach Chicago. I figured we could purchase the tickets once we arrive at each depot so we could be more flexible on times . . ."

I stopped speaking as Will stepped away from me and toward a young couple at the information booth. It was an Army private and a beautiful, dark-haired girl with a bright gold band gracing the fourth finger of her left hand. They turned to Will as he approached.

"Did I overhear you saying you're headed to Chicago?" he asked.

The man—barely older than a boy—smiled. "Yes, sir. I'm bringing my new bride to meet my family. She's French."

I watched with growing trepidation as Will studied the soldier's service ribbons and division patch. "You were at Normandy?"

"Yes, sir. First Infantry. Omaha Beach. We were in the thick of it."

"Yes, you were," Will agreed, an odd smile on his face, and I knew what he was about to do. He handed them the tickets. "Here's a wedding gift to you and your bride. Best of luck to you both."

The soldier stared at the tickets in his hand, the *Twentieth Century Limited* logo emblazoned on the top along with a picture of the train at the bottom, and his eyes widened with recognition. "Thank you. Thank you, sir!" he said, his free hand squeezing his bride closer to his side. He was still thanking Will as Will walked away toward me.

"Too refined for me. I hope you don't mind," he said, assuming I would. He began walking toward the ticket counters. "I guess we'll need to buy two train tickets home."

I looked over at the exuberant couple who were still embracing and speaking rapidly in a mixture of French and English, and I wasn't sure if I should laugh or cry. I hoisted my bag and followed Will to the ticket windows, refusing to complain. Will was *alive*, and I was going to bring him home, and it was enough.

He didn't acknowledge me as I stood at his side in the line; rather, he stared stoically in front of him. My hands stung, but I wouldn't let him know it. *One thing at a time.*

My thoughts were distracted by a flash of yellow from the corner of my eye, the color a surprise in the wash of mostly browns and grays. It was a young girl wearing a crumpled silk dress and carrying a small suitcase, her hat as weary as her face. She was walking quickly, and as she passed where we stood in line she began to run toward one of the track entranceways shouting, "David!"

I watched until she'd disappeared from view, hoping from the earnestness in her eyes that she would find him in time.

Will's voice startled me. I glanced up to find those eyes, both familiar and not, staring at me. "Thinking about home is what got me through the war. Please don't ruin my memories now by talking about my brother."

I thought of the letter nestled against the bottle in my carpet-bag, wondering now what my purpose had been in bringing it. What my purpose had been to even come to New York.

We remained silent except for the words necessary to navigate our route, and then to hurry down the ramp to the platform where our train waited, our tickets for the slower and less opulent *Wolverine* clasped in our hands. We boarded our train, preparing for the long journey home, both of us thinking about all the things that had changed in the last three years. And all that had not.

2

We changed trains in Chicago, embarking on the *City of New Orleans*, and again in Mississippi where the colored passengers, even soldiers in uniform, had to ride in the seating areas of the baggage car. Things changed slowly in the South, and sometimes one had to wonder if things ever changed at all. Some say it was the oppressive heat that slowed any kind of momentum. And as we traveled farther and farther south, I was tempted to agree.

On the way to Chicago on the first leg of the trip, Will did not speak to me except to find our way to our seats and then later to seek out the dining car. We joined a woman wearing a large, feathered hat and dining alone at one of the communal dining tables. She kept staring at us, assuming by our silence that we were having a lover's spat. At least Will's concentration on his food meant I could watch him, could study him as he ate, could be thankful for each breath he took.

The woman finished and left while we were halfway through our dessert, and Will watched her leave, his fingers drumming on the table just as he'd done as a boy when he was working up his courage. He put down his fork. "Why did you really come to New York, Ginny? It couldn't have been just to let me know about my daddy. You could have told me that in a letter or a telegram."

Because I need to tell you a secret. I took a sip of water. "Because Tug asked me to. And I . . ." I faltered. *And I've missed you so much, but I couldn't tell anybody because you were no longer mine.* "There's something you need to know . . ." I started, each word heavier than the last.

"What happened to your hands?" he asked softly.

He'd been so busy ignoring me that I'd forgotten to try and hide them. "I've been helping out. In the house and around the farm. Sometimes in the fields if Amos needs me."

He reached out and took my hands in his, turning the reddened palms up to face him. "You've been working in the fields?"

I nodded. "But I'm glad, Will. Glad to be useful, to contribute for the first time in my life."

Slowly, he placed my hands on the table, leaving me bereft. "I suppose that's a better use of your time."

I flushed, remembering. "It was only a kiss, meant to make you jealous." I paused, feeling as if I were talking about a stranger.

Which, I supposed, I was. "I knew how Johnny felt about me, and how easy it would be to hurt you. I was just a stupid, stupid girl."

"Yes, you were." Will had never been one to strain his words through a filter.

"And you went straight to the enlistment office and signed up. Then you were gone. You didn't give me a chance to tell you that I was sorry. That I loved you." *That I still do.* I looked down at the slim gold wedding band I still wore on my left hand even though Johnny had been dead for over a year. "Things have changed, Will. *I've* changed. There are things I need to tell you . . ."

He stood, swaying with weariness. "I'm tired, and I'm done fighting battles. I just want to go home." He scrubbed his hands over his face, as if trying to erase the past few years. "Please, Ginny. Just leave me be."

I breathed in deeply, tasting disappointment and relief, and placed my napkin on the table. Will helped me stand, then escorted me to my sleeping berth before leaving me after a brusque good-night.

I watched him walk down the corridor, knowing now how useless my words would be. He'd survived the war, and that would have to be enough for all of us for now. He'd see the changes soon enough, recognize them as a shedding of skin, and a leaving behind of an old life.

As I lay on my berth, listening to the silent breathing of the two other women in my compartment, I stared out the window as the moon flashed through the trees and thought of all that I'd left behind me, and all that I had gained from loss.

The muggy air of an early Mississippi morning swaddled us as we stepped off the train at the Indianola depot. Will had wired ahead to let his family know what train we'd be coming in on so we could be met at the station. I was exhausted and travel stained, the swaying motion of the trains staying with me even as I stood on the platform waiting as Will retrieved our luggage.

I removed my jacket and gloves, desperate to feel a breeze. The humidity always made the heat worse, but it made the chill of winter even more biting.

"Mr. Will!"

I turned to see Lucille's husband, Amos, walking toward us down the platform. He wore his uniform of worn denim coveralls and a plaid cotton shirt, neatly starched and pressed by Lucille, sweat making his bald head gleam. Will set our bags down and met Amos halfway, throwing his arms around the older man.

Amos held Will at arm's length. "You's too skinny. You needs some of Lucille's fried chicken. My George say he gained five pounds since he come home on account of his mama's cookin'." He grinned widely, but I could see the worry in his eyes, too. I'd seen it when George came home, the look of joy at reunion stirred with the worry of how much of their souls they'd lost in the killing fields of Europe.

Will gave an uncomfortable shrug, then picked up our bags before Amos could grab them. "I'm so used to carrying my gear that I need to hoist something."

"That's good to hear, 'cause you be hoisting a big cotton sack right soon. Been a good summer. Fields are just bustin' out with cotton."

We began walking toward the old pickup truck that Amos had been driving since Herbert Hoover was president. Its red had long since faded in the Mississippi sun to the color of an autumn cypress, but Amos kept the engine in perfect condition.

"How's George?" Will asked as he tossed his bag over the side of the truck bed, then placed mine carefully next to it.

A broad smile split his face. "He doin' real good. He grown some, too—might be taller'n you now." His smile faded. "Says he movin' to Chicago. Will just about break his mama's heart, but he say there're better jobs there for him." He opened the passenger side door for me to slide into the middle. "All them boys comin' back from the war don't want to work the cotton fields no more. Things are changin'. Yes, sir, things are changin'."

The cloth seat burned from sitting in the sun, my blouse sticking to my skin as I leaned forward away from the seat back. Amos settled himself behind the steering wheel as Will climbed in beside me, doing his best to avoid touching me.

Amos pulled the truck out onto Highway 82, heading west. A warm breeze blew through the open windows, bringing with it the smell of rain. "We could use some rain," I said, eager to change the subject. "It's been dry the last couple of weeks."

I turned my head toward the window, desperate for the wind to hit my face. Will and I remained silent as Amos kept up a constant chatter about the crop and the farm, about people Will had known all of his life. Will nodded occasionally, but his gaze never left the broad sweep of level lands that made you feel as if you could see all the way to the edge of the earth. When we were small, Will, Johnny and I had started walking just to see if we could reach that horizon that seemed so close. It had been near sunset before our parents found us less than a mile from Greenville. We'd all been punished severely, me most of all. I'd been sent away to school in New Orleans where the scent of the river was different and the accents of the people foreign to me. But I always liked to think that a part of that adventure stayed with us, reminding us of the day we'd believed that it was possible to touch the sky.

"Stop here."

There was something in Will's voice that forced Amos onto the gravelly roadside. Without a word, Will left the truck and moved to the edge of the road in front of a field of what Delta farmers called white gold. Rows of cotton plants pregnant with white bolls seemed to stretch out like fingers all the way to where the land ended and the sky began.

We watched as Will scrambled down the side of the road into a turnrow, then bent to snap a cotton boll from one of the plants. He stared at it for a long time until his broad shoulders began to shake. I slid toward the door, wanting to go to him, but Amos placed a staying hand on my arm.

I looked back at Will, imagining thousands of soldiers around the world standing in different fields, and in vineyards, and port cities, on old familiar roads and front yards, touching home again.

I glanced down at my ruined hands, thinking of Johnny and all the boys in the county who would never be coming home. I wanted desperately to hold on to this moment for Will, to allow him to believe that while he'd been away we'd held on to the life he remembered so he could slip back into it like a familiar bed. But time could not be fenced no matter how hard we tried.

Clouds scuttled overhead as we drove the rest of the way home, turning onto a dirt road right past the stone pillars that announced the entrance to the home where I'd grown up, Oak Alley. I no longer accidentally turned too short into the wrong drive, finally realizing where my home truly was.

Will leaned forward slightly as the wind picked up, rushing through the open windows of the truck, the wheels kicking up dust as we drove under the canopy of oaks, maples and gum trees until we reached a clearing and the house the Claibornes had called home for almost a century.

It was a simple whitewashed two-story farmhouse with a chimney on each end and a wraparound porch. My great-grandfather had lost this part of his property at auction to pay his taxes after the Civil War. A fence had always separated the two, fostering generations of mutual hatred, at least until I was born and the lure of the fence had proved too tempting.

Two figures sat on the steps of the porch, and my breathing became short and shallow until I forced myself to fill my lungs with the heavy air. Amos took our bags from the back and carried them to the covered porch as Will climbed from the truck and held the door open for me. Before I'd even set both feet on the ground, I heard my name called.

"Mama! Mama!" John-John's bare feet raced over the yard toward me.

I bent down in time to catch him in my arms. "Hello, sweetheart. Mama missed you so much."

I lifted him when I stood, reveling in the weight of him. Closing my eyes, I breathed in the earthy scent of little boy and a trace of soap Lucille must have forced on him.

I turned as Will approached, then watched him and my son regard each other with open curiosity through identical hazel eyes set beneath dark brows and hair.

"Will, this is John-John. Sweetie, this is your uncle Will."

"Soljur," John-John said. "Like Daddy."

I kissed his temple. "Yes, darling. Like Daddy."

They continued to take each other's measure, and I shifted my feet uneasily in the grass. "Today's my birfday," John-John said, his face serious. He held out a hand with three fingers just like I'd been teaching him. "I'm free."

The corner of Will's mouth lifted. He reached over and ruffled the little boy's hair. "It's good to finally meet you, John-John. And Happy Birthday." He studied him for a long moment. "You look just like your grandpa, Tug, don't you?"

John-John lifted his right hand. "Erich make dis. It's a top an' it spins."

The man who'd been on the porch with my son when we'd first driven up approached. I felt Will stiffen beside me as he took in Erich's pants with the large letters PW stamped in blue across each thigh.

In one of our few conversations on the train, I'd told Will about the German POW camps that had been established in Indianola and around the country to provide local farmers with much-needed labor. But I'd stopped from telling him more when I'd seen the look of disdain that had curled his lips and darkened his eyes.

"Will, this is Erich Schumacher. He was a big help to Amos during the planting, and he'll be here for the harvest. He's a good carpenter, too. He's done a lot of the repairs . . ."

Will cut me off. "Where's home, Mr. Schumacher?"

He gave Will a measuring look before answering in good English, his accent apparent from the heavy consonants not usually found south of the Mason-Dixon line. "Near a small Bavarian town called Freising, about thirty kilometers from Munchen."

"You're German?" Without allowing Erich to answer, Will turned on Amos. "You let this *German* near my nephew? Near my mother and father? On my *land*?"

All of the endless travel, the heat and my sore hands finally overtook my already frayed nerves. I put John-John down, his arms clinging to my leg like kudzu. "It wasn't Amos, Will. It was me. We needed help with the cotton, and the Germans were the only labor available. So I hired them. We had Erich and a bunch more during the planting season, and I've already asked for the same men for the harvest."

I'd only seen the look on Will's face once before, nearly four years ago when he'd found Johnny and me beneath the three-hundred-year-old cypress tree that had their parents' initials carved into it. Right in the same spot where Will had asked me to marry him, and I'd said yes. I'd hoped to never see that look again. It was more than anger and hurt. It was the look of a starving man right after you'd snatched the last bread crumb from his hand.

Will turned in a circle as if looking for someone. But that person had been in a wheelchair for the best part of a year and couldn't help him now. "Why?" Will asked. I knew he wasn't asking me to repeat what I'd already told him. He was simply asking the same question I'd been asking for three long years that no one on this side of heaven had an answer to.

"Because someone had to make sure that you'd have a home to come home to." Taking John-John's hand, I turned to Amos. "Please take Erich back to the camp now. You can bring him back tomorrow to get started on repairing the roof on the mule barn."

Erich nodded, then followed Amos, his eyes carefully avoiding Will's. The front door of the house opened and we all turned as Lucille came out, wiping her hands on an apron, Will's mother, Marjory, following closely behind her. Marjory's knees buckled at the sight of Will, and Lucille placed an arm around Marjory's too-slim hips to hold her steady.

Will walked quickly toward his mother, her dark eyes never leaving his face. Lucille let go only after Will had reached them and his arms were safely around Marjory, his face reflecting a grief I was already too familiar with.

Marjory Claiborne had once been a force of nature in Indianola, small of stature and soft of voice, but wielding so much authority and conviction that people seemed to forget that she was half their size. She ran her house and her two boys with stern discipline, never one to adhere to a spare-the-rod philosophy—not that it helped corral the Claiborne boys. But even with them she commanded respect and devotion.

But the war had killed a part of her, almost as if she'd stepped on a mine and it had blown up half her heart. I'd begun to believe that only the hope of seeing Will again was what got her out of bed each morning. It was one of the reasons I'd agreed to go to New York, to be a surrogate protector for the one thing the war had not taken from her.

Will cradled his mother's head against his chest, patting her back much as I imagined she had once done when he was a child. Her tears bled dark spots onto his jacket, and I wondered if they would stain. Not that it mattered. I doubted he'd ever want to wear his uniform again.

Lucille clasped his arm in her large, black hand, her lips clamped together and trembling as she worked hard not to cry. Will smiled at her, but it didn't lift the bleakness from his expression. "Amos is gonna bring George up to the house for birthday cake after supper tonight. He gots lots to tell you."

Will nodded, but anything he was going to say got stuck in his mouth as his attention turned toward the doorway. For the first time in his life, Tug Claiborne appeared smaller than his wife. Even his large personality had shriveled to fit inside the shrunken body folded into the wheelchair like a rag doll.

A guttural sound emitted from the older man's throat, his eyes wet with tears he wouldn't let go. His strength had deserted him, but his stubbornness would not. For a moment, Will hesitated as if he didn't recognize this man, or these people, or the life they represented. Before he could realize that he was right, he bent toward his father and grasped his hands.

"I'm home, Daddy. It's going to be okay."

Lucille's eyes slid to mine for a moment before she turned back to Marjory. "Let's go start makin' dinner. We gots two things to celebrate today. Praise the Lord, yes we do. We gots your favorites, Mr. Will. Collard greens and fried chicken, and my beans done in fatback just like you likes them when you was a boy. Don't figure that much has changed. Your mama done made her peach cobbler, the one that took first prize at the church fair three summers ago. We've got to fatten that boy up, don't we, Miss Marjory?"

Marjory stared blankly as Will pulled his father's chair back into the house, followed by Lucille holding tight to Marjory. I stood where I was, needing to be quiet for a few moments. My son sensed this and held on to my hand without complaint as the wind picked up and the late-morning sky darkened.

Long rows of cotton plants in the fields behind the house bobbed their puffy heads like old ladies in church praying for rain. The water-saturated air tasted bitter and sweet, an odd concoction of celebration and grief. But I couldn't stop myself from believing that there was hope there, too; that hope existed in the endless cycle of sowing seeds and reaping cotton from the dark, alluvial soil. I had to believe that. I had to for John-John's sake. And for Will's.

A small flock of white-throated swallows flitted up above the trees, nervously chattering as they circled the house before settling on the roof and chimneys like children returning home to roost. Fat slaps of rain hit the ground around us, splattering my shoes and stockings and speckling John-John's bare feet with dirt. Holding tightly to his hand, I led him toward the house and up the steps as the sky relinquished its rain. My shoulders ached as if I'd been hauling a cotton-filled sack through muddy furrows, and I straightened them, lifting my head. I entered the house with purposeful steps as the rain fell on the thirsty fields and the white house, turning the dust to mud.

~ 3 ~

It was still dark the following morning when I padded quietly into the back office that had been carved out of the parlor. I'd have preferred to use the dining room table for farm business, still feeling as if I were intruding into Tug's life by sitting at his desk and writing checks from his checkbook, but the dining room had been converted to a bedroom for him and Marjory.

Amos and one of the tenant farmers had carried their bed from upstairs as I watched with Marjory and she silently cried. That's what had finally broken her. It was as if moving that one piece of furniture was the beginning of a funeral cortege for the life she'd always expected to have. She was different after that, easily letting go of the yoke that had tethered her to the farm and allowing me to slip it around my own neck.

I'd watched with the same dry eyes I'd had when I'd packed up all of Johnny's things and stored them in a suitcase in the back of our bedroom closet. I didn't have time for tears, or looking back, or wishing for something that wasn't to be.

I flipped on the desk lamp and sat down, then heard Lucille come in through the kitchen door. I waited for the smell of coffee to drift into the office, more grateful than I should have been that coffee was once again in regular supply.

I started with the mail that had accumulated while I'd been gone. The first was another letter from the Southern Tenant Farmers' Union protesting our use of POW labor. I rubbed my temples, wondering how long it would take the coffee to brew, and if I should bother with a reply explaining yet again the shortage of workers and my inability to pay the higher wages the remaining ones demanded.

I looked again at the teetering stack of mail, then slid the letter from the STFU into the wastebasket. I pulled out the ledger and began logging the bills as I paid each one, then wrote out the checks. I didn't sign them. I brought every check to Tug, who seemed grateful to make a semblance of a mark in the signature line. It was accepted at Planters Bank in Indianola, who'd done business with the Claibornes since it had opened in 1920.

A steaming mug of coffee was placed on the desk in front of me. I looked up, surprised to see Will. He was dressed in a plaid cotton shirt and dungarees, and if I hadn't seen his eyes I might have thought it was the old Will, the Will with the easy laugh and big dreams. The Will I'd fallen in love with when I was six years old and never stopped loving.

"Good morning," I said, putting down the pen and picking up the mug. "Thank you."

His response was a short nod. "Lucille told me I could find you in here, and that you'd be wanting coffee. I thought she was joking. You've never been the kind of girl to get out of bed before noon." He took a sip from his own mug.

"There's work to be done. And John-John will be up soon, which makes it hard to concentrate." I indicated the ledger and the piles in front of me.

His jaw tightened as he glanced at the papers on the desk. "So Daddy . . ." His voice faded away, leaving a trail of incomprehension and confusion.

"Tug's still there, Will. Beneath the man you see, the father you used to know is still there. It's just harder for him to communicate and get around. But he still signs all of his checks—as best he can—and I always go to him with my questions. I can usually figure out what he's saying."

He stared into his coffee mug like it had answers. "Poor Mama. She's loved that man her whole life. And now she's like a ghost. Not dead, but not alive, either."

I remained silent, not wanting to show any disrespect by agreeing. Or by telling him that I'd learned in the past three years that some people break in a strong wind, while others learn to bend into it.

He looked down at my hands, and I fisted them, as if I could hide what he'd already seen. In a quiet voice, he asked, "Why didn't you go home, Ginny?"

I stood as if to emphasize my words, as if to convince him that I was sincere. "Because this is my home now."

We stared at each other across his father's desk for a long moment, listening to the clanging of pans in the kitchen as Lucille prepared breakfast. The sound had come to mean home to me, along with the braying of the mules, and the spring song from the family of warblers that lived in the magnolia tree outside my window. And the sweet notes of my son's voice as he pretended to read one of his father and uncle's childhood books that remained on the bookshelves in their boyhood bedroom, which John-John and I now shared.

Living at Oak Alley with my parents and brother, I'd never heard any of those things. I'd been insulated and isolated from the rest of the world. And from the person I never knew I could be.

"For now," he said, his voice hard as if shutting a door. He moved away from me, toward the window that showed a slowly brightening sky. "I'm walking the farm today with Amos to get a handle on things, figure out when to start the harvest—looks like the fields are almost ready. You won't have to deal with any of this anymore. And no more German labor, Ginny. I can't abide it."

I was unprepared for the surge of anger, for his easy dismissal. "Save yourself the trouble of trying to find labor to work the harvest. So many of the tenant farmers moved up north to work in the factories for the war effort and they're not coming back. And those who stayed are working for higher wages than we can pay. My own father is paying them twice per pound what we can. If we don't use the Germans, our crop will rot in the field. Just ask your daddy. It was his idea to begin with, and it took me two minutes to realize that he was right."

His stranger's eyes flickered in the light from the window. "A German bullet killed my brother. Or has everyone already forgotten that?"

I looked away, unable to meet his eyes. "There are lots of empty spots at kitchen tables all over the country. We're not likely to ever forget that—and we shouldn't. But we can't change it, either. It's hard to walk forward if you're too busy looking behind you."

I thought of his mother, and her empty eyes, and was suddenly exhausted. I sat down, leaning against the back of the chair. "If we have a good harvest this year, we might be able to afford one of the new harvesting machines everybody's talking about. The Germans will be gone after spring planting. If we can get one of those machines by next fall, we'll be fine. We just need to make it through the spring."

My gaze moved past him out the window where the sun was just beginning to stretch its legs over the horizon. In my old life, I'd never witnessed a sunrise, and the thought shamed me. After four long years of war when it seemed the whole world was on fire and the news was full of so much death and destruction, to take for granted the glory of a sunrise seemed a lot like working in the fields without a hat. Sooner or later, you'd end up with scars from wounds you didn't remember having.

I flattened my palms against the ledger, then swallowed to clear my throat so I could say the words I'd been rehearsing all night while I'd lain in bed listening to my son's breathing in the bed next to mine. "I can leave now, if you want. Or I can stay through the harvest and help Amos handle the POWs so you don't have to. Just promise me that you'll do what needs to be done with the farm for your parents' sake. They already lost so much. They can't lose the farm, too."

I focused on breathing slowly as I waited.

"Do you want to leave?"

"No," I said quickly, surprising myself with my honesty. I'd never been one to give a straight answer, not when a half-dozen vague responses would do. "But I won't stay if my being here makes you . . . uncomfortable."

The sun crept higher in the sky, making the walls of the office blush pink. He turned toward the window again. "I wanted every-thing to be the same as it was," he said softly.

I closed my eyes, seeing again the flat horizon on that long-ago day when Will, Johnny and I walked toward the sky. "Don't look back, Will. Don't. It's like swimming with a stone around your neck. It'll drag you down so deep that you can't find your way back to the surface." I shut the ledger book and rested my hands on top. "Moving forward is the only way I figure I can honor all those boys who aren't coming home."

He finished his coffee, then faced me, his face hard. "Stay through the harvest, then. I don't want to have anything to do with the Ger-mans."

Joy and desolation battled inside my head as a thump sounded from my bedroom upstairs, followed by the quick patter of little feet running toward the stairs.

Will moved to the doorway. "Can he make it down the stairs on his own?"

"Yes," I forced out. "He crawls down backward on his tummy. Johnny told me that's how your mama taught the two of you."

His old smile lit his face as he watched John-John's progress down the stairs. "And it worked until we discovered that sliding down the banister was faster." He laughed, and I found myself smiling at the sound, worried it had died alongside so many of his friends.

John-John rushed into the room wearing his red drop-seat paja-mas and holding something in his hand. I drew in a sharp breath as I realized he must have been clutching the glass object as he climbed down the stairs. "Mama!" he shouted, running forward. "What's this?"

It was the blue bottle I'd unpacked and left on the dresser. Will crouched down in front of him. "It's a bottle from Lucille's bottle tree. Why don't you and me go put it back now so it can be with all its friends?"

John-John scrunched up his eyebrows. "Why?"

"Because we need it to catch all the evil spirits before they can get into the house."

He thought for a moment. "Why?"

Taking the bottle from John-John, Will said, "Maybe Lucille can tell you better than I can."

He held out his other hand and John-John reached up to grab it. After a brief backward glance from Will, they left the room with the bottle to return it to the bottle tree. For a long time I stared at the empty space where they'd been, hoping that they weren't too late.

Hours later, as I settled John-John back into bed for his nap, I glanced over to the dresser where the bottle had been and then to the spot next to it where I'd placed the letter, relieved to find it still there. I slipped the letter into the top drawer, then slid it closed with a soft snap.

4

The harvest began the following week. As promised, Amos drove the German POWs to the fields each morning, then returned them to the camp behind high barbed wire fences after the iron bell announced it was quitting time.

The fields were bisected by the highway, and Amos and I arranged it so that the Germans worked the north fields, while everybody else—the seasonal field hands, Amos, Will, George—worked the south fields. I rotated between the two to supervise. I couldn't pick the two hundred pounds of cotton per day that the other workers did, but at least my labor was free.

By the time the dinner bell rang at noon on the first day and all the field-workers collapsed in the shade of the back porch and under the trees, my shoulders ached, my fingers were bloody and raw and my eyes stung from the brightness of the sun despite my wide-brimmed hat.

Will and I sat on the back porch with John-John on my lap, eating Lucille's fried chicken and dumplings. Since our conversation in his father's office, he'd been avoiding me, only speaking to me when we needed to discuss the farm, or when he asked me to show him the ledgers. We were dancers at a country dance, coming together only briefly, but always aware of the proximity of the other. He sat eating his lunch at the other end of the porch, his back to me.

Erich removed himself from the POWs clustered in the group beneath a shady elm and approached the porch. He stopped at the bottom of the steps, his straw hat in his hands. Will put down his knife and fork and fixed a hostile stare on the German.

Addressing me, Erich said, "I would like to have the wood left from the barn repair if that is all right. I have a project . . ."

"We don't need any of your projects," Will interrupted.

To my surprise, Erich climbed the steps and approached Will, stopping a few feet behind him.

"I apologize. I only wish to help." Will continued to glare, his fingers tapping hard on the table. Erich took another step forward.

"We are not so different, you and I," he said softly, his fingers worrying the brim of his hat.

Will jerked to a stand. "I beg your pardon?"

Erich didn't step back. "The war is over, and we are not soldiers anymore. I am a farmer, like you. I want to return to my fields and to my wife and son. It was dreaming of my home each night that kept me alive. I imagine you and I shared the same dream under the same stars." His fingers tightened on his hat. "And we both lost our brothers."

Will took a step toward the German, his hands in fists. I turned John-John's head away, pressing his face into my shoulder.

"Do not speak of my brother," Will spoke through clenched teeth.

Erich's face showed no alarm. "Our brothers are dead, Herr Claiborne. But we are not, yes?" He offered his hand to shake, and it hovered in the space between them like a white flag.

Without a word, Will stepped past Erich and stormed down the porch steps before disappearing around the corner of the house.

For the remainder of the harvest, Will remained aloof, our conversations only about soil, and weather, and the price of cotton, avoiding the subjects that floated between us like a poisonous cloud, waiting to be inhaled.

But I'd sometimes catch him watching me with wary eyes, like an owl in a tree waiting for darkness. We seemed to both be waiting for the inevitable confrontation, yet reluctant to let go of the peace of our false innocence. John-John took turns following Erich and Will down the rows, carrying his own small sack as he wrestled the puffy bolls from their stems. He kept up a steady stream of conversation with each man, and more than once I caught Will stopping to laugh and rub John-John on the head. When Lucille came to gather him for his nap, Will seemed disappointed to see him go.

I found I couldn't dwell on Will and his demons. Watching the men weigh their stuffed cotton sacks at the end of each day and seeing the mule carts tote the cotton to the shed filled me with as much joy and pride as I'd once reserved for a new dress and matching shoes. I relished the new calluses and blisters on my hands, wearing them as proudly as medals.

Slowly, the fields lost their bloom of white, the furrows returning again to dark brown. The air turned crisper in the evenings and the bald cypress trees that fringed the swamps around Indianola transformed themselves into clouds of russet leaves. The harvest had been a good one, but its end was bittersweet knowing that as soon as the cotton was ginned, I would be leaving.

On the last evening after the quitting bell had rung and our sacks had been emptied, we trudged silently from the fields to the house. Tug sat in his wheelchair on the porch with Lucille and Marjory, with Amos's truck parked in the drive, the tailgate open as Erich and the other POWs lifted something from the back and placed it on the porch steps.

Erich held John-John, but jumped down and ran to Will as we approached. "Look, Uncle Will! Grandpa has a hill!"

We stopped at the bottom of the steps where a wedge-shaped ramp had been made to fit over each rise, the flat top wide enough to accommodate a wheelchair. Tug's face was lit from a lopsided grin as Erich moved behind his wheelchair and slowly pushed him to the bottom. Tug reached up with his good hand and patted the German's arm in thanks.

"You made this?"

We all turned to Will, unsure how to read the roughness in his voice.

"Yes. To thank you all for many kindnesses shown to us here. I wish to have made it sooner so your father could greet his son when he came home, but I had no more wood."

Will's gaze took in the man standing before him, then moved toward his parents, John-John, me. And then toward the tidy white house with the wraparound porch and the harvested fields behind it with rows that reached out toward the horizon as if he were seeing a dream come to life. And maybe he was. Maybe this is what he'd dreamed of under the same stars that twinkled light over sleeping soldiers and his Mississippi home. He looked like the boy who'd awakened as a man to find that there was no longer a bigger bed to crawl into.

His gaze returned to Erich. After a long pause, he held out his hand. "Thank you."

Erich placed his hand in Will's and the two men shook.

Will cleared his throat. "John-John tells me that your son's name is Hans."

A slow smile lifted Erich's lips. "Yes. And when he grows up he wants to be a horse. Or a farmer like his father."

Will reached down and placed a hand on John-John's head. "I guess boys are pretty much the same everywhere. John-John told me yesterday that he wants to be a mule."

The men's voices carried softly across the yard as they spoke of the next generation of young men, hope in their voices that they might grow up to be farmers instead of soldiers.

I slipped past the cluster of people and went inside to grab a sweater, then headed out the back door toward the bayou that

edged the southeast boundary of the property. The family cemetery lay beside it, cocooned in the shelter of the cypress trees. It was
the best spot to watch a Delta sunset and to finally say good-bye.

I hadn't been there since Will's return, but now, with the harvest over, I didn't know when or if I'd be back. I walked through
the wrought iron enclosure and found Johnny's marker. There was
nothing of him buried beneath it except the miniature Civil War
cannon and soldiers that had been his favorite toys as a child.

I watched as the sun gently eased itself through the autumn
sky, peering through the sinuous arms of the cypress trees. Insects
pricked the dark water of the swamp, the soft gloaming light settling onto the surface for a good-night kiss.

"You're going to miss supper."

I turned at the sound of Will's voice. "I didn't want to miss the
sunset. I don't know when I'll get another chance."

He came to stand next to me, neither of us speaking for a long
moment. He squatted down next to Johnny's marker, his finger
tracing the letters of his brother's name. "You'd think growing up
with a person would make you really know them. I always thought
Johnny put himself first. But that's not true, is it?"

A vine of dread slipped up the back of my throat. "Why do you
say that?"

He stood and faced me, his serious eyes reflecting the fading
sun. "He loved John-John like his own, didn't he?"

Slowly, I nodded, unable to force any words from my lips.

"It wasn't until I came back and John-John told me his birthday
that I figured it out. I was angry with you at first, because you
didn't tell me. And then I realized that I never gave you the
chance. I just signed up and shipped out, thinking I could leave you
behind."

I swallowed. "Johnny was a good father. It made him grow up a lot."

Will was silent for a moment. "Johnny will always be his father. I don't want anybody to think otherwise."

I nodded, understanding the complicated yet unconditional love between brothers.

"You don't have to leave, Ginny. I'd like you to stay. Johnny would want you to."

I looked up at him, unable to speak.

"He wrote to me the day before he died. It was almost as if he knew . . ." Will shook his head. "He asked me to tell Mama and Daddy good-bye." His eyes held mine. "And to take care of you and John-John."

He paused as a flock of white-throated sparrows exploded from the treetops, swirling above us for a moment before flying into the dusk. They would head north in the spring but would return again to the Delta the following winter. It was as if a giant magnet pulled us all back toward home, back to the place where we began.

I closed my eyes, seeing Johnny's impatient scrawl in the letter he'd written to me on the same night he'd written to his brother.

I'm walking into enemy lines tonight because I'm too much of a coward to face another day of fighting or to put a bullet in my own brain. You made me happy, Ginny, and I hope now you can find your own happiness. I wish I could see one more Delta sunset. Maybe when you see one, you'll remember to think of me and how much I loved you.

I knew then that I wouldn't show Will the letter, that I would destroy it so Johnny's last words would be the ones he'd written to

Will about his love for his family. He would always be a hero to those who had known and loved him.

"Can we start over, Ginny?"

I thought for a moment. "We can never go back to the people we were, and I don't want to." I touched his arm. "But maybe we can start again. As the people we've become."

The sun dripped yellow over the horizon like butter melting in a frying pan, and my vision blurred. "Johnny wanted me to remember him when I saw the sunsets."

Will put his arm around me, and I rested my head on his shoulder as if I'd always belonged there. "It's a good memory to have."

"Yes," I said. "It is."

"Will you stay, then? With us?" I felt his breath on the top of my head. "With me?"

The last edge of light glimmered in the sky, a last good-bye. "Always."

In the last four years we'd changed, leaving behind who we'd once been. But we'd learned that change is more than leaving behind; it's a gathering up, a harvest of newness and possibilities.

But some things would never change. The flat landscape of the Mississippi Delta with its fields of rows carved from the rich alluvial soil. The sunsets that sank into the cypress swamps and into the great river whose bends and curves defied again and again the human need to contain its borders. The cycle of seasons telling us when to sow, and when to reap. Johnny would stay the same charming boy of our memories, never growing old, never changing. Always a hero to his son.

With Will's arm still around my shoulder, we turned back toward the house where the light gleamed from the windows, welcoming us home. The last of the daylight sank into the dark earth as we put the war and the past behind us and stepped into our future. And I pondered how sometimes the best secrets are those that are never told.

$$\sim\!\smile\!\!\sim$$

ACKNOWLEDGMENTS

My heartfelt thanks go to Kristina McMorris for spearheading this amazing project and getting nine other authors to wholeheartedly agree on the story concept. *Grand Central* would never have happened without her. Thanks also to our editor, Cindy Hwang, for seeing the potential for an anthology centered around a New York City icon at a pivotal time in history—truly a writer's dream!

Thank you to my father, Lloyd Sconiers, and to Andrew Zappone for your detailed knowledge of the U.S. military in the 1940s. I wish I were writing something longer because I certainly had enough details from you both to fill an entire novel! Any errors in using your meticulous research are my own.

Thanks to train enthusiast John Osgood for your helpful suggestions, and a huge thanks to Robert Holland, whose knowledge of trains and the railroad system was as astounding as it was interesting. Thank you for finding those elusive facts that were so critical to my story.

My biggest thanks go to the servicemen and women of our country, both past and present, whose sacrifices I appreciate more than I can ever express with mere words.